JO HARKIN

tell me an ending

HUTCHINSON
HEINEMANN

1 3 5 7 9 10 8 6 4 2

Hutchinson Heinemann
20 Vauxhall Bridge Road
London SW1V 2SA

Hutchinson Heinemann is part of the Penguin Random House group of
companies whose addresses can be found at global.penguinrandomhouse.com

Penguin
Random House
UK

First published in the United Kingdom by Hutchinson Heinemann in 2022

www.penguin.co.uk

A CIP catalogue record for this book is available from the British Library.

ISBN 9781529151374 (hardback)
ISBN 9781529151381 (trade paperback)

Typeset in 11/15.5 pt Sabon LT Std
by Integra Software Services Pvt. Ltd, Pondicherry

Printed and bound in Great Britain by Clays Ltd, Elcograf S.p.A.

The authorised representative in the EEA is Penguin Random House Ireland,
Morrison Chambers, 32 Nassau Street, Dublin D02 YH68.

Penguin Random House is committed to a sustainable future for
our business, our readers and our planet. This book is made from
Forest Stewardship Council® certified paper.

For Cian

'I, not remembering how I cried out then,
Will cry it o'er again –'

Shakespeare, *The Tempest*

PART ONE

Noor

'Just a few more questions,' says Noor. 'Box ticking. And then we're all done.'

She remembers from her training, years ago, that she's supposed to give a reassuring smile at this point, to let the client sitting in front of her know that the difficult bit is over; that this is just a small matter of paperwork, before they can begin their new, happy life.

Noor said to Louise at the time that the clients Noor forgets to smile at probably feel *more* reassured than the ones who receive a smile, see the forced nature of the smile, and start worrying what Noor might be hiding, but Louise said it didn't matter.

Nobody expects it to look authentic, Louise said. You look like a competent professional doing a token smile, and that's perfect. That's all they want from you.

Noor smiles at her client.

'Great,' says the client. He rubs his face. His body softens into his chair. He's only about thirty; his notes say he saw a man being sucked into a snowblower at a ski resort. 'Good to know.'

'So. Since your deletion procedure, have you experienced any insomnia, unexplained mood changes, symptoms of paranoia, hallucinations or visual disturbances, headaches, anxiety, depression?'

'No,' says the client. 'Does that stuff often happen after a wipe?'

'After a *removal*,' Noor says, because Nepenthe doesn't like the word *wipe*. They prefer *targeted removal solution*. Not that it matters. Slang is slang: they can't fight the tide.

'None of these are common after-effects,' she continues. 'In fact, incidences are far lower for our clients than for the general population.'

'Cool,' says the guy. 'Well, I haven't had any of those.'

'And you say your PTSD symptoms have subsided.'

'Yep. All gone.'

'Well, that's certainly good news,' she says. She stifles a small burp, apple-flavoured. It reminds her that the apple she ate for breakfast was a while ago. She wonders how long she's got until lunch.

Noor is the head of the aftercare team. She doesn't usually conduct follow-up interviews personally, but she's doing a few to test out the new script. She's looking forward to the end of them.

There are two kinds of clients at Nepenthe: self-informed and self-confidential. The self-informeds know that they've had a memory removed, the self-confidentials don't. Self-informed clients tend to be people who have witnessed terrible but relatively simple events, like snow-blowing accidents. In most cases these clients are content with knowing that they saw these things, without being able to remember the thing itself. It's enough that the incident has become . . . abstract.

The self-informed clients usually arrive for their interview a month after their procedure, say they feel great, and leave. Even on the rare occasion that someone *doesn't* feel great, they're usually civilised about it. Before Noor started working at Nepenthe, she thought that she'd be facing a lot of chair smashing, desk tipping, door punching. But in fact the clients are almost uniformly well behaved.

It's because we're messing with their brains, Louise says. Makes people very polite.

Noor never meets any of the self-confidentials. Their procedures take place at night. And nobody interviews them afterwards. Obviously. Noor gets reports from their GPs instead, which usually reach the same conclusion: the patient, to all appearances, is feeling great.

'I do have one thing I was just . . . wondering about,' says Noor's client now. 'Maybe it's stupid.'

'Please,' Noor says. 'There's no such thing as a stupid question.'

Her stomach mutters, as if to disagree. She folds her hands over it.

'I remembered something I read, about how life is like a symphony, and what Nepenthe does is edit out the wrong note. But then I was . . . I mean, I've been kind of unmotivated, I've been wiping out on the mountain bike a lot, I was wondering the other day if I'm in the right job. And I'm thinking – what if I accidentally deleted a *good* note along with the bad note? Or even if it was just the bad note, if I needed that note to, well, be *me*.'

What a bloody stupid question, thinks Noor.

Instead she says, 'Your state of mind goes through changes all the time. You're only noticing it now

5

because – post-procedure – you're on the alert for side effects. It's a well-known cognitive phenomenon. When the brain takes up a theory, it focuses on gathering evidence to support it, and ignores everything else. It's not objective.'

'Huh,' says the client. Eyebrows up, slow nod. 'That's nice. Reassuring. They should tell people that earlier.'

Noor waits.

'Oh,' says the client. 'They already did, didn't they?'

'In your first appointment, yes. In fact, your notes indicate you felt positive about it then too.'

'So I *am* still the same person,' the client says. 'That's good.'

'Absolutely,' Noor says. She sighs. 'So, last question: do you feel that every element of the unwanted memory has been completely removed?'

The client stops smiling. He frowns.

Noor knew he would. This is part of the new script; reworded in a hurry not by the psychology department but by Nepenthe's legal team.

'Is this about traces?' says the client.

'How do you mean?' asks Noor. Neutral tone.

But she knows exactly what he means. Over the years since Nepenthe opened, there have been a small but vocal number of people claiming to be former self-confidential clients who've been left with part of the memory intact – or else that part of the memory has somehow regenerated. The media picked up the story and blew it out of all proportion. *Traces* was the word they came up with for the phenomenon. Which hadn't *been* a phenomenon until the media decided that's what it was.

Are you *suffering from traces?*

Documentaries were made, interviewing mostly mentally ill people about their unexplained visions. Films, TV dramas, novels followed – usually clenchingly moralising, usually having puns in their titles – and Noor considered them a good thing in that they managed to trivialise the whole issue. The phenomenon eventually dropped off the front pages. People moved on to new phenomena.

Then about a year ago, Nepenthe scientists discovered that deleted memories weren't actually gone for good. That – with another procedure – they could even be recovered.

Oh no, Noor remembers thinking when she found out. *Please, no.*

But yes. And once *that* got out, a significant number of people who claimed they'd been tormented by traces argued that they should have the right to know if they were former self-confidential Nepenthe clients – and not only that, to get their memories *back*. It became a class-action lawsuit in several countries, and – in most of these – the former clients had won.

Hence: the restorations.

Noor knows her client knows all of this. She's just not sure how much he'll feel emboldened to ask. She sits back and allows her smile to fade into her usual expression, which she's been told variously is one of coolness, flatness, hostility.

'I mean,' says the client, with a look of minor defiance, 'are you checking to see if I have any traces –'

'Regarding the alleged phenomenon known as traces,' Noor says carefully, 'the company's official position is that evidence of this is only anecdotal. There are yet to be any peer-reviewed, methodologically sound studies proving their existence, let alone explaining what they are or why they occur.'

'Sounds very formal,' the client says. 'But this is about that whole fuck-up, right? Excuse my language. The . . . eff-up. You know. Didn't you guys have to give all the night clients their memories back because they were getting traces?'

'It's true that the former self-confidential clients who claimed to be experiencing traces happened to be the ones who brought the lawsuits,' Noor says. 'But the argument wasn't about whether or not traces exist. It was about the right to have a memory restored, now that restorations are a possibility. Any former Nepenthe client could have brought that case. It's just that the only people who cared enough to do it were the ones who believed they were experiencing traces.'

'I just don't see why they cared,' the client says. 'I mean, given the absence of any peer-reviewed, methodologically sound research proving that they *ought* to care.'

Is he taking the piss?

Noor sighs.

Yes, he is definitely taking the piss. He's forgotten that he's afraid of Noor, and Nepenthe. Noor blames the fuck-up, personally. It's undermined their authority.

After the client has gone, Noor carries her cold cup of tea down the long, glass-walled corridor, divided by geometric patterns of light, to the staff kitchen. She's pleased to see there's nobody else in there. She tips the tea away, puts the kettle on and allows herself to lean against the

8

empty worktop, enjoying the moment despite the continued keening of her stomach.

Before the moment has a chance to get going, several technicians and a nurse arrive.

'Hi, Noor!' the nurse, Ben, says. He's about thirty, new and persistently friendly. Noor's heard him in the kitchen before, trying to find out everyone's *story*.

You're barking up the wrong tree, Noor said to him. This is where stories come to die.

'We were just talking about holidays,' Ben says. 'Summer's nearly over. Are you planning a late getaway, Noor?'

'Somewhere to *unwind*,' says a technician called Jennifer. She casts a meaningful glance at one of the other technicians, whose name Noor can't remember.

'I don't plan on it. Unwinding,' Noor says. She rinses her mug. 'It sounds dangerous.'

'Well, *I'm* going to the Maldives,' says Jennifer to Ben and the technicians.

'Which island?' Noor asks her. 'Hotel island or burning trash island?'

Jennifer doesn't have much to say about that. She goes into a corner and becomes very involved with the preparation of her herbal tea. The technician whose name Noor can't remember laughs uncertainly.

Two of the therapists on Noor's team – Monica and Nij – arrive. The kitchen is beginning to feel overcrowded. Noor nods at them.

'How's the new script going?' Monica asks Noor.

'It's a disaster,' Noor says.

'Is it going to be fixed?'

'Probably not,' Noor says.

'But aftercare don't even deal with the self-confidentials! The self-informed aren't getting restorations, right?'

'Nope,' says Noor.

'Do the self-informeds even *get* traces?' Nij asks. 'And do they mind if they do?'

'Don't call them traces,' Noor says. 'We don't know if they exist. Remember that.'

'But we're asking clients questions that are obviously about . . . er, them.'

'Yep,' says Noor. 'Like I said. It's a disaster.'

Monica opens her mouth. She looks at something behind Noor. Then she closes her mouth again.

Noor turns round.

'It's good to see you on message as usual, Noor,' Louise says, from the doorway. 'Afternoon, everyone.'

'Hi, Dr Nightingale,' the others say. Then they go quiet. The air fills with the effort of thinking of something to say to Louise that will mark the sayer out as an interesting, well-informed and promotable individual. Noor, enjoying the return of the silence, spoons three sugars into her tea and stirs it gently.

'Don't rush on my account,' says Louise to Noor.

'Good tea can't be rushed,' Noor says. She picks up her cup and heads out of the kitchen. Louise, holding her own takeaway coffee, follows her.

'That is *not* good tea,' Louise says. 'Three sugars?'

'I started drinking tea when I gave up smoking,' Noor explains. 'I needed – wait, why am I explaining this? Do you know you're ten minutes early? Normally you're exactly on time.'

'I do know that, and I went to your office to wait, but it was locked,' Louise says.

Noor could remind Louise that offices aren't meant to be left unlocked, but it's been a very long time since the two of them stood on any kind of ceremony.

'Crowshill,' Louise says meditatively. 'I lived here for years, but I never enjoy coming back. There's something wrong with the atmosphere. A big clinic in a small town. It feels off. The other regionals are the same.'

Louise is based at the company's London headquarters, but she visits regional clinics every month. Technically Crowshill – the flagship facility, and only five minutes outside the M25, a border town between London, Surrey and Kent – isn't a regional clinic. But Noor knows how it is. She saw it that way herself, before she moved here from London. *Regional* is the word for the pleasant square with its plane trees, the fifteenth-century pub where Alexander Pope once had an ale, the Waitrose, the coffee shops and charity shops and independent butcher with halved pigs hanging in the window, the 1960s Baptist church and old chequerboard Catholic church, the Victorian primary school and the tabby cat that sits at the end of Noor's drive most mornings.

Noor's come to like it.

Louise sits down, takes her phone out and starts tapping at the screen. 'So, first things first. They've finally worked out the schedule for the disaster – I mean, the upcoming restorations. The self-confidentials will all be informed about their status in September. The restoration procedures will start in late October. You shouldn't see much disruption. New self-confidential procedures will remain suspended for the foreseeable, so Crowshill will be closed at night from now on, but that obviously doesn't affect you personally.'

'Nope. I spend my nights sleeping,' Noor says.

(This is a lie.)

'Good for you,' Louise says. 'How is the new script going?'

Noor just looks at her.

'I thought so,' Louise says. She looks at her phone screen. 'How shall I word it? New script causing consternation? Anxiety? Suspicion?'

'All of the above,' Noor says.

Noor's thinking, now, about sleeping. The possibility of it. Wondering if maybe this might be the time to ask Louise the favour she's been thinking – for the last year – of asking. But how should she word it? *Hey, boss, any chance you could sign off on a slightly dodgy memory deletion for me? It's not illegal, exactly, just unethical. No need for consternation, anxiety or suspicion.*

She decides against it – but not before Louise notices her expression. Which is annoying, because Noor thought she *had* no expression.

'Everything okay?' Louise says.

'Yes,' Noor says. She tries to think of a change of subject. 'Are you going on holiday this year?'

'What?' Louise says. 'You sound like a hairdresser. *Are* you okay?'

Noor feels mildly offended. 'It's a perfectly normal question,' she says. 'It's generally considered to be acceptable small talk.'

'Have *you* ever asked anyone that before?'

'Of course not.'

Louise laughs again. 'Well, maybe leave the acceptable small talk to other people.'

'Fair enough,' Noor says. Louise is still looking at her, with more, not less, curiosity. Noor wishes she'd stop it.

And as if in answer to her wish, there's a loud scream from outside, in the direction of the gates.

'*Liars! Thieves!*'

'Shit,' Louise says. 'That made me jump. Oh, for fuck's sake. My coffee.'

There's a brown stain on the knee of her pale grey trousers. Noor reaches for the box of tissues, but Louise shakes her head.

'I'll go to the loos and wash it properly,' she says. 'Back in a sec.'

After Louise closes the door, Noor's mobile phone goes off: a reminder alert. She thought she'd put it on silent. She picks it up, frowning. The reminder says *RASA*. Noor has no idea what that is. And she can't find out, because her phone keeps rejecting her password. By her third attempt it becomes apparent that this isn't Noor's phone at all. It's Louise's. Noor's own, identical phone, is still lying on the desk. She puts Louise's phone down, just as Louise herself comes back in. There's a large wet patch on her leg.

'This had better dry before my board meeting,' she says. 'Bloody idiots.'

Noor is surprised to see that Louise looks angry – at least, she does for a moment, before she recalibrates. Louise isn't usually someone who gets angry over coffee spilling, or protesters screaming. But lately, she has seemed more . . . edgy. And when she picks up her phone, the sense of edginess around her deepens.

Of course (Noor reflects with some pride), very few people besides Noor herself would even be able to detect this edginess. Louise always looks the same: cool oval face, every surface perfectly smooth. It's not easy to pin anything on a face like that. According to Nat, a doctor on the removals team, Louise has had 'work done', but Noor isn't sure that's relevant. She can't remember a time when Louise's face was what you'd call *expressive*. While her skin might be available for inspection, what's going on underneath it is anybody's guess. Take now, for example. Louise has put her phone down and turned, expectant and calm, towards Noor. Leaving Noor wondering if Louise really did look edgy a second ago, or not.

If maybe the only edginess is within Noor herself.

'What are we meant to expect?' Noor asks. 'Regarding the disaster, I mean. The fact that in three weeks' time, all the self-confidential clients will know who they are. Are we . . . prepared?'

Louise does the kind of laugh people do to let you know they find something utterly laughable. The laugh sounds furious.

'So that's a no,' says Noor.

'God knows what's going to happen,' Louise says. 'And God help us all . . . Wouldn't it be nice to believe in God at times like these?'

'Instead of playing him?' Noor says. She remembers her tea, and picks it up. It's cold.

Louise sighs. 'Unfortunately, we've already made our choice,' she says.

Noor hasn't seen the emails that are going out. But she imagines they go something like this:

Dear former client,
Do you want to know a secret?

It's about you.
It might make you happy, or it might be something
unimaginably horrible.
Once you know it, you can't unknow it.
Please get in touch!

Some people would immediately delete the email.

But not everyone.

There are people who, once they read those words, would find it impossible to resist. And then, what would they get back? Noor thinks of the clients who'd deleted the discoveries of their dead parents being rapists, paedophiles, Nazis.

Louise once said to Noor, early on, that *Do No Harm* is an impossibility. *Do Least Harm:* that was Louise's ethos.

Which is why Louise said the restorations were a mistake. Based as they were on the philosophy of *Protect Nepenthe from Harm, and Fuck Everybody Else.*

And Noor, as she usually did, agreed with Louise.

Noor had to look up the word Nepenthe before she came to work here. It occurred to her on the way to the interview that she had no idea what it meant – if it was a scientific term, or a surname, or what – and she might well be asked about it.

She found out that most people *think* the name comes from 'The Raven', the poem by Edgar Allan Poe.

She read the poem, which was basically about a raven bothering a man grieving his lost lover. The unhappy man cries, *Let me quaff this kind Nepenthe and forget this lost Lenore!* But there was no Nepenthe for him. Just his own increasing madness, and an annoying raven.

In actual fact, Noor discovered, the word Nepenthe came from the *Odyssey*. There was a magical potion called nepenthes pharmakon, *a drug to quiet all pain and strife, and bring forgetfulness of every ill.* Helen of Troy got hold of some of it. She used it to spike the drinks of veterans of the Trojan War – which she technically started, so it made sense that she'd want people to forget about it.

Noor can't remember everything about that interview. It was ten years ago. Some of it – the view from the window, her painful new shoes – is clear and bright, other parts are in darkness.

She remembers Louise saying: The procedure was originally only available via the NHS, for people like soldiers and terrorism victims, but of course the technology has been commercialised, and now – so long as no laws have been broken – anyone with enough money can remove a memory of almost anything. Exciting, isn't it?

Louise didn't *sound* particularly excited. But then she'd have rattled off this explanation hundreds of times, probably several times that day alone.

But Noor was excited.

I'm very excited, she said.

Right, Louise said. What excites you, specifically? Why do you want this job?

This was when Noor realised that it was possibly a mistake to have spent the train journey looking up poems. That she probably should have spent the time preparing an answer to this particular question.

She embarked on an answer anyway. She went with the truth. It still makes her cringe to think about it. She talked about her background in coding, drew some clumsy links to neuroscience, getting more and more earnest as she went.

She can hear herself now:

You see, we're all coded, we're all running programs. The goal is simplicity, elegance, orderly cooperation, to produce an effective and bug-free whole. Obviously the human brain is more of a challenge. When you don't know the operating rules, problems seem impossible to fix. But they aren't. To understand the underlying system, the rules, like Nepenthe does, and then use them to *fix* a, a malfunction, in this case a PTSD response – that's just a . . . beautiful concept. Actually I don't think there's anything more beautiful than that.

(She realised she'd been leaning forward and holding the edge of the desk. She let go; put her hands in her lap.)

You didn't mention morality, Louise said.

Well, no, Noor said. Health, function – those aren't moral matters. It's not a moral matter when a program isn't working. It's a practical one.

Louise looked at her for a long time.

I understand, she said.

On the train home Noor, knowing she had the job, was able to find it a little bit funny that she'd thought she might have been asked about Helen of Troy.

Helen, thinks Noor.
Helena.

Elena.

The problem with thinking about forgetting things is that it always makes you think about the things you want to forget.

Noor hasn't thought about Elena in a long time.

That's a lie.

At first Noor thought about Elena a lot. Over time, she thought about her less. There may have been a period of time – a month or two – when she barely thought about Elena at all. But then the news about restorations arrived, and with it: Elena.

Not the real Elena, who by now was far away in time and space, but the Elena in Noor's head: less understanding than the original, more devious than the original, and much, much harder to dislodge.

Noor was ready for Elena by then, though. She armed herself with a range of CBT and neuroplasticity techniques, visualisations and circuit reshaping exercises, with the end result that Elena didn't get so much as a *foot* over the threshold of Noor's brain.

Apart from just now, obviously.

Noor feels embarrassed at this failure. In fact she could quite happily remove the bit of her brain that was responsible (the amygdala. As per usual). Remove, wipe: the terminology doesn't matter. She could put a pencil up her nose, right now, at her desk.

A targeted removal solution.

Ha.

*

By the time Noor finishes work a dark cloud is spreading over the sky like spilled paint, making for Crowshill. The glass corridor outside her office is dim. It feels colder now, though rationally Noor knows the clinic temperature is maintained at exactly 23 degrees.

One of the first things people ask Noor when they find out what she does for a living is, *What's it like inside the clinic?* For some reason, they all want to know.

It looks like what you expect, Noor says.

What do you mean?

Well, imagine a place where you go to get your memories removed. What does that look like?

White, says everyone. Futuristic. Sci-fi.

There you go, says Noor. It looks exactly like that.

Noor's got no idea why the collective idea of the future apparently came to a stop in the sixties. At some point in that decade it was decided that the future looked smooth, curved and white. And now it *is* that future, but our idea of the future hasn't changed. Noor wonders if the smooth, curved whiteness will ever really come to pass, or if it will just stay in the places it lives now, the lobbies of companies who want to be seen as futuristic.

She passes through Nepenthe's reception area (all white, with two curved white leather sofas and a large white desk like half a Polo mint) and goes out through the landscaped grounds to the car park. She nods to the security guards. All of them ignore the noise the building has just started making, a low, long *ooooooo*.

The clinic was originally designed with a large, circular reception area at its heart, and two wings on either side. The wings curved inwards and the central portion curved outwards and the whole thing was glass-faced from floor to ceiling. It looked good. Sci-fi good. The problem was that after it was built it became apparent that, at a certain time of day, the concave glass parts focused the sun so that it burned large brown patches in the grass and melted the paintwork of the cars. It also dazzled anyone walking past. Clients had to approach the clinic slowly, squinting in the blinding light, through which they could just about make out their own frighteningly deformed reflection.

Hardly *striking the right note*, was how Louise put it.

So in the end, after a lot of meetings, shutters were put up over the windows. Now on windy days the air is funnelled between the glass and the shutters and a kind of low fluting or moaning note can be heard in all the front-facing offices, including Noor's. She barely hears it these days herself, but sometimes it startles the clients.

The future is here, thinks Noor, and it wasn't thought through.

What's that? Elena – or: *the client*, as she was then – had said. That whistling?

It's the shutters, Noor said.

I thought maybe it was all the memories, said Elena. Being released from vents.

Noor didn't know what to say to that.

So she said: Shall we continue?

Sure, Elena said. She moved her hair (shiny brown, wavy) off her shoulders. As soon as she did it the hair started to slide forward again. Noor wondered if this was a gesture she'd adopted years ago, as a little *did you notice I'm a very attractive woman, do you see how elegant and also vulnerable my neck is* kind of thing, and now just performed without even knowing she was doing it.

According to Elena Darke's notes, she had deleted the memory of a helicopter crash in which she was the only survivor. The case got some press attention, not least because it involved the CEO of a big company – her boss, and a married man – and Elena wasn't supposed to have been in the helicopter with him.

In answer to your previous question, Elena said, I wasn't sleeping with Guy. I think he wanted to sleep with me. I mean, who invites a random marketing executive to travel with them in the company helicopter to the AGM? But then, what random marketing executive would say no? I'm actually 90 per cent gay. I've had a few sexual relationships with men. But those were years ago. Though I did wonder if I would consider sleeping with Guy for a promotion. It's the kind of thing that crosses your mind, right? He wasn't unattractive. Would I do it for 40K? 20K? A better company car? I think now, on balance, I probably wouldn't have. And I'm not saying that just because, you know, he's dead.

Right, Noor said.

She looked back at the previous question.

It said: *Is there anything about the care you received during your procedure that you feel could be improved?*

And I know what you're thinking, Elena continued. I got the job purely on merit. I've always worked hard. And I've had a good career. Having said that, I'm not sure how I'm going to present this latest development. It's not great on the CV, you know?

There was a short pause. Noor realised, with dismay, that she was about to laugh. And then Elena caught her eye, and was so obviously willing Noor to laugh that Noor ended up not being able to help it, and did.

At *last*, Elena said. She sat back in her seat with evident satisfaction.

Sorry, Noor said. That was inappropriate.

I enjoy inappropriate, Elena said.

Noor found Elena difficult to look at, suddenly.

The way Elena was looking at her was making it difficult.

She went on to the next question.

Have you experienced any feelings of regret concerning the procedure?

That's an interesting one, Elena said. Sometimes I wonder if it's a good idea to vaporise your memories. And then I think: no, good riddance. If I had the money I'd wipe more. Childhood, most of that.

Childhood? said Noor.

She wasn't supposed to ask questions like that. She was supposed to refer clients like Elena for further therapy. There was a script.

. . . *Having concluded this assessment, I feel that in this instance it would be helpful for you to discuss your thoughts and feelings further, with one of our team of memory specialists.*

She'd wondered in her interview if it had been appropriate to compare clients to computers. Now she wondered what the difference was between her own job and that of the customer service employee for a Wi-Fi provider. Both of them working through their script, switching things off and on, giving up, booking an engineer.

Yeah, Elena said. Childhood was fairly shitty. But not in any original or interesting way.

Yes, Noor said. Uh. I mean, I understand. And I think, with your agreement, that it might be helpful if I refer you on for some therapy sessions with our team of memory –

Sure, sure, Elena said. Why not. I can tell them about how I'm currently trying not to drink, but that's difficult because I live above a cocktail bar. In Fitzrovia. It's called The Cat and Pigeon. I end up in there every Saturday night, pretty much.

(None of this was appropriate – not at all – but it would have been stupid of Noor to point that out, given that Elena had already identified herself as a person who enjoyed inappropriate things.)

Elena looked at Noor. She pushed her hair back over her shoulders. The sunlight from the shutters sliced her neck.

So, Elena said. If anyone was looking for me. That's where I'd be.

The lowing of the building fades as the wind drops, leaving the grounds nearly silent, except for the occasional clattering wood pigeon, the hiss of the security guards' radios. On the other side of the pines and the tall flint wall that divide the clinic from the town, there will be the noise of cars, and music playing from windows, and the idle chat of the protesters, placards downed, sharing Thermos flasks. Soon the gate will start to open and they'll have to stand to attention, ready for Noor's car to pass.

As Noor drives out, the protesters – for the most part – keep back. They're waving their signs and chanting various slogans. There's a girl aged around six here today, standing with her mother. She's holding a sign that says 'Pray to

God for Forgiveness'. Noor, against her better judgement, looks at the girl. The girl looks surprised. Then she sticks out her tongue.

Noor edges forward. A couple of wilder-looking protesters jostle around her bumper. Soon a security guard will shoo them off. She turns up the music: Haydn's *Orlando Paladino*. The chorus inside the car swells, the chorus outside the car vanishes.

The first Nepenthe clinic opened in '98, or '99 maybe. Noor can remember the uproar. The ado, the to-do. It wasn't only the protesters: everyone had an opinion on whether or not memories should be deleted. Religious groups worrying over the sanctity of the soul, human rights groups worrying that the technology would be abused by repressive regimes, conspiracy theorists worrying about everything. Journalists, celebrities, MPs, genuine experts, fake experts, genuine angry mobs both online and IRL. Preachers shouting outside the clinic, war veterans shoving the preachers, people turning up apparently from nowhere and throwing bricks.

But as Nepenthe expanded, and reported year-on-year increases in profits – because the majority of people didn't really care about souls or human rights abuses – attendance outside the clinic gates gradually dwindled to no more than ten or so protesters. (Except for one notable day in 2013, when the council announced it was planning to cut down a hundred-year-old tree to build new offices in the centre of town. The tree protesters got themselves muddled up with the Nepenthe protesters, but because all the placards said things like 'Don't Chainsaw the Past' and 'Respect our History', it took a while to work out that there'd been a misunderstanding.)

Those occasions aside, the protesting had gone on peacefully. The regulars tended to be on first-name terms with security and each other. There were old women on folding chairs, knitting. There was a camaraderie. But now – since the fuck-up, the disaster – the clinic gates attract a large and varied crowd. Liberals and reactionaries, Christians and Muslims, concerned parents and anarchists – as likely to shout at each other as they are at the staff.

'Thieves!' It's the same voice as before, closer now. 'Liars!'

Noor looks out of the window with interest. She sees a man of about sixty, with a beard, holding a placard that says 'RASA Cover Up'. There are already two security guards, in fluorescent orange, on their way over to him. One makes a grab at the placard; the man dodges and darts back, towards Noor's car. The guards follow; the placard is taken, the man gripped by both arms. The crowd boos. Just before the guards can pull the man away he twists, turning his head backwards, and something hits Noor's passenger window. Then, in a violent bustling of hi-vis, the bearded man disappears.

Noor realises that the thing that hit the window was spit. It sits there at eye level for a second, before sliding slowly down the glass. There's a lot of it. How long was this guy preparing it? His one almighty gob.

She turns off the music. As if she's controlling the volume outside too, the crowd quietens. Perhaps because the security guards are moving among them now, clearing them out of the way of the car, perhaps because – like Noor – they were taken aback by the man's vehemence. A line has been crossed, and now they're all waiting to see what happens.

RASA, thinks Noor. She's never heard the word before, and now she's seen it twice in one day.

She squints at the crowds, but the man is gone.

One of the security guards taps on her passenger window. She opens it.

'Sorry about that, Dr Ali,' he says. 'We've got it under control now. Everything's under control.' He looks proud, as anyone would if they'd managed to get every single thing under control. 'You want someone to clean that for you?'

'It's fine. I need to get the car washed anyway.'

'Right you are. Have a nice evening, Dr Ali.'

As it turns out, the sky – which had given itself up to the darkness – cracks open while Noor is waiting at the traffic light, and a heavy rain comes down. It beats at the top of the car, sluices down the windows, erases any trace of spit. The sound of rain makes a pleasant backdrop to the Haydn, which she's turned up again. By the time she gets back to her house she's in a nearly good mood. Then she pulls into the drive and her car crunches over an egg carton, then a foil takeaway tray.

She gets out. There's rubbish scattered across her driveway and lawn. The house next door to her is divided into flats. Outside the garden flat is a torn-open black bin bag.

'Idiots,' Noor mutters.

She's talked to the neighbours about this before. Noor doesn't like having to *call round* on neighbours. Before she moved into her house she'd discreetly checked out the people on the road, to make sure that they weren't the kind of people who would necessitate being *called in on.* They weren't. But then the old woman in the garden flat died and – much to Noor's annoyance – a young couple had moved in, and then this young couple couldn't be bothered to put their bin bags in the actual bin, and of course some nocturnal animal had pulled the remains of their fried chicken meal deal into Noor's garden to eat.

And so there Noor was, *calling round.*

The girl explained to Noor apologetically and charmingly, leaning in the doorway wearing a Pixies T-shirt and a pair of pants (her legs long and tanned, which is as much as Noor noticed in the fraction of a second she allowed herself to look at them), that they'd put their bin bag in the porch, to take down to the wheelie bin at the foot of the drive when they were –

Less stoned? thought Noor. (The scent of marijuana coming over the fence being impossible to avoid on sunny afternoons. And grey afternoons. And evenings. And mornings.)

– dressed, says the girl.

Well, as you can see, the foxes and cats get into it, Noor said.

I'm so sorry, the girl said. She had a low, slightly hoarse voice. She looked earnest. I wouldn't want wild animals to eat it. Or, like, a vole could get stuck in a crisp packet. We'll do a litter pick this afternoon.

But that day was windy, and the rubbish all blew away.

Noor decides not to call on the neighbours again. She goes in, closes the door, takes off her work clothes and changes into leggings and a T-shirt. She makes herself some pasta. She googles *Nepenthe, RASA.* The results are not

27

enlightening. The only thing that seems even vaguely relevant turns out to be some conspiracy theorist rambling on a forum about how Nepenthe has a top-secret programme called RASA that's stealing large chunks of human memories to build lifelike robots. The robots could already be among us. The person knows all this because they themselves can't remember several years of their own life.

Noor shouldn't laugh. But she's at home alone, so she allows herself a smile, a real one. She picks up her pasta and takes it into the sitting room. She switches on the TV, chooses a show about people buying houses in hot countries, and allows the day – restorations, emails, snowblowers, spit, neighbours – to gradually fall away.

Mei

Mei is sitting cross-legged on her own bed, her iPad propped on a cushion, headphones in, listening to Zizi TellsIt saying,

Obviously, I'm sharing this with you guys because there are no secrets between us, right?

This is how Zizi TellsIt often starts one of her videos.

What exactly is a Zizi TellsIt? Mei's mother asked her once.

Zizi TellsIt is a brightly lit blonde girl who sits on a sofa in her beach house, and shares things. Advice, tips, stories from her own real life. She started as a model and fashion blogger, then she got into clean eating, and now she's also a mental health brand ambassador and she talks about being bipolar as well as her new range of vegan coconut wellness juices.

Soo, I'm gonna be real with you guys about the memory traces I personally have been experiencing lately, Zizi says. *The first one happened when I was arriving at this hotel. So, just as I walked in I, like,* remembered *this man's face. And I straight up* don't know *this guy! I was like, what the hell is happening right now?*

A voice cuts in above Zizi's. 'Several beers later! . . .' it says.

It's coming from outside the headphones, from the other room: Mei's dad, telling a story. Mei recognises it as an old favourite: a misunderstanding in Thailand. His voice goes up as he gets towards the punchline.

'It was a bloody *woman* after all!'

Laughter.

Mei turns up the volume on the iPad.

. . . *so then, the next week, I'm going back to the same hotel,* says Zizi. *And as I was leaving, walking through the foyer, I remembered the* same *face. Out of, like, no-where. Let me tell you guys, it freaked me out.*

Mei takes her headphones out. She closes Zizi's window, opens Instagram, and searches for #memorytrace. A few new stories pop up. Some nobodies, then an influencer Mei recognises, who's posted a black-and-white bikini picture, looking out over an infinity pool with a sad expression. *Wondering what I've lost,* is the caption.

Mei sighs. She opens Reddit, then closes it again. She spent four hours on Reddit last night and then she couldn't sleep. She's starting to think maybe it's not good for her brain to absorb so much raw internet all at once.

On top of whatever else is wrong with her brain.

The first of Mei's own memory traces came to her a month ago, when she was eating breakfast (9 a.m., scrambled egg on toast), and the second arrived in the shower (7 p.m., grapefruit and ginger shower gel) a week later. Since then she's been eating the same breakfast and showering with the same products at the same times every day, but nothing else has come back.

She looks out of the window that spans the north wall of her bedroom. The early evening Kuala Lumpur skyline is softened by a heat haze, a silver-grey humidity – not that she can fell it in here, with the aircon on full-blast. Mei's dad has adapted, he claims. It's a point of pride with him to have a tropically hot bedroom, as it is to barter down a rendang at the night market, demand the best view at his favourite whisky lounge, to have mastered chopsticks, if not the language. Mei herself isn't sure if she made a mistake coming here, and she doesn't know how long she'll stay. So she moves from air-conditioned building to air-conditioned car to air-conditioned building, not adapting.

Her phone buzzes. It's a message from Katya.

Mei? says the little preview on the screen. *It's so weird to hear from you . . .*

Mei had half been expecting Katya not to reply. It's been nearly a year since Mei left uni, and they haven't been in contact since. If it hadn't been for the traces, Mei would never have texted her. And Katya, equally, has no reason to respond. Except – perhaps – to vent some anger. Even in the dry chill of the air conditioning, Mei feels an anticipatory sweat starting. She pulls her T-shirt away where it's clinging to her back.

She opens the message.

. . . I have to be honest, Katya has written, *I was legit hurt the way you left things. I'm over it now tho. We're cool. I guess you had stuff to deal with, or whatevs (shrugging emoji). What did you want to ask me?*

Huh, thinks Mei. That wasn't so bad. She puts the phone in her bag, gets dressed and goes out into the apartment.

Her dad, his girlfriend Keiko, her dad's boss and his girlfriend, and another couple of people from her dad's office are in the sitting room, on the long sofas in front of the long glass window, drinking champagne. They'd concluded some sort of work deal today, Mei remembers. She wonders if she can sidle out without being spotted. Her dad is pretty drunk. His eyes look like small buttons in his tanned face. He's a handsome man, even so. That has to be the explanation for why Keiko puts up with him.

'Hi, Mei!' Keiko says, seeing her. She slurs the words slightly. She's scared of heights, and she has to take a Valium before she can visit Mei's dad's apartment. (Mei's dad: '. . . *I always say, once you pass the fortieth floor, there's no going back down again.*') The pill obviously hasn't mixed well with the champagne.

'Hi, everyone,' Mei says. They all turn towards her. 'I'm going out. Not sure when we'll be back. Bye, everyone.'

'That's my daughter,' her dad says proudly. 'Parties like her old man. Have fun, darling.'

Mei was startled when the first trace came to her. She was standing in the shower and there it was. A trace of a place. She'd rinsed herself off, got out, and written it down in her phone:

A row of houses standing above a river. One is dark red, the next one is a burnt orange colour, another is pale brick red. They are all four or five storeys, and all their window frames and gables are white. Each of them has a different roofline and its own quirky brickwork. The water of the river is busy, all the time, and their reflections are just moving colours.

Where is it? she thinks, now. Not Kuala Lumpur, not London. And where am *I*? In the scene she's a nothing. A set of eyes, opposite these houses. Floating. *Listening.*

And who is she with?

Who is talking?

Bold moves aren't such a big deal. Almost as soon as you've made one, it doesn't feel bold any more.

She hears the man speak, but she doesn't recognise his voice.

Mei takes a taxi to Chinatown, to a cafe off Jalan Petaling. She gets out next to a crumbling old colonial building with vines bursting out of the upper shutters. The humidity closes over her, with finality. Walking a few metres down the crowded street, dodging a durian seller, a friendly woman with three small dogs and a piece of plywood bridging a half-finished pavement, overwhelms her. She's relieved to walk into the cafe. The place has a familiar feel to it: green plants, exposed brickwork, metal chairs. Admit it, she thinks: it's just like every independent London coffee shop. She doesn't go to the malls – brighter, cleaner, bigger, more luxurious than the ones back home – but she doesn't go to the night markets either.

Not adapting, she thinks. Not to anywhere.

She stands at the counter; breathes in.

And . . . *there it is.*

The edge of the memory. Sometimes, like now, she can almost feel it in there. It's like a shiny reflective *presence* sitting right in the middle of her brain. Like the creature in that old film, *Predator*. She can catch its movement, sometimes, but when she moves in to investigate, she loses the sense of it.

Mei's googled the science behind memory traces (no way was she going to ask her parents), but there wasn't anything useful on the Nepenthe website. Of course there isn't. Nepenthe still tries to deny the existence of traces, even though nobody believes this. Even though there's a growing body of anecdotal evidence, as Mei's mum might put it, that traces are more common than Nepenthe would like to admit.

Also, if the row of houses and the conversation *aren't* traces, then Mei is just going mad.

She's *almost* sure she's not going mad.

Admittedly, she came off her antidepressants recently without consulting her doctor, which even Google said was a difficult and dangerous thing to do, but also, the internet is full of people talking in forums about how to come off them in stages, gradually lowering the dose, which is what Mei did. And she's okay. She doesn't feel happier, exactly. She feels . . . different. More alert to her own feelings – even though the feelings sometimes alarm her, the way they arrive out of nowhere: fright, shame, anger. It's like they've been queued up for months, long since the incidents they were originally attached to, just waiting for the neurochemical door to open.

And with the feelings came the traces.

The problem is that Mei can only remember those two traces. They repeat, but they don't develop into anything. She can't see anything *around* the houses, no wider view. She can't see anything around the words, either. She has no idea what they could mean in relation to Mei herself. She's never made a bold move in her life. Even coming here to Kuala Lumpur wasn't bold, in the end. She's just moved under a different wing.

Without any way to recover more memory, Katya is Mei's main hope.

The other day, one of Mei's apps suggested Katya to Mei as a friend, which is what always happens when you delete people: they get served up to you again, and again. But before Mei dismissed the pop-up, she noticed that Katya's profile picture showed her beside their other friend Sophia, and a shoulder that Mei is *sure* is her own, with a sunny park in the background.

Mei has no memory of sitting in that park.

She felt a chilly electricity run through her at the thought that this might be the same place as the one from the memory trace. Followed by a more straightforward chill: at the prospect of getting in touch with Katya and – without getting into why Mei left uni, and why Mei hasn't spoken to any of them for a year now – trying to find out where exactly that place was.

Mei orders a flat white, sits down with it, and picks up her phone. WhatsApp shows Katya is online, her picture smiling up at Mei. Mei feels a sharp shove of dread.

Hey, she writes. *How are you?*

Lol, Katya replies. *Stressed out with finals (exploding head emoji). Guess you wouldn't remember it's finals. You left all that behind (laughing emoji).*

It's hard to guess at her tone, or if the emoji is meant to be a gentle laugh or a nasty one. Mei might as well get to the point. It's not like she's going to convince Katya that she just wants to catch up.

I wanted to ask about your profile pic, she says. *Was I in it, originally?*

There's a long pause. The screen says *Katya is typing.* Then there's nothing, for so long Mei wonders if she's gone. Then again, *Katya is typing.*

You're seriously getting back in touch after ghosting us for months to ask if I cropped you out of a freaking photo??!?

Not really, Mei writes. *I'm sorry. I know it sounds weird, but I think I maybe got a memory wipe. I think maybe I went somewhere. With you? But I can only remember a couple of things about it.*

A string of shocked emojis, exclamation points and question marks arrive.

WTF????

Mei sends a shrugging emoji. She's not sure what else to say.

You're saying you don't remember Amsterdam????

Amsterdam?

But it makes sense: Amsterdam. Home of canals, tall houses, parks.

Please tell me about it, Mei writes. *I'm serious. I don't remember any of it. I must have got a wipe after I left uni.*

Got kicked out, you mean.

Ok. Do you know why I'd have wiped that holiday?

This is so freaking weird. OMG. I can't believe you're asking me this. You were shady AF on that trip tho. You totally ditched us (eye-rolling emoji). We went for a week and we saw you for two days of it. You vanished. I thought maybe you met a guy.

I didn't tell you who I met? Or where I went?

36

No. Like I said. You ditched us (shrugging emoji). BTW I have to go out soon.

Mei doesn't know what to say. Obviously what Mei did, leaving uni before the end of the second year and ghosting all her friends, wasn't cool. But on the other hand, Mei was having a hard time at that point. And it's not like Katya and Sophia were going to get any friend-of-the-year trophies either.

Mei's not coming out tonight, said Sophia to Katya.

Mei's like, crying in her room or something, said Sophia to Katya.

I'm kind of over Mei crying in her room.

Mei needs to get her shit together.

(The walls of their student flat were thin.)

Ok, Mei writes now. *Thanks for letting me know. Sorry about everything. Good luck with finals.*

Uhhh ok, writes Katya. She sends an eye-roll emoji. Then, a moment later, she appears to relent. *Bye Mei. Good luck with whatever you're doing.*

When Mei gets back she runs into her dad and his colleagues coming out of the lift, talking loudly. The noise of them clatters all over the marble foyer.

'Mei-mei!' says her dad. 'Back already? We're going out for more drinks. Come with us!'

'Sorry,' Mei says. 'I'm really tired. Have fun though.'

'Fine, fine,' her dad says. 'Hey, do me a favour and call your mother, would you? She called me earlier. She does that when you ignore her. She comes after me.'

'Okay,' Mei says.

37

Her dad turns to the others. He says, 'My ex-wife is terrifying. Very probably a psychopath. That's the real reason I fled England.'

They all laugh.

It's funny, Mei thinks, how when she was living with her mum she used to feel affectionately towards her dad, and now she's living with her dad she's started to feel more affectionately towards her mum.

'I'm going now,' Mei says. She moves in the direction of the lift.

'Bye, darling,' says her dad. 'And seriously, call your mum back, will you?'

Mei sits on her bed, watching the sky darken – grey, to blue, to purple, to black – and the towers of the city light up. She orders some sushi, then calls her mum: the idea being that after no more than twenty minutes the sushi will arrive, and she'll have to go.

'Plum!' says her mother when she picks up. That's what Mei's name means. Beautiful and gracious, says Google: also, a tiny, sweet fruit. She's not sure how you can be a gracious plum. The name was presumably intended to honour her heritage while at the same time remaining easily digestible to Westerners.

'Sorry I haven't called,' Mei says.

'*I'm* sorry for being a clichéd mother and worrying.'

'You're not a clichéd mother,' Mei says. She knows that's what her mother would like to hear.

'Well, no,' says her mum. 'But I'm not immune to *concern*. How are you? Is everything going well?'

'Uneventful,' Mei says. 'I'm looking at universities online.'

'Yes?' her mum says. 'What sort of thing? Still philosophy?'

She says this carefully. Mei had originally been studying philosophy at Edinburgh. This had puzzled both her parents. When she started applying for courses her mum said, But, Plum, I understand you enjoy it, but have you considered what you'll *do* with it? What are you going to do, become a philosophy lecturer? You got top marks in core sciences. Think of the future potential there.

I'd really like to be a philosophy lecturer, actually, said Mei.

Oh, said her mother. Well. A very rewarding profession. Obviously I totally support your choice.

Her dad was more direct. He said: Teaching is for people who can't do anything else. But you *can* do something. You could go into politics. Better, go into the City. Make some real money.

'Yep. Still philosophy,' Mei says to her mum now.

'Ah. I thought you might feel like starting . . . afresh? After your previous experiences.'

'There wasn't anything wrong with the *course*,' Mei says. 'I loved my course. I failed because there was something wrong with *me*.'

There's a silence. The silence is full of things that have been, demonstrably, wrong with Mei. Her earliest memories are of her own lazy eye, her habit of wetting the bed. Her mum fixing her: with corrective lenses, night alarms. Her mum put the incontinence down to the trauma of Mei spending her first six months of life in an orphanage in Guangzhou. But the orphanage is a long time ago now,

39

and Mei's not sure she can blame it for her failing her course.

The thought of the orphanage makes Mei feel weird. It always does. She can't put a name to the feeling beyond *weird*. It's another place she doesn't remember: she never will, and the idea of that makes her uneasy, like waking up after a night of drinking and thinking: *what happened?*

She focuses. It was a mistake to think about the orphanage when she's talking to her mum. Mei needs to stay composed and alert. She can't waver, or she might cry.

'There's nothing at all wrong with you,' her mother says. 'You just needed more help than you were getting. It's not *wrong* to have areas of vulnerability, or to struggle to cope. The next time you go into that situation, you'll have that support.'

'More drugs,' Mei says.

'I can't tell over the phone if this is a dry humour thing or if this is something we seriously need to talk about,' her mother says.

Mei covers the handset. She sighs. Then she takes her hand away and says, 'It was humour.'

'Good. Anyway, how are you for money? I put some into your account last week.'

'Thank you,' Mei says. 'I'm not really spending it though.'

'You should. Enjoy yourself. Think of it as a summer off before you come back for university.'

'Right,' Mei says.

She hasn't told her mum that she isn't sure yet if she *does* want to come back to England. That she's been looking at universities in Italy and Germany and France. She's not sure when to have that conversation. The thought of it makes her face feel hot, then abruptly cold, as the beginning of sweat meets the powerful air conditioning.

Not now, she thinks. It doesn't have to be now.

'And everything's going well with your dad?' her mum asks. Her tone here is neutral.

Mei's not going to say: actually, I thought moving here would make it easier to just . . . *be*, but it turns out that while I don't feel exactly the same *type* of pressure I felt living with you, I still feel a pressure, and I still don't know how to be.

How can she even describe that pressure, anyway? Her mother would say she just wants Mei to be supported. Her dad would say he just wants Mei to have fun. Mei can't articulate what her actual problem is with either of those wishes.

'It's fine,' Mei says.

'Well, good,' her mum says. 'I imagine he's still telling people I'm a psychopath.'

'Not every day.'

Her mum laughs. 'Obviously I think your father is a flashy, irresponsible egotist,' she says. 'But he does adore you. I respect that. And so I hope you don't feel like there's any issue of loyalty here. Of omertà. You can tell me if things aren't going well, you know. And it's okay if you do want to come home.'

When Mei's mum says this, tears rise up, in Mei's eyes and her throat. She's annoyed at the tears for falling so quickly into line. She swallows them back.

'I'm having fun here,' she says. 'I'm happy.'

'Well, I'm glad to hear it. No other news?'

Mei looks at her laptop screen, which is open on a website that scans the internet for the cheapest flights, in this case to Amsterdam.

'Nope,' she says. 'Nothing I can think of.'

Mei's read a lot, now, about memory wipes.

She would have been a night client: collected in a black car, in darkness; driven to the clinic nearest her house. Crowshill. There, around midnight, she'd have had the procedure. (Which isn't done by lasers, like everyone assumes, but by a little capsule, a plastic cup of water, and a mild electrical current.) Afterwards, Mei would have been given another drug, to stop new memories from forming, so that she'd forget she'd been to Crowshill. Then she'd have been put into another black car and driven back to bed; everything that happened that night vanishing behind her, as if someone was following her with a little broom, rubbing out her footsteps.

Back at home, she'd have taken the last pill. One to put her into a sleep lasting for a thousand years – or ten seconds: in the morning she wouldn't be able to say.

She'd be calm. Groggy.

None the wiser.

Mei's heard that traces can come back in dreams. But she's never dreamt about Amsterdam, or the conversation she must have had there.

And yet, there's a dreamlike sense to the traces. The way she's present but not present. Watching; bodiless. The light that flickers on the surface of the river, the tall houses, the man saying, *Bold moves aren't such a big deal.*

How can you have nostalgia for somewhere you don't remember being? How can you long, in a painful way, for something you don't even know?

But she longs, all the same.

It turns out that Mei's mum has put enough money in Mei's bank account to cover the flights and a few nights in a small hotel near the Bloemenmarkt. She thinks she can probably get some more cash from her dad before she goes.

Mei feels bad about lying to her parents. After the failed year at university, she'd agreed with her mother that she would be honest and open about her feelings. But she's already failed at that, by not telling her mum she stopped taking her pills. And anyway, what else can she do? It's almost certain that her mum – and maybe her dad, too – knows Mei had a memory removed. In which case, they would definitely *not* want Mei to rush off to Amsterdam to try to get it back. To them, this would look inconsistent, and unstable, and would remind them of other times Mei has been inconsistent and unstable. They'd worry, and they'd stop her going.

She clicks continue; purchase; agree; confirm.

When everything is settled and paid for, she feels a sharp rise of emotion. It's not easy yet to tell – since coming out of the muffling blanket of antidepressants – what these kinds of sudden, piercing emotions are, where they're coming from. It takes her a minute to recognise a feeling she once had all the time: fear.

But there's also relief. And . . .

. . . excitement?

Excitement! It's been a while since she felt that one.

Her phone chimes and lights up, like a dog picking up the mood.

You are going on holiday! Here's everything you need to know for your flight on 26 May.

May, Mei, she thinks.

It's her month, after all. May Day. Isn't that what people say when they're in trouble? Not May Day, but *m'aidez.* Help me.

Mei's helping herself.

Maybe this is it, she thinks. A bold move. At last.

She lies back on the bed, the phone resting on her heart, and laughs.

Finn

Finn is walking back to his car from the bakery, trying to remember if there are flowers at home, or if he needs to buy some, and if the florist will even be open by the time he gets there.

It's almost six o'clock. The Sedona sun is already withdrawing from the windows of the shops. Once it's taken itself away from the street it will begin the process of unfastening itself from the landscape; the trees, the desert, the unearthly red rock buttes last of all.

For now, though, the sky is preposterously blue, and the sun is in it. Finn should really try to notice things like this more, not think about twilight, or parking tickets, or grey hair, or the stealthy descent of his own balls towards his knees – the way they never seem to do it when he's watching, like a game of What's the Time, Mr Wolf? – or whether the bread he has just bought will still be springy tomorrow morning.

He tries to focus on the street. Sun, cars, cafe tables, a waft of smoke, of coffee.

Coffee.

Ri, his daughter, aged fourteen, has left the family home to go on a four-week tour of Europe. She goes to a progressive private school that values experiential and intuitive learning, which apparently makes it okay to miss almost a month of actual syllabus.

They do extra work at other times, Mirande said.

Yes, but what's the work? said Finn. Contemplating sunsets? Wasn't that one assignment? Going to the cinema. Taking ayahuasca.

You liked that school up until now. You just don't want her to go away. Admit it.

I admit nothing. All I'll say is: she still drinks chocolate milk.

What?

She says coffee tastes like poison, said Finn.

It *is* poison, said Mirande, sipping her espresso.

The point is, her taste buds are childlike, said Finn. Too young for olives, dry wine, coffee. How can she cross an ocean and leave us, with a tongue as young as that?

He gets into his hot car and turns on the air con. The harsh cold, scything his face, is as close as he'll get to an Irish climate. He feels envious of Ri – who will probably get rained on in Europe, hailed on if she's lucky – envious, and something beyond that. Some premonition of melancholy. Then he realises he's done it again. He's meant to be trying to live in the moment, or at least that was the idea a moment ago, before he forgot.

Note to self, remember to live in the moment.

Finn, Mirande and Ri live on the outskirts of town, in Oak Creek Canyon. Their house is a long, sub-Mies van der Rohe box, stark white, floor-to-ceiling glass windows on most sides. Apparently it had replaced a historic (*for Arizona*, Finn feels compelled to add) house that had been owned by one family for over a hundred years, until it burned down. All that was left was the garden and an adobe wall with wonky gateposts and a noisy wrought-iron gate.

When the landscaper they hired to sort the garden out arrived, he said, So you're replacing all this.

It wasn't a question.

Actually, no, said Finn. It makes me smile. The old meeting the new.

I see, said the landscaper. It's clever. The gate is your joke.

Sort of.

But not a very good joke.

Maybe not.

Not a *funny* joke.

Right.

That's how you know it's clever.

Finn didn't try to explain that the gateposts were part of the reason they'd bought the house. They'd been living in California at the time. Mirande had seen it online, sent a picture to Finn. No subject line, just an exclamation mark.

It was their *thing*, that's what it was. Finn and Mirande's thing, born on a spring afternoon in Southwark. (This is one of Finn's favourite stories, albeit one he doesn't tell at parties, because that day Finn and Mirande, the main characters, were actually accompanied by Finn's girlfriend Diana and Mirande's boyfriend Max, the supporting cast. Plus David, who knew Mirande from medical school, and David's girlfriend what's-her-name. Extras.) Anyway, it was the mid-nineties, and they'd all had lunch at some restaurant that didn't exist any more. Afterwards they wandered around the South Bank, and everyone else walked, talking, past the two remaining walls of the old Winchester Palace – everyone except for Mirande, who'd stopped, and was looking up at them.

Finn stopped too. Diana, who'd been holding his hand, rolled her eyes and went on ahead.

I didn't know this was here, Mirande said.

City ruins, Finn said. What I like about this particular ruin is that it's half built into that building. I don't know why. But I prefer it to something old that's been left on its own, and I definitely prefer it to something new that's totally new.

I understand that, Mirande said.

She didn't seem inclined to move on. She looked up at the fractured rose window thoughtfully, as if she had a question for it. The others were almost out of sight. They'd been wandering too long, and the general consensus was that it was time to find somewhere to sit down and get pissed.

One of the best ruins I ever saw, said Finn, was in Wales. It had the same quality to it. It was an ancient dolmen.

The big rocks balanced on top of each other? The old tombs?

That's it. Thousands of years old. Anyway, this one was right in the middle of a suburb. There was this empty space, interrupting a row of new houses. With a dolmen in it. You walked into this cul-de-sac, and in a square of grass there it was: a Neolithic tomb. I can't explain why I liked that so much.

It's an absurd juxtaposition, Mirande said. Unexpected dissonance. Didn't someone once say that all jokes were the result of that?

Those are exactly the right words, said Finn, enjoying them. Absurd juxtaposition.

Behind them, David came round the corner. He looked pleased to see them.

How did you do that? Finn said to David. I thought you were ahead of us.

Had to go to the cashpoint, David said. You two look like you're scheming.

Scheming about ancient bits of masonry, said Mirande.

David said: I *love* ancient masonry.

Oh, do you? thought Finn, as David went on, enthusing about a particular stone circle in the Scottish Highlands, which wasn't crowded by modern buildings, like this poor palace, but was instead in the middle of absolutely nowhere – absolutely nothing there, really, but you and the circle and the rain and the far-off sheep and this feeling of almost . . . portentousness. Anyway, it was a pretty powerful experience.

David smiled.

Mirande nodded and smiled.

Finn nodded and smiled.

Thinking: *Ha! You fool! You clot! You blew it!*

Finn isn't expecting to see Ri when he gets into the house, and of course she isn't there, but something about her not being there still surprises him. He walks from Ri-less room to Ri-less room – feeling quietness and tidiness, for the first time, as absence. The absence is loudest in the kitchen, which is pristine. If Finn squints he can almost see the ghost of his daughter, upper body sprawled across the kitchen island, school bag collapsed on the floor beside her, stealing the canapés Finn left out to cool.

Mirande comes in, looks startled at the sight of him, then smiles.

'I didn't hear you get back. Oh, you brought peonies,' she says. 'They're beautiful.'

Finn springs over to Mirande and catches her in his arms. She puts her head on his shoulder. He feels the bones of her back, the layer of yoga muscle, the soft skin, the silk jersey. She looks almost the same as she did when they met. More care goes into it these days, over twenty years on; she's elegant where she used to be hippy-ish, though she still has something hippy-ish about her: her hair not quite as long as it used to be, blonde, in a carefully half-arsed chignon. A tall woman; a long-footed woman; slender fingers; queenly nose.

'Remember Winchester Palace?' he says to her.

'Of course I do,' she says.

Mirande and Finn, thinks Finn, into her hair. Scrappy Finn, from the poorest of Irish council estates. Beautiful Mirande, descendant of rich Dutch merchants.

An absurd juxtaposition.

Perfect.

In the half-hour before the party, Finn is restless; pacing the house, rearranging things, putting them back. Mirande comes in, smelling of tuberose and orange blossom.

'Mbali is coming,' she says. 'Oh, and Natalie and Viv DeWitt! They're new here and I want them to be our friends, so make sure you charm them. Though I suppose I don't need to tell you that.'

Finn acknowledges it, his ability to charm. To put on the Finn Show. A generous host, a compliment for everyone, a joke for every awkward moment – a whole repair kit of jokes.

An empty glass! says Finn. Let me fix that for you.

It is *a Kofod Larsen, says Finn. I'm impressed you noticed. It isn't often one gets to meet another true sideboard enthusiast.*

Your wine? On the rug? says Finn. Don't apologise! Blame the dog! There is no dog? Then that's your first mistake. Always bring a dog.

Mirande is the quieter one of the two of them. Not because she's shy. She's never anything other than perfectly at ease with herself. Unlike Finn, she just doesn't feel the need to make quite so much noise. She doesn't feel so much *need* full stop.

Of course, it helps to be beautiful.

The doorbell rings.

'I'll get it!' Finn says, leaping (the Finn Show begins!) across the room.

'And the project?' says Mbali to Finn. 'How's that going?'

Finn's the architect in residence on a social housing and neighbourhood regeneration project in South Phoenix. People tend to get very solemn and admiring when they find out. To keep his ego in check, Finn's developed a little spiel in which he gives all the credit to his hero, Samuel Mockbee.

'Mockbee wanted to make buildings not an egoistic thing but something collaborative, socially responsible,' Finn tells Mbali now. 'I try to think what he would have done here. Talking to the community, for example.'

'Working without ego is quite an achievement,' says Mbali, gazing at him approvingly.

Finn, flattered, says, 'Oh, no, I haven't transcended ego. With something like this, I *can't* impose my own identity. What I mean is, when you disregard the community you get the spaces wrong. You have to think about how people move around. Where they have to squeeze past each other, where they feel cornered, where they feel safe. So really, I *have* to be collaborative, but I act humble about it. And then people praise me for being humble. So maybe my ego has just found another way to feel superior.'

'Now I don't know whether to praise you for being honest or whether this is another act to get more praise,' says Mbali.

'Oh, we're only about halfway through my ego layers,' Finn says. Mirande has appeared next to him, topping up his and Mbali's drinks.

'Your what?' says Mirande.

'Layers of self,' Finn says. 'And the question of whether, if you peel them away one by one, you're left with anything at all.' Reaching back, blind, he finds the base of Mirande's back, slides his thumb along the channel of her spine.

'That's horrible,' says Mbali, with a delighted laugh. 'Surely you're left with whatever you *really* are, deep down.'

'I'm watching a TV series right now,' says Finn, 'and one character just told another that they don't believe in deep down. They said all you are is what you do. I agree with that. If someone's 90 per cent awful and 10 per cent great, everyone says that *deep down* they're great. Like they're an iceberg but all the greatness is under the water – and invisible. But actually, the truth is, they're just 90 per cent awful.'

Other people have joined the conversation. 'That's the show with the talking horse, isn't it?' someone says.

'Mr Ed?' says Mirande. 'Mr Ed said that?'

Everyone laughs. 'No,' says Finn. He prides himself on staying abreast of the zeitgeist. 'It's a cartoon horse. A depressed one.'

Mirande says, 'Well, I'm not sure we *are* the things we do, either. This is what I've never understood. We're told to just be ourselves, right? But we're also told we can be whatever we want. Where does that leave us? What *is* "myself"?'

'That doesn't make any sense,' a man says. Finn has no idea who this man is. The fat husband of Mirande's attractive book club friend, is all Finn knows of him.

'*She would not say of any one in the world now that they were this or were that,*' Finn says to the man. 'Mrs Dalloway.'

'Who?' says the man.

'She works in one of the many jewellery shops of Sedona and says really quite profound things,' Finn says. 'You should look out for her.'

'I'm on the side of "we can be whatever we want" then,' says Mbali. 'Because most people are terrible. At least if they can be whatever they want, there's a chance they'll *improve*.'

'Well.' Mirande considers this. 'I think it's very rare for people to even have that level of self-awareness. Let alone change their behaviour.'

'Okay. That's . . . truly disturbing,' Mbali says.

'Don't worry,' says Finn. 'As I always say: it's not a party if you're not left questioning the nature of your own existence. More wine?'

Later, after everyone has gone home, Mirande and Finn lie in bed. The house beyond the bedroom walls is very quiet. The most silent silence, after the noise is gone.

'Sweet of you to defend my honour, against Lily's husband.' Mirande moves herself closer to him. Her skin is cool, even in a warm room. 'I love you,' she says. Then she starts to laugh. 'I love how proud you are of knowing about a depressed cartoon horse.'

'Nothing gets past you,' Finn says. 'I'm fifty. But I still want to be relevant. Is that ridiculous? It is ridiculous.'

'You're relevant to me,' Mirande says. She kisses him.

'Oh God,' Finn says. 'It really is all over. We should go shopping for gravestones tomorrow.'

'We'll get you a really fashionable one,' Mirande says, yawning. 'All the kids will be taking photos of it for Facebook.'

'It's Instagram now,' Finn says, unable to help himself. Then, 'I have a question.'

'Yes?'

'What you said about not having a true self, or however you put it. Do you . . . believe that?'

'Oh, maybe. I don't know. I like the idea of it.'

'Do you? It bothers me. I mean, if you could become something different at any second, there's no guarantee you'll wake up tomorrow and still love me.'

'Oh, so this is about *you*.' Mirande says.

'It's about us. Finn and Mirande. They met, they fell in love, they lived happily ever after. Right? Not: they met, they fell in love, they lived happily for a while, they became completely different people.'

'I like the first one,' Mirande says.

'But can you guarantee it?'

'Whatever "I" am guarantees it, sure.'

'Thanks. I feel so much better.'

'Finn.' She puts her face close to his. He can smell the night transmuting on her skin: wine turned to ethanol, her perfume a vague sweetness. 'Didn't I say how impossible it is for anyone to change? We're stuck with the selves that love each other.'

'That's what I wanted to hear,' he says.

'Mmm.' She yawns again. 'I'm tired now. Aren't you?'

'Definitely. Speaking of gravestones. I'm going to design a house for Ri next to an ancient burial mound. I could get us buried there too. In among the Beaker people. Or as near to them as we're allowed. I'm drunk, yes. But wouldn't it be the perfect cycle? Us ending where we began. Ruins, and death, and life going on. We might need permits.'

'Sounds lovely,' Mirande says. 'Let's get some sleep.'

'Okay,' Finn says. 'Sleep it is.'

And so they go to sleep, in each other's arms.

(No they don't. Mirande falls asleep and Finn, as usual, thinks on.)

*

It's the morning after the party and Finn is lying in bed, enjoying not having a hangover. He drinks (*Of course I drink!* he says. *I'm Irish*), then gets up the next morning feeling young, refreshed and more than a little smug. *Got away with it again, Finn, you old fox.*

He gets up very quietly, without waking Mirande – who has not been similarly blessed – and gets into the shower. He dresses and goes downstairs.

'Ri?' he calls, before he remembers.

Silence. Broken only by the pert whistle of Mirande's phone, lodged between the sofa cushions. He plucks it out. It's a message from Nepenthe. The memory-removal place.

Weird time for them to be sending out marketing texts, Finn thinks. Trying to attract new customers while still paying compensation to the old customers – or giving them their memories back, or whatever it is they're being forced to do. There are ads running on TV at the moment: a man in a suit asking: *Are you unhappy about your memory removal?*

(The man is trying to be stern and sad at the same time: stern about the company removing memories, sad for the people who've had their memory removed.)

Do you feel misled? Traumatised? You could be in line for compensation. Call our dedicated legal team NOW.

Finn brews silver needle tea, arranges two cups and the phone on the tray and carries it back to their bedroom. The bed is empty: Mirande is up, brushing her teeth in the bathroom.

'Goo' mor'ing, my 'arling,' she says through the froth. 'I fee' awfu'.'

'There's tea here. And there are some emails and texts for you.'

'From?'

He unlocks the phone. 'The DeWitts, Mbali, a couple of other people.'

She turns delicately away to spit out the toothpaste, then holds her hair back with one hand, puts her head under the tap and rinses. 'Would you read them to me? I haven't got my lenses in.'

'Sure. You've got something from Nepenthe . . . here we go: "Dear Mirande, we are writing to inform you of your full medical history, in accordance with a change to our company policy. Recent developments in memory removal technology have brought about a change in the law concerning our service, and we are now required to notify all Nepenthe Memory Solutions clients of their status —" what? What is this?'

Mirande comes over; he holds the phone out to her. They read in silence.

. . . As you may know, Nepenthe clients must decide whether or not to be aware that they had a memory removed. You underwent a procedure at one of our clinics to remove a short period of time (of no longer than a week) from your memory, and you opted not to know about this procedure. We are unable to give you any information about the procedure itself, including the date it was carried out . . .

Mirande's hand falls to her side, still holding the phone. She stares at Finn. Her mouth is very red from the pressure of flossing, the blood all risen up to the surface.

'This has to be a mistake,' Finn says. 'They're saying you had a memory wiped, you can get it back. Which is ridiculous. You haven't had a memory wipe.'

'No,' she says. 'I *can't* have.'

They stand there for a minute, staring at each other. Then Mirande says, 'But . . . how would I know?'

'Okay,' Finn says. 'You wouldn't know. But *I'd* know. Wouldn't I? I remember when they started up. We were together. It was in the late nineties. Remember, when we were house hunting and that estate agent said it would give everyone brain damage? You were explaining neurons to him . . . We laughed about it. Remember?'

'I remember,' she says slowly. She's reading the email again. 'But, okay, why would *you* know?'

'Well, if the technology only came into existence while we were together, surely I'd know whatever it was that you were getting deleted.'

'Not if I chose not to tell you,' she says. 'Not if something terrible happened to me and I knew immediately that I would get it erased. I wouldn't tell you, because then you'd have to keep the knowledge a secret from me, or get a wipe yourself.'

'Okay. Right. But . . . surely there would have been some sign that something terrible had happened to you? I mean, if you came home hurt, or upset, I'd *know*. I know you. You couldn't have hidden it from me.'

'I don't know,' she says. 'I just don't know.'

She frowns, evidently trying to remember. It's like watching someone reaching for a phantom limb. Mirande hates any failing of her own brain, always has: taking it badly when she can't remember a surname, or calculate a sum in her head. She looks pained, now. It's painful to watch.

'When I was in Singapore,' Finn says. 'We weren't living together then.'

She shrugs, shakes her head. She looks like she's about to cry.

Finn takes her hands and presses them.

'Listen, don't be upset. They've clearly just fucked up. Why don't you call them first thing on Monday? Find out what the situation is. In a day's time we're going to be laughing about this.'

'Okay,' she says.

But later, Finn thinks: that was a mistake. To say *we're going to be laughing about this*. To think *when everything is sorted out*. It was the most basic tempting of fate. Schoolboy error.

So it's Finn's own fault, then, when a week later, over dinner, a colleague of Mirande's named Liz says to them:

'I hear an old friend of yours is here.'

Finn has never really thought of himself as having psychic abilities. He doesn't believe in them. There's always an explanation. Still, it's strange how when Liz says *I hear an old friend of yours is here*, turning to Mirande, Finn *knows* who it must be. He doesn't feel it as a frequency, a vibration picked up from either of the two women – rather, it comes from Finn himself. The knowledge rises up through him. It's simple and clear. The question is posed, and something in Finn answers:

David.

Mirande blinks. 'Oh?' she says. 'Who?'

'Well, it's a funny story. I was at the hospital, and there's a British surgeon here teaching some reconstructive surgery techniques. He's here for a few weeks. David Schafe. He's very good, we're lucky to have him. Some of his grafts . . . Anyway. I got chatting to him, found out he was from London, studied at Cambridge, and I wondered if he knew you. He said, Mirande O'Connor? Yeah, just a bit.'

They all laugh.

'David,' says Mirande. 'Of course.'

'Wouldn't he have let you know he was coming?' Finn asks.

'Actually he did. He emailed. But things have been slightly . . .'

Finn wonders how she's going to explain *things* to Liz.

Things being that Mirande had secretly had a memory deleted – had been told later, on the phone, that no, this wasn't a mistake, Nepenthe didn't make mistakes like that. And no, they couldn't tell her when it had been done, on the basis that if Mirande chose not to restore the memory, she'd retain her original right not to know anything about it.

The news had upset her. It was still upsetting her. She'd been frowning into space a lot, and biting her cuticles. One was bleeding. Finn himself was slightly upset. Not that he'd mention it. *Things* were bad enough as they were.

'. . . chaotic,' Mirande continues. 'You know how it is . . .'

'Oh, lord, tell me about it,' says Liz.

'. . . and I forgot to follow up.'

'And now he's here,' says Finn.

'What a small world it is,' says Liz, and starts talking about the really very beautiful job Dr Schafe did of putting someone's ears back on.

Mirande's face is pointing at Liz, nodding, but Finn can see her gaze is passing straight through Liz's head and out the other side. Across the garden, over the desert and forests, not stopping until it reaches the Mayo Clinic in Scottsdale, in which David Schafe is probably doing something beautiful.

Finn has been aware of the various Nepenthe court cases, obviously. He was interested at first, checking the news, but legal action turned out to be very, very slow. And as it had nothing to do with him – or not until a few days ago – he'd mostly tuned it out.

He's known a few people who've had memories erased. Like the woman at his office whose husband was shot in a robbery. She knew it had happened, but had no memory of the incident. She was doing okay, he heard, or as okay as you can do when your husband has been murdered.

Finn also knew that there was another kind of Nepenthe client: the ones who chose not to know about their procedures. The night clients. Finn never knew any of those people, because they didn't know themselves. Or not until a few days ago, when it turned out Mirande was one of them.

Or not until a few days ago. Finn wonders what else about his life is going to end up with this qualifier.

During those last few days, Finn and Mirande have acquired an exhaustive knowledge of the subject of memory removal. Via Google, obviously.

'I can't believe the ruling,' Mirande says. She looks tired, and unhappy. 'That all the night clients have to be notified. It's insane. Don't I have the right *not* to know? Isn't that what I paid them for?'

'Apparently that original agreement is void,' says Finn, internet legal expert. 'Nepenthe argued that patients had signed to opt out of having the memory. But the lawyers bringing the case argued that the contracts were based on the premise that the memory was gone in perpetuity. And so it wasn't fully informed consent. Legally there's no precedent, it's –'

'It's insane,' says Mirande, again. She takes off her reading glasses and rubs her face.

'Well,' says Finn, 'it might help the people who were getting those traces or memory flashbacks or whatever they were, and didn't know if they were going mad.'

'A *fraction* of the total number of clients,' Mirande protests. 'Less than 1 per cent!'

'Still: a lot of people. Thousands,' Finn says. (Wondering: what is he doing? How much does he care about these people?) But on he goes: 'Their quality of life –'

'What about *my* quality of life?' Mirande says. She's started to cry. 'What about *me* going mad?'

'I'm sorry,' Finn says. 'This isn't abstract. It's not a debate. I'm an idiot. I'm sorry.'

He hugs her. Over her shoulder he sees himself in the glass of the window, superimposed on the red rock formations.

He doesn't like his own expression.
He closes his eyes.

When did you two meet?

That's what people like to ask couples who've been together for a long time. When he's asked, Finn doesn't tell the story of Winchester Palace – though, privately, he considers that to be their true origin story.

Instead he'll say: There was this wedding in Cornwall, 1996, and Mirande and I danced together, and pretty much straight after that, we both broke up with the people we were with at that time, and then we got together.

It was *not* like that, Mirande will say. (Mirande's role in the story being to deny, to roll her eyes, to laugh.)

She left him for me, Finn will say.

I did not leave him *for* anyone, Mirande will say. We parted on mutual and very good terms. It was actually months before Finn and I got together.

She just didn't want to have chucked this guy for someone else, Finn will say. She told me she wasn't ready to start a new relationship so quickly. She calculated that she would need six months exactly, to think.

(Laughter)

Chuck is a very harsh word, Mirande will say.

Then Finn will tell them how Mirande said Finn could still come over, of course, as a friend. And maybe they ended up kissing, on one of Finn's friendly visits. Because, *obviously*, she couldn't resist him.

Mirande will laugh, take Finn's hand, shake her head. The joke lying in her final acknowledgement of Finn's story: that she really *couldn't* resist, and the thinking period was reduced to three months – early release for good behaviour, as Finn says.

And whoever they are telling it to will say, *Isn't that lovely?* Or something along those lines.

Sometimes Finn worries that the more he tells a story, the more the original events fade away. Certain elements get left out. Over time they get forgotten entirely – or at least until something stirs them back up again.

For example, David Schafe.

David and Mirande were friends for years before Finn met Mirande. They'd studied medicine at Cambridge together. Then they lost touch for a while, with Mirande living in London with her boyfriend, and David in Surrey somewhere, which meant Finn spent the first months of his own friendship with Mirande not knowing that there *was* a David, until one spring – the spring that Finn suspected that Mirande and her boyfriend were on the outs – he was told that Mirande had a close friend called David, and he'd just moved back to London.

During Mirande's three-month thinking period, Finn was aware that she was also spending time with David Schafe. They went to the cinema together, exhibitions, ate lunch – and why not? They were friends, after all.

Also, Mirande had already told Finn that she wasn't asking him to wait for her. In fact, she said he should consider himself to be single. They mustn't have any expectations of each other.

And so Finn couldn't have questioned her about David, even if he wanted to.

(He wanted to.)

Another of Finn's stories:

A few months after Finn and Mirande's wedding, 2002, Finn was offered the opportunity to work in Singapore for eighteen months. He talked it through with Mirande and she said she understood. Mirande herself was hoping to go to Africa with Médecins Sans Frontières. She was staying on in their house in Pinner while she waited for her application to be processed. It took longer than she expected, and Finn hadn't had as much time off as he expected, and by the time six months had passed their marriage mainly consisted of one visit and a lot of arguing over the phone, terse back and forths zapping over oceans and continents.

Mirande explained, later, that it was after one of these arguments that she'd decided to surprise him.

It was either that or divorce you, she said.

How did you decide? asked Finn.

Flipped a coin, she said.

(*And I'm still not sure if that was a joke*, present-day Finn will say.)

And so Finn got back from work, on a day of warm, heavy rain, to find Mirande waiting for him. She was sitting under an umbrella with her suitcase, on the step outside his apartment block. Even a hundred feet down the street he knew it was her, from the men passing, looking, turning their heads to carry on looking.

It turned out that once the oceans and continents were cleared out of the way, there was only love left. They spent the rest of the weekend in bed.

A few weeks after her surprise visit, Mirande called to tell Finn that she was pregnant and that she wanted to have the baby.

(Up until then neither of them had intended to have children. Mirande had brought it up when Finn proposed. The champagne was still fizzing when she said,

I probably won't ever want children. Is that all right?

Fine with me, said Finn. I don't see the point of them at all.

So that was that, and they could clink their glasses.)

I know this isn't what we planned, she said. I wouldn't blame you if you didn't want to do this.

It's fine with me, said Finn.

And it was.

So Mirande told MSF that her circumstances had changed and she wouldn't be able to join them, not yet. Finn left Singapore and came back to London. Ri was born. It was genuinely beautiful. He found his daughter beautiful even though she wasn't beautiful, not then, and had done unspeakable things to her mother's body. He took hold of the damp bundle: forgave her immediately, loved her immediately.

(And present-day Finn will often have to stop talking at this point, because there's something in his eye.)

'Why don't you invite David over for dinner?' Finn says to Mirande, once Liz has gone.

'David?' she says. 'Really? I was just going to meet him for a lunch. You want to see him too?'

'Why do you look so surprised? He's one of our oldest friends.'

'Our? I didn't think you even knew him that well,' Mirande says.

It's true: Finn never did get to know David, really. There was a short period in London when they all saw a lot of each other, but then, not long after Finn and Mirande got together, David moved to Edinburgh. By the time David came back to London, to work at Great Ormond Street, Finn was in Singapore. A year later, David moved to Canada. He met a woman there, and got married. Finn met his wife once, apparently, but can't remember much about her, and then she and David got divorced, and David moved back to England, to Crowshill. By then Finn and Mirande were in America. David kept in touch with Mirande by email, and Mirande would pass on significant details – marriage, divorce, emigration – to Finn.

'That's just situational,' Finn says. 'We've just never been in the same place long enough. It's like Clark Kent and Superman. Out of modesty, I won't say who's who.'

But he doesn't find his own joke very funny. He feels annoyed, even, at the thought of sharing a comic book with David, the same feeling he had when he and Mirande were looking at Winchester Palace and David turned up behind them.

Mirande frowns. She's visibly choosing her words.

'I suppose I thought it might not be a great time. With this Nepenthe decision hanging over me. Us.'

'But we're carrying on as usual, aren't we? You said you didn't want anything to change, that you needed a bit of time to absorb it, but that we'd still live our usual lives, and then –'

'Yes. I remember. It's just. You know, David isn't part of our usual lives. I thought, maybe, he'd be an additional . . .'

'Additional what?'

'An additional strain.'

Silence. They look at each other. Then Mirande raises her hands, helplessly. 'Come on, Finn! We both know you've never liked him particularly.'

'What? When have I ever said that?'

'Years ago. You said you didn't like him; you didn't trust him.'

Finn does vaguely remember something like this, now that she says it.

'Years ago,' he says. 'Before we were together?'

'No. It was when you were in Singapore. He was back in London, I was spending time with him. And you said he was trying to . . . move in. On me. I remember the expression because it was the first time I'd heard it.'

That was it.

'Well,' he says now, 'that was a long time ago. I was away from you, I was insecure. I was being ridiculous. But the fact that I could barely remember *not* liking David ought to demonstrate that I like David now.'

'Hmm,' says Mirande. She looks like she might say something else, then she hesitates, and sighs. 'I could invite him on Thursday?'

'Good idea,' says Finn. 'I'll cook.'

Oscar

Oscar, for the twentieth – maybe even thirtieth – time since he got here, is lost in the medina.

The problem this time is that his phone has died, so he can't use it to navigate, and he has no cash, having given it to a man whose wife was dying and needed medical care. (A man who, in retrospect, might not have been telling the truth.)

The medina is a maze as mysterious to Oscar as the many branches of his own misfiring neurons. Circlings; dead ends; occasional, unexpected connections. Above it all, the call to prayer, rising and undulating, in a language he can't interpret. Which means Oscar can't have grown up here.

Useful information. One country, Morocco, ticked off the list.

One hundred and ninety-four to go.

Everyone says you can navigate Marrakech by using the main square and the minaret of the Koutoubia Mosque as reference points, but the minaret isn't usually visible from the ground, and while getting to the square is easy, leaving it to go somewhere else isn't so simple. Oscar ends up arriving back at it over and over again, until the snake charmers and orange-juice salesmen stop calling to him, and look suspicious, as if he is wasting their time. In the end he gives up. He'll just have to get a taxi, and get fleeced.

He's also going to have to go to a cashpoint.

There's no way round it. He thought he'd be able to avoid it for a bit longer: that noisy machine, telling tales. When the screen lights up and bleeps he wants to cringe away.

Here you are! it says. *I see you!*

At least, he thinks, this machine is at the opposite end of the medina from the last one. If someone wants to search every street for him they can go ahead. The thought cheers him up. A hundred entrances. A thousand blind corners. A million (or thereabouts) heavy studded doors set in blank, lumpy walls.

Oscar takes out as much money as the cashpoint will allow. He avoids looking at the balance on screen. Another thing he doesn't understand, another thing that frightens him.

All that money.

Oscar doesn't think about the money, if he can possibly help it.

It's a strange place, Oscar's hotel. It looks like a dictator's palace – like the kind of place you'd see on TV getting turned over during the Arab Spring. He can't walk through it without hearing the ghostly cries of revolution. It feels *temporary*, as if the chandeliers, the velvet cushions, the giant bronze sculpture of a lion attacking a camel are all already halfway out the door, hoisted on the shoulders of looters. There they go down the road, like the dancing furniture in that Disney film, to the sound of singing, the occasional gunshot.

Oscar's never been in a revolution. Not to his knowledge, anyway. Though it is exactly the kind of thing he'd get accidentally involved with. Someone would hand him a placard or a machete and off he'd go, in over his head, as per usual.

A memory comes back to him.

This isn't the first time you've got into trouble, said a woman. There was a folder in front of her. Oscar tried to read it upside down, but she closed it. She didn't sound particularly angry. She just sounded sad, at all the trouble Oscar had been getting into.

Who was she? A teacher? A policewoman? But no. No uniform. But the sense of her – of that talk – is drifting away, turning to fuzz. He sees the woman in a corridor. It's not a school; there are too many adults around. But the harder he tries to remember that moment the less grip he has on it, like squeezing a rubber ball until it shoots out of his grasp.

'Oh!' the receptionist says when she sees him. 'There have been calls for you, Mr Levy. One moment, sir.'

Calls?

Unwillingly, he crosses the slippery marble floor to the desk. The receptionist smiles at him, says, 'Excuse me for one minute,' then disappears through a door.

What calls? Oscar wonders. Nobody should know that he's here.

Calm, he thinks to himself. *Calm.*

He considers turning and walking straight out of the hotel, before the receptionist comes back.

Except, he remembers, his passport is in his room.

Fuck.

The receptionist gets back, smiles again, and hands him a mock-croc folder. The excess ceremony – the five-star insistence on hiding everything in folders and under silver lids – isn't calming. Each of his fingers leaves a dark sweat print on the leather.

The names inside aren't any he recognises. Are they the same names as before? He can't remember. The messages are brief and polite. Why are they always polite? It seems like a strange, nastily delicate way of messing with him. Like the leather folder, slipping in his wet paws.

'We didn't have any instructions, regarding callers . . .' the receptionist says. She looks wary, as if Oscar's about to start upending gilded chairs. Why is she wary? What are his eyes doing? They could be up to anything. Staring wildly, darting shiftily, glaring psychopathically (is that a word?). If only he could see what they were doing, maybe he could stop it.

'I wasn't expecting calls,' he says. 'But I should have known they'd find me.'

'They?' she asks, looking confused.

Was that a weird thing to have said?

Yes. Yes, it was.

'Oh . . . the world,' he says, trying to sound like a jaded businessman avoiding the office. He's never been very good at impressions. Another thing to tick off the list of Stuff Oscar Might Have Been In His Former Life: actor.

'Oh, right,' she says, and smiles. 'Would you like to leave us instructions now?'

'Right. Yeah. If you could just tell . . . whoever calls that I've already checked out. Thank you.'

Her smile is ghostly thin now. 'But some of the callers said it was urgent?'

'They're lying,' he says quickly. No – this isn't good. The smile is gone. 'Er, I mean, they always say that. You know what people are like. Everyone's urgent, to themselves.'

But it seems like this isn't quite the right thing to say either; he is sounding less and less like a jaded businessman every minute, and so he stops talking.

Why is the receptionist staring at him? Oh, right: he hasn't given her an answer that makes sense yet.

'Just tell them I've left, please,' he says. 'I . . . I am busy. I am not, I repeat not, to be disturbed.'

He says this with all the businessman-authority he can channel, then turns, almost collides with a chair, and flees.

Later Oscar lies in the sun, facing away from the pool, towards the hotel gardens with their dazzling flowers, strange foliage, monster-outer-space cacti.

There's a sound of splashing behind him.

He ignores it.

Most of the other sunbeds are drawn up almost to the water's edge, like chairs pulled up to a fire. Like it's a *view*, not a flat turquoise rectangle smelling of the death of millions of microorganisms. In fact the only other person who hasn't fallen under the spell of the pool is a little kid. He's sitting on the grass not far from Oscar, playing on some handheld thing. Oscar glances at him and the kid looks up. They share a look. There's something amused in the kid's expression, like somehow he knows Oscar isn't really a man lying by a pool on holiday. The kid's look says, *Hey, it's okay, I'm not really a nine-year-old playing on a handheld device either.*

Oscar feels like this kid gets it. He smiles at him.

'It's meant to be warm once you're in it,' the kid says. (He's American, or maybe Canadian. Hard to guess which, and guessing causes offence, so Oscar doesn't.) The kid indicates the pool behind them. 'But I don't believe them.'

'You don't swim?' Oscar asks.

'What's the point?'

'I'm the wrong person to ask,' Oscar says. 'I haven't been in a pool for a long time. I think.'

But he has; as he says it he remembers it, the chemical-scented turquoise of it rippling over his skin. A few years ago, in Spain. It obviously didn't bother him then, the water. But now he feels a little sick quiver travel up his body. It's in his throat, for a moment. Then it sinks away.

'You don't have to go in,' he says.

'One of the other kids said he'd throw me in,' says the boy. 'But he's gone home now, and he never did.'

He sounds almost wistful.

'You've got no brothers or sisters?' Oscar asks.

'They're not here. That's my mom.'

Oscar follows the jerk of the kid's head, across the water to a sunbed with a tanned foot hanging off it. Presumably the body attached to it belongs to the kid's mother.

'My name is Atticus,' the kid says.

'That's quite a name.'

'It's awful. But it's from a famous book.'

74

'Is it? I don't read much. I'm Oscar.'

'What are you doing here, Oscar?' asks Atticus.

Oscar studies him. Is Atticus all he seems? But surely they wouldn't send a small boy to spy on him.

'I pretend to be sunbathing,' he says.

Atticus laughs. Then he gets up. 'I have to go,' he says. 'Will you be here tomorrow?'

'I don't know. Probably.'

'Then I'll probably see you tomorrow.'

Memory is a strange thing. Floating in the water, like a jellyfish. Gelatinous, both sticky and slippery.

Translucent.

Venomous.

A couple of years ago Oscar wrote down everything he knew about himself, in a notepad he'd bought for the purpose. He stalled after filling half of the first page.

He realised the notepad was a pointless purchase; he could have fitted his autobiography on the back of a receipt.

– Name: Oscar Levy (at least passport says so)
– Age: 28 (see above)
– Lives in: England in late teens, went to school there. No fixed address since then. Early years = ??
– Likes: animals, people, music, Monty Python films, TV shows about weird facts.

– Dislikes: liquorice, jazz, water (bodies of). (Why?)
(drinking water = fine.)
– Has something wrong with brain. (What?)
– Has a lot of money. (How?)
– Has memories that don't make sense (gun, white
room, men in suits).
– People are looking for him (see above).

He tore out the piece of paper and kept it for a while,
to check that he wasn't forgetting *more* stuff, but then it
began to depress him – this ninety-two-word life story –
and he threw it away.

Oscar can't remember anything at all before he was about
sixteen. After that the memories start appearing, in an
unpredictable, stop–start way, like a sputtering tap, until
his early twenties, after which he can remember mostly
everything. He *thinks* he can, anyway. There's no way to
know for sure.

One of his clearest early memories is of being seventeen,
and hanging out at his friend Lonnie's house. Lonnie's
dad was American, had been a rock star in the eighties.
Big hair, sparkly leggings, sort of thing. This was when
Oscar was at the boarding school for rich people's children.
Oscar isn't sure why *he* was at the school, or how long
he'd been there. He wasn't a new boy, he knows that
much. He'd had a different accent from everybody else,
a non-rich accent. So his parents, who he can't remember,
probably weren't rich. But he didn't have *the money* back
then. Not yet. *This* was before all *that*. So who was paying

the fees? He doesn't feel like he's smart enough for a scholarship.

The whole thing is very confusing.

Anyway.

Lonnie had a gun.

Oscar found this out on a day when a few of their friends were at Lonnie's dad's house in the country, sitting in the garden. Lonnie's dad was away. It was a calm October afternoon. The sky was grey and quiet and minding its own business, but Lonnie, unmoved, took aim and shot it.

Oscar, who'd been facing away from the French windows Lonnie had just strolled out of, had no idea what had happened. Except he also did. He heard a sound he couldn't have identified, and yet he understood what it represented – his body *knew* it, on a deep and instinctive level. Not that an evolutionary theorist would agree with that, but how else could you explain Oscar throwing himself off his chair, his hands over his head?

Nobody else had reacted like Oscar did. Drinks were spilled, someone exclaimed *shit!* and someone else – everyone denied it being them – let out a shrill squawk. But when the ear-noise had died to a slight hum, everyone looked at Oscar.

You okay, Ozzie? someone asked.

Did you see him? That was like, some fucking SAS shit. He dropped and rolled.

Ninja reflexes.

The rest of us just did a ninja piss in our pants.

(Lonnie was piqued at this. Came back over and put the gun down on the table, to remind them what the main event was.)

Where the fuck did you get that?

It's antique. My dad's. Totally illegal. He got it off someone who knew Jimi Hendrix.

Maybe it's the gun that killed Jimi Hendrix.

Was he shot?

Yeah . . . think so.

I thought he committed suicide.

That's Kurt Cobain.

More than one person's allowed to commit suicide, you know.

Oscar picked up the gun. It was so old that the metal bits were covered in a curly filigree pattern. The handle was made of wood.

If he were better with words he'd have tried to think of a limerick. Lonnie, Lon. Fun. Gun. Run. Done.

There was young man called Lon
Who stole his father's gun.

Careful, Lonnie said, taking it away from Oscar. You got a weird look in your eye, you know that?

There was a young man named Oscar . . .

But nothing rhymes with Oscar.

Sound works interestingly in Marrakech. It sits low, unable to clamber over the high roofs of the riads, or find a way into the gardens of his hotel. In those walled spaces only the birds can be heard, the clinking of the silver teapots.

Then Oscar leaves the hotel – he's going out now to buy a book, a Rubik's cube, anything to occupy his thoughts – and the city hits him like a train. Carriage after clattering carriage, swaying and spilling over with patterned ceramics, braying donkeys, barrels of spices, pierced brass lanterns, leather bags with their rich smell of shit and tanning, designer knock-offs, curly toed slippers. A smell of burning and grilled lamb and exhaust and incense. Oscar's head is wall-less: the sounds and smells pour right in and fill it up.

Then one voice cuts, suddenly, over the others. It's a flinty little Home Counties 'Excuse me', and it goes straight into Oscar's ear and sparks up a memory of another:

Excuse me. Excuse me! Hey!

This is a known memory of Oscar's; it wasn't that long ago. She'd come up to him, this girl, in a club. Oscar was nineteen or twenty. He had taken a pill someone had given him, then another, and his good time had risen, risen, then tipped slowly (he watched it happen, helpless) into a *bad time*. The club was underground and the surface felt a long way up. The music crashed against him. He felt like he was in a metal bin being beaten by a giant. The girl trying to get his attention looked as wired as he felt, white and shiny with sweat.

It's Oscar, right? she shouted.

He was startled, and didn't reply immediately. She came closer to his ear, became louder.

Do you remember me? Theresa? Lawrence's sister? Lawrence . . . from school?

Oscar's understanding came slowly; he nodded before it had fully arrived.

I can't believe you're here! Theresa shouted. I mean, nobody knew what happened to you after school. I mean, you were like, so – shit, I'm embarrassing myself now – and when you just vanished it was like . . . devastating. We used to wonder where you were. We used to make up stupid stories. Everyone thought you might have . . . Er. Anyway.

(She was going to say *died*, Oscar realises.)

Her hand is still on his arm; she's drawn him outside – how? – into the quiet night air.

I'm talking too much, she said. But I just have *so* many questions. What are you doing now? Where do you live? God, I can't believe I'm here talking to you. I almost want to take a picture of you. I mean, the others might not believe me otherwise.

I don't think you need to do that, said Oscar, alarmed.

Then Theresa started telling stories of Oscar, first-hand or second-hand or maybe not even true: the time Oscar jumped onto the bonnet of a passing car; the time Oscar came to school on LSD; the time Oscar passed out drunk in art class and had to be hidden in the cupboard. All the time Theresa's hand was on his arm, like a magic spell of compulsion, like Oscar couldn't move while that hand was there – though he wanted increasingly more desperately to throw it off, to twist away. He didn't remember any of her stories except for the car, though in his memory he didn't jump, he was hit, and this freaked him out – remembering the way the windscreen had cracked like a frozen lake, the groan of glass crushed against glass.

'*Excuse me?*' says the present-day voice, again.

*

80

He returns to the medina, locates its owner. Narrows it down, anyway, to a trio of English girls: sunburnt nose-tips, messy ponytails, harem pants. They have a *day two* look about them.

'Yes?' he says.

'Hi! Sorry to bother you. Could you please point us in the direction of the main square?' This is the middle girl speaking. The other two are half a step back, flanking her. If they were a girl band, she'd be the one about to leave and go solo.

'I can show you,' Oscar says. (Can he? He hopes so.) 'I'm going that way anyway.'

'Are you sure? We've been trying to get there for like, half an hour, and we're out of change so we can't tip anyone –'

'I get it. It's this way.'

'Thank you *so* much.' The girl falls in next to Oscar and her two friends follow on behind. 'You must think we're pathetic.'

He glances at her. *Pathetic* isn't a word that has occurred to him. He guesses she said *pathetic* for the benefit of her friends, with whom she's clearly impatient. She's enjoying herself, they're not. One of them is obviously pissed off, and the other jumps whenever a moped gets too close to her.

'Chill. They're like pigeons,' says the girl next to Oscar, back over her shoulder. 'They won't hit you.'

'I once saw a pigeon fly into someone's head,' says her friend.

'It's perfectly safe, isn't it?' the lead girl says to Oscar. 'Tell her, won't you?'

Oscar, who has been clipped by several mopeds and had his foot run over, nods. He says, 'Just watch out for the donkey carts.'

'I'm Jess, by the way,' the lead girl says.

'Oscar.'

'Hey, why don't you join us for some food, Oscar? We're just going to get a sheep's head . . . oh, come *on* –' this aimed at her friend – 'I'm *joking*.'

'Sure,' says Oscar. 'Why not?'

'What's that necklace?' Atticus asks.

Oscar opens his eyes. He's been dozing under a tree a little way from the hotel pool, sleeping off the large amount of lamb he's eaten. The blinding green of the grass dazzles Oscar's fuzzy eyes. He blinks. Still, better over here than gazing out over the surface of the pool; the lace of light weaving, shifting over it. The tiny waving arms of bugs drowning. He gets stressed hoping someone will fish them out in time, but doesn't want to attract attention by doing it himself. Maybe he could get Atticus to do it. Nobody questions a kid like they question an adult.

'What?' Oscar says.

'What's that necklace?' Atticus repeats. Oscar notices he's pulled up a lounger right next to Oscar's own.

Oscar's fingers go up to the necklace. It's a thin gold thread, with twenty knobbly gold lumps attached to it. He guesses the lumps are meant to look like gold nuggets. He's had it for as long as he can remember, but he has no idea where the necklace came from. He gets asked about it so often, though, that it was easier just to come up with a story.

Story meaning: *a lie.*

The problem is that lying to Atticus – a child – seems worse to Oscar than an adult-on-adult lie. Maybe that's because adults already exist in a twilight world made up of half-lies, delusions, things left unsaid, outright fraud. But meeting Atticus's eye, like he does now, and telling him, 'It was my mother's. I kept it after she died . . .' feels like a bad thing. Like he's taken the kid by the hand, led him one man-sized step, down into the shadow realm.

'Oh,' Atticus says. 'Sorry.'

'Don't be, man. I can't even remember her.'

(At least this is true.)

'You've got a book today,' Oscar observes, to change the subject.

'I'm meant to read it for school. It's boring.'

'What is it, maths?'

'I like math.'

'Really? Good for you. Maths is important. I've never understood it myself. I do like fractals though. There's this thing called Koch's triangle that has an infinite per-imeter but a finite area. Try thinking about that when you're sto— just try thinking about that. Anyway, if I were good at maths I'd be a professor of fractals. But I'm not.'

Atticus has got closer and closer to Oscar's sunlounger and is now leaning in, mouth slightly open. It seems Oscar's uselessness has mesmerised him. 'What *do* you do?' he asks.

'I lie on sunloungers,' says Oscar. *Ha*, he thinks. *Lie*, in both senses of the word.

'No, what's your job?'

'What are you, the FBI?' (Oscar aims for a jocular tone here. The tone falls somewhere between jocular and alarmed. The effect is odd.) 'Hang on – what do your parents do? They're not in the FBI, are they?'

'My mom's a real estate agent. My dad's in futures and derivatives.'

'At least estate is real,' Oscar says. 'Derivatives are not real. Futures are definitely not real.'

'Can I tell him that?'

'No.'

'Okay. I won't tell him. *If* you tell me what you do.'

'Fu— Jesus Christ. Okay.' Oscar looks around. What might he do? Pool cleaner, gardener, hotel manager, sun-lounger repairman? His gaze falls on Atticus's book. 'I design book covers,' he says.

'But you said you don't read books?' Atticus says.

'You really do remember everything, don't you?' Oscar says. 'Well. Book cover designers don't have to know what's in them. In fact it's better if you don't.'

Atticus's mouth opens, clearing the way for another question, no doubt, but at this point Oscar's phone rings. It makes him jump. But it's okay, it's the girl from the souk: Jess.

'Oscar! So, we're coming to your hotel this evening. How fancy is it? Will they let us in in flip-flops? Anya says she's only got flip-flops. They're gold though, apparently . . . what? He doesn't need to know that. Oh, for fuck's sake. With diamanté detailing. Anything else? No? Well, if the gold flip-flops with diamanté detailing aren't as impressive as Anya seems to think, could you sweet-talk someone . . .'

Oscar doesn't try to explain that his days of sweet-talking the receptionists might be over. That, lately, they've started looking at him – with what? Curiosity? Suspicion?

He can handle a few strange looks. Just about. It's not as if they're going to kick him out, is it? Not with the money he promises, even if it is lumps of soft and dirty money from the cash machine, not the high-level spiritual communication the hotel would prefer, between his microchip and theirs.

Microchips.

Who else was the hotel's chip talking to?

Because that's *it*, isn't it? That's how they found him. They probably already knew he was in the city: the cashpoints would have ratted him out. But after that: it must have been the card at the hotel, that first day.

Oscar had thought he was being clever, booking the fanciest place in town. Imagining them hunting for him in all the dusty corners while he sat on the terrace in the full sun, drinking his strawberry daiquiri. But when he arrived with his cash all ready to pay in advance, the receptionist said they still had to swipe his card. Just to 'put him on the system'. Oscar asked what happened to the card details, once they were in the system. They reassured him that nothing would go on the card unless there were outstanding bills after he left.

But nothing else? he asked. The card details don't . . . *go* anywhere?

They didn't understand.

Your details are safe with us, Mr Levy.

Mr Levy.

He didn't like having to be Mr Levy; not here, not anywhere. He felt his shoulders drawing in, as if to protect him from Mr Levy, an unwelcome arm slung over his shoulder. *Hello, mate, I'm Oscar Levy. Why don't we buddy up? You're stuck with me now, so you may as well.*

But maybe – maybe – strange looks is all it is.

He sends a silent prayer up into the hard blue sky. A plea for strange looks. That the receptionists just think Oscar's a bit weird. That's all. They've done what Oscar said, and told the people calling him that Mr Levy has checked out. They haven't got talking to the people calling, or asked them who they were, or why they're looking for Oscar. They don't know anything more about Oscar's life than he does.

'Oscar? You still there?' says Jess.

'Yes. Flip-flops are fine,' Oscar says.

'Cool. So, what's your room number? That's where the fourway will be, right? Oh, for fuck's sake, Anya, I'm *joking*. We'll see you in the bar, Oscar. Call you later!'

Oscar takes the phone away from his ear. He looks at it with interest. He realises Atticus, who has moved to sit next to him, unnoticed, is doing the same thing. Did Atticus overhear any of that? But no, it's the phone itself that intrigues him.

'I've never seen a phone like that before,' he says.

'That's because it's a cheap pay-as-you-go non-smartphone,' says Oscar. (The other day, suddenly paranoid, he'd swapped it for his iPhone, to the amazement of a street vendor.)

'A what?'

'Never mind.'

'Was that a girl?' Atticus says. 'What did she say?'

'Never mind.'

*

Jess throws herself onto Oscar's bed, arms spread out across the heavy gold bedspread, cushions scattered all around her like she fell out of the sky, flung-open hotel bathrobe for wings.

'I love this place,' she cries.

She's wearing nothing but a pair of red pants under the bathrobe. Her nipples point at the ceiling, neat and cocky, like they have a right to be here. He suspects they do. She pretends awe at the hotel ('These bathrobes must be like three feet thick!'), but there's something knowing about it. She's one of the rich people, really, albeit one who ate half a sheep's head in the name of authenticity. No wonder her nipples look so confident.

They have sex, twice, before Jess falls asleep suddenly, as if she's been hit on the head. Oscar finds himself awake and alone.

His mind twitches, wanders. Here and there it goes, forwards, sideways and finally backwards –

– ending up with the gun.

Oscar stole Lonnie's dad's gun.

He doesn't remember why.

He does remember – guiltily – Lonnie's agitation when he found out it was gone.

It had to be someone at the party, Lonnie insisted, but nobody took that seriously. They were making jokes about Cluedo, guessing who among them was the killer.

Nobody guessed Oscar.

Later, Oscar held the gun in his hands. It was cold and dense, like a dead fish. The filigree was agreeably textured under his own whorled fingertips. After a while of holding it, it got warmer, as if it was getting to know him.

Why did he want it so much?

Maybe it was just the law of Chekhov's gun. Once it had appeared, it couldn't just go safely back into Lonnie's dad's safekeeping, could it? No. That was against the rules.

The gun has been shown: the gun must now fulfil its destiny.

William

William and Annetta are waiting in Marian Dunlop's small study, on a blue sofa, flanked by boxes of tissues, flimsy white flowers stirred gently by the small wind coming in the top of the window.

Not knowing – as usual – what to talk about.

Small talk seems ridiculous, big talk equally to be avoided – what's the point, after all, when they're paying someone else to talk about all that with them?

And so, as if in agreement, they sit in silence.

Marian Dunlop arrives, with two glasses of water, which she puts down next to the tissues. She's a young woman, much younger than William. She has little glasses and a tightly wound bun, like a librarian in a film. Maybe the glasses and bun are an attempt to compensate for her bird-boned slenderness, her lack of visible pores, the reediness of her voice. William tries not to think of her as a whippersnapper. Or to wonder aloud what a girl her age knows about marriage, or life, or death. It's a test of his prejudices. He needs to make an effort to pass.

'So,' Marian Dunlop says. (She's asked them to call her Marian, but she'll always be, in William's mind, Marian Dunlop.) 'In our last session, Annetta was explaining that she felt she lacked insight into how William has been feeling. Which is where I'd like to pick up today. Annetta, did you mean William's feelings concerning the issues in your relationship – your living separately – or the PTSD symptoms, or something else?'

'Anything,' Annetta says. 'Everything. When it comes to William I have literally no insight into anything at all.'

'Well,' Marian says, 'that's quite a broad scope. William, are there any general feelings you'd like to share, having heard that?'

'Uh. Nothing springs to mind,' says William.

'Okay. Maybe it would be helpful to start small when it comes to feelings,' says Marian. 'Why don't you tell me about your morning, maybe? How did you feel this morning?'

William thinks about his morning, which could be any morning: all William's mornings are the same. His alarm goes off at seven, so he can start work – his new job as a gardener – at eight. He gets up, goes to the bathroom, brushes his teeth with the toothbrush kept in the ceramic pot with a picture of a smiling frog on it, shaves with the electric razor in its own corner of the mirrored cupboard – his corner – even though the rest of the cupboard is empty. He dresses, goes downstairs. He puts Radio 4 on and listens to the news, or as much of it as he can. Bombings, shootings, stabbings. He turns the radio off. He eats his breakfast in silence.

'I felt fine,' he says.

'So, you don't usually experience any flashbacks or episodes in the morning?' Marian Dunlop asks.

'No,' William says. 'Sometimes.'

'Okay,' says Marian Dunlop. 'And how do these episodes usually –'

'I already filled in your questionnaire,' William interrupts. 'It's all on there. Do we have to go over it again?'

Marian Dunlop pauses. Then she says. 'We don't have to go over anything if you don't want to.'

'Okay,' he says. He's ashamed of himself for snapping at her. 'Sorry.'

'Wait,' Annetta says. 'I didn't know about a questionnaire.'

'We can look at it now, if William feels comfortable with that,' Marian Dunlop says. 'It might be an easier way for him to share his experiences. William?'

William nods.

Marian Dunlop picks up the folder next to her. She takes out a piece of paper.

'Here we are,' she says. 'Number one. *I persistently avoid discussing or thinking about the traumatic event.* William's ticked that one.'

'No shit,' says Annetta. 'Er. Excuse my language.'

'Number two. *I have full or partial amnesia of the event.* William hasn't ticked that one. Number three. *I experience intrusive, recurrent recollections and flashbacks.* That's ticked. Number four. *I experience feelings of distress or intense physical reactions when reminded of the event (e.g. sweating, pounding heart, nausea).* William has ticked all of these.'

'Oh,' says Annetta. She takes a breath, lets it out through a thin gap in her lips. The sound of it fills the silence.

'How do you feel, hearing that?' Marian Dunlop asks her.

'That I can't believe I have to hear it read out like that,' says Annetta. 'This is what I mean. Communication! It's like I'm always trying to get William to speak, and he just . . . won't. But how can anything be fixed if he can't *open up?*'

She looks desperately at Marian Dunlop, like she's willing her to get out some sort of trepanning equipment, a hammer or saw, and physically force William open.

Marian Dunlop doesn't oblige. She leaves her usual pause, then says, 'And how do you feel, William, about what Annetta's saying?'

They both turn to look at him.

William knows Annetta's right about him. In the box on one of the homework sheets Marian Dunlop had given them early on, the one that said <u>Communication</u>, he'd have liked to write, *No thank you.*

'I'm sorry,' he says to Annetta.

'I don't need you to apologise,' Annetta says. 'I want you to talk. I want to *understand*.' She turns to Marian. 'It's like talking to a brick wall. A wall that just keeps saying sorry.'

There is a short silence.

'You're frustrated,' observes Marian Dunlop.

'He didn't even tell me why he left the police force,' Annetta says. 'It took me months before I got even a clue. All I know is a few scraps. I don't even understand why *that* case caused all this. But then he never talked about any of his cases. The upsetting ones. He never talks about his childhood, like how his dad died when he was really young. And now he's got PTSD and he doesn't want to talk about that either. He just wants to, to *skip it*, and get a memory wipe.'

'Would you like to talk about the death of your dad, William?' Marian Dunlop says. 'I don't think we've touched on that before.'

'Because it's not relevant,' William says. 'I've only had these symptoms in the last few years. So that can be ruled out as a factor.'

'The Chief Inspector has spoken!' Annetta says. 'Case closed.'

Marian Dunlop says to William, 'It seems like something you'd rather not discuss?'

'There's just no point,' says William. He knows he sounds curt, and that he can't apologise for his curtness now either.

'Okay,' Marian says. 'And I take it you'd still like to get a memory deletion?'

William can feel Annetta looking at him. He doesn't want to look at her in case there are tears in her eyes.

'Yes,' he says. 'I do.'

'And you've spoken to your GP? Did they give you the information booklets, paperwork and so on?'

'Yes.'

'Okay,' Marian says. 'Okay. It's probably good that you have time before the next session to read the Nepenthe material and have a think. Then we can talk about it next week.'

'Thank you,' Annetta says to Marian Dunlop. Her voice is tight.

William knows that this thank you really means, *thanks for nothing*.

He thinks Marian Dunlop probably knows that, too.

(William knows Annetta wants to understand. The problem is that *he* doesn't understand. He doesn't know how to

93

explain it to her. It's a feeling, he knows that, but it's not classifiable. He has no name for it. He definitely doesn't know where it came from. It's like a shadow passing over him, vague, too big to see how big it is.

But: big.

The shadow arrives, that's the only way he can describe it.

The shadow arrives, and everything under it looks different.)

William reads Nepenthe's prospective client advisory material over breakfast, a bowl of slightly soft cereal, a brand once loved, then abandoned by the kids. It's a glossy, heavy brochure, like something you'd pick up in an expensive shop. William wonders if these things are actually *displayed* anywhere, to tempt potential clients. Where does human regret live? Police stations, hospitals. Courtrooms. Hotel bedrooms – bedrooms in general. They should advertise on pillowcases.

It's not only the flashbacks and anxiety, says the leaflet. *A traumatic memory can impact on your own sense of your personal life story. Over time it begins to skew your perception of the world. Our PTSD clients often describe their traumatic memories as 'swelling', 'distorting' or 'taking over' other parts of their lives.*

Which sounds about right.

(The prospect of the memory shrinking, his life expanding to its usual size, is almost unbelievable. An escape, a reprieve. He wants it so badly that it's too painful to think about.)

*

It's Sunday afternoon, and Fiona – William's daughter – wants to go to the park.

'*All* my friends are there,' she says. She's managed to invest the words with considerable urgency. The way she fixes him with her expectant gaze reminds him of her mother. Like Annetta, Fiona is stiff and quiet with new people, which sometimes leads them to assume that she is a meek or placid character. As with Annetta, this is not the case.

'All your friends?' says William. 'So is Jack going to be there?'

At age eleven Fiona has a pretty decent poker face. She got that from William. She assumes it now. 'Jack *is* one of my friends, so yes.'

'Your mother says that Jack's your boyfriend,' William says.

(William doesn't actually care about Jack. Now that it's been established by Annetta that Jack isn't some 23-year-old from the internet but another kid in Fiona's class with a set of train-track braces and a pet dog he himself named Pickles, William is relaxed about Jack. In truth, William's playing for time. He's feeling edgy. He needs to work out whether the edginess is reasonable.)

'Oh, so you're comparing notes on me now?' says Fiona with disgust.

'Something like that, yes.'

'Okay. Whatever. Can I go?'

William smiles blandly. He wants to say no. The *no* is so near to his closed teeth. A pressure. *No.* He keeps it back; tries, again, to think.

William knows it's hard for Fiona and Milo. He used to be a background figure in their lives, a permanent, ignorable presence, but now *time with Dad* has become an end in itself. It's artificial. No child should have to go on dates with their dad, for God's sake. Plus, he doesn't stand up very well under the increased scrutiny. He has the kids one night a week and every Sunday. The problem with Sundays is becoming apparent. It's late summer, Fiona has a boyfriend, and he's at the park with Fiona's friends. Correction: *all* her friends.

'Well,' he says. 'Um. Do you have your phone?'

She nods vigorously.

William sighs.

'So, I can go?' she asks.

'Where's Fiona going?' asks Milo, coming downstairs.

'To the park.'

'Oh! Can I go to the park too?'

'*Dad*, no. Please no. He'll try to embarrass me. Please don't make me take him.'

'He'll *try* to embarrass you? Surely that's not true. I can see how it might happen by accident. But it's not fair to infer *intent* –'

'He told everyone my poem,' Fiona says flatly.

Milo looks immediately abashed.

'What poem?' says William.

'A poem I wrote. He found it and he learned it off by heart, and then last week at the park, in front of *everybody*, he started reciting it!'

Milo has gone red. 'I didn't mean to!'

'You didn't mean to recite a poem?' William says. Unlike Fiona, whose composition is so clearly 50 per cent William, 50 per cent Annetta, Milo's nature is mysterious. For example, William has no idea where he got his love of performing. Milo's good at it, too; his King Herod, both magisterial and sympathetic, stole the show from Mary and Joseph at last year's nativity play.

'I didn't mean to embarrass her!' Milo cries.

It turns out that Milo had been allowed to hang out with Fiona and her friends, just once, on a strictly trial basis. Fiona had watched him suspiciously, but her friends had been nice to him. Milo wanted to offer something in return. He also wanted to show that he had been entrusted with this: a beautiful poem, his safe passage to the world of the big children.

Of course he didn't phrase it like this; it was all broken up because he was trying not to cry, but William got the gist.

'Okay,' William says, cutting them off. 'How about Milo promises not to recite any more poems, and Fiona accepts that he meant well . . .'

Fiona is looking hostile.

'. . . and I'll let her go to the park this afternoon alone for a couple of hours?'

'Yes. Agreed,' Fiona says quickly.

'And, Milo,' William adds, before his son's dropped-open mouth can form a wail, 'we'll walk Fiona to the park then we'll go to the cafe next door. I can keep an eye on your sister, and you can have a sundae.'

The wheel of fortune turns. Whoops from Milo. Fiona looks stricken.

'Can't *I* have a sundae, Dad?'

'Of course. But, sweetheart, you don't have time for a sundae *and* the park. I've got to sort dinner out then take you guys back to your mum for seven.'

(How casually he says it!)

'Huh,' Fiona says, drifting towards the stairs to put on her shoes. Invisible thought bubbles float from her head.

Then she turns, and – miraculously – says, 'I think I'll have the sundae, if that's okay?'

William nods. (Careful not to celebrate too conspicuously. Celebrating inside, within his ribcage, which has expanded with the joy of not having to spend the afternoon stifling fears of his only daughter being injured or mugged or abducted or murdered.)

We live in Malting, he tells himself. A tiny, quiet outpost of the quiet village of Hassocks. He knows for a fact there's been no abduction, rape or murder in Malting since 1980. That's why they moved there, for God's sake.

Malting hasn't changed.

Something has gone wrong with William, that's all.

At the cafe Fiona has a knickerbocker glory and Milo a double chocolate cherry cream sundae with extra sprinkles. It's dinnertime in two hours. William isn't sure whether this is good parenting but what the hell, Milo and Fiona are talking animatedly about some teacher they both hate and the sun's coming in through the window and warming the side of his cheek like someone's put a hand there, and he's still got four hours before the car journey to Annetta's mum's house.

And – there – the thought is in his head.

The car journey to Annetta's mum's house.

William tries, and usually manages, to live in the moment. Not for any healthy, happy reason. More because the past and the future are often too much to think about.

Take this thought, for instance.

Break it into its components.

Car journey.

. . . A half-hour of limbo; broken-up chatter; heavy, contemplative silences; occasionally tears. A tumour feeling in William's stomach.

Annetta.

. . . Wondering if Annetta will come to the door. When she does, it's painful. When she doesn't, it's painful. He isn't sure which he hopes for.

Mum.

Judy. She came to the UK from Jamaica when she was a child. She now suffers from arthritis, and has lived alone since the death of her husband, George; she was half grateful when Annetta came to live with her, half angry. Throughout the separation she'd unashamedly sided with William. He didn't even *have* a side, for Christ's sake – he knew he'd shut Annetta out, he'd made it impossible for her – but Judy managed to find one. She told her daughter she expected too much – she was ungrateful; she should be happy to have a man who worked every day and fed his family – and generally pissed Annetta (a maths lecturer) off so much that Annetta frequently forgot her intention not to get drawn in, and would argue with her. Then Judy would cry.

House.

William worries, privately, about whether living at Judy's is damaging for the kids, who've heard their share of muffled arguments already. He'd offered to move out of the house in Malting, but Annetta said she needed to look after her mother, and anyway she didn't like the thought of William in some shitty flat. She thought it would depress him. It depressed her, just thinking about it. William didn't tell her that there was a different kind of depression in his living alone in their family home. Coming out of the house on a sunny weekend to see all the other families along the road doing their family things: two boys on bicycles riding up and down the road, chased by a small girl on rollerblades; a woman watering a lavender bush; grass flying behind a man pushing a mower back and forth. People actually washing their cars on a Sunday.

William never lingers for long outside his house. He doesn't want to be noticed, to have to answer any questions, asked or not asked. And – less rationally – he's wary that something about him could start to bother the functioning, unbroken families around him. Not consciously. But in the way that birds suddenly unite to drive off one that's sick or injured. He doesn't think they'd turn up at his doorstep with makeshift clubs or anything. Not in the suburbs. But they could start a petition.

He told his friend Matt this and Matt laughed.

Divorce *is* contagious, Matt said. One of my colleagues got divorced, then three others followed within a year.

I'm not divorced, said William.

Oh yeah, right. Sorry.

William had also suggested to Annetta, early on, that the kids live with him. He could take them to school: his job was more flexible than hers in that respect.

They like the bus, Annetta said. Their friends take the bus.

But –

Look, William. It's not just that. I don't want to be the one to point this out, but what about your . . . bad days? The zoning out. The . . . amount you drink. Your sleep thing.

He considered telling her that the last two had never been separate, concurrent problems, but one problem (night terrors) that was then replaced by another problem (drinking in the evening), which, actually, was replaced in turn by another problem that she wasn't even aware of (benzos): so technically just one problem overall. He'd started drinking a couple of whiskies before bed on the basis that it was preferable to the thrashing, the shouting. The accidental hitting of Annetta during the night. That had happened a few months before she moved out, William waking up in the final notes of his own, shouted *No!* The blood welling slowly through her fingers.

What *did* you dream about? she'd asked in the morning. There was a bruise on the bridge of her nose.

I can't remember, he'd said.

(A lie.)

Then later, after Annetta left, it turned out that benzo-diazepines did a better job than whisky of stifling his dreams, and made it easier to get up in the morning, with plenty of time to take the kids to school.

But then there were still the bad days, and the zoning out.

He sighed. She looked softer. He could tell she understood he'd given up.

I'm sorry, she said. I know you miss them.

Everyone says they know how much William misses them. He isn't sure they *do* know.

Milo looks up now, an ice-cream squiggle dried onto one hot cheek.

'I miss home,' he says. 'When can we come back?'

'Ah,' says William. He can only repeat the line he and Annetta have agreed on: that Annetta needs to help Judy, and it's not forever.

As expected, it fools Milo but not Fiona, who says, 'But how long for? Until she *dies*?'

'No, until we come up with another plan.'

'Ugh. That's a *lie*,' says Fiona. 'Granny told Mum she didn't need her and she should go home. You're both lying. Granny knows it and we know it. You and Mum are getting a divorce, and you think we're stupid and we won't realise.'

She stares at him.

William can't think of anything to say. Long seconds pass; the sunlight turns sticky; a sugar hangover; a curdling. It dawns on him that Fiona didn't actually *believe* this: that she was asking him, not telling him. The realisation comes along a few seconds after her eyes fill with tears. Late again.

'I thought the police weren't even *allowed* to get memory wipes,' Annetta says to William.

'We – *they* aren't allowed to wipe crimes,' William says. 'Or cases they've personally worked on. Or if they were the subject of an investigation. But this memory doesn't fall into any of those categories. So all I need is sign-off.'

Annetta shakes her head.

'What are your thoughts, Annetta?' Marian Dunlop asks her.

'My thoughts are that this is crazy!' Annetta says. 'Sorry. But. We came to you to *talk*. As an alternative to William destroying his brain cells. Can't we do that?'

'It's my professional responsibility to talk – neutrally – about all the options available to you,' says Marian Dunlop.

'The procedure doesn't destroy anything, anyway,' William says. 'The booklet says it's a chemical blocker. Every time you remember something, the memory has to be physically rebuilt. The brain has to make new proteins. It's called reconsolidation. So the drug blocks the formation of the proteins, and the memory . . . goes.'

'Right,' Annetta says. 'Can I just point out that you seem to have a lot more to say on the neurochemistry or whatever of Nepenthe than you do about our marriage?'

'I was just trying to explain what was in the booklet –'

'I read the booklet too,' Annetta says. 'But I still don't know what a chemical *blocker* does to someone's brain. What the side effects are. This procedure has only been around for twenty years. How can they know everything about it?'

'They can't,' says Marian Dunlop.

'See?' Annetta says to William. 'That's neutral advice. And isn't there the risk, Marian, that it can make people feel worse?'

'That's very rare for the people who know they had the procedure,' says Marian Dunlop. 'According to research, the vast majority seem happy with the knowledge that something happened, but not the detail. Though recent studies have shown that the *concept* of memory loss can be very troubling and destabilising to some people. Identity –'

'I'm not troubled or destabilised or struggling,' William says. 'And I don't care about identity. I just want to get on with my life. If one of my fingers was infected and was poisoning my blood, I'd amputate it. It's simple.'

'But it's *not* simple,' says Annetta. 'Didn't you say you thought it was weird that this particular case triggered PTSD? Because there was nothing very unusual or horrible about it? And you said that there were things about the memory, things that didn't even *happen* –'

'Little things,' William says quickly. He feels pained by Annetta's obvious distress, but at the same time he wishes she'd stop talking. *So I have communicated some things after all,* he wants to say, *and look what happens.*

He turns to Marian Dunlop and says, 'It's not much. Just small details. Like I remembered her face differently, I thought she was holding something different.'

'This is the photo of the girl who died, is that right?' Marian Dunlop says. 'The picture that triggered the PTSD response.'

He nods.

'But it's so specific,' Annetta says. 'He said he remembered she was holding these sweets. The sour jellied ones. Sour mix. And there were no sweets in the photo. So why would you remember something so specific?'

'Witnesses get details wrong all the time,' William says. 'The longer it's been, the more wrong they are. I must have got confused at some point. Included the . . . sweets.'

But saying this is a mistake. The word sweets connects up to the picture of sweets. A bag of them scattered through the broad puddle of blood on the ground. He can see the sugar on them. Sparkling, like real crystals.

The shadow is coming; he can feel it at the edge of his awareness. He focuses on the room; stares at the box of tissues standing in front of the open window. He holds on to the sound of Marian Dunlop's voice like it's a rope, hoisting him out of a well.

'Well, what you're describing isn't that unusual,' Marian Dunlop says to Annetta. 'Nobody really remembers events accurately. Even in a wider sense: we tell a story of ourselves, and edit our memories so they fit that narrative. If the story we decide to tell changes, the memories change. We see memory as creating the self, but the self that's created looks back and changes the memory.'

'So that's it?' Annetta says. 'It's settled? William's just going to go to Nepenthe and get a wipe and we won't ever talk about anything ever again?'

'This upsets you,' Marian Dunlop says.

'Of course it does!' cries Annetta.

'Okay. How about we talk about *talking*,' says Marian Dunlop. She asks Annetta if she would say it's true that William was never much of a talker.

'He never really spoke about his feelings,' Annetta says. 'But he was always so kind, and generous, and a good listener, and he showed he cared – just in more non-verbal ways.'

'And this was attractive to you?'

Annetta blinks. She says, 'I don't see why this is suddenly about *me*.'

(William shares her concern. If Marian Dunlop cures Annetta of her attraction to William, what's going to happen then?)

'And it *wasn't* attractive,' Annetta continues. 'No. I *liked* to talk. But I made the best of it. I used to say to people: what would you rather? An imperfect man who could talk to you all day about his problems, or a perfect man who didn't talk at all? But then that wasn't the choice any more. Because then William did have problems, and he wouldn't talk about them. He was more and more shut off. Cold, actually, if I pushed him. And I know he's suffering now, but it's like it's going on behind a . . . a closed door.'

William was staring at a closed door when it first happened. It was four years ago, the morning meeting at work. Someone else had been assigned to the case, and William, for whatever reason, had been shown the photograph.

William had excused himself and gone to the loos. He went into a cubicle, shut the door, put the lavatory seat down and sat on it. He stared at the advisory poster on the back of the door with a cartoon picture of E. coli being spread around the workplace. *Now Wash Your Hands*, said the picture.

It was the first time he felt it, whatever it was. It was like he was at the bottom of the sea. It was cold there – inhumanly cold – and there was a great shadow passing over him, like the underside of an impossibly big ship. The ship moved over him but it was so big that even when everything had gone black there was still more to come. William held his breath. He couldn't surface. He had to wait for it to pass. Having the sense – even then, the first time – that if he could keep control of himself and just hold on, the shadow would, at some point, move on. The feeling was temporary; the feeling would lift.

Just a matter of waiting it out.

*

'Who does that girl think she is?' Annetta says, outside. They are standing by their cars, which are side by side in the small car park. It's a warm, grey day. The aftermath of a summer rain rises humidly off the tarmac.

For a moment William thinks she means: *the girl*. Then he realises she's talking about Marian Dunlop.

'How do you mean?' he says.

'How old is she, anyway? Twelve?' She mimics Marian Dunlop, '"I *know* it's difficult for you, Annetta." How can she know? She's not the one living with her bloody mother, dealing with questions from her children every bloody day.'

There are tears in her eyes. William wants to put his arm around her – maybe, sneakily, inhale her hair. One of the things that has come up in the sessions had been his inability to show spontaneous physical affection. Annetta said he didn't shrug her off, exactly, but sometimes his look of surprise when she took his hand made her feel . . . unnecessary. Unasked for.

Of course, now that he can't touch her, it's all he can think about.

'It's shit,' he says. 'I'm sorry.'

'It's just . . . how long has it been? A year? Living like this. Not knowing what's . . . I don't know.'

He puts his hand out, lightly touches her arm. She has her head bent, looking in her bag for a tissue. Then she looks up, suddenly, and he reflexively pulls back the hand. The touch was so tentative, the removal so fast, that he's not sure she even realised it happened.

She wipes her eyes; blows her nose.

'I can't do it any more,' she says eventually. 'I can't. I'm scared about what will happen. But I'm not going to fight you. If this is what you're sure you need to do, go ahead. I'll support you. And I'll . . . I don't know. Try my best to understand.'

William fills out the application form for a Nepenthe consultation. While this is being processed he needs to get senior management at his old unit to sign another form, confirming that the case in question had nothing to do with him, wasn't a crime, and so on.

'It should be simple,' is what his GP says. 'After the procedure you'll obviously know – very generally – what happened that morning. That you were shown this photograph. But you won't remember what was in the photograph, or any of the details of the case.'

William feels uneasy. He prefers to do a thorough job. He'd like every element of the memory gone, nothing left behind.

'It couldn't be one of those self-confidential procedures?' he asks.

'I'm afraid not. That's only for personal memories. This is professional, which means it has to be self-informed, and it'll go on your police record, by law.'

'Yes,' says William, because he already knew that.

He's meant to get a call from Nepenthe within a week, inviting him to visit their clinic in Brighton to explain to a psychologist there what this particular memory has done to offend him. After that he'll spend a mandatory twenty-eight days thinking it over.

Or:

Choosing not to think about anything to do with it at all, until the twenty-eight days are over and he can go back to Nepenthe, sign the waiver, and pay the fee (£4,000: most of his savings – as Annetta could but would never remind him).

Then he will go to the clinic and tell them about his problems and watch them disappear, the moment they hit the air.

The shadow will lift.

Life will resume.

PART TWO

Noor

'Don't worry if the Maranta dies,' David says. 'It's been unhappy for a while.'

'Which one's the Maranta?' Noor asks.

'Dining-room window. Big leaves. Brown at the edges.'

'Right.'

There's a loud laugh from behind Noor. She turns round – a mistake: it's her other neighbours, and they catch her eye and wave, smiling. Irritated, she waves back.

'My biggest fear is that those two idiots will get it into their stoned heads to have children,' she says to David.

'I thought they seemed sweet,' David says.

Noor supposes they are. In some ways. They walk out of their house arm in arm, they walk back up to it arm in arm, with their matching wool hats, sleepy eyes, wavy hair. Once the window was open and she heard the guy singing, a nonsense song about how beautiful the girl was. Then a sudden, high giggle, like he'd just picked her up and spun her round. The glimpses of their closeness sometimes bothers Noor more than the rubbish from their abandoned bin bags. On balance, she'd prefer to deal with a vole trapped in a crisp packet.

David gives her a door key. 'I think that's everything,' he says. 'I really appreciate this, Noor. I told you about the back door sticking?'

'You did,' Noor says. 'You didn't tell me when you'll actually get back from this residency, or whatever it is.'

'I'm not totally sure yet myself,' David says. 'Sorry. I'll text you.'

'Okay. Just bear in mind that the longer I'm in charge of the plants, the less likely they are to survive.'

'I really appreciate it,' David says. 'You're a good friend.'

Friend? thinks Noor. But she supposes, yes, that's what David is. Not that she calls him that. If she ever talked about him she'd say 'my neighbour'. It's the same with Louise. Louise is technically Noor's friend. But Louise is also her boss, and that's what Noor calls her. So really she has two half-friends, adding up to one friendship in total. And she's happy with that number. She wouldn't want to have to water any more plants, for a start.

Louise and David actually used to know each other years ago. They shared a flat after university, when they were both grad students working at St Helier's. When Noor made the connection and told them that she was their mutual half-friend, Louise and David reacted the same way. They both said what a small world it was, except David's eyebrows went up as he said it, and Louise's eyebrows drew down. Both of them were wrong, though, Noor thought. It's Crowshill that's the small world. With both Nepenthe and St Helier's based nearby, it's the Silicon Valley of UK medical tech. On the cul-de-sac Noor and David live on, there's a cardiologist, an oncologist, a paediatrician, a Nepenthe technician and a Nepenthe therapist. As David said once, it would be the best place in the world for something terrible to happen to you.

Anyway, after the eyebrow activity, neither Louise nor David seemed that interested in the connection. It was a long time ago, was what David said.

David's talking about something else now, some friends he plans to catch up with. Noor's lost the thread, but it doesn't matter. They're just making small talk while they wait for his taxi to appear at the bottom of the road. She tries not to look over David's shoulder for it. It's a mild day, grey, with sudden shots of sunlight across the roofs of the houses. Leaves have just started to fall, lining the sides of the road.

'How are *you*, Noor?' David says suddenly. 'I know there's a lot going on at your work. From the grapevine, I mean. It's not like you tell me anything.'

'I'm okay.'

'What do you do in your spare time? In the evenings? Do you see people?'

'That depends on the evening.'

'Okay. What did you do yesterday evening? Saturday night.'

'I watched an old *Star Trek* on Netflix.'

David sighs. 'You can just tell me to mind my own business, you know.'

'You don't believe me?'

'You've always said you hated sci-fi. Which struck me as ironic, given your job.'

'I could tell you what happened in the episode.'

'Please do,' says David.

'It was about Captain Kirk falling in love with a robot called Rayna. There was a love triangle with Kirk, Rayna and the guy who made her.'

David's looking at Noor closely. He's frowning. 'Why this story?' he says. 'I mean, why did you pick that episode?'

Noor frowns back at him. 'I don't know. Why do you ask?'

'Nothing. Go on. What happened?'

'The two men fought over Rayna. But then Rayna died. It turned out all the new emotions she'd acquired were just too much for her. They blew her circuits, or something. Kirk was very upset.'

David's taxi turns in to the road, and makes its way towards them.

'Here it is!' Noor says, with relief.

David's shaking his head, grinning. 'I'm going to re-member this morning, Noor. I've learned something new about you. A secret love of *Star Trek*. I'd never have guessed.'

He looks so pleased that Noor doesn't have the heart to tell him that this is the first and only *Star Trek* episode she'll ever watch. 'Well, enjoy it,' she says.

'I will,' he says. He's laughing as he gets into the taxi. Before he closes the door he gives a Vulcan salute.

If she'd known how easy it was to amuse him, she thinks, she'd have done it sooner.

. . . But who is she kidding? Of course she wouldn't. Almost as soon as she thinks it, she recognises that this thought is essentially bullshit.

*

Outside the clinic Noor recognises Imran, the security guard from yesterday. She waves at him and he comes over to the car window.

'How's it going, Dr Ali?' he says. 'Hope you weren't upset by yesterday.'

'Oh, no. I'm fine.'

The other guard, whose name Noor doesn't know, strolls over. This isn't exactly what Noor had in mind, but she smiles at him anyway.

'Dr Ali was the one that got spat on by that nutter,' says Imran.

'My car was spat on,' Noor clarifies. 'And it's made a full recovery.'

'Effing maniacs,' says the other guard.

'I actually wanted to ask: who was he?' Noor asks.

The two men look at each other for a moment. Then the guard Noor doesn't know says, 'No idea. We haven't seen him before. We told him to move along. And he did.'

'It's just that you seemed to be after him already,' Noor says to Imran. 'Before he spat on the car. I wondered if it was something about the placard he was holding.'

Imran looks at the ground.

'I didn't read it,' Imran says to the ground. 'Sorry, Dr Ali. He'd just been kicking off earlier. That was why we were after him.'

'Sounds like you've got your explanation,' says the other guard cheerfully. Noor is starting to dislike this man.

'Yes,' she says. 'So long as he's not going to be an on-going nuisance. That's the important thing. Have a good day, both of you.'

*

Noor makes a tea in the empty kitchen (she'd taken care to arrive early enough that this would be the case). She eats her apple while she waits for the kettle to boil. Then she takes the tea into her own office, opening the blinds onto the view of the grounds – or, more accurately, fifty-seven very thin views of the grounds. The room fills with divided morning light.

The first thing she does is log on to the computer and search the system for the word *RASA*. She doesn't really expect anything to come up, and nothing does. So she texts Louise, and asks Louise to call her when she can.

Noor has a couple of client interviews that morning. The first client is someone who saw a shooting at a pop concert and developed agoraphobia as a result. Now it's gone. She sits happily through Noor's checklist. At the end she says she's glad to have had the procedure.

'I feel like the world's been given back to me,' the client says. 'Because it was ruined before. It sounds dramatic but I honestly couldn't see anything without seeing . . . it. But now the world's *back*. In fact it's better than it was before. I'm going to . . . well, I don't know. I'll just do something better with my life, I think. Be better. Something like that.'

'Good,' says Noor.

Better than before, writes Noor, on the form.

Unfortunately the next client isn't quite as easy. She arrives and starts to cry. After about five minutes of crying, while Noor tries not to look at the clock, the woman finally says: 'You deleted too much!'

'Excuse me?' Noor says.

'You deleted extra memories. On Monday I forgot the name of the hotel I stayed in in Greece last year, and then

I couldn't remember what I needed to buy from the shop, and then, when I was thinking back, there were all these things I couldn't remember. Totally random things, like what year I got married, and what my grandmother's maiden name was.'

Noor tries not to sigh.

'Did you read your aftercare guide?' she asks.

'Yes,' says the client. 'Well. Most of it. It was *so* long. And then I googled –'

'Don't google,' says Noor. 'Did you end up on a forum?'

'Yes.'

'Don't go on forums.'

'Oh. Sorry.'

Noor fixes the client with a stern look. Then she says, 'I hear what you're saying.'

'You do?'

'These sorts of fears are very common. But in fact, there's a safeguard built into the system itself that makes what you're describing impossible. The procedure uses a drug activated by a gentle electrical stimulation. Before the procedure even begins, we can see the areas of the brain that are to be activated and targeted. The second your attention moves away, to the wrong areas, the current shuts off and the procedure stops. Once your attention has moved back and the correct areas of the brain are activated, we continue.'

'Okay,' says the woman.

On Noor goes, reciting the aftercare guide. Except when she's finished the woman still looks anxious.

Okay, thinks Noor. Let's have Phelps.

'Want to hear how reliable memory actually is?' Noor says.

'Uh . . .' says the woman. 'Yes?'

'Not long after the Twin Towers were attacked, a scientist called Elizabeth Phelps surveyed several hundred people about their memories of that day. Then a year later, they were surveyed again. The second time around, their memories were only 63 per cent consistent with their original accounts. After another two years this had dropped to around 50 per cent. And these inconsistencies weren't just minor details. Some people even claimed to have been in a different place when the planes hit.'

'They were lying?'

'No. They genuinely believed in their latest version of events.'

'That's . . . terrifying.'

'But the thing is: if there hadn't been a study, nobody would even have known they were wrong. Just like you're only noticing how unreliable your memory is because *you're* studying it now. Does that help?'

'I find that . . . quite disturbing, actually,' the woman says.

'Okay. Well, there's good news.' (Noor remembers to smile here.) 'The same people were surveyed again ten years later, and this time their answers weren't much more inaccurate than the last lot. Which shows at least there's a limit to how wrong we can be.'

'Right,' says the woman.

She frowns, apparently falling into her own thoughts.

'All right,' Noor says briskly. 'I feel that in this instance it would be helpful for you to discuss your thoughts and feelings with further therapy. I'm going to refer you to our team of dedicated memory specialists. They'll be here to support you in every way.'

At this the client finally perks up. It's the *dedicated team offering full support*. This is what the anxious clients like to hear.

But from what Noor can remember of her days as an interviewer, the anxious clients used to be more . . . reassurable. It never took this long to get them out of her office; she rarely sent anyone to the therapy team. It's the restorations again, she thinks. The clients' trust is wavering. And it's not surprising. Nepenthe promised people that their memories had been removed forever. Then it turned out to be wrong. Why? Because of science. Clients aren't very convinced by science at the moment, and they definitely aren't convinced by Nepenthe.

Noor shows the woman out and sits down. She takes a sip of her tea. It's cold.

At almost the same time that Noor, gazing out of the window, notices that Louise's Tesla is outside – parked in the spot usually occupied by the clinic director Jim – a voice startles her.

'Dr Ali?'

It's Marie the receptionist, or at least her head, hovering hesitantly in the doorway.

'It's Dr Nightingale,' she says. 'She asked to see you when you have a spare minute.'

'I suppose that means now,' says Noor.

'Yeah. That's the impression I got,' says Marie.

A moment later Louise is in Noor's office. She smiles and sits down.

'I didn't realise you'd be coming in today,' Noor says.

'Well, I got your text and rushed right over,' says Louise.

'Really?'

'No, of course not. I'm here to go over some restorations stuff. What was the text about?'

'It's going to sound weird,' Noor says. 'But there was a protester yesterday who was causing a scene. Obvious mental illness. But I was curious about him. I felt like he might have had some connection to us – have been a client, maybe. I was wondering if there was a way we could find out more about him –'

'To do what?' Louise says. 'If he's mentally ill, you know we can't help him. We can't do removals *or* restorations.' She shakes her head. 'Don't worry, I'm sure our underfunded NHS will look after him.'

'It's not just that,' Noor said. 'It's that he was holding a placard. It said RASA Cover Up.'

She waits. Louise looks back at her, blankly.

After a long moment Louise says, '. . . And?'

'Don't you know what RASA is?' Noor asks, confused.

'Not a clue,' Louise says. 'So, are you going to enlighten me?'

Noor opens her mouth. She hesitates. The problem is that she had genuinely expected Louise to say, *Ah yes, RASA, not many people know about it, so keep this under your hat, but* – and then explain who or what RASA was.

'I just thought . . . I'd heard it somewhere round here before,' Noor says.

'Really?' Louise leans forward slightly. 'In what context?'

On your phone, Noor could say.

'I don't know,' she says. 'I'm not even sure now where I heard it. I certainly don't know what it means.'

'Okay,' Louise says. She sits back. 'So . . . that's what you wanted to ask? That's why you texted?'

And for a second Noor actually feels *embarrassed*. Before she reminds herself that she had every reason to text. That Louise, watching Noor with this slightly amused, slightly curious smile, has just told an out-and-out lie.

That's how good Louise is.

'Yep, that's it,' she says. 'I just felt bad for the guy.'

'I know. It's a shitty system,' says Louise. She says this with real feeling. Then she pushes her chair back. 'Listen, Noor, I need your co-authorisation to access another client file. Would you mind?'

The co-authorisation system is meant to protect client confidentiality. To look up a client's contact details, two senior doctors need to sign off on the action. It applies even to someone at Louise's level. (According to rumour, the system was implemented after a psychologist decided he was in love with a client and started stalking her: a story that never fails to make Noor squirm).

Louise has had a few of these requests for Noor lately, post-fuck-up. The problem with the self-confidential patients, Louise explained, is that over the years some of them have changed their contact details and not registered their new email addresses with their GP practice. As a result Nepenthe is having trouble getting the emails out to them. Louise has had to step in and get their home addresses.

Noor is supposed to carry out a few basic checks on what Louise is doing; which clients she's looking up. She's definitely not supposed to type in her password and leave Louise to it – which is what she's always done up until now. But now, Louise has officially lied to her, and Noor's feeling somewhat *unsettled*.

As a result, she hesitates before she says, 'No problem.'

Which was stupid. The hesitation is tiny, and the *no problem* emphatic, but she knows Louise will have noticed it. And yes – she glances up – Louise's head is on one side, and she's looking at Noor closely.

Before Noor became one herself, psychologists were, in her mind, something akin to hypnotists or wizards. She used to believe that they could tell when someone was lying. Now, she knows they all do the same thing that Noor herself does: carry out basic checks. Not so much detectives of the mind as security guards: going round the perimeter, the same route night after night.

All done here. Nothing unusual to report. Let's call it a night.

The exception to this is Louise: one of only two people in the world who has ever been able to tell when Noor is lying. So when Louise says, 'You look troubled. What's wrong?' Noor knows there's no point saying, *nothing*.

'Just the clients,' she says. 'You know they don't believe anything we say any more? All because of this restorations fuck-up.'

Louise brings her breath sharply in between her teeth. 'Restorations,' she says, with some bitterness. 'The public don't hate us because we played God. It's because we *weren't* God. We got something wrong. They've realised we're humans. They'll never forgive us.'

Louise has always been opposed to the restorations. She'd wanted Nepenthe to resist the public pressure. If they'd just held out for a terrorist attack or an earthquake, Louise said, it could have all blown over.

'Could it . . . bankrupt us?' Noor asks. 'The cost of all the restorations?'

'No,' Louise says. 'If Nepenthe'd had to compensate people, that would have been expensive. But it can't be held responsible for scientific advances – that was the ruling. We didn't know memories could be restored until the Glanzman study with the snails. And don't – don't – say the word *traces* or I'll literally have to sack you. Anyway, do you know the cost price of a single restoration? It's about £300. It's not an issue. The thing that will hurt us is bad publicity. Do you know that a man on YouTube who says Nepenthe was set up to wipe the memories of people who found out the earth is flat has 3 million subscribers? That the Twitter account NepentheRunByAliens has 10 million followers?'

'That's a lot of ill-will,' Noor says.

'Yes. And at some point they're going to focus on something that's actually true.'

'So *that's* when we're bankrupted?'

'If people stop getting deletions, yes. And if I were you, I'd stop thinking in terms of *we*. There's no we, not in the company's eyes. There's you. And there's Nepenthe. And in fact it would be no bad thing for the former to have some leverage regarding the latter.'

'Some what?' Noor asks.

'Leverage. Dirt. Bodies, location of? Are you following?'

'Right,' Noor says. She laughs, partly because she thinks Louise is probably joking, partly because she's worried that she's not.

Louise looks at her for a minute, until Noor feels compelled to shift in her seat, crossing her legs, feeling less comfortable, uncrossing them – then she smiles too.

'My next patient is here in twenty minutes,' Noor says. 'I'll go and make another cup of tea and you can do your thing. Is that long enough?'

'Plenty,' says Louise. Noor gets up, and Louise takes her place. Noor leans over Louise and types her password into the authentication screen. Louise averts her eyes comically high, out through the skylight.

'Looking for a signal from our alien overlords?' Noor says, heading for the door.

'I'm glad you can see the humour,' Louise says. 'Because we have to, don't we? And on that note, our beloved head of operations Clifford Byrne will be coming in with me in a couple of weeks for a walk around, which will be another thing for us to see the humour in, I hope. See you later.'

Noor's final appointment of the day is a client who chose to remove the memory of a rape rather than report it to the police.

Noor, though she isn't really supposed to, asks the client why she decided not to press charges. But she already knows. The law against tampering with neural evidence means that crime victims and witnesses aren't allowed to delete the memory of a crime until a ruling has been made, and any appeals are over.

The client says that she didn't want to wait years before she was allowed to have the wipe. The man was untouchable anyway. She only wanted the memory gone. That was it. And now it's gone, and she's been feeling better.

'Okay,' Noor says. 'I . . . Okay.'

She writes: *Has been feeling better.*

Tell me a story.

Once upon a time Captain James T. Kirk, of the starship *Enterprise*, fell in love. But Rayna, the woman he fell in love with, died. Or maybe it's more accurate to say that she suffered a *systems failure*. She broke down, and couldn't be repaired. This loss left Captain Kirk incapacitated with grief. One night he said to his first officer, Spock, 'If only I could forget.' Then he put his head on his arms, and fell asleep.

Spock decided that what would be best for Captain Kirk was if he, Spock, used a mind meld to erase the sleeping Kirk's memories of the woman he loved.

So he did.

And that was the end of that. The theme tune began. The credits rolled. And by the next episode Kirk was his usual untroubled self, and nobody ever mentioned Rayna again, which you'd think might have happened by accident, at least once or twice.

So. Do you think it worked? Noor asks Elena. *Do you think Kirk really was his old self again?*

Elena doesn't answer. She stares out of the window, the light cutting its lines across her forehead, her cheek, her mouth, her neck. It's not very helpful. Actually, it's rude. But Noor guesses that's what you get, asking imaginary people questions.

The real-life Elena was more forthcoming.

For example:

You have beautiful hair, Elena said. You should let it loose.

It struck Noor how strange it was that she knew quite a lot about Elena, while Elena knew nothing about Noor, and yet it was Elena looking at Noor with something almost nostalgic in her friendliness, as if they'd known each other for a long time, and had just been reunited. And, this being the case, that it would seem natural for her to reach out and touch Noor's hair.

Panic comes out oddly in a voice. In Noor's case flat and affectless, like a recording warning commuters to move back from the train doors.

It's difficult, she told Elena. We're not allowed to have any kind of, uh, personal relationships with clients.

The two of them were outside The Cat and Pigeon, where Noor, arriving, had walked straight into Elena coming from the other direction, her small face barely visible above her large fake-fur coat. The night was black and sooty. Lights fizzled in the damp air; a fine sleet blew sideways.

Is that right? Elena said. She was standing too close. Of course she was. It made Noor aware of their breath – commingling, communicating, or just shot down by the rain.

I could be fired just for coming here, Noor said. And it's not a *turning a blind eye* kind of situation. They're very security-conscious. I know they check up on us.

So you came here just to tell me that? Elena said.

Yes.

Quite a journey, said Elena. I mean it. It was very kind of you. In fact, I feel like I owe you a drink. You may as well have one seeing as you're already here. Not in the bar, don't worry. Somewhere totally anonymous. A top-secret location. Screened for bugs and enemy agents. What do you say?

Noor's attention returns to the office. It's time to go home. More than time to go home. If she doesn't hurry the chemist will close, and she needs to pick up her sleeping pills. She ran out yesterday, and had to spend the night listening to the sounds of her neighbours having a party. On a Wednesday. They'd turned the music down, probably after another neighbour complained, but people kept going outside to smoke, their voices rising straight up through the still air, as loud and emphatic as flying geese.

Nina, the boy shouted from inside. Nina, dance with me.

How old are they to be living together anyway? she wonders. Playing house. Going to work after getting no sleep, in smart clothes that look – on them – like costumes. Don't they know the stats on the likelihood of it working out?

Noor saw the girl sunbathing topless in the garden one Saturday. She turned away from her naked breasts, fiery white in the strong sunlight. A wince on her behalf. *Be careful*, she wants to say to her. *Please look after yourself.* Then that night the two of them played drum and bass until 4 a.m. and she thought: I hope your tits got burnt.

But then: the day after that she saw them in the garden looking at a bird, a greenfinch, on the feeder, with their arms around each other's waists, heads tipped back, and she felt a moment of intense pain and longing.

In short: the neighbours confuse and bother Noor and she wishes they'd move out. Or – as it's inevitable – just break up. Get the hurt over with.

She exits the clinic via a side gate, and walks down the hill towards the high street. It's been raining while she was indoors – she didn't notice – and the air smells of wet tarmac and wet grass.

The chemist is on the main square of the town, next to the handsome clock tower and opposite the large oak tree. A popular local claim is that the tree was once used as a gibbet to execute Cornishmen. Apparently at the end of the fifteenth century the Cornish rebelled against the king and marched on London. After they were defeated some of the rebels fled to whatever Crowshill was called back then, where they were caught and hanged, three a day, until all thirty-three of them were dead. The story actually comes from the neighbouring town of Horsfield Heath, but that hasn't stopped the Crowshillians claiming that after the hangings the sky above the town was black with crows for days, which is how the town got its name. They've also been known to claim that the Nepenthe clinic is here because of the famous crow from the Edgar Allan Poe poem, which makes absolutely no sense at all.

Locals, Noor thinks. She's waiting behind two of them right now, in the chemist queue. They're talking about the clinic.

'It's a magnet for lunatics and criminals,' one woman is saying.

(Noor has to give her that one.)

'I know,' says her friend.

'The infant school is only a few yards down the road!' the woman continues. 'All the parents having to walk past the protesters every day. It's only a matter of time before something terrible happens.'

'It's awful,' says her friend.

It's already happened, thinks Noor drily. *And you're right: it is awful.*

(It's only later that it occurs to her that true awfulness doesn't become apparent all at once. It arrives in bits and pieces, dribs and drabs; it drips, then it roars; it rains and then it pours.

But she didn't know that then.)

The first drip of awfulness comes at the end of September, with the visit from Clifford Byrne. He arrives with Louise and a couple of other senior management people, and is met by Jim Stokes, the clinic director. The five of them walk around, looking at the treatment rooms that have been repurposed for the restorations.

Other than Crowshill, the only clinics carrying out restorations are in Manchester and Scotland. This is because, as Clifford Byrne puts it, the restoration programme has been mobilised reactively with ambitious time scalings and streamlined resourcing.

They've cobbled it together, is how Louise puts it. *They don't have enough units. They don't have the staff. They have no fucking idea what they're doing.*

Noor stays in her office. After a while the tour approaches her door. It's closed, but she can already hear the commanding voice of Clifford Byrne in the corridor outside. She imagines the voice rattling the slanted glass panels of the roof; startling the wood pigeons.

By contrast, Jim Stokes's voice is hardly audible. He's a pleasant man who probably wishes he was in his own office, but isn't allowed to be because after working for the clinic for twenty years he's attained enough importance to stand within commanding distance of Clifford Byrne.

Noor stretches, comfortably, in her chair. She allows herself to feel smug about the way she has evaded real importance over the years. Louise has tried to put her forward for further promotion a few times, but Noor has got out of it – not with argument or active resistance, but by making herself very heavy and limp, the way you're supposed to if someone tries to drag you somewhere you don't want to go.

'Thanks, Jim,' Clifford says. A dismissal.

Louise's voice takes over from Jim's. It's a mellow sound, relaxing yet capable. It's clearly aimed at Clifford Byrne, and soon he laughs.

As the party reaches Noor's door she hears Louise saying: '. . . all the research shows that a sense of personal identity, narrative continuity, goal motivation and fulfilment can remain robust even in cases of severe episodic amnesia. The self might be a convenient fiction, but it's a remarkably resilient one.'

Someone says something inaudible in response, and then all the voices pass beyond hearing.

*

Noor first encountered Clifford Byrne in 2008. Not that he'd remember meeting *her*. He was preoccupied at the time with propranolol – the drug everyone was hoping could cure PTSD sufferers without removing their memory – and what could be done to cast doubt over its efficacy and/or the reputations of the researchers.

Noor said to Louise she'd rather, on balance, not have met Clifford.

Why? Louise asked. Giving Noor an *aren't you funny* look.

I expected him to be more . . . not noble exactly. But him and the rest of the board. They're just like board members anywhere else.

You should meet the scientists, Louise said. They're even worse. I met the guy who basically invented the procedure and he ate with his mouth open. Also, he smelled.

But *they're* more principled, surely, Noor said. The scientists?

Louise's *aren't you funny* look deepened. Took on other elements. Noor thought she could make out *how sweet*. Or maybe it was *wake up, idiot*. Then it was nothing at all except Louise's warm, sincere smile.

Sure, said Louise.

How much does Elena remember? Noor wonders.

Does she remember throwing herself back on her pillow, saying, Hey, you want some wine? I did promise you a drink. Do you prefer red or white? Or spirits? Hang on – do you drink?

Why do you ask? Noor said. Because I'm Arabic?

What? No! Good lord, are you always so defensive?

Sorry.

Some of us white people don't drink either, you know, Elena said. My mum didn't. That's partly why we never got along. Family, right? Do you get on with yours?'

What?

Your family. You know: mum and dad. Ma and pa.

Ah . . . no, Noor said. I don't see them.

There was a silence, and then Elena said, thoughtfully, You don't like talking, do you, Noor?

Not this sort of talking. I'm not great at it.

But you talk for a living.

That's different, Noor said. I'm not personally involved. I prefer it that way. An observer of people, rather than a participant.

Elena gave her a sly smile. She had very white teeth. Noor had noticed that the inside of her mouth was very pink. A vivid, bright mouth, always ready to drink, lick, taste, bite. And talk.

You seemed to be participating just now, Elena said.

Well, I've never done this before.

You've never – Shit! What, you're a . . . ?

Noor nodded.

There was a long silence.

Wow, Elena said, at last. She'd raised herself up to peer straight into Noor's face, which Noor tried not to mind, and now she laughed and collapsed back onto the bed again. Her hair rolled over the pillow, the tips of it touching the tips of Noor's own unloosed hair.

Why didn't you say something? Elena asked.

Why, what would you have done differently? said Noor.

I don't know . . . lit candles? Elena said. Well, I've got to say, I do feel pretty smug about that. Have you not been tempted before? What's the closest you came, I mean, to *this*?

Not very. And not very.

Okay, sorry. Shit, you weren't playing around. You really *don't* like questions . . . It's fine. We don't have to do that. There's other stuff we can do.

Oh? Things are looking up, said Noor.

Let's . . . let's tell *stories*.

Stories.

Don't look like that. I don't mean personal stories. *In fact*, the rule is that they aren't allowed to be personal in any way at all. I'm with you on that, believe it or not. You never tell your stories, well, I've told mine too often. I'm sick of them. I only told you because I wanted you to hear everything about me upfront. See whether you'd still come here.

That's why? I thought you were slightly unhinged, Noor said.

Is that a professional diagnosis? Well, maybe I am a bit unhinged. But you're still here. So. Tell me a story.

I think you've gravely misunderstood how creative I am, said Noor. I can't just make up a story.

Tell me a story made up by someone else, then, said Elena. Oh, and the other rule is: it has to have a happy ending.

Noor thought for a while.

Okay, she said. I have one. *Orlando Paladino*. An early example of someone actually benefiting from the removal of their memory.

Who? Is this one of your patients? That's cheating.

It's an opera. By Haydn. Orlando Paladino is a knight. In fact he's a maniac who spends most of the opera stalking and harassing a princess named Angelica. Angelica doesn't love him, but Orlando doesn't care. He's obsessed. He tries to kill any other man she so much as glances at. In the end Angelica's saved by a sorceress named Alcina.

I like that, said Elena.

Alcina takes Orlando to the River Lethe. That's where souls who are crossing over to the lands of the dead drink to forget their lives on earth. The boatman dips Orlando into the water, and Orlando forgets all about Angelica. His love vanishes; his rage vanishes. He's cured. He goes back to his previous existence, Angelica can get on with her life, and everyone's happy.

Interesting, said Elena. But okay. I have questions.

Like?

What else is gone? What's left? What would have happened to him if the boatman had dropped him and he'd been in the water for hours before they fished him out?

No idea, Noor said. You wanted a happy ending. You didn't say you wanted answers.

Elena threw herself down on the pillow again, and laughed.

Once Clifford Byrne and the others have gone, Louise comes to Noor's office. She seems to be in a good mood.

'It went well, then?' Noor asks.

'What? The walk-around? No. It was a shambles. But it's over now. Anyway, before I go, would you mind signing me off on a client file? Another of the elusive self-confidentials.'

'Sure,' Noor says. No hesitation. 'I was about to make a tea anyway. Want one?'

She gets up; Louise moves into her chair.

'Would I . . . ?' Louise is already clicking on files. 'Oh. Tea. No, thank you.'

Noor, leaning over Louise to enter her name and password, notices that Louise still wears the same perfume. The scent of it takes Noor back to that first interview with Nepenthe, when she was so impressed with the company, and Louise's expensive-smelling perfume, and the sci-fi technology literally saving lives, and Louise's referring casually to the architect working on her modernist Japanese-influenced house and her way of smiling when Noor answered a question right, as if she were willing Noor on, saying, *Come on, you can do it, you too can wear expensive perfume and administer life-saving sci-fi technology and live in a modernist house and know when and how to smile.*

The kitchen is empty when Noor arrives. There are no windows to look out of so she watches the temperature gauge on the kettle and feels –

What?

By the time Noor gets back to her office Louise has finished what she was doing and is just closing Noor's door behind her. She's got her bag and coat. Her good mood has apparently vanished. Her expression hasn't changed, but all the bones of her face look locked.

'That was quick,' Noor says.

'Actually, I didn't manage to get everything done,' Louise says. 'A bit of a pain, really. I've got to leave now.

I've got a meeting. I'll try to get back in next week or something.'

'No problem,' Noor says. 'See you soon.'

Noor logs back in to her computer, sitting in the warm chair – which, shaped to Louise, feels momentarily unfamiliar. When she picks up her phone to call reception, even the *phone* feels unfamiliar.

Then she realises that this is because the phone smells, quite unmistakably, of perfume.

Noor brings the handset to her nose. She sniffs. Words like benzoin, ambergris, oud come to mind. Gold-lidded, square-cut bottles, displayed on shelves in the marble bathrooms of modernist glass-walled houses.

Louise.

She must have been calling reception, or Jim, Noor thinks, as she presses the Last Dialled button.

She isn't sure why she does this. Or why it doesn't surprise her when the phone doesn't connect to reception or Jim, but trumpets a sharp tone in her ear, and informs her that *this number is out of service.*

Noor puts the handset down.

Now, Noor thinks. There's nothing technically *wrong* here. Louise must have called a private number. Louise has every right to use Noor's phone to make personal calls if she wants to. *More* right, in fact, than Louise has to delve alone into client records.

Which she was also doing.

Sitting at the desk, looking up client records, making calls.

Huh, thinks Noor.

She tries to imagine why Louise, being the owner of a perfectly good phone – a phone Noor has seen her using already today – might decide to use Noor's phone instead of her own.

Does Louise remember Noor's previous career? is what Noor wonders, then.

Noor had gone into her first interview planning to talk about her background in software development and cyber security as little as possible. She didn't see much difference between coding and psychology, but she was aware that other people did, and that dropping one to retrain in the other could have cast doubt on her personal consistency – her character itself. In the end Louise made it clear she didn't believe in either concept. Which was lucky, because Noor had spent most of the interview going on about coding.

So probably Louise does remember, but just hasn't realised how easy it would be for Noor to do what she is now doing, which is to log in to the system as an executive administrator, and retrace Louise's own steps.

Or – more probably – Louise knows all of this, but would never have suspected that Noor would check up on her.

Noor herself isn't 100 per cent sure why she's checking up on Louise.

Something to do with expensive perfume, maybe.

The way Louise said, *Anyway, before I go.*

Louise only looked at two pages, it seems. The first thing she did was exactly what she said she was doing: she looked up a client's contact details. The problem is, while Noor can see the type of page that was accessed, even in admin mode she can't see who this person is. Not without getting a co-authorisation herself, which would draw attention to her activities, or hacking into the page, which would draw more. Noor's good, but she's not better than Nepenthe's cyber security team. They'd know there'd been an internal breach immediately.

The second page Louise viewed is from the clinic's calendar. This isn't sensitive data: Noor could have accessed it just by pressing the *back* button. Louise was apparently looking at the first week of November, a schedule of all the appointments at the Crowshill clinic. Four people are coming in that week – presumably to get restorations, as no new procedures are being carried out. Noor supposes that one of these must be the person Louise was trying to call, as she's clicked through straight from a client page. Again, she has no way of knowing *which* person Louise is looking for. She makes a note of the four names anyway. None of them mean anything to her.

'Okay,' Noor says, out loud.

As if Louise herself is in the room. Which might be why Noor's *okay* sounds not resolute (*Okay, Louise, you asked for it*) but almost pleading. (*Louise? Is this okay?*)

In the absence of a response from Louise, Noor looks up the last quarter's CDR report for her own phone. It's not difficult to find the numbers Louise called: Noor herself tends to use her mobile. There are eleven unfamiliar numbers on the list, all of them made during – Noor checks her diary – Louise's last visits.

. . . *Huh*, she thinks, again.

There's not much Noor can really do with a list of numbers, most of them mobiles. She goes back to the page log and scrolls back to the dates Louise visited. As she expected, each time Noor co-authenticated Louise's activity, Louise went straight to a client's contact details page. So she was calling clients. But why would she do that?

Noor can see, too, that on several occasions Louise also looked up clinic schedules, and – most importantly – client case notes. She looked up the case notes for eight out of the eleven people she called.

These are pages Noor, as a senior psychologist, *can* access.

And does.

It seems that the clients Louise looked up are all self-confidentials, which might have been the only thing she was honest about. Case note pages for self-confidentials don't actually contain much information, because Nepenthe isn't allowed to keep a record of the deleted memory. (In fact, the only person in the entire world who ends up knowing what the memory was is the psychologist who deals with that client. The treatment doctors strolling around the Nepenthe corridors are living libraries of exiled memories.)

In addition, all the people Louise looked up were once her own clients, presumably from the long-ago days when she had clients.

Not so strange, necessarily.

The strangest thing – the worst thing, the thing that Noor can't make sense of – is the status report for each client. Louise had told Noor that she was trying to track down self-confidential clients who had moved house, or dropped off the map, or whatever. But Noor can see that nobody has in fact moved house or dropped off the map. And that all these people, every single one of them, have *already* been tracked down.

Every one of these people had responded to the email from Nepenthe, most of them weeks ago, to say they'd like to take up the offer of a memory restoration. But then every one of them – within days or even hours of being called by Louise – got in touch with Nepenthe and said they didn't want a restoration after all.

Which means Louise's calls to these people weren't on the record. They weren't authorised. They weren't legal. And whatever Louise said to these people *definitely* wasn't legal.

Louise could get sacked for this.

Noor could get sacked, for co-authorising it.

Fuck, Noor mutters under her breath. She's cold with fright.

Fuck, fuck, Louise, what the fuck?

None of the clients gave a reason why they wanted to cancel their procedure. *Change of mind*, was the box that was ticked.

Ha ha, thinks Noor. Literally, a change of mind. No changing back.

Ha very not very ha.

Mei

Mei's dad gives her a lift to Kuala Lumpur airport.

'You know, this is a *great* plan,' he says. 'This is the sort of plan I'd have made, way back when.'

Mei's dad thinks that Mei is going to London to meet some friends for a weekend of partying, a trip which is to be kept secret from her mum. Mei couldn't tell him the truth, that she's chasing a memory trace to an unknown city, alone. He wouldn't have understood. Every now and again Mei's mum and dad call an uneasy truce in order to share information about how well – or not – Mei is doing. And the truth is exactly the sort of thing that could bring about a truce.

But a clandestine weekend of getting fucked up in the very city her mum lives in, without her mum's knowledge? Mei's dad is delighted at the thought.

'This is what you need, darling,' he says. 'Your mum worries about you. But that's no way to live. That's why you came to stay with me, right? I mean, she's always been overprotective. No wonder you ended up depressed. All that . . . at uni. She didn't get that this is the sort of thing you *ought* to be doing. Getting out there, drinking, having fun.'

'Absolutely,' says Mei.

Her dad had always been confused by the hows and whys of Mei failing her second-year exams. It wasn't the kind of failure he understood. Mei didn't fail because of recreational drugs, she failed because of study drugs. Modafinil in the day, Xanax to sleep at night. Mei could tell at the time that he thought the real problem was that she was doing the wrong drugs.

Good clean fun, that's what his smile says now.

Meanwhile, Mei's wondering how wise it was to be taking advice from a disembodied voice about bold moves. *Almost as soon as you've made one, it doesn't feel bold any more.* She's not sure the voice was right. Because the move isn't feeling less bold. It's feeling *more* bold. Nearly unbearably bold. She stares out of the window, trying to reel her anxiety back in.

'Here we are,' her dad announces, redundantly, when they get to the airport. He helps her with her case; darts in – exuberant, almost shy – for a kiss on the cheek. Mei almost holds on to him then, wanting to cry out:

I lied! I'm scared! I don't know what I'm doing!
Take me home!

She takes a long breath, and the feeling passes.

'Have a blast, darling,' her dad says. 'And mum's the word, right? Ha. Literally.'

The airport is very new and very sleek. A curving false ceiling, like an idea of a bird's belly, is held up by curving pillars like the idea of trees. Above that there's glass, behind which is real forest, or what Mei thinks is real forest. Maybe it's a holographic forest. Mei gets herself a flat white and a pastry, tries to regulate her breathing – which has been short and panicked since she watched her case disappear down the conveyor belt – and gets down to business. Business being: going through Katya's and Sophia's social media feeds.

When Mei left uni her mum had encouraged her to cut ties – real and digital – with both girls. From a purely Pavlovian point of view they were a bad thing, she said. She'd already got Mei to tell her that Sophia had been the one who sorted out the drugs for them all – though in Sophia's defence she did warn that modafinil was called that because it was just for finals, and later she said that she thought Mei was using the Xanax for coke come-downs, not to, like, get *dependent* on.

None of it was really Mei's friends' fault. Mei had been feeling sad and unmotivated before she got behind with work. She can't remember *why* she'd been feeling that way, which she guesses is the fault of the wipe. Then, when she realised she'd got properly, irreversibly behind, she started to panic. She decided she'd get a little extra bit of chemical help, to get back on top again. And then it was only a couple of months before the drugs made her feel genuinely insane, and she started crying in the library and couldn't stop, and that's when they called her mum.

Mei had deleted all her past chats with Sophia and Katya on various apps, untagged herself from their photos, and removed them as friends on others. Standard practice, according to Mei's mum's guide to Ending Unhealthy Relationships. Standard practice, Mei now thinks, before a memory wipe. Anyway, she was worried that she wouldn't be able to find out any information about their trip at all. But, *thank God*, and *of course*: both Sophia's and Katya's feeds are public.

Mei scrolls through the last couple of years, until – just next to a video of Katya twerking on a loop in cut-off denim shorts – she spots the first canal boat. None of the hashtags are enlightening, but in the next picture there are three beers sitting together on a sunlit upturned barrel, the name of the bar – Cafe Belgique – clearly visible in the background. In another picture there's a latte with a heart drawn on it, and a napkin next to it with the name of the *koffiehuis*, Armand's Coffee. There's Sophia eating a hash brownie in a large bar with purple lighting. There are Katya and Sophia on bicycles, next to a sign saying Vondelpark. Mei isn't in any of the pictures. But that's not so strange: she probably got deleted after they fell out.

Mei favourites all the identifiable places in her phone's map app, and makes a note to look for the others. She's already tried googling *Amsterdam canal houses, tall houses dutch canalside, red house orange house*, and so on – but she can't find the ones from her memory trace. She's hoping that she might just pass them, by chance, as she walks from one favourited place to the next.

She's frightened that she won't pass them.

She's frightened that she will.

Mei's mum once told her about some study to do with rats. Mei can't remember what the study was, but she remembers her mum saying that at some point the rats became depressed.

Wait. How did they *know* the rats were depressed? asked Mei.

There's a simple test, her mum said. The float test. They put the rats in water. A happy rat will swim, to survive. A depressed rat just . . . floats.

Oh, said Mei.

A couple of months ago, her mother's story came back to Mei. She'd had been living at home for a few months by then, though the day she'd packed her things and left university seemed like a long time ago. She wasn't going out, though she told her mum she went for walks each day. She held books and pretended to be reading them as she stared out of the window. She looked at celebrity gossip pages online and told her mum she was looking up university syllabuses. She sat at the dinner table and asked questions about current affairs, and pretended she was interested in the answers.

Then one day she thought: *I'm a floating rat.*

So she stopped taking her antidepressants. This had mixed results in that she felt sharper, more *feeling*, but she also found it harder to be around her mum. The feelings Mei's mum provoked were . . . mixed. So Mei went to Kuala Lumpur, and now she's in the middle of the mixed results of *that*.

And where is Mei now?

She considers it. She definitely *feels* more, which is a good thing.

She's also telling a lot of lies. And she's anxious a lot of the time.

But on the plus side, she thinks: *I'm swimming.*

Mei arrives in Amsterdam at night. She doesn't have the energy to find the right tram, so she gets a cab as far as it can take her, a couple of streets away from her hotel, and walks the rest of the way, dragging her case over the cobbles. Once she's in her room, she stands and looks out of the window at the busy street and canal below. She's taken a lot of flights in her life. She knows that she's tired. She ought to go to bed. But all she feels is a peppery, agitated wakefulness.

Get moving, get moving, it urges. *Let's get started!*

Mei takes a taxi to the first of the destinations on her list, the purple-lit bar. She'd managed to Google Image search it and find out its name – Neuhaus, off the Amstelstraat. But as soon as she gets there she finds she's exhausted. She sits on a shiny banquette with a beer, recognising nothing, then, after about an hour, walks back to her hotel.

There's a group of people about Mei's own age in the lobby. They're gathered around a boy who's lying on one of the sofas. Mei can just see his arms waving above the cushions.

'I can't do it, I can't go on,' he's saying, in a loud voice.

Mei slows down, alarmed. But as she gets closer it becomes apparent that the group is laughing, the boy is laughing. Two girls take a hand each and start trying to lever him up from the sofa. When they give up, one of the girls turns, still laughing, and catches Mei's eye. She smiles at Mei.

Mei, embarrassed at having been caught watching them, looks away. It's only a half-second before she realises she ought to have smiled back, but by that time the girl has turned away again.

Mei goes upstairs. She shuts the door of her room and feels, suddenly, like crying. I'm tired, she thinks. That's all. She sits on the bed and pulls the duvet and blankets in around herself until she's cocooned like a pupae. She used to wrap herself up like that when she was very young, she remembers. It's comforting to do it now.

She thinks: *I'm not just tired*. Well, she is, but she's also – piercingly – miserable.

She's *lonely*.

But she's going to *do* something about that. She's going to find out what's wrong with her, what happened to her – and then she's going to take part in things, and be happy, and have friends, and roll around with them on sofas and laugh. And furthermore –

(Sleep.)

Mei wakes up early the next morning. It's a sunny day, so she walks to the second place on her list, Armand's Coffee.

She orders a flat white, sits in a corner, and looks around. It's a single room with a worn parquet floor, white walls and a collection of lights hung at different heights over the tables. There's a fiddle-leaf fig in the corner and a counter with pastries on top of it. Behind the counter is a girl in a coffee-stained apron. Across the room there's a guy working on a laptop, wearing headphones. There's a woman at the counter deciding on a cake.

So far, so . . . nothing.

Mei isn't sure what she was expecting. She didn't re-member the hotel, the bar last night, and now she doesn't remember this coffee shop. She knows she's been here, but she has no memory of it. The sensation is strange. It's the opposite of haunting. She feels disturbingly *un*-haunted.

Disappointment rises. Then frustration, at herself, for expecting the impossible.

Stupid, she thinks. She already *knew* that revisiting the scene or object of a deleted memory couldn't bring back the memory itself. It always used to annoy her mum when it happened in films. Some character would have something deleted at a Nepenthe-esque clinic, then come out and see the person they were trying to forget, and it would all come flooding back.

Preposterous, said Mei's mum.

So Mei should have known better. She'd just thought she knew *better still*. That maybe she'd be the exception. When the only thing she's ever been exceptional at is getting things wrong.

Mei realises that the girl across the counter is looking at her. She wonders what she's been doing with her face. Screwing it up, probably. She makes an effort to look smoother.

'Do you want something else?' the girl says. 'Because I'm going to have a break and call my mother, and I want to make sure I won't be interrupted by customers ordering things while I'm doing that.'

'Oh,' Mei says, taken aback. 'I'll have another coffee.' She hesitates. 'If that's okay.'

'I can do that,' the girl says, with a magnanimous wave of her hand. Then she pauses, and looks at Mei more closely. 'You've been in here before?' she says.

'I'm not sure,' Mei says. She feels a tremor of something, a twitch: the kind of excitement detectives and journalists are always experiencing. *This could be it*, she thinks. A *lead*. 'I *have*. I think.'

The girl nods. She turns away and starts making Mei's coffee.

'But . . . you remember me being here?' Mei asks. She wants to lean over the counter and get hold of the girl's uninterested shoulders. 'Who I was with? What was I doing?'

'I don't know,' says the girl. '*You* should know these things.'

'I . . . have memory problems,' Mei says.

'You were probably stoned,' says the girl. 'You tourists always get too stoned.'

Mei gives up.

'Okay,' she says. 'Thanks.'

Feeling disappointed, she takes her coffee and sits down. The girl picks up a *pain au chocolat* and takes a seat at one of the tables outside. She starts talking on her phone. Mei puts some money down on the counter and walks out of the cafe. She tries to catch the girl's eye as she passes, so she can smile and point at the money she left, but the girl is talking loudly in Dutch, and doesn't notice her go.

It doesn't take Mei long to visit the other places on her list. It's not like she, Katya and Sophia roamed very far. She spends a day walking around the city. She hasn't walked for a while, and quickly gets a blister. She goes to the Belgian cafe with the beer-barrel tables outside, and orders a beer. The cafe is canalside, but the houses opposite it are wrong. Mei's seen so many gabled houses now that she's made a little sketch of the ones in her original memory, in case they get overwritten. She knows that's something that can happen.

By the end of the day she's in the last of her destinations, the Vondelpark. It's very pretty, with the late-afternoon sun coming through the trees that her phone tells her are birch, plane, red chestnut. People cycle along the wide paths through the patches of sunlight.

The Vondelpark reminds Mei of various other parks she's been to. It does not remind her of itself. At all.

What now? she wonders.

But she already knows: there's nothing now.

Mei walks back to her hotel as evening falls. A feeling jolts her as she walks: anger. She's angry at herself.

Mei's mum always says that being angry with herself is pointless and damaging. But in this case it seems appropriate. There's a part of Mei that Mei wasn't previously aware of, and this part of herself has made the decision to erase some of Mei's memory. And it won't explain why. Mei is chasing this partial self, and it's running away. And yes, it might be pointless and damaging but Mei still wants to get hold of that treacherous partial self, wrestle it to the ground, twist its arm and not let go until it gives up all its secrets.

The really frustrating thing is that Nepenthe could actually give Mei her memory back if it wanted to. There's been an ongoing court case, and at the end of it Nepenthe might be ordered to give everyone their memory back. But the case has been going on for so long; it could go on for months or years more, according to Mei's mum.

Mei realises how tired she is when she sees her bed. The adrenaline of the hunt has staved off the jet lag, but that was never going to last forever. Now she feels like she's been shot with a tranquilliser dart. The anger she felt earlier is gone; submerged. She remembers she was supposed to email her mum, and sends her a brief, bright email about how she's tried a couple of new restaurants in Kuala Lumpur and is reading a good book. She lies down on the bed, on her back, and texts her dad for good measure: an emoji of a martini glass. He texts back an emoji of a thumbs up. She drops the phone on her face.

Ow, she says.

Then she must fall asleep, because it's light suddenly, and she's lying in bed with the phone next to her, ringing.

It's her mum.

Mei lets it go to voicemail, then listens to it.

'Hi Plum,' (says Mei's mum) 'I got your email. You sounded . . . odd. A little too determinedly *upbeat*, perhaps. Is everything okay? Call me.'

Mei winces.

She doesn't want to talk to her mum. Mei's heard of insurance companies installing lie-detecting voice software on their phone lines, to tell if customers are making fraudulent claims. Mei's mother is like the human version of that.

But then, Mei can also tell when her mum is lying. For example, her mum said that she liked Mei's chess club friends, but also, she thought Mei would enjoy spending time with different people too. Her mum said Mei was capable of dealing with her own problems, but also, Mei should probably take some antidepressants. She said that Mei could make her own choices, but also, given Mei's *history*, and Mei's *challenges*, Mei might need extra help and support, and – oh, *those* are Mei's choices? – in which case Mei *might* want to give them some more thought.

Especially in light of the choices she's made so far.

Mei's mum didn't say that last bit, exactly. But Mei knew. Aside from anything else, Mei's fundamental patheticness (*issues*, says her mum), her utter stupidity (*faulty reasoning*, says her mum), and the epic failure (*learning process*, says her mum) that was her university career speak for themselves.

And now she's in Amsterdam, realising that maybe she hasn't made a bold move, just a stupid one. Maybe it's another consequence of coming off her meds so abruptly. Maybe she's not rational.

Mei realises she's wrapped herself in the duvet again. She's wound it too tight this time; she's feeling hot, and slightly panicked. Her breathing is short and fast, reminding her of a rabbit she held once at a petting zoo. Is she going straight from floating rat to frightened rabbit? She struggles free and gets out of bed. She takes off her clothes from the day before, showers, and gets dressed again.

She refocuses.

She has one more full day in Amsterdam. Plenty of time for investigating. The problem is, she's not sure where to start.

In the absence of a plan, she goes back to the coffee shop, Armand's. She liked it in there. The young woman from before isn't working today, which is a relief. Mei sits in the window and texts her mum, a slightly less upbeat message. She hopes that'll give her a little more time.

'I told you,' says a man's voice. 'There's a whole box of oranges downstairs. That should be enough.'

Mei's hand is holding her cup halfway to her mouth when she hears this. The cup halts and tips. A splash of coffee hits the table.

The man who is talking has just come into the room from a door leading to some stairs. He has his back to Mei and is speaking to the younger guy behind the counter. He has curly dark hair and wide shoulders. She can't see his profile.

For a moment she stares at him, incapable of moving. Is she even *breathing*? No, she is not. Fear has switched her off. She tries to breathe, succeeds; inhales – too much – almost coughs. But now her arms and legs are back, thank God, and she can slide out of her seat, gather up her stuff, as quietly and quickly as she can. She turns her face away from the man, towards the door, not looking up – or back, not even once she's out in the street again, and safe.

There's a whole box of oranges downstairs.

Bold moves aren't such a big deal.

It's the same voice. She doesn't have to think about it: she knows. A European accent. Mid-pitched. The tone is the same; friendly, relaxed about both oranges and bold moves.

It doesn't relax Mei. It agitates her. The agitation disturbs her, because she doesn't understand it. She isn't sure if it's excitement or dread that stirs her stomach up, if it's longing or fright that jolts her.

Mei hadn't *actually* thought what would happen if she found the owner of the voice. But now she has, and she has no idea what she's going to do about it.

155

Introducing herself is out of the question. She needs more information, for her own protection. Better, she decides, to follow the man for a little while. Find out where he lives, who he is, why she might have been talking to him.

Why she didn't want to remember anything about him.

She spends her afternoon sitting at a bar across the road from Armand's, watching the man in the cafe. She sips a beer slowly and writes things down in her phone:

Seems to be owner or manager.

Nice to customers. (He jokes with people when he carries their drinks out to the small tables in the sun. The customers laugh back.)

Dark curly hair, needs trim. Tan. Long eyelashes. Hot. (Something the customers also seem to notice. At least one woman watches him through the glass; others flirt with him. The man doesn't pay them any particular attention. When they leave, he doesn't watch them go.)

In a relationship?? writes Mei.

After the cafe closes, the man goes back to his flat. Mei pays her bill in a hurry and follows him, walking on the other side of the street. It's a ten-minute walk, and he walks quickly, going finally into a tall, old house divided into flats. Mei stops short, slightly out of breath. They're on the Prinsengracht, the Canal of Princes. She hasn't walked along this part of it before. She turns and looks up. Above her there is a row of town houses. One is red, one is orange. Mei stands on the pavement and gazes at them, standing against the blueness of the sky.

Underneath the houses is a small Surinamese restaurant, just opening up for the evening. She goes in and asks for the table in the window. She spends the evening ordering dish after dish, eating slowly – all the time: watching.

Mei's feeling a bit uneasy about that by now. It's one thing sitting at a cafe with a glass of beer opposite a *koffiehuis* and watching what goes on inside. The cafe is technically public space. But it's another thing sitting opposite a man's apartment, watching him move around his own home. It's true that he has no curtains, or he's left them open, and the lights are on. But that almost makes it worse, the openness. The man lets himself be watched because he assumes nobody *would* watch. It hasn't occurred to him that, like the prostitutes in their windows, he has an audience.

Right now the man seems to be watching TV. The screen is out of Mei's limited viewline, but she can see his head, tilted upwards, unmoving.

She writes,

Lives alone?

'Is there anything else?' the waiter asks her.

He's looking at her dubiously, because Mei's already ordered a snack, two courses, two cups of coffee, and an ice-cream dessert she left unfinished. What else could there possibly be? She glances again at the flat opposite. The man seems to have gone to bed. The rooms are in darkness.

It's half past ten, and she still doesn't know anything about him. She could cross the road, ring the bell for his apartment, wake him, talk to him – but the thought of it frightens her. To face him would be to face their inequality: Mei standing at the bottom of the mountain of *this is what happened*, the man at the top.

She'd have to trust him to pull her up.

She doesn't *feel* trust. She's getting quicker, now, at identifying her feelings. What are they?

Worry.

Fear.

She won't face him. Which leaves her with . . . what? Back to the hotel, to bed. Her flight is early tomorrow morning. When the staff unlock the door of Armand's coffee shop, water the flowers, and put its tables and chairs out, Mei will be sitting in a departure lounge waiting to go home.

Is there anything else?

The problem with her plan is that it didn't have an anything else.

'I'll get the bill, please,' she tells the waiter.

He gives a small bow. Then he looks past her, towards the counter on the other side of the restaurant. 'Hello, Mr Armand,' he says. 'Takeaway? One moment please.'

Mei looks up. The man is waiting at the counter with a menu in his hands. For the first time, he realises that he's being looked at. He looks up, directly at Mei.

He blinks.

'*Mei?*' he says.

Oscar

Oscar wonders how much power the people looking for him actually have. They can track his credit card, he's guessed that much. Early on he had a scare when a man approached him outside his hotel in Brighton, asking, 'Mr Levy? Can I talk to you?' before Oscar escaped, dodging around him and running into the Lanes. Since then he's kept moving: using cashpoints, then leaving for another town.

Eight or so years passed uneventfully. So much so that Oscar had started to relax. In April, in Budapest, he'd been putting rounds of drinks on the card, swiping it in taxis, buying pastries from bakeries. And then the girl he shared a flat with at the time, Karolina, said a man had approached her in the bar where she worked and asked her where Oscar was. The man said he was a friend of Oscar's. Karolina knew it was weird because Oscar had no other friends.

Maybe the police are looking for you, Karolina said, smiling.

Oscar couldn't speak at first. There was absolutely no way his body could push enough air out for an answer, let alone move his tongue and lips. Then he realised it was a joke, and came out with a weird, throttled little laugh.

So, who was it? asked Karolina. *Do* you have a secret friend?

Sure, Oscar said.

Cool, she said. I told him that you usually drink here, so he should come back tomorrow.

Oscar made some excuse, and fled the bar. He was hurrying back to the flat when he noticed there was an expensive car parked on the road opposite it. Cars like this were not usually seen outside Oscar's flat, in the shabbier part of town. There was a man in the car. Oscar moved back behind a van and watched the man. For ten minutes the man didn't move. He sat perfectly still, watching Oscar's flat.

Fortunately, Oscar had his passport with him – by luck not design: it had been in the same pocket of his backpack since he arrived. So he turned his back on the flat and Karolina, and walked until he got to the station. Then he got a train to the airport, and left Hungary.

Oscar isn't frightened of airports. Whoever is after him seems to have no power there. When Oscar's passport goes under the various scanners no alarms squawk; nobody goes poker-faced and asks him to hold on a minute, as they turn away and pick up a phone. This doesn't surprise him. He suspects his pursuers are as far outside the law as Oscar himself. Their resources seem to be bribes rather than warrants, surveillance rather than raids. Not that there's much to surveil, with Oscar. He hasn't done anything remotely illegal, not since he left England. Before that he can't remember much.

Except for the drugs, and stealing a gun.

He'd give anything to remember what he did with that gun.

As Oscar is lying on a lounger in the hotel gardens, a decent distance away from the pool, he remembers a hippy he met once in Amsterdam. The hippy told Oscar a word Oscar had never heard before. *Synchronality*, or something. The hippy said that apparently meaningless coincidences actually do have meaning, and they show us that we're all one, all part of the universal connectedness. Oscar liked that idea.

He's not sure how much he likes it now that lying on a sunlounger next to him is a book that says, in large yellow letters:

A Trip to Remember: Murder, Memory Removal and Madness.

The book has been lying there for a few hours now. Oscar can't see anybody who looks like they might be its owner. Maybe someone left it there by accident when they went back to their room. How ironic, forgetting a book about memory. Oscar wonders if a joke could be made out of it, but his heart isn't in it. It's the book. It's ruining his pleasant mood. He can feel it sending its snarled, synchronous energy in his direction.

It's not a coincidence, not really. The book is a bestseller. It's everywhere. Oscar's seen it already, at an airport. It's about a woman in America named Carol Kurtz, the woman who killed somebody and lied about it.

He picks up the book and reads the first couple of pages.

Apparently the set-up at Nepenthe makes it impossible to cheat the system. Patients describe the memory to a psychologist, that's how it works. As they're talking about the memory, it's getting vaporised by drugs or electrical currents, or something. Despite this, people try to lie. They try to describe something and think about something else at the same time. But apparently anything like this is painfully obvious, and if it happened the technicians would just switch off the electrical current.

Carol Kurtz tried something a bit different. She gave a *partial* version of a memory, in the hope that the whole thing would be wiped. She told the clinic that she had had a secret fling overseas and fell in love, but now she wanted to erase the memory of the affair. What she didn't tell them was that when Carol's lover told her he didn't see it as anything more than just sex, they argued and she pushed him off a cliff. Nobody had ever suspected she might be responsible for the guy's disappearance, or at least they didn't until Carol, driven mad by nightmares and partial flashbacks about killing a person she'd never met in a country she'd never been to, ended up confessing most of it by accident to a friend.

Oscar feels sick. He puts the book back on the lounger. Unsatisfied, he gets up, picks up his towel and moves to another lounger, further away, where he can't see the book any more. He chooses a spot under a tree, so it looks like he's just got too hot in the sun. As he sits down he gives a little approving look up towards the branches, as if to say: *There. That's better.*

'What *are* you doing?' someone says, just behind him.

Oscar jumps violently. Then he realises it's only Atticus. He should have guessed. The kid has been preoccupied lately with what Oscar is *doing*. What Oscar's doing in Morocco. What he's doing when he leaves Morocco. What he did before he got there. Is it normal for kids to be this nosy? Is Atticus possibly a ghost? Or a figment of his imagination?

'You shouldn't move so quietly,' he says. 'People might assume you're a ghost.'

'You shouldn't read other people's books,' says Atticus, sitting on the lounger next to Oscar's.

'Fair point,' says Oscar. He calls a waiter over, and gets him to bring them two milkshakes.

'I thought you didn't read books,' Atticus says. 'Because you do the covers.'

'Well, I'm on a holiday from that,' Oscar says. 'Which means I can read if I want to.'

'Oh,' Atticus says. 'Are you married?'

'We're back to the interrogation, are we?' Oscar says, amused. 'No, I'm not married.'

'I didn't think so. Do you have kids?'

'Nope.'

'I didn't think that you did.'

'Maybe you should just go with your gut instinct, and then there'll be no need to ask me questions.'

'You can ask *me* questions, if you want.'

'You already tell me everything. Like yesterday you told me about your maths homework, and what you had for breakfast, then more homework, then how much iPads cost, and that you're going to the souks later but there's nothing there you want to buy, and you miss your best friend at home, and you don't have a girlfriend but you want one.'

Atticus looks offended. His woundedness is vast and dignified, like a Siberian plain. He stands in the middle of it, a lonely figure, slurping his milkshake.

'I didn't mean that you talk too much,' Oscar says. 'I like talking to you.'

'Hm.'

'Oh, shit. I didn't mean it like that. I'm sorry.'

'It's okay,' Atticus says.

'Good,' says Oscar. He lies back and shuts his eyes. Heat patterns dance on the inside of his closed eyes, red on black. He can hear the distant plash of the pool, ploughed by a tanned man in small pants; the chirrup of the blackbirds in the gardens. He can hear – he swears it – Atticus being sad.

Oscar opens his eyes and it's as he suspected. Atticus's eyes have filled with tears.

'Hey,' he says. 'What's up? Was it what I said?'

Atticus shakes his head. He wipes his sleeve across his face. 'I'm not crying,' he says.

'Of course not,' Oscar says.

'It's . . . I haven't been having a very nice vacation,' Atticus says. 'My parents are busy, and my brother didn't come because he isn't speaking to them, and I . . . I'm lonely. I'm just lonely.'

Oscar shuts his eyes. 'I'm sorry, man,' he says.

After a short while, Atticus says, 'Oscar? Are *you* okay?'

'I'm okay,' Oscar says. 'I'm just a bit lonely too.'

*

To Oscar's surprise, Jess calls, and comes over again. The two of them sit on Oscar's balcony and share a bottle of wine. The creeper above their heads is covered in gold flowers, like frozen flames. Jess sticks one behind her ear. Then she asks him to slap her when he fucks her, and call her a bitch.

'What?' Oscar says, shocked. 'No way. I can't do that.'

'You can.'

'I definitely, definitely can't.'

'Just try saying it, then. Say, *You dirty little bitch*. Or, *Suck it, you slut*, or something like that. Improvise.'

He tries it, without making eye contact, and she laughs.

'Oh dear. You're lucky you're pretty,' she says.

(Oscar's been told this before. He can't really see it himself. He's stared at his own face in the mirror, looking for clues as to his own origins, but nothing strikes him. He has no striking features at all, in fact. Indeterminate colour eyes. Brown hair. Beige skin. Symmetrical face. An *average* face, like a computer composite of every single face in the world.)

After Jess leaves (the two of them having settled on no insults, but a bit of hair-pulling), Oscar lies on his back in the bed. His thoughts drift, loose and undirected.

A door opens, and he finds himself back in the past.

He's standing in what was once a supermarket. The supermarket hadn't been closed for long, but that made it more creepy. The signs for the aisles hanging above him like ghosts, signposting other ghosts; the spectres of confectionery, pet food, detergent. The shelves hardly even dusty. It was like the very recent end of the world.

Oscar hasn't come across this place before, in his memories or otherwise. He's accordingly suspicious. Is this a real place? How likely is it that anyone would be inside a closed supermarket at night? Come on. Chances are it's either a moment from a bad dream or a horror film.

Or: it's what happens when you fall in with the wrong crowd.

Oh yeah. That was it.

Oscar was what, late teens? He isn't sure. He'd started doing heroin by this time. A lot of the usual time-markers – birthdays, Christmases, jobs, holidays – had slipped away. Lonnie was long gone too, vanished along with the rest of Oscar's school friends, gathered up in a tornado and carried away to Oz. No, that's not right. Oscar was the one in the tornado. Oz-car. And, with him, Lonnie's gun.

Who were these people he was with?

He can't remember their faces. He probably wouldn't have called them friends. They had heroin though, which made them all right in Oscar's book. Without really liking them he shared beds with them; without trusting them he let them tie up his arm and administer substances that could be anything, really. He only understood what hit him once it hit him.

Without any real thought he'd showed them the gun, which had been under his bed for a few years now, doing nothing. And now they'd brought it here, to the former supermarket, to debate what it *ought* to do.

Which is where the memory, to Oscar's intense anguish, ends.

Oscar really had believed he'd get lost here in Marrakech. Fall through the cracks, slip into the woodwork. But instead, without planning to make friends, he's got two, Jess and Atticus. Without intending to make enemies, he might have made one of those too, in the shape of Zineb, the customer service manager. She's standing in front of him now. Oscar was walking towards the pool, when Zineb stepped in front of him, carrying a silver tray with an envelope on it.

Oscar swallows. He'd had to pass quite close to the pool to make his way through the sunloungers, and then Zineb moved in, blocking his way forward, and now he's stuck with the pool behind him and Zineb in front of him, her eyes hard to read – what's that Oscar makes out? An accusation? *Interloper, fraud* – at the same time as her mouth is saying, 'I have a letter for you, Mr Levy. We were asked to sign for it at the desk. It is urgent, apparently.'

In the corner of Oscar's eye, water splashes, making small smacking noises against the tiled sides of the pool.

'Do you . . . do *you* know who it's from?' he asks. Stupidly.

'No, sir,' Zineb says. She extends the silver plate. Does he have to take the letter? What are the rules here?

Oscar takes the letter.

'Didn't you tell them, when they called, that I wasn't here?' he asks. (Another suspect thing to ask, but fuck it: the gig – or is it the jig? – is most definitely up.)

'We did tell them, sir, as you asked. But that was only two days ago. The letter must have been sent before then.'

Could this be true? Oscar tries to count the days backwards. *Plap, plop, shplap,* goes the water – and how is Oscar meant to think with that racket going on?

'Is there anything else, sir?' Zineb asks.

The letter-writers could be on their way here right now, thinks Oscar. They could be here already, and as soon as Oscar's out of sight, Zineb will pick up the phone and say, *Yes, he's here. Heading for his room. Please don't make a mess when you remove him.* Sweat is being pushed up to the surface of Oscar's skin, thousands of tiny pinpricks. Water, closing in.

'No,' he says. 'Thank you.'

And Zineb, miraculously, turns and walks away.

Relief floods Oscar.

No: flood is the wrong word. Forget flood.

What can he do? All he can do is run. He's got his passport in his pocket, his phone, his untrustworthy credit card. He'll leave everything else in his room. If he just walks out and leaves his room exactly as it is – as if he's coming back – he might even win a head start.

He strolls, in a chilled-out manner, in the direction of the gardens. He finds a bin and posts the letter into it. Then he walks back into the hotel, down the wide corridor, across the great marble floor of reception – trying not to think of it as a frozen lake, trying not to imagine the creaking underneath him. Nodding to the receptionists, the bell hops, the doormen –

Nod, nod, hello, good morning, nothing suspect here. Just another rich person. Businessman. In derivatives. The London office has been an utter shitstorm lately. Yeah. Don't even mention New York . . .

– aiming all the while for the square of blue sky he can see beyond the pillars of the hotel entrance, the several sets of steps, nearly running down the steps, until finally he is out – out! – on the street.

*

Oscar walks into the medina with a broad and stupid grin. People smile back at him as he goes. He wants to open up his arms and shout it: how much he loves this city, the beautiful twists and turns of it, like the heaps of snakes in the main square, the inked labyrinths of henna.

The thing that takes the smile off his face is the thought of Atticus. Who is probably on his way to the pool at this moment, looking for Oscar. Which is stupid really: it's not like Atticus will care if Oscar says goodbye or not. What was Oscar even going to say? Wish him a pleasant life, good luck with the maths homework, see ya around?

And even if Atticus did care, it's not like Oscar owes the kid anything. He's only known him a few days. And Atticus is a nosy bastard. He was a nuisance, in fact. He'll probably find someone else to annoy. Is probably at it right now.

Oscar stops, causing a small crowd of people to concertina up behind him. He looks back, in the direction of the hotel. Dimly aware that he's being glared at; a few angry words in various languages.

'Sorry,' he says.

He walks on.

What else can he do?

After an hour or so of wandering the medina, Oscar calls Jess.

No, she says, she doesn't find his idea weird. She'd love him to come and stay at the same riad as her. It's half empty, apparently. She tells him to get his arse down there, asap, because she's missing him. Not just missing the arse. Missing the whole lot.

Oscar wonders briefly if Jess is an undercover agent.

Then he thinks no, she's just a girl who now apparently likes him for more than just his arse.

Which is another set of problems.

But he can think about that later.

Jess was right: Oscar has no trouble checking in at her riad. His room overlooks an ornate central courtyard, a lagoon of shade disturbed only by the twitter of tiny birds and the clonk of the maid's bucket as she moves in a methodical circle over the emerald tiles, mopping up the tiny birds' tiny shits.

He feels suddenly shaky. The adrenaline from earlier is all gone. His body feels scraped out and floppy, like the cowhides slung on walls to dry in the sun. He probably *smells* like a cowhide, his anxiety sweat from earlier attracting the dirt of the medina, the dust and smoke, forming a paste.

He goes to the bathroom and washes his shirt out in the sink. He turns on the shower and gets in. The shower drips a small amount of cold water on him, then stops. He twists the valves back and forth; nothing happens.

He gets out.

He looks at the bathtub.

. . . Is he scared of *baths* now?

*

Oscar's unease about water is something that arrived gradually. It crept in, like a leak. He's never been much of a swimmer, as far as he knows. But he used to be fine with water. He once swam in a mountain lake in Switzerland, floating on his back. Then the next time Oscar tried to float like that, he found he'd lost the knack of it. He panicked, his legs fought, he'd flip back up, like a cork.

Later still, without any real reason he can remember, he stopped bothering with water. Lakes, seas, swimming pools. He only realised how urgent 'not bothered with water' had got when he was supposed to be boarding a ferry in Croatia and he couldn't get on it. The thought of all that water under him, slopping away at the sides of the boat like something greedy and messy, a big dribbly mouth, sucking at the painted metal.

Now the prospect of a bath is . . . well, it's not great.

He catches his own eye in the mirror.

Oscar, Oscar, Oscar. Has it come to this?

<u>No</u>.

He is going to stop being a pussy and run himself a bubble bath, like a *man*. With some of this nice lemon balm bath foam the riad has thoughtfully laid on. And so he does. And aside from having misjudged the temperature somewhat, the hot water stinging his skin and making his face sweat, it actually ends up being a very nice bath. He begins to relax. So much so that he starts to doze off; and there, in the suspended place between awake and asleep, he sees

the room.

Oscar knows this room. He has a lot of part-memories like this; bits and pieces of the past. This is a memory he's familiar, if not comfortable, with. It starts with a closed door, with a strange light coming from underneath it, a flat lifeless light. Behind the door is a white room, with no windows, just fluorescent lights. There's a noise, a high buzz. There's a white coat, hanging on the back of a door. A chair, the reclining type, with a plastic cover on it. And . . .

That's it.

There's never any more than that. The room and the chair, it's as far as he ever gets.

He lies back.

A new memory arrives.

Not an early memory, this time. A recent one, only a couple of years old. He knows it immediately.

Carol Kurtz.

The woman who went mad because she did something bad and tried to lie about it to the people who were remodelling her brain.

In the article Oscar read, a journalist had interviewed Carol in prison. The journalist said that Carol didn't look evil. She looked dazed. She was on a lot of meds, obviously. The journalist struggled to identify her with the murderess she'd read about.

Not a flicker, said the journalist, of whatever she'd been before.

The journalist asked Carol Kurtz if it was true that she didn't intend to apply for parole, or for early release. Carol nodded.

I'm safer here, she said.

The journalist asked if Carol was afraid of other people's reactions. Vigilantes, and so on.

Not other people, Carol said. *Me. I don't know myself. I don't trust myself.*

Oscar doesn't know himself.

He doesn't trust himself.

(Why did he want that gun? What did he *do* with that gun?)

William

William takes Milo and Fiona to the park. It's a hot, still day, the heat pushing up from the tarmac in waves. As Fiona chats to a couple of her friends and Milo queues again and again for the helter-skelter, William sits on a bench, keeping them discreetly in view. In the late-afternoon sunlight long shadows extend from the feet of the children; dipping and flaring along the grass.

Any day now, William will hear back from Nepenthe. He feels strangely peaceful, as if the clanking of the swings and the shrieks of the kids and the cawing of the seagulls are a gentle sonata. He hums along to it for a moment – a kind of Sinatra/seagull medley – before he realises he's humming, and stops.

Just in time too: Fiona's coming over. There's a slight, unfamiliar boy next to her. William knows from Fiona's somewhat defiant saunter, as well as the dog trailing at the boy's heels, that this must be Jack.

Interesting choice on Jack's part, William thinks, to seek out his girlfriend's dad. A man who could have been so easily avoided. There are nine boys here, five dogs. Jack and Pickles could have blended with the crowd, but no: here he is.

Jack is shorter than Fiona, which seems to be the general rule for kids this age, but he has the same kind of pent-up grace as his whippet. Maybe that's the attraction for Fiona: that or the blond curly hair, half of it in the kid's eyes. How can he see? Maybe he came over here by accident, thinking he was headed for the ice-cream van or the dogshit bin.

It turns out that Jack wants to be a policeman when he grows up.

'I wondered what it's like being Chief Inspector,' he says, peering sincerely at William from under his weight of hair.

(*It's? It was*, or *it is?*)

'A lot of hard work,' William says.

'Oh, right. Have you ever been shot?' asks Jack, apparently thinking that hard work means gunfire.

'No,' says William.

'Have you ever shot someone?'

'No.'

'Have you ever seen someone who's been shot?'

'Yes.'

'Oh,' says Jack. He looks dismayed. 'That's sad,' he says.

'I told you,' Fiona says importantly. 'He's seen *loads* of dead people.'

'All right, Fiona,' William says. 'No need to dwell on that.'

A new thought occurs to Jack. 'Do you ever let school trips come to the police station? My friend did that, once. He saw the cells, and the evidence room, and they dressed up in riot gear.'

William looks at Fiona. She isn't looking at William, but casually scuffing a hole in the grass, pretending not to be listening. She's a cool one. Anyone else would be signalling with their eyes: *Please don't tell him you're not a chief inspector any more. Please don't give me away.*

'I'm sure that could be arranged,' says William carefully, and Jack does a fist pump, and then Fiona drags Jack off to see the labradoodle puppy that's causing a commotion by the seesaws – all this without so much as a look at William, who's left with no idea what he was meant to do, and if he did it or not.

He's seen loads of dead people, Fiona said. Where did she get that from? The television? William's never told Fiona about any dead people.

I used to know when someone had died horribly, Annetta said to Marian, in their last session. William was more . . . brusque those evenings.

Brusque, said Marian, noting it down.

I looked it up in a thesaurus, Annetta said. I didn't want to use the word cold. And hostile was too much. But quiet wasn't enough. I needed a word in between the two. It was either brusque or breviloquent.

Both Annetta and William started to laugh.

Marian smiled at them.

Laughter is good, she said.

(Which obviously killed the joke, faster than a speeding bullet.)

Then Annetta said: What I don't understand is, why *that* girl.

Which is, coincidentally, what William would like to know.

Why her?

It ended his career. A career that had included worse sights, by anyone's standards. Though God knows there can't be many jobs that invite the ranking of horrors. Sitting on a break with Carey discussing over a KitKat what you'd rather be called out to: a tramp set alight, or a parent who'd killed their children then failed, messily, to kill themselves. He can't remember which he chose. Not that it mattered: after a while he saw both.

When William was Chief Inspector, a new officer said to him, I'm struggling. To cope. I don't know if this is the right career for me.

Why are you telling me this? William asked. I can't tell you whether it is or not.

The new officer just stared at him. He looked like he might cry. William did not want this to happen.

You should be discussing things like this with the welfare team, William said. That's what they're here for.

After the officer had left the police force to retrain as a primary school teacher (which William personally thought would be far more traumatic), he told Carey the story. Carey had known William for a long time. They were partners in Brighton when they were both PCs. Carey didn't say anything. He just gave William a strange look.

What? said William. What's that look?

I was about to accuse you of being stuck in a previous decade, Carey said. But this *is* your decade. You really ought to familiarise yourself with the customs.

How do I *cope*, William said. That's what I get asked. Like there's a manual. But there's no answer. It's like asking an insomniac how they sleep. They'll have a load of advice for you. But if you ask a normal sleeper how they do it, they don't know. They just . . . sleep.

Right, said Carey. He sighed.

Either you cope or you don't, William said. Welfare and talking won't do a damn thing to help you.

Christ, Carey said. Just don't say that to new recruits, okay?

That was before, obviously.

Before the girl.

Sometimes William thinks about the look Carey gave him. There was something knowing and sad in it. As if Carey *sensed* what would happen to William himself, in just a couple of years' time.

William's wondered before if the girl was a last-straw kind of thing. Something cumulative. But surely, then, he would have sensed it building up? But there was nothing. He'd been fine. Maybe he didn't confide in Annetta; maybe he'd been *brusque*, at times. But he was able to go home from a violent crime and make a spaghetti bolognese, or help the kids with their homework, then maybe have a glass of wine with Annetta, watch a box set of a prestige drama.

But then he saw the photo, the girl

arm
hand
road

and the shadow came, and he couldn't do that any more. Couldn't get on with it. Couldn't *cope*. And eventually his behaviour in the office was noticed – the zoning out, the long periods away from his desk, as if he'd be able to hide from a shadow (a shadow!) – and rather than go to therapy, or make things awkward for everyone, force them to keep on carrying him, he quit.

It's ten days since William sent off his application to Nepenthe. He's getting impatient with the delay. His GP isn't sure why it's taking so long either, but could only suggest that William give them a follow-up call if he still hasn't heard from them after a week.

In the meantime, William makes an appointment with someone from Sussex Police HR and someone from the welfare team to get his sign-off for the procedure. He doesn't recognise either of the names – he doesn't even know the person who answers the phone. It's only been a year since he left. A year of trimming roses and routing greenfly infestations, sun and showers, blisters, cups of tea, cut leaves piling up – and up, and up apparently, because in the meantime everything has changed.

When William arrives at the headquarters in Lewes, the young man on the gate doesn't recognise him either. He lets William through once he's confirmed he has an appointment, and gives him directions on where to park.

William doesn't say, *I know*, or *I worked here for ten years*, or *when were you even born?* He doesn't linger in front of the handsome red-brick buildings, or try to catch anyone's eye. He walks straight inside and goes to a room he's never been in before, the room in which former officers go to petition for their brains to be rewired, where Michaela from HR smiles and says that she doesn't see any issue here, given that the incident was four years ago, wasn't unsolved, and didn't actually involve William directly, and Lucas from the welfare team notes that William is currently in therapy, which is good, very good – and then sits in silence, as if he's not sure why he was called in at all.

Neither Lucas nor Michaela say: *All this over a photo of an unexceptional death that had nothing whatsoever to do with you?*

And William doesn't say: *Thanks for not mentioning how ridiculous this is.*

They all shake hands. Michaela says that William will get the paperwork within seven days.

'Great,' says William. 'Thanks.'

He's keen to leave, now. And while he doesn't believe in premonitions (obviously: he's not an idiot), the fact that he registers his own keenness to leave about twenty seconds before Tim Carey appears and says, 'Hall!' is, well. Premonition-like.

'Hi, Carey,' William says.

After William left, Carey replaced William as Chief Inspector. William meant to congratulate him, then didn't. It's been over a year since they last saw each other. Carey looks mostly the same. Less hair. More stomach. That's it. William wonders briefly what Carey sees as he looks at William. More tanned, more lean, more emotionally disturbed?

'You should have told me you were coming in,' Carey says. 'We could have got lunch. It's been too long. I mean, I don't want to come off *needy*, but a pint once in a while would be nice.'

He laughs, but he's looking at William with something that – if William had to name – he might call hurt.

Because the two of them used to be friends. Probably best friends. They went about their best friendship mostly in silence, mostly brusquely, but William understands, now: that's what it was.

'Looks like you found me, anyway,' says William.

'Detective work,' says Carey. 'It's how I got this job.' He coughs, and looks awkward. 'Anyway. Did that go okay?'

Of course, Carey knows exactly why William is here. Stupid of William to think his appointment wouldn't be noticed.

'Yeah,' William says. 'All signed off.'

'Good,' says Carey. 'And it's just that . . . photo? Right? Leona Samways?'

'Who?' William asks. Then he realises that must be the girl's name. He hadn't remembered that. Just the pictures of her, passed to him in that morning's Daily Management Meeting. The high tops, a gold and black star pattern, the way they lolled at a relaxed-looking angle, as if she was asleep in the sun. The hair bobble with two little cat faces. The way her head lay, so that her face was turned away, her stretched-out, empty hand.

The girl, Leona, had killed herself, said the PC on the case. They weren't sure at first whether to consider it suspicious as she was from a criminal family in Newham, London – her dad was a dealer – but it was looking like suicide. She was only twelve. She'd stolen a load of the dad's pills and overdosed. She'd also cut her wrist before she passed out, as if wanting to make extra sure that she'd definitely end up dead.

What was it about the pictures? The fact of the high tops and the little cats having been chosen, by this girl, who was no longer technically a girl, was now the body of a girl?

The blood fanning out around her?

All of it, maybe.

Excuse me, William had said. He had got up and gone to the loos, and as he'd sat staring at the Now Wash Your Hands poster, the shadow had entered his life.

'Yes,' he says to Carey now. 'Just that photo.'

Carey still looks confused – wary, even – but he doesn't ask anything else about it. He talks about the latest news: people getting married, people retiring, people dying. Carey's former boss, Chief Superintendent Rathbone was one of the last. He died only a few months ago, of prostate cancer.

'I'm sorry,' William says. He feels ashamed. Rathbone was basically Carey's mentor. The two of them were close. This is the kind of thing that William should have known about. But Carey doesn't reproach him. When they get to the door he tells William – that mildly hurt expression, again – that the two of them really should go for a drink.

'I know,' William says.

'I mean it. Keep in touch,' says Carey.

William nods. Then Carey goes back to his office, which was once William's office, and William drives home.

The next time Fiona and Milo come it's Annetta and not Judy who brings them. She smiles at William, shyly, over the tops of their heads. Happiness fills him.

'Did you want to come in?' William asks her.

'I can't; I'm driving to Warwick. A symposium on derived categories and applications.'

'I hope it's fun,' William says politely.

'It actually will be,' says Annetta.

'Don't forget your calculator,' says Milo, and they laugh. Half a laugh for Milo, half a release of the skittish, hopeful energy that has collected between William and Annetta. Milo beams at them both, pleased to have entertained, even if he wasn't actually joking.

Once inside, Fiona and Milo give him their own news, in the usual rush, and William makes fish pie and mash. It's their favourite, but he's made it for the past three visits, and he's wondering when they're going to call him out. He peels potatoes, exposing the raw white flesh underneath. For some reason the process reminds him of Marian Dunlop. The prospect of not going back for more sessions – to sit cringing as the blade descends on his knotty skin – is a relief. To put himself instead in the more businesslike hands of Nepenthe. The word 'targeted': that was what he liked about their marketing material. Targeted like a laser, like keyhole surgery, expert and precise. A more appealing alternative to being flayed alive.

He isn't bothered by the news that Nepenthe has discovered a way to get memory back, or the court case that just got settled. The hysteria around traces he's dismissed. If a trace does come back and starts to bother him, he'll just go back to the clinic, waving his receipt, and get the trace re-zapped.

What if that's why there's a delay with your application? Annetta said. What if they're going to stop the procedures?

They won't stop, William said. They just might have to rewrite the contracts or something.

You think? she said.

William said, I think if they have an opportunity to charge people for erasing the memory, and then charge them for putting it back, they'll find a way to make that work.

William looks through to the sitting room, where Fiona and Milo are watching a film about some CGI animals. He can hear them giggling.

William's relieved to hear the laughter. He's wondered before if his children will be tough enough in the world. Tougher than William, is what he means. But they seem well adjusted. The way they took the news of their parents' separation, for example. They ticked off a few of the emotions on the photocopied 'What to expect when you're on a trial separation' sheet Marian Dunlop gave him – sadness, confusion, anger – but then they'd be talking about cereal again, or some grievance about a purple biro.

William lays out a cloth over the kitchen table; tries and fails to fold napkins. He has the urge to make things nice for the children – though maybe it's just adding another layer of weirdness to the already weird experience of being visitors in their own home. He tidies up, wipes the worktops, then picks up his phone.

He's got an email.

Dear William,
We are writing to inform you of your full medical history, in accordance with a change to our company policy. Recent developments in memory-removal

technology have brought about a change in the law concerning our service, and we are now required to notify all Nepenthe Memory Solutions clients of their status . . .

William reads the email.
Reads it again.
Starts on the fine print.

. . . Nepenthe Memory Solutions admits no wrong-doing or false advertising. The original claim made by Nepenthe guaranteeing the 'permanent removal of memories' is not technically incorrect, as memories can be considered to be permanently erased *unless* reinstated, therefore the terms of the original con-tract . . .

But he doesn't finish all that, because his eyes have apparently stopped working. He can hear the potatoes boiling over on the stove next to him, smell the pie burning, see the kids sitting, oblivious, watching the television. But the words right under his eyes are playing some kind of game with him: dodging, darting, running up and down the page, shrinking and looming, until he feels sick, and puts the phone down.

'Marian said she can't fit us in until next Wednesday,' Annetta tells him. 'Apparently it's all these Nepenthe clients, and their families. Everyone's been booking appointments.'

'I don't mind waiting,' William says. 'I don't know what to say to her anyway.'

The first thing William had done was call the clinic. They said they couldn't tell him anything about the procedure at all, because he was a self-confidential client.

What? So the memory was *personal*? William said. Not a police thing?

That's correct, said the woman at the clinic.

Which made sense, because if it had been a police thing it would have been on his record, he'd have known about it. But he asked anyway:

Are you sure this isn't an error?

This is definitely not an error, said the woman at the clinic. The way she said it, William realised that all the people who'd got this letter had immediately called Nepenthe to tell them it must be an error. He was annoyed with himself, for being *people*. He was annoyed with the woman for making that clear to him. Well, thanks for nothing, he said, and hung up.

In the meantime, Annetta had cried, and puzzled over what had happened, and then she concluded that William must have had the procedure after he saw that girl, and it backfired, and that's why he was so – she tried to find the right word – *troubled*.

William reminds her that it wasn't anything professional. It was something personal.

'It must have been before I met you,' he says. 'I couldn't have had it done when we were together. I would have –'

'Told me?' Annetta asks.

There's a short silence.

The obvious thing – that he wouldn't have told her, of course he wouldn't have – flares, dies unsaid between them.

'Well,' Annetta says, 'forget when it was. And okay, so it's not that girl. It must be something else. What if your PTSD symptoms are just a weird side effect of that wipe? The wipe went wrong in some way? And the symptoms don't have anything to do with that photo at all?'

'I don't know,' he says.

'Have you thought more about it?' she asks. 'I mean, it's been a week since you got the letter. You still haven't said what you want to do.'

Annetta wants him to get the memory back. Having decided that a botched wipe must be at the root of his problems, she thinks undoing the procedure will undo the problems. She seemed shocked that William didn't immediately get on the phone to ask Nepenthe to sort out a happy ending for William and Annetta. (Even *more* happy than the ending William himself had envisaged, actually, because this time it'll be free. They could spend the money on a holiday, she said.)

'I don't like it,' William says. 'The idea of getting it back.'

'But why?' cries Annetta. He can almost see her agonised expression, on the other end of the phone.

'Because I *chose* to forget it. Whatever it was. I obviously had my reasons.'

He thinks about the William of the past. This William is a stranger. He knew something Present-day William doesn't, and he chose to hide his knowledge forever. He did that by killing himself. And Present-day William is . . .

Okay with that.

And now he's being asked if he wants to resurrect Past William: to – effectively – kill his unknowing present-day self. And if he did it, brought Past William back – would Past William, who presumably had his own good reasons for killing himself, be happy about that?

'*Chose?*' Annetta says, startling him. 'It went wrong! You didn't choose this! It hasn't turned out the way you *chose* at all.'

'In which case,' William says, 'it makes sense to leave the deleted memory as it is, and book in another procedure to wipe this new thing. Even if it is a side effect.'

'But –' Annetta says.

'It's like a rose bush,' William says.

'A *rose bush*?'

'If it gets an infestation of aphids, I spray it. If I don't catch all the aphids, and they start to cause problems again, I'm not going to put all the original aphids back. I'm going to spray it again, and make sure they're all dead this time.'

'But this isn't an infestation,' Annetta cries. 'It's your *self*.'

'Not any part of me I recognise,' William says. 'Or want.'

'You want to insecticide your brain?'

'I want to work again,' he says. 'I want to sleep at night. Christ. I want to be a functioning husband and father.'

His voice has risen. He realises it in the silence that follows; how very silent it suddenly seems. It's a while before he hears a small sound: Annetta is crying.

'Annetta,' he says, 'I'm sorry.'

'No. *I'm* sorry,' she says. 'I don't want to pressure you.'

'Don't apologise. That's my job, isn't it?' He waits, but she doesn't laugh. 'Look. Let's talk about it with Marian next week.'

'Okay,' Annetta says eventually. There's a small, damp noise, as of someone wiping their noise. 'I understand.'

She sounds slightly more optimistic.

William can guess why. She thinks Marian Dunlop is going to see the same thing she does. That Past William was fine, and now he can come back.

Of course, Past William never told Annetta why being Past William was so intolerable, or why he'd chosen to die – because he never told Annetta anything, and so no wonder Annetta can't understand why he shouldn't be brought back to life.

I'm trying to understand you, pal, William says, to Past William. *I know you must have your reasons.*

But.

Did you have to be such a dick about it?

There are days when William is not at work, and it's not his time to look after the kids. These are not good days. He usually needs to find something to keep him busy. He's cleared out the gutters, creosoted their fences, tiled the wall of their bathroom that's been unfinished for five years. Today he cleans the entire house. Not that there's much to do. William is army-tidy; it was Annetta who was (*is*, he thinks, is) the messy one. But he finds work. He mops, dusts, disinfects – goes into the children's rooms and straightens up the unused duvets even, pulling the wrinkles out of the cartoon faces. He cleans his (their) own bedroom last, crouching down to push the Hoover under the bed, where it chokes on something on Annetta's side.

He pulls out the item: an old T-shirt with a picture on the front, black-and-white fractals. William shakes the tiny dust tumbleweeds off it and holds it to his face.

It smells of nothing.

He gave it to Annetta, their first Christmas together. He didn't even know if Annetta's kind of maths had anything to do with fractals. He'd got her some other things too, nothing very clever or thoughtful. The closer the moment got, the more he was dreading handing them over.

Annetta gave him her present first: the 1955 pressing of *In the Wee Small Hours*. It had exactly the sleeve he remembered from his childhood.

Oh God, William said. This is too much. And how did you know?

Your mum told me. That last time we saw her, before she died. She said how much you and your dad used to love all those old singers. How your dad used to sing 'That's Life' to you when you were a kid.

William remembered it: Ercol chair legs, cigarette smoke, wine-coloured deep pile carpet. Textbook seventies flashback. His dad singing away, Brummie Sinatra.

She told me to ask you about your dad's records, said Annetta. Get you to play some. But I didn't think you had anything like that?

The records? William said. No, we haven't had those for years.

Well, I don't know. That's just what she said.

I think she must have been confused, William said. I don't have any, unfortunately. She or my dad sold them years ago. There were rare ones . . . I think they probably got a lot of money for them. Though I wish they could have kept at least a couple.

That's sad, said Annetta. But you've got this one now, at least.

William was suddenly worried. His mum had got pretty senile towards the end. She'd liked Annetta, though; she'd spent a lot of time talking to her.

Did she say anything else? William asked.

About what?

About, uh, my dad?

Not that I remember. Why?

He tried to smile. He said: Just for nostalgia's sake.

Oh, William. I know it must be hard. An awful accident like that, when you were only little. I can't imagine –

It's okay, said William. No need to dwell on it. Anyway: this is your first present. It's probably terrible. No. It *is* terrible.

Annetta opened it. She laughed.

You know, there's not much maths merch out there, she said, holding it up to herself. I mean, it's not like being a musician, when everyone buys you stuff with musical notes on.

I'm not sure if that means it's a good present or not?

I'm not sure either, she said. But I love it.

When William looks up, it's night-time. He's sitting on the floor of the bedroom, holding the T-shirt. He must have zoned out again. Well, never mind. What has he lost? Part of a day he didn't want anyway. And now it's evening and he can put on Netflix, and scroll through the Recommended For You section. Not that any of the recommendations are actually *for* William. Most of them are prompted by Annetta's favourite shows of last year and so he is presented with a selection of dark Scandinavian dramas, true-crime documentaries and Jane Austen adaptations.

William can't watch anything about crime or murder. Nor is he in the mood for unspoken tension, even dressed up in bonnets and breeches. In the end he puts on the documentary with the least violent-sounding title – which is so boring that he falls asleep.

This is a mistake.

William isn't usually a napper. Because of this, he doesn't see the nap coming. It's like a cosh coming down over his head.

Thump.

Lights out.

And his nightmares are especially pissed off, after being ignored for so long. They've been trying and failing to get the attention of William, drugged-deaf as he usually is, drugged-blind. Now it's their chance. They get hold of him and force him down flat onto the ground. He turns his head to look at his hand. And there it is: the ghostly other hand overlying his own. It's holding something colourful, and crumpled. An empty plastic bag. There's blood all round the hand.

It's a dream, he realises. All he has to do is wake up.

. . . *wake up!*

He wakes up in a smaller shape, Child William, scrabbling at a door. Behind it his dad is locked in a room with no air. If William can't get the door open in time, or break a hole in it, his dad will suffocate. But at some point it becomes clear that his dad is dead, he died a long time ago, and William's the one in the airless room. He doesn't shout for help. He already knows nobody can hear him. So he gives in.

Yes, he says.

If this is it, then: yes.

Finn

David stands in Finn and Mirande's garden, admiring the view. He stands in profile, the four o'clock sun stretching his shadow out beyond the gateposts, out for miles.

David is still, Finn has to acknowledge, very good-looking.

One thing Finn has always been proud of is his hair. Not that he'd admit it. It's slightly thinner than it once was, but most of it is still there, and the grey suits him. But then David arrived and took off his panama hat and out came the most ridiculously thick, dark head of hair. An unreasonable amount of hair. Finn doesn't know how it's possible, either, that there's so little grey in it. Is it possible to dye hair, then add a few natural-looking grey highlights back in?

Finn's thoughts run on. David is a surgeon. Possibly this hair was not acquired by fair means. David could literally have stolen it off the top of someone's head. And then his muscular shoulders: implants. The way his shirt tucks so flatly into his waistband: liposuction. His sad wrinkles filled out; distinguished ones added. His nose and jaw – but those were always impressive. And he's still slightly shorter than Finn; he hasn't had extra vertebrae added, or lifts in his knees. But then it can be argued that Finn himself is on the awkward side of tall.

'This house is *exactly* what I'd pictured,' David says to them now, smiling. 'I don't have the taste or vision to dare to own a house like this.'

'Finn's taste,' Mirande says. 'Finn's vision. I'm hopeless. Shall we go inside? Well, inside, then outside. We can sit in the sun in the garden. It's a lovely aspect.'

She's talking faster than usual.

'What was here originally?' David asks, as he turns towards the house. 'The gateposts look older.'

'A house that burned down,' Finn says. 'The gateposts are all that's left.'

'Is that why you kept them?' David asks.

'Finn has a thing about old and new,' Mirande says. She laughs. Finn isn't sure if he's on the inside or the outside of her laughter.

'I remember,' says David.

'Really?' says Finn. 'You've got a very good memory. Either that or I was a memorable bore.'

'Oh, no,' David says.

'I mean, how many years has it even been?' Finn says. 'The last time we saw each other? I was saying to Mirande that you and I always miss each other. I remember I came back to London from Singapore just as you were leaving for Canada. Which makes sense, now I think about it . . .'

Both David and Mirande look visibly taken aback here, before Finn continues,

'. . . I must have been *really* fucking boring.'

And then they laugh. David and Mirande enthusiastically, Finn less so, because it wasn't all that funny. Maybe relief made it funnier.

'Right,' Finn says, 'I've got to check on the food. You two can get the saving lives chat out of the way while I toss the salad.'

Except when he comes back, half an hour later, the saving lives chat is still in full swing, and goes on for what feels like a long time after that. Every now and again either David or Mirande will try to explain a word, or a procedure, which further postpones the prospect of *not* talking about saving lives.

'I understand,' Finn says. 'No, no, carry on. It's fascinating. Really.'

Eventually David says, 'You know, I don't want to talk shop. I want to talk about architecture.'

'Now now,' says Finn.

'I do. I love buildings. I just don't know anything about them. I need someone like Finn to tell me what to think. I want to know what's good. Like brutalism. Am I a hopeless case if I don't like brutalism?'

'Well,' says Finn, torn between honesty and pretension.

'Finn hates it!' laughs Mirande.

'It's true. My rational mind tries to like it. I just can't make my eyes like it.'

'What do you like?' asks David.

What does Finn like? There's something in nearly everything. Modernism, minimalism, postmodernism, even –

But then he sees himself, and the two of them, and has the distinct suspicion that he's being indulged. Or distracted. As if he can be so easily manipulated into going on about himself, wound up and set off like a little barking Finn-dog.

Mirande says, 'Finn likes beauty.'

'How dare you,' says Finn.

'And you like . . . old and new?' says David.

He certainly *sounds* sincere.

'Yes,' says Finn. 'More like past and present. But don't ask me to articulate why. It just ends up in a load of bullshit about dialogue and vernacular and continuity of narrative.'

'What's a good example, then, of old and new together?' David asks.

'Very few,' Finn says. 'Bringing them together is a delicate business. Achieving collaboration, not conflict.'

Bark, bark – he can't help himself. But David is leaning forward, keen to join in.

'Absolutely,' says David. He hesitates, then says, 'I really like what Foster did with the British Museum and the Smithsonian. I don't know if that's the equivalent of, you know, liking Renoir or "Clair de Lune" . . .'

Finn's smile tightens on his face. Because he also loves those glass ceilings, really loves them, rising up diaphanous and buoyant as a sail. He doesn't particularly want to admit that to David. But then Mirande knows how he feels about Foster, so he has to say, 'No, I'm with you on that.'

And David looks delighted.

At the end of the evening, they offer, again, for David to stay the night, but he refuses. He says he has to work the next day, he's already got a taxi coming. On the way to the front door David spots a picture of Ri on a small table.

Finn sees him spot it.

David sees Finn see him spot it.

'I haven't seen any pictures of your daughter,' David says. He sounds formal, suddenly, though they talked about Ri earlier, her progress across Europe, her failure to send them photos, to phone at regular hours. 'She looks like a lovely girl.'

He doesn't say 'She looks like you', to either Mirande or Finn – because the fact is Ri has never, at any stage of her childhood, looked anything like either of them. They thought a resemblance might emerge as she got older – her hair might get darker, like Finn's, or blonder, like Mirande's, her eyes might stop dithering at grey and decide on brown or blue – but no, here she definitely is, light brown hair, freckles, grey eyes, stubbornly herself.

'I know what you're thinking,' Finn says. 'But she's not adopted.'

They all laugh.

'Actually I was just thinking I could see Mirande's jaw. And your brow area,' says David. He gestures at the photo with his finger, professionally, as if the picture is an X-ray.

Finn wonders for a second about himself, as if watching himself. Is Finn, he wonders, going to look at the photo, and then at David?

No, he is not. He will never, ever do that.

'My mother had freckles,' says Finn. 'They multiplied in the sun. We make Ri wear sunscreen when she's here, but I keep thinking: I bet she won't be wearing her sunscreen in Rome, or Paris, or wherever – and I try to imagine how many freckles she'll have when she gets back.

I suppose if she doesn't have any new ones we'll know she listens to her parents.'

(What is he talking about?)

Mirande turns to look out of the window, where the two lights of David's taxi are crawling up the dark road.

'Oh, here it is,' she says.

'Ah yes,' says David.

But it isn't here, not quite. The drive up to their house is long and bumpy, and the taxi comes on slowly, and they all fall silent, waiting for it to get to the door.

'Have you thought any more about it?' Finn asks Mirande, the next day. 'The restoration?'

'Yes. No. A little.'

'What are you thinking?'

'That it's just . . . impossible. Whatever it was, it was so terrible that I went to dramatic lengths not to know it. I'd like to know what it was, but then I'd get it back. The terrible thing. I'm not sure I *want* the terrible thing.'

'Well, I was thinking about it,' Finn says. 'And I thought that whatever it was you saw at the time must have felt impossible to live with. Back then it had only just happened. You didn't see how you'd ever be able to manage it. But now, right, if you got the memory back it would arrive years old. I mean, maybe the length of happy life you've had since it happened would show you that it's okay, there's no danger to you, no need for any sort of PTSD response.'

She doesn't say anything to this.

'Or do you think maybe it's not something you *saw*?' he asks (bland, curious). 'That it could have been something you did?'

She looks at him sharply, and he wonders if he's gone too far. Then she shrugs, and whatever had galvanised her sinks away, until she just looks sad again. His wife, sitting on the edge of the bed, looking sad. He takes her hand. The back of it is silky under his fingers. There are tiny hairs there that catch the light, too small to feel.

'I don't know,' she says eventually. 'I mean, there were cases back in London I wish I could forget. Abuse, violence, rape, torture. What I don't know is why I would have picked one out.'

'I could go with you,' Finn said.

'What?'

'To the clinic, I mean. So you wouldn't be alone.'

'I know what you meant. I'm just surprised. You seem to *want* me to do it. Is that it? Do you think I should?'

'No, no,' he says. 'It's not my decision. I'd never want to decide for you. I just see that you're unhappy, and I think maybe you won't feel at ease until you know. That you – being who you are – can't be okay with *not* knowing.'

She looks away.

'Is that right?' she says.

Their usual lives go on. On Saturday they have a party. Finn invites David. He says to Mirande that they might as well make the most of David, while David's here. And now David stands with the mountains behind him, one hand casually resting on the back of Finn's favourite chaise, a glass of wine in the other, telling a story. He finishes speaking, and everyone around him bursts out laughing.

Yes. Finn remembers this now. In the years that David hasn't been around, Finn's been able to think of himself as the more personable of the two men. Funnier, quicker, more articulate. But the truth is that while David is mostly serious, every now and again he'll say something that isn't just funny immediately, but is smart, layered, the kind where people laugh once, think about it, and laugh even more. A small, carefully curated selection, David's jokes. Compared to hundreds from Finn. Throw it at the wall and see if it sticks, that's always been Finn's motto.

Finn can tell, looking at the people around David, that they already think David is very witty.

How big is David's penis? wonders Finn.

He'd rather not be wondering things like that, but now that it's occurred to him, it turns out to be a difficult thing *not* to wonder.

Finn moves from group to group, topping up glasses, stopping if something interests him.

Here's Mbali:

'. . . so nice not having everything explained to me,' Mbali is saying. 'Not that all scientists are like that. Maybe just my ex-husband. A sample-size of one, is what he'd say now.'

'Scientists,' Finn says, seizing on his moment (why? Because he can't not), 'are not to be trusted.'

'You know some?'

'No. But I watched a documentary about memory deletions. Did you know it was a *snail* that started off this whole memory-restoration thing? Well, probably not just one.'

'Uh, what?' says Mbali.

'Apparently the idea that memories could be erased for good was based on a misunderstanding. At the time everyone thought memories were made in the synapses of brain cells. They thought they could delete memories by burning out the right synapses.'

'Human synapses?'

'No, rats'.'

'What?'

'They – the scientists – did all these studies involving rats. That's how they found out they could delete memories in the first place. They frightened the rats by giving them electric shocks. Then they burned out their memory of the fear.'

'Bastards,' says Mbali, becoming animated. 'The past is a foreign country, right? And you know what happens when foreign countries are first discovered. Massacres, that's what. My ex-husband –'

'Exactly,' Finn says. 'But that's just the start of it. Nepenthe's memory tech is based on that early research with rats' synapses. But it's all wrong! Years later, this scientist, Glanzman, found out memory *actually* happens in the nucleus. The heart of the cell. Not in the synapses at all.'

'Did he shock more rats?'

'Marine snails this time, actually. He didn't know what he was about to discover. He just thought he was deleting memories the usual way, but then, *later*, the snails got their memories back. Apparently the snails formed new connections at the synapses. Some of the connections were the same as before and some of them were totally random. And that's how they worked out they couldn't delete memory forever.'

'Poor snails,' says Mbali. 'Scientists are psychopaths.'

'Not even accurate psychopaths,' says Finn. 'And yet, people trust them enough to let them mess with their brains. What do you make of that?'

'Um,' Mbali says. She hesitates.

Mbali's from South Africa, which was one of the countries that banned Nepenthe clinics on religious grounds (Christianity, like most religions, has generally taken a dim view of Nepenthe). Finn isn't sure if Mbali is religious or not. Is her expression disapproving? Warning? Perhaps Finn should drop the subject.

'Would *you* get a wipe?' he asks. 'Or, if you found out tomorrow you had a memory removed, would you get it back?'

'I have no idea,' Mbali says. 'I can't even imagine –'

'Is it a religious thing?' says Finn, because he can't help himself.

'No,' Mbali says. 'I just . . . don't know. Sorry.'

The next day, when Finn gets home from work, Mirande doesn't call out a hello. Finn looks for her, finding her in the kitchen: leaning on the worktop, elbows down, face in hands, crying.

In that moment Finn is certain that Mirande is going to leave him.

He grips the door frame. He doesn't want to ask her what's wrong. He'd rather hurry back into his study, pretend he never saw anything, wait in there, for years if he has to, until she changes her mind about what she's about to say.

But he asks, because he can't not: 'What's wrong?'

When he speaks, she jumps.

'Oh! Finn! I didn't hear you come in.' She wipes her eyes, gestures at her mobile. 'I was just talking to Ri.'

'Oh,' says Finn. Then: '*Oh*. Ri! Have I missed her?'

'I told her to hold on but she had to go. They were getting on a coach to the Sacré-Coeur or something.'

'Fuck. Did she say when she'd call again?'

'Maybe tomorrow? She sent her love. Sounds like she's having a blast.'

She's teared up again. Blast comes out with a small jerk, breaking it in half. *Blah-hast.*

'Of course she is,' Finn says. He moves some hair out of Mirande's eyes, puts it gently behind her ear. 'Now now. Did you think she'd be missing us?'

Mirande laughs. 'I didn't let her hear me cry,' she says. She blows her nose on a bit of kitchen roll. 'Even when she said she'd done some drawings for us. One of the Arno. The Tiber, too, I think.'

Finn's gaze goes to Ri's drawing of Cathedral Rock, hanging on the wall. He'd had it framed: white mount, simple black metal.

Urgh, *Dad*, Ri said, when she saw it.

You should be proud of it, Finn said. It's very expressionist. Very Munch.

But it turned out it wasn't the picture Ri objected to, it was the frame. If she'd had her way it would have been something rococo. Gold, curlicued, cherubs in the corners blowing trumpets.

God help me, said Finn.

That's what proper art gets, Ri informed him. I've been to galleries. All the proper art is in big gold frames.

Now listen, said Finn. Because your dad is going to tell you all about a man called Peter Behrens, and about –

Ri interrupted him.

I don't mind the frame. I mean, it's so boring. But I know it's what *you* think is nice. It makes me think of you. So I . . . like it.

'Finn?' Mirande says. 'Are you all right?'

'What? Me? I'm fine.'

'Okay,' she says. 'Well, I'm going to have a shower. We could have dinner after, if you haven't eaten?'

'Perfect,' says Finn. 'Perfect, perfect, perfect.'

Mirande says to Finn, after dinner: 'Mbali thinks you want to get your memory wiped.'

'She what? Oh, for God's sake. That's ridiculous.'

'You were asking for advice?'

'It was nothing like that,' Finn says. 'I didn't say anything that – I honestly have no idea where she got that from.'

'She said you seemed bothered by the idea of it. That you sounded, uh . . . *unlike* yourself. Maybe she read between the lines.'

'Clearly she read altogether too much into it,' says Finn. He's annoyed with Mbali, then remembers he has no right to be annoyed, then feels annoyed about not being able to be legitimately annoyed.

'But you were talking to her about it,' Mirande says. 'So it's obviously on your mind.'

'Well. Maybe it is. But I don't want to keep badgering you about it. Not when it's a painful subject.'

'Finn . . . are you angry with me for not telling you about whatever it was?'

There is a moment of silence. He looks, but he can't see anything in her expression beyond sincerity; concern.

'Of course not,' he says.

'Right,' she says. 'Okay. Well, that's good.'

She puts her head on his shoulder, apparently reassured. Finn probably ought to feel reassured too.

He is, he tells himself.

Finn is reassured.

Finn works from home at least one day each week. When that day next comes around, he waits until Mirande has gone to work, goes into her study, and takes her antique marquetry chest down off the shelf. The chest contains letters, ticket stubs, Ri's baby hair, and other sentimental things. And it is *organised*. Everything piled in order of time, with the most recent years at the top. Not long ago, a research paper came out about vertical filing, which said that the most efficient way to manage paperwork is to pile it up in the order that it arrives.

The scientists must be spying on me, Mirande said.

I did see a drone the other day, said Finn.

Drones are entry-level, said Mirande. I hear it's not long before they put cameras on bees. I mean, the spy could be literally anything.

Your own husband, thinks Finn – but he won't be shamed, not now. He's opened the box before, fossicking out letters or photos to show people. It's not as if Mirande's forbidden him from looking through it without her.

The question of motive, he ducks.

He takes out the contents of the box. There's a piece of notepaper in between each layer, with a time period written on it. *Childhood* is the first one. Then *Amsterdam*. *Eighties*. *Uni*. The pre-Finn era.

The next layer is called *London*. The beginning of the Finn Age. The Finnthropocene. After that comes *Millennium*, *Wedding*, *First House*. Finn takes them all out and lays them to one side. What he's looking for is the year that he was working in Singapore. When he gets to that time, he begins going through everything, piece by piece.

It takes a while because he keeps getting sidetracked. He finds letters he wrote years ago, telling Mirande stories which make him laugh again now. There's a picture someone sent her, a big group of people in what looks like a beer garden. *Cambridge reunion*, it says on the back. Finn's at the very edge of the picture: he recognises his own cheekbone, an ill-advised haircut.

There was something else about that night, he remembers. His body is uneasy, as if it's braced against that particular memory. But what was it?

A woman. That's it.

A woman saying to Finn:

You're very tolerant.

He can't remember anything else about it. Not a face, not an identity. Nor why it would bring up this unpleasant feeling of – what? – of dread?

All Finn knows is that someone he didn't know at the time, in that particular bar, said to him: *You're very tolerant.*

He decides it's more likely to come back to him if he stops trying to remember and goes back to his task. But the task is a waste of time. It's all innocent, it's nothing. There are tickets for art exhibitions, on dates when he knew he wasn't in the country – but so what? Tickets for Kew Gardens, for Christ's sake. Even if she'd gone there with David it's not like the two of them could get up to anything humid in the glasshouses.

What am I doing? thinks Finn.

He looks at the piles of paper all around him, his and Mirande's story gutted and divided and spread out across the floor. He's been shamed, after all. Shame fills him, *from the crown to the toe top-full.* He starts putting everything back into the box.

As he does, a card slips out of another heap. It's an old-fashioned anatomical drawing of a heart, its parts labelled. Finn opens it, already smiling, expecting to see his own handwriting.

It takes him a moment to realise that it's *not* his handwriting. The writing inside the card says:

The way we were.
Happy birthday.
David
X

The way we were? Finn thinks.
And how, exactly, *were* they?

*

The problem, Finn thinks, is that David and Mirande were something – whatever that was – before Finn and Mirande were anything. The two of them had been friends for years, after all. They'd had a whole layer of Mirande's marquetry chest to themselves, before either of them had even heard of Finn.

In Finn's stories David is usually a background figure, which is funny, because in David's memories of the exact same moments Finn himself must be the shadowy man – half in and out of sight, or not even there at all. Finn remembers his joke about Clark Kent and Superman. But it's not like he and David are the same man in two different roles. They're two men, inconveniently occupying the same role.

Two men sharing one story, each of them having half – and one of them looking over the other's shoulder, trying to read the rest.

Unfortunately, there are things Finn can't ask David outright. Like, for example, *So, did you hear Mirande had a memory erased?*

Or: *What exactly do you want from her?*

So he asks:

'How does it come about, this teaching visit? I mean, do the doctors here write and ask you to come? Or do you decide you want a change of scenery, to share some techniques, or whatever, and . . . offer your services?'

'A little of both, I suppose,' David says, casually vague, like a man who knows that Finn knows nothing about how these things are done, and – furthermore – isn't going to be able to phone up his workplace and check. 'I can't pretend I wasn't looking forward to a bit of a break. And the pace is easier. But mostly I enjoy comparing notes with other people. It's like what you say about your work: sharing ideas, cooperating.'

'Of course, of course,' says Finn. 'Collaboration is the thing.'

He asks:

'So, are you seeing anyone at the moment?'

David hesitates, then says, 'It's . . . uh, it's a bit soon after the divorce, I think. Well, I suppose it's been two years. At some point I'd better get back *out there*. Grim as that sounds.'

'I sympathise,' Finn says. 'I mean, I can't even bring myself to buy new shoes. Was it a bad break-up, then?'

'She cheated,' David said. 'A mutual friend. Maybe for the best. They're still together.'

He says this in short bursts, like he's tapping out Morse code, without much apparent feeling. Finn can't tell if David's battling great emotions or whether he genuinely doesn't give a shit.

Cold, he decides. Cold, and controlling. Finn's already noticed that David refuses more wine after having exactly three glasses. Every time. The man could very well be a sociopath. Possibly this is why his wife fled.

'Do you want children, David?' he presses. 'Did your wife?'

David blinks. Finn wonders for a moment if he's going to answer at all. Maybe he's going to tell Finn to fuck off. But eventually, after a long time, he says,

'I wanted children once. But we were busy, and then we were unhappy, and so it never happened. Obviously I didn't want them that much.'

'I shouldn't have asked,' Finn says. 'Sorry.'

'Not at all. It's probably good for me not to avoid the subject.'

'Absolutely. I expect you'll see some health benefits over the coming days,' Finn suggests.

'I'll monitor my blood pressure, shall I?' David says. He smiles, but his smile seems sad to Finn.

Perhaps David isn't cold. Perhaps he's just sad, and doesn't want to talk about it. Finn tries to remember what David used to be like. Maybe he always had this barely detectible melancholia about him. Maybe Finn's just reading into it and David's not sad at all. He's just older. Maybe it's Finn that's old, and sad, and he's projecting that onto David. Finn's been doing a lot of speculating and projecting lately. He needs to watch it.

But sometimes, Finn will look up at David and catch David watching *him*, Finn, with this *expression*. It's not alert, or wary, or anything like that. It's just curious. Almost like he's watching a bird behaving weirdly on a lawn: hopping about, flapping its wings, not really achieving much. And David has paused for a moment to watch it, wondering what the bird might do next.

A week, that's what Nepenthe says.

Finn's looked it up. They won't erase more than one period of time, lasting no longer than a week.

Which means whatever Mirande erased probably only happened once.

Either that or it was something that happened all the time, was commonplace, even – until one day, when it was something else.

Did Mirande call David, the day she got the email? What did she say to him?

David, I've worked it out. I never understood it before – why everything between us ended so suddenly. But now I know what I must have deleted. David, I thought my marriage was over when you and I were together. But I changed my mind: I chose him. And then later, when I found out . . . I wanted us to be a family. Me, Finn, Ri. That was the choice I made. And now . . . I don't know . . .

Or was it David who called Mirande? Or – came here to speak to her in person?

To say to her, *Mirande, did you think I'd forget how extraordinary you are? How could I? I want you to leave Finn. I want to be with you, to make you happy. I want you to love me and question me, like you do with Finn, the way you expect him to be thoughtful and intelligent*

and kind, as if you truly believe he is all these things, and
when he gets angry over nothing or does something ri-
diculous or gets carried away making generalisations or
pompous statements of fact, you laugh at him, or you ask
a couple of well-placed questions that make him stop, and
look sheepish, but never make him feel small, or unwanted,
and that's an art in itself, a kind of love, too, and you're
so good at it – except of course you haven't been doing
it so much lately, have you?

The David voice is rambling somewhat.

Or . . .

. . . maybe Mirande had already worked it out long ago.
Maybe they'd already discussed it. And the call was
nothing more than:

David, I'm not sure I did the right thing after all.

And David replied:

I'm on my way.

PART THREE

PART THREE

Noor

Your turn. Tell *me* a story, said Noor.

They're lying in bed, Elena's body alongside Noor's, heating up her right side, from her arm to her toes. She strokes or taps Noor's shoulder or face when she wants to make a point. Noor's trying to work out if she likes this or not.

She thinks, *yes*.

She does like it.

Okay, Elena said. There was a couple who were in love. Then they broke up. Afterwards, the woman deleted the memory of the relationship, without telling the man. Her name's Clementine by the way. I can't remember his name.

Clementine? said Noor. I feel like I've heard this before.

Anyway, Elena said, the guy is really upset when he finds out Clementine wiped him, and so he decides to get his own wipe. I mean, fuck *her*, right? But then, halfway through the procedure, he realises he's making a huge mistake. This machine is zapping his memories, one by one, and he's trying to hide his memory of Clementine, to keep it safe.

What? That's not how it works.

Shh. What he does is make up a *new* memory of the two of them together. They're at this place by the sea. Montauk, where they met.

Hang on, Noor said. This is that film. *Eternal Sunshine of the* something.

And why not? said Elena. I like that story. It's got a happy ending. Sort of.

Has it? I never got to the end. I couldn't get past the science. I mean, they were trying to delete a long-term relationship. If that were possible – which it isn't, by the way – it would be a *nightmare*. Can you imagine? You'd be bombarded with hundreds of inexplicable things. Friends' slips of the tongue. Small talk with dog walkers. Christmas cards from distant acquaintances. Utility bills. The electoral roll. *Social media*. And that would just be the outside world.

That's not – said Elena.

And that's just the half of it, continued Noor. What happens in your own head? Surely you wouldn't forget everything that had anything to do with that person. *Years* of your life would be blank. But then if not, how do you remember the bedroom you shared? Films you both watched? The holidays? Do you remember the country you visited, but when you try to remember the person next to you, the picture just . . . fuzzes out?

I feel that these are rhetorical questions, to which you already know the answer, Elena said.

The answer is no, Noor said. It's impossible, clearly. You'd go mad.

Okay, Elena said. Never mind that. *I* think the main question is: can you really undo love? Can you undo heartbreak? Or do you think they'd sort of . . . *do* something to you? Leave something with you?

I feel like you're asking these ridiculous questions just to provoke me, Noor said.

They were both laughing now. Elena stroked Noor's face, slid her thigh over Noor's legs.

Story time is over for today, she said.

Noor isn't enjoying this memory. *Fuzz out*, she commands Elena.

And Elena, surprisingly, does.

She's replaced by Louise.

. . . Something Louise said to Noor, years and years ago:

What do you think is the number-one least-wanted memory among prospective Nepenthe clients? The type of deletion requested by a whopping 72 per cent of the people that call the clinic?

. . . You guessed it. The memory of a past relationship. People come in and say they want what the guy had in *Eternal Sunshine.*

The dream of nepenthe lives on, whether or not any such thing exists.

*

Noor has always taken pride in her professionalism. Everything she does, she does properly. And so when it comes to applying herself to the task of investigating the illegal behaviour of her boss, mentor and friend Louise, she does it properly.

She closes her door and sits at her desk with a notepad and a cheap pay-as-you-go phone that she bought at the supermarket last night. (Noor knows from TV shows that this is a *burner phone*, but she refuses to call it that.) She logs in as an administrator and goes back to the case notes of the people Louise called.

Noor can't see all of them, because Louise herself hadn't opened the case notes for every person. The last person Louise tried to call is a mystery. Louise hadn't looked at their case notes, only the clinic schedule for the first week of November, before she made her call. Noor guesses that person has a procedure booked that week. And the call itself was to an out-of-service number, so that leaves Noor with nowhere to go on that one.

Instead Noor writes down the names of all the other people Louise called whose case details she can see. There are eight of them. She can't look up their addresses, but she can see their names, the details of their local GP, their age and job description. It's more than enough to find most of them on Google within the hour. She feels a small pulse of smugness – only for a moment, before the next moment brings the awareness that this list of people makes absolutely no sense at all.

Noor wasn't really sure what she was looking for in the first place. Maybe she expected the people to be obviously connected to Louise somehow, or have something to do with Nepenthe. But they don't seem to have anything to do with anything. Least of all each other. There are a couple of executives – one at an energy utility, one at an arms manufacturer. There's a former soldier who left the army to set up a business making environmentally friendly cleaning products. A woman who appears to be a house-wife in Kent. One person has served a prison sentence for fraud, but another is a solicitor.

Noor looks at her notepad. She's not quite sure what the point of it was, now. To write a list of names, appar-ently. Then to draw a large question mark next to them.

She underlines the question mark.

Then she looks at the phone. Thinking: *burner phone.*

Because she may as well give in to the inevitable.

Noor is going to have to use this phone for something illegal, and then throw it away.

Tell me a story.

. . . But no.

It wasn't like that. It wasn't even exactly a story.

But it was the closest thing to a story Louise ever told Noor, and ever since Noor found out about the clients Louise – no, Louise and *Noor* – had looked up –

No.

Ever since Louise lied about the word RASA.

Since then, Noor's been thinking about that story.

Have you heard of Richard D. Rubin? Louise had asked Noor. It was a sunny day, back before the shutters had been installed. The two of them were sitting in Noor's new office, watching the reflected light toast the grass outside. Every now and again a security guard would walk past, hand up to his face to protect his eyes from the glare.

No, said Noor. Should I have?

Not many people have, said Louise. He was really the first person to discover memory deletion. Except he didn't know that's what he'd done: his study wasn't seen as anything but a one-off, a curiosity. And now he's probably dead.

That's unfortunate for him, said Noor. But when did he discover it?

Back in the seventies, said Louise. Before they tightened the rules about what you can and can't do with patients in mental hospitals. Rubin gave ECT to twenty-eight people suffering from paranoia and hallucinations. Obviously ECT is usually only given to anaesthetised patients. But Rubin kept his patients awake. He encouraged them to think about the things that frightened or disturbed them most, and while they were doing this, he shocked them.

What? said Noor. Why the hell did he do that?

Well, it was known back then that ECT caused memory loss. A few hours, even a whole day. Rubin's idea was that if the ECT coincided with one of their active episodes, like a hallucination, the patient would just *forget* that they were mentally ill. It was insane, obviously. But as it turned out, nearly all of Rubin's patients saw a dramatic improvement in their conditions.

That doesn't surprise me, said Noor. I'd dramatically improve too if the alternative was going through ECT again fully awake.

Louise leaned forward. She said: But you see why it worked?

Sure, said Noor. (Always trying to please teacher.) I guess he interrupted the memory of their fear or delusion, and stopped it from reconsolidating –

Yes, yes. (Louise waved a hand, to forestall any more explaining.) We know that *now*. But people didn't know about memory reconsolidation for decades after that study. They had no idea what was going on with the neurons.

Okay, said Noor warily.

Louise had leaned back again. Her face blinked out, turned dark against the window behind her. But Noor had the feeling that Louise was looking at her the way she'd looked at Noor in her job interview, only a few weeks before.

What do you think about that study? Louise asked.

Well, said Noor, I feel like my answer is going to end up being unintentionally revealing of my ethical beliefs. Whether I'm a moral absolutist or a relativist. And that also, if I answer, it could lead to more questions that are harder to answer, until we end up with a thought experiment like the trolley problem. Which I don't have anything against, but honestly, I've gone over that so many times I'm quite happy to let them all die under the trolley, even the ones who weren't in danger in the first place.

Louise smiled.

And? she said.

And so I'd prefer not to answer, if that's okay with you.

Of course, said Louise. Listen, what are you doing this Saturday? I'm having a party. I think you should come.

Which was good and bad: good because Noor knew she'd passed the test by refusing the test, and she felt an immense (almost painful) need to pass a test set by Louise.

But also bad, because now she was going to have to go to a party.

Noor opens her notepad. On one page she's written what basically amounts to a script. It's a little different from the usual Nepenthe script.

Hi! (goes Noor's script.)

Am I speaking to (insert name)?

Great. Hello (insert name). This is Laura Honeywell from the Nepenthe clinic. This is just a follow-up call, as I understand you've already spoken to Dr Nightingale?

As I understand it, Dr Nightingale has discussed your upcoming restoration with you, and you made the decision to cancel?

Would you mind taking part in a brief feedback survey, over the telephone? It should only take five minutes and is designed to help us tailor our treatment to our clients' needs, going forward.

Wonderful. First question –

Except it doesn't ever get that far.

The executive at the energy utility says he hasn't spoken to Dr Nightingale. Not at all. Never heard of her. The former soldier (flustered) has heard of Dr Nightingale, but only because she was the one who conducted his wipe, and when Noor expresses surprise that he can remember anything about the procedure, he hangs up. The arms manufacturer executive hangs up immediately. The person who has served a prison sentence for fraud says he won't be speaking to anyone from Nepenthe without a solicitor present. The solicitor says he won't be speaking to anyone from Nepenthe at all, let alone Laura Honeywell. That *is* her name, isn't it? And what is her job, if he may ask? Who, exactly, authorised this call?

The Kent housewife – Barbara Key – is the most surprising. By the time Noor gets to 'this is just a follow-up call', Barbara interrupts and says,

'Journalist, is it?'

'What?' Noor says. 'No, it's –'

'Fuck off,' says Barbara, and hangs up.

Interesting, thinks Noor. She circles Barbara's name a few times, slowly. Then she looks her up again. It turns out that Barbara is the wife of a former East End gangster, now in prison. Barbara wasn't implicated in his crimes, and so she kept her six-bedroom house in Sevenoaks, new Range Rover and ownership stake in a wine bar called Grape Expectations.

It feels like a significant discovery. Noor just doesn't know what the discovery *means*.

She draws some more question marks on her notepad. These marks deeper than the first, more darkly scored.

She'd like to push these people further. Prod, pry, provoke, whatever it takes to get something illuminating out of them. They might not be good people – a number of them at least are definitely criminals. But the fact remains: they're clients. She has a responsibility towards them. Maybe Louise's actions have already made duty of care a lost cause, but there might still be something to protect. Noor doesn't know how much they know, or how vulnerable they are. They could be victims, not co-conspirators. So she can't mess with them too much.

What next?

She opens a new page in the notebook.

Noor only ever went to one of Louise's parties in the end. The news that she was invited caused envy and consternation among her colleagues, none of whom had been invited to Louise's large, expensive house – let alone any of her parties. Noor could have told them not to worry. It only took one party to establish that Noor was happier not attending Louise's parties, and she imagined Louise was happier not having her there too, because there were no more invitations after that.

(Why this? Why this particular memory? Is it because she's been wishing for the Elena memories to let up, and so now she has to be punished with something that's almost worse?)

The walls of Louise's house were white and there were a few sofas scattered around. The tall windows looked out onto a garden that was lit up with floodlights, firing the undersides of the trees. It reminded Noor of Nepenthe – not in any way that she'd ever seen it personally, but the way it must look to the self-confidential clients, arriving at night.

(She allowed herself a nostalgic thought of her own office. Noor inside. Door closed.)

Louise – or her husband – seemed fond of Japanese woodcuts of mountains and villages and the sea. There were a lot of them on the walls, lit up with tiny spotlights. Noor became quite fond of them herself. They allowed her to stand in front of them with her untouched glass of champagne, pretending to be deep in contemplation. Every now and again someone would approach her and make conversation, and she'd try to look like she was happy that they'd done this. She tried, but she could tell they could tell she wasn't quite sincere.

So, how do you know Louise and Alistair? asked one man. His name was Bob Rathbone. He was actually very pleasant. He asked her about her working relationship with Louise, and Noor was glad to have the chance to say something with sincerity. She told him that Louise was a kind of mentor; that Noor was very grateful Louise had seen something in her despite Noor not having much of the right kind of experience.

Well, that's Louise's gift, said Bob. Knowing when to go by the book, and when to read between the lines. I imagine you're the same?

Oh no, Noor said. Not at all. I'm a coder, really. If the lines don't cover every eventuality, I believe they need to be rewritten.

Exactly, Bob said. Then – Noor was almost *sure* – he winked.

At that moment Louise appeared at Bob's side, and asked to borrow him for a moment. Noor was grateful for the interruption. The conversation hadn't been bad, but winks? She didn't know what to do with a wink. It was exactly the kind of between-the-lines interaction she thought she'd been very clear about not liking.

Alone again, she noticed that one of the windows to the garden was actually a door, and that it was slightly open. The air coming in was warmer than the air inside the house. It was perfumed, too, with moss and roses and faint woodsmoke.

She slid the door the rest of the way open, and went outside.

The garden went back a long way. Noor found herself out of the range of the floodlights, and still there was no end in sight. What exactly was she doing, anyway? A little further off she could make out what looked like a white, vaguely human shape under some trees. As she got closer she realised it was a figure of a girl, floating above the lawn.

She'd never believed in ghosts, but that didn't seem to matter: she was about to meet one. Her heart rate hurried, but she carried on walking. (Noor still isn't sure why she did that.)

As she got closer still she realised the figure was a real girl, about twelve years old, sitting on a swing.

She remembered that Louise had mentioned she had a daughter, adopted when she was a baby. A clever girl, according to Louise, but fragile. Something like that. (Louise had looked suddenly uncertain, when she said this. Noor hadn't seen that expression before, or since.)

Hi, Noor said to the girl. You look like a kid in a horror film. Didn't anyone ever tell you not to sit on swings in the dark late at night? You could give someone a heart attack.

Noor was looking at the girl with curiosity. She couldn't have imagined Louise wanting a child so much that she'd source one from another country. But here she was: a sweet, soft-looking girl in white pyjamas, with a blunt fringe and a ponytail.

Sorry, said the girl. Is your heart okay?

Seems to be working, said Noor. What are you doing out here?

But as she said it the *out here* enveloped her; the warmth of the night, the smell of the slightly damp grass – and there was an owl hooting, which was ridiculous, because this was London and surely owls were extinct here. At this distance the lights of the house and the people moving silently inside looked beautiful. There was something almost poignant in how beautiful they were. It was obvious why the girl was out here.

(*Mei*, she remembered. That was Louise's daughter's name.)

I'm seeing what it feels like to be an outcast, Mei said.

You're what? said Noor.

My mum's always saying if I don't stop doing x or start doing y, I could end up a social outcast. So I'm seeing what it's like. Because I *might* decide not to do what she says, and just be an outcast.

Maybe not so soft after all, thinks Noor. She can see more of a resemblance to Louise, now.

Right, Noor said. Except then you're not really an outcast. You can't cast yourself out.

I can, said Mei.

No, I mean: it would be called something different if you chose to walk away.

Mei smiled. An outwalk, she said.

Noor was watching the house. Louise had come close to the window now. She was talking to someone; smiling and moving her hands. For the first time, with the sound taken away, Noor saw that Louise wasn't quite like the other people around her. As if Louise was *there*, talking and laughing and entertaining, but also: she wasn't.

She looked at Louise again. Louise looked totally normal. Still, Noor didn't feel like going back to the party. So she said goodbye to Mei, walked back down the garden, left via the dark side entrance of the house, and went home, gratefully, to bed.

Later, Noor understood her own mistakes at the party. She'd been too obviously insincere, then too sincere. She should have been perfectly insincere: sardonic, jokey and light. She should have behaved like Louise's drunk but charming husband Alistair, joking that every time he won an argument Louise wiped his memory. Referring to Nepenthe as the *brain drain*. Noor didn't find that one funny. She was surprised that Louise would tolerate it, actually. But Louise just raised her eyebrows and smiled.

And then later Alistair made a joke that Noor thought Louise *definitely* wouldn't have found funny, which might have been why Alistair said it quietly, to a friend of his. The friend was as drunk as Alistair. Neither of them had noticed Noor standing near them, pretending to inspect the art. They were talking about investments.

Thanks for sorting out the KL property, Alistair said. That was a good shout.

Any time, said the friend.

How about soon? said Alistair. You know how Louise's income is. We can't keep up. It's like a fucking oil well. What are they called? Geysers? Gushers.

The friend said something crude then, and Noor moved away before they realised she was there and felt embarrassed.

Though she thinks now: they wouldn't have been embarrassed.

It wasn't the friend's joke that really irritated Noor. It was Alistair's laugh at his wife's expense. He was obviously the one with the money. Noor had checked out the payroll at Nepenthe (an early hack) and Louise, while on a decent salary, wasn't rich. There was clearly no way the two of them could have afforded the house in London and Alistair's Maserati and the overseas property on her income. Noor thought it was tasteless of Alistair to draw attention to this inequality. She wondered why Louise – never knowingly tasteless – would marry a man like him.

What Noor admired about Louise, more than anything, was her infallible judgement. She didn't want to admit Alistair into that picture of perfection. She didn't want to have to think, about Louise: *what the hell was she thinking?*

So: she just didn't think about it.

Noor calls up the clinic schedule for the first week of November. She makes a note of the people who are supposed to come in that week to have their bad memories put back into their heads.

M. Lewarne
M. O'Connor
W. Hall
O. Levy

She clicks through to the case notes for each of them, one by one. There's nothing unusual about them. She realises M. Lewarne's appointment is actually a follow-up, with their actual restoration taking place the week before, so Noor rules this person out on the basis that if Louise was trying to intercept them, she'd have been looking at a different calendar page. None of the others have cancelled their restorations yet, which makes sense as they're still in the calendar. She can't work out which of them might have been that last person Louise tried and failed to call, the one with the disconnected number.

She gets to O. Levy. There's something strange about these case details. When Noor clicks on his or her name, an error message pops up:

ACCESS DENIED

She tries again but gets the same result.
Huh, she says.
This is something she hasn't ever seen before.
She looks up the call log again, before she remembers that she won't be able to see the number Louise tried to call, as it never connected.
O. *Levy*, Noor writes in the notebook.
Question mark.

And of course the problem with Louise not getting through to this person – who *has* to be O. Levy, surely? – is that Louise will probably try to contact this person again. She will probably expect Noor, unwittingly, to help her with that.

Noor isn't sure how she's going to get out of that one.

It would be reasonable to suppose, thinks Noor, that this mystery about what Louise is up to would be Noor's uppermost concern right now.

Because of *course* it should be. Clients could be at risk. The company's reputation would definitely be at risk. Louise could lose her job. Noor could lose her job. Criminal charges; *prison* may not be out of the question.

And yet: that's not the case. It's like when children wonder if there'll be enough love to go round when a sibling arrives. And the parents say, *love is not finite*, or something to that effect. It turns out that worry is not finite either. The disturbing thoughts about Louise haven't supplanted Noor's disturbing thoughts about Elena. Rather, her worry has expanded, embracing them both.

It's Noor's own fault. She knows how neural pathways work. She's the one who started thinking about Elena again. She's reinforced the pathway, over and over again. The more she thinks about Elena Darke, the more she thinks about Elena Darke. Until the most tenuous things remind her of Elena Darke.

And some of them are *really* fucking tenuous. Like a glass of wine, and there she is, puff of smoke: *red or white? Or spirits?* Or a pillow. Noor looks at the empty pillow and there's Elena, throwing herself back, laughing.

She sees her young neighbours, walking through the park, talking and laughing. Yesterday they were arguing; something about decisions.

. . . *Just insane*, the girl said. Why? Why would you want that? The boy kept saying, But I have to, I can't not. It ended with a fuck off and a door slamming at 2 a.m. Now they're arm in arm. The whole thing looks exhausting.

Noor finds herself pausing, turning, as they dawdle past. They don't see her; they're engrossed in their own conversation. But she feels embarrassed, and annoyed, seeing herself watching them. The neighbours are nearly at the park gate when they stop and draw together in a kiss, the girl's arms wrapped tightly round the boy's neck, the boy's hands pressing into the denim above her arse. All this totally in the way of people using the gate, of course. Noor wills somebody to walk into the park and tut at them.

(Nobody does.)

And what am I *doing?* Noor thinks. Is this who she is? A disapproving old bag, at the age of thirty-six. Hanging around parks in order to get her fix of outrage. Is that it?

There's a low vibration of pain in her stomach that says: that's not quite it.

Maybe it's that (admit it) something about the girl reminds Noor of Elena. She's smiling; she gestures with energy; she throws the full length of her body into a kiss. But there's a look she has – surfacing again now, as the two of them disentangle and walk out of the park – that seems somehow . . . fatalistic. It's not exactly the right word. Noor doesn't know the right word. Something

234

like: being in the epicentre of happiness, knowing that this happiness won't be around long, but making peace with that.

Elena often had that look.

And there she is, Elena, saying, *What would you get rid of, if you had to get rid of a memory?*

No idea, was what Noor had said.

Something from childhood? pressed Elena.

You can't delete anything from childhood, Noor said. Childhood is too far back. Too . . . woven in. Nepenthe doesn't usually delete things if it's been longer than six months. The longer you wait, the more chance you'll have talked about it or thought about it in the interim.

And what happens then? Elena asked.

You get . . . fuzzy patches. That's not the scientific term. That's how people often describe it. So if you deleted something very integral, very early, a lot of your life would be a fuzzy patch.

They'll be able to one day, I bet, Elena said. Delete childhood. So, *theoretically*, would you delete anything from yours?

Well, theoretically, ethics would prohibit –

It's very obvious when you avoid personal questions by the way, Elena said. You get very academic.

What do you want? Noor said. A tale of woe? Well, my childhood was ordinary. That's it.

And it's true, she thinks. It was an ordinary kind of bad. Nothing startling, nothing original. Noor was gay, and an atheist. Her family were straight, and religious. It wasn't a good mix.

Elena looked at Noor for a while. She said this carefully:

235

Do you think it's fair to say you aren't a very open person, Noor?

Absolutely, said Noor. Being open isn't the same as being honest. I think honest is important. Open, not so much. Especially in the modern sense, when it's most often used to justify rehashing one's traumatic past endlessly – and usually unproductively.

Right, Elena said.

Noor doesn't say that sometimes she'd rather Elena was less open. Noor doesn't know how to respond to the confidences Elena drops on her, without warning. First of all, Noor deals with that kind of stuff every day in her professional life. Talking about it out of hours is like bringing work home. Secondly, she can't even respond as she would at work: neutral, detached. There's a pressure on her to be warm, empathetic – even to give up something personal of her own. She never trained for that.

The second time they spent the night together, Noor was about to go off to sleep when Elena said,

I thought I was done with all this. Sex. I've been celibate for over a year. Since the helicopter accident. What's awful is, when I saw them taking Guy away, what came into my head was: that's a mistake I won't be making. I mean, I was always getting drunk, or bored, or lonely, and sleeping with people. I might have slept with Guy. If he'd caught me in the right mood. It's pretty cold to think that when you're looking at someone's dead body though, isn't it?

You were probably in shock, Noor said.

Noor really didn't want to hear about Guy. She didn't want to hear about any of the people Elena had slept with when she was drunk, or bored, or lonely.

I did mean it, though, Elena said. At that point I started to get sick of sex. I got sick of other people. Which is stupid, because how can I blame other people? It's not like they're one homogenous mass. I mean, it's my fault for being attracted to the wrong type of people.

Noor wasn't sure what to say to this.

In case you're wondering, Elena said, you're the right type of people.

She rolled over to face Noor and smiled. One breast had slipped out from under the sheet. It was velvety and full. The nipple was a pale salmon pink; a tender, almost painful softness. Noor had never seen another woman's nipple so close. It was like an unblinking eye she didn't know how to meet.

Open, she thought. One door closes, another door opens.

Noor: closed. Elena: open.

Elena was so open it was frightening.

Hang on, Noor thought, later, after Elena had gone to sleep, and couldn't be asked:

How can you remember the accident?

Noor isn't one to dwell on past failures. Granted, access has been firmly denied to the clients Louise phoned, and to O. Levy – and, before that, to an explanation of RASA (something she thinks, now, must be connected to the phone calls somehow, if only because it's clearly secret and it also involves Louise). But one thing Noor has learned from that innocent time when she worked with computers rather than people is:

There's always access. One way or another.

There's always a way in.

(The same does not go for people.)

Noor waits until she gets home to begin implementing her plan. More accurately: the last of her plans. She's got no idea what to do if this doesn't work.

She gets onto Google and searches again for Nepenthe and RASA, looking for the forum in which a poster – TotalWipeOut73 – mentioned the two in connection. Some theory about robots with human memories. She finds it, then scrolls through the rest of the threads; reading about MK Ultra and Illuminati and Wouter Basson and Area 51 and what this might have to do with Israel, the Queen, fluoride in the water, genetically modified weaponised ravens – before she thinks: *That's enough*.

She sets up her own blog with an amateurish font, a few stills from the *Terminator* films, and a disjointed but passionate diatribe about the web of lies and corruption at Nepenthe, and calls the whole thing Truth About RASA.

Then she goes back onto the forum and tells TotalWipeOut73 that he's mostly right, except for a few crucial details, and posts a link to her new blog.

When TotalWipeOut gets there he's going to find that the Truth About RASA is that Nepenthe are taking human memories to implant them into genetically modified ravens. She's even included a few lines from the Poe poem, for extra credit.

It doesn't matter if TotalWipeOut73 agrees with Noor or not about the ravens. She plans to talk to him if she can, but if not, she'll be able to get his IP address as soon as he visits her web page. And then she'll be able to find out if he was once a Nepenthe client, and how he got hold of that word: *RASA*.

It's 2 p.m. Noor's interviewing her last client of the day. After this the trial period of the new script ends, and so does Noor's contact with the general public. The prospect of paperwork and management duties never seemed so sweet.

'I feel like I've meddled with something I shouldn't have,' says Noor's client. 'I tampered with my own memories.'

'That's a very common feeling to have after the procedure,' Noor says.

'Really?' asks the client.

'Let me tell you about the Phelps study,' Noor says. 'It's very enlightening. We *think* our memories are pure and uncorrupted, but this is a delusion. Every time we access a memory we rebuild it. Every time it's rebuilt, things are added and things are lost. In fact the more we remember something, the less resemblance that memory bears to the original event. We *know* that memory is fallible – or we know it but we don't really believe it. If someone says we remembered something wrong, we argue over it! We fight for the honour of our memories. Maybe it's like religion, or love. The more flimsy something is, the more fiercely we believe in it.'

'So, this is . . . Phelps?' the client says. 'Phelps says this?'

'Not exactly,' Noor says. 'Uh. Sorry. Let me restate that.'

She manages to get things back on track, but after the client has left (on time, for once), she thinks:

Well, Noor, what the fuck was that about?

It's been a few weeks since Noor saw Louise. This is unusual: Louise usually visits Crowshill every week. Noor's not sure what to make of her absence. At the end of every day she's relieved that she hasn't seen Louise, but every day her dread of Louise's inevitable appearance is sharper.

The clinic is busy these days. Bordering on chaotic. Nobody was able to accurately predict how many of Nepenthe's self-confidential clients would end up going through with a restoration. A couple of hundred, so far, think that they will. Two hundred and thirty-seven people have replied to say *I'd like my memory back. I don't want my tonsils, my appendix, my tumour, my rotten right toe. But I do want this.*

There are new staff members arriving, people training them, people carrying equipment into offices and therapy rooms. People filling up the kitchen. It's nearly impossible to avoid people. Noor's been having to make small talk all week.

One of the main perpetrators of the small talk is Dr Karine de Oliveira, who has taken an empty office in the opposite wing of the clinic to Noor's. Karine's got the job of comforting and calming the clients who get their memories back. She has a convincing smile, maybe even a real one. She's very warm and approachable. Noor doesn't approach her. Karine drinks fennel tea, and Noor's heard she does yoga in her office, so she already knows they have nothing to say to each other.

And the busier the clinic gets, the more resonant Louise's absence is. After three more days go by, Noor goes to the clinic director, Jim Stokes, to ask if Louise's visits have been postponed, while the restorations go ahead.

'No,' Jim says. He looks alarmed. (Louise alarms him.) 'Are you expecting her?'

'No,' Noor says. 'I'm just organising my diary. She won't be coming in this week then, you think?'

'I have no idea,' Jim says. 'She used to put her visits in the system. Lately she doesn't turn up for them, or she arrives at different times. I have no idea what's going on. Actually, I thought *you'd* know. You tend to know more about her visits than I do.'

Noor imagines Jim saying this to the board members. *Dr Ali was the only one who spoke to Dr Nightingale. I had no idea what was going on.*

'I wish that were the case,' she says quickly. 'Dr Nightingale's schedule is a mystery to me too. A complete enigma.'

She smiles.

Jim looks confused.

Maybe she shouldn't have smiled. The best thing to do is behave normally, which in this case would be – what?

No smile. A short nod. An *I'll let you get on.*

Yes. And with that she's out of Jim's office, thinking: *Thank God normal Noor isn't a small-talk person.*

Around this time, it occurs to Noor that maybe Louise hasn't *got* another way to contact the person she's looking for, O. Levy. Maybe there's only one phone number on the system, and no other way to track this person. Which would mean that Louise doesn't need Noor to co-authorise another view of the same client contact page. Which is why she hasn't bothered coming in.

But what she might do, what would make *sense* for her to do, is to come to the clinic instead, on the day of O. Levy's appointment, and speak to him or her in person.

And what will Noor do then?

TotalWipeOut73 won't speak to Noor, as she expected. She sends him a PM under a different name, but he's immediately so suspicious of her that she starts to worry she might be putting him under too much stress, and stops. She doesn't really need to talk to him anyway. She's got his IP address now, has found his real name – Nigel Potter – and looked him up in the Nepenthe system. He's another ACCESS DENIED. Noor feels elated by this discovery for at least three seconds. That's about as long as she gets to celebrate each breakthrough, before realising every breakthrough makes the whole picture harder to understand.

There's not much else Noor can do with TotalWipeOut73/ Nigel Potter. As a former Nepenthe patient who says he's lost several years of his own life, he's hardly going to be able to remember anything useful. She writes a question mark under his name in the notebook.

But something else potentially interesting has come out of Noor's blog. About twenty other people have followed the link to it. And the very first person to click is someone who works for Nepenthe. From the speed of the click, whoever it is must have a keyword search alert set up. The words being *RASA + Nepenthe*. Unfortunately, the IP address covers the whole of Nepenthe's London head-quarters, so the visitor checking out Noor's blog is one of hundreds of possible employees. And the Nepenthe IP is so guarded against hackers there's no way Noor could get any more information about the specific user.

Is this you, Louise? Noor wonders at her laptop. *What are you up to, out there?*

She goes through the rest of the people that followed her blog link. It doesn't take her long. Most of them have a loudly troubled online presence, with the focus of their rage falling on things like blood-drinking celebrities, crop circles and so on. They don't care about Nepenthe, particularly.

But then she sees one social media profile she recognises. In fact, it makes her flinch, a delayed physical reaction. It's the protester with the RASA cover-up placard. She remembers the beard, the grey hair, the antagonistic look in his eye. Last seen glaring behind a large globule of his own saliva, travelling towards Noor's face.

Noor is delighted to see him.

Martin Noye is his name. His profile is private: the only other picture of his she can see is a black Labrador in the back of a Volvo estate.

Noor creates a fake social media profile of her own. She puts a lot of care into finding a photo: attractive blonde in her forties, dressed neutrally in a shell-pink blouse. *Who could spit at this woman?* Noor thinks fondly. She names her Isabelle Blanchard and gives her two golden retrievers and a farmhouse in Cornwall.

Isabelle requests Martin as a friend. Martin accepts.

Hi Martin! Isabelle messages. *This sounds weird, I know, but I have something I was hoping to talk to you about. Privately, I mean. To do with RASA. Can we talk over the phone?*

It's not even a minute before Noor's burner phone is clattering on the desk. She's a little taken aback. She picks up.

'Hello?' she says, in what she imagines is an Isabelle voice.

'I know what you're doing,' says Martin Noye. He seems angry. (Already?)

'I'm sorry?' Noor says.

'You must think I'm stupid. If you know about RASA, you know about the non-disclosure. You think you're going to catch me out that easily? I'm not bloody stupid. Do you understand me? One day your bosses are going to get found out and then they'll be fucked, like they fucked me, and that means you get fucked too, you lying bitch.'

Martin hangs up. The sound of his furious voice seems to leave the phone slowly, as if the handset is gradually cooling.

'Well, you really ruined that one,' Noor says to Isabelle, deleting her.

She goes back into the system and looks up Martin Noye.

ACCESS DENIED.

'*What?*' Noor says under her breath.

Boss*es*, she thinks. *Multiple* bosses. *Non-disclosure.* Whatever RASA is, more than one person at Nepenthe is involved. Which she should have suspected sooner, because it's not like Louise sent that message to herself.

Up until now, Noor has had only one vague theory. More of a hope than a theory. She knows Louise doesn't like Clifford Byrne, their head of operations, and Louise's immediate boss. Louise also doesn't like the damage that restorations could potentially do to vulnerable clients. (It's not like the memories can be removed again. It was tried with rats and the results were 'not promising'.) Nor does Louise like the way Nepenthe has ignored the issue of traces; staying stubbornly silent, refusing to investigate, even though everyone *knows* they exist. And Louise doesn't like the way clients who develop mental illness are effectively shut out by Nepenthe.

And Noor agrees with Louise. She agrees with her about traces, and restorations, and Clifford, and basically everything else Louise has ever said. And so Noor's been wondering if this – admittedly very serious – wrongdoing on the part of Louise could perhaps have an underlying reason that Noor, too, might agree with. Unfortunately, while Noor thought restorations were just something she and Louise bitched about together, maybe Louise has decided to stop bitching and start phoning clients to warn them they're making a terrible mistake.

The problem with that theory is this: why Louise would only try to talk a tiny handful of clients out of getting their memories back. Louise has had hundreds of clients over the years. Why these few?

Noor had come to assume that the Access Denied clients, RASA and Louise's phone calls were all part of the same wrongdoing on Louise's part. But now it's clear that while RASA definitely has something to do with the Access Denied clients, and Louise has something to do with RASA, Louise hasn't called any Access Denied clients – only the usual kind. Nor is there any sign Louise tried to contact either Nigel or Martin. And so there's no reason to think that O. Levy was the person Louise was looking for on the clinic schedule.

Noor is embarrassed by her own bias. She's assumed that Louise was only keeping one secret from her. And why? Because she finds it painful to believe that Louise is involved in separate misdeeds. As if Noor can perhaps handle the personal betrayal of Louise having one secret, but two is just too much. When, rationally: if Louise is breaking one rule, she's probably broken more.

Anyway.

Noor has to assume that Louise could have been looking up one of the other people due to have a restoration that week. She looks up their names again.

M. O'Connor? W. Hall?

There's no way to find out.

Ugh, Noor mutters. She rubs her scalp, as if she can massage the answer out of it.

Another problem is why Louise would knowingly implicate Noor in whatever it is she was up to. It might be that she believes so passionately in whatever she's doing that she expects that Noor would want to help her. But then why not tell Noor about it?

Noor has to admit that there's a strong possibility that Louise isn't as good a friend as Noor would hope. That maybe 'do least harm' doesn't cover Noor quite as comprehensively as Noor would like.

Please, no, Noor thinks.

Even though it's too late for Noor to be pleading with Louise. Whatever Louise is doing, she's already done it. So what, exactly, is she pleading for?

Noor can't sleep. It's been two hours, and she's been thinking about Elena, then Louise, then Elena, then Louise, and so on. She's getting pretty pissed off with the pair of them. But then she thinks: it's hardly their fault. Come on. Elena *Darke*. Louise *Night*ingale. No wonder they pop up at times like these, when the curtains are drawn.

Noor gets up. She takes another sleeping pill. She doesn't read the fold-up paper instructions that come with them. (What's the worst that can happen? She never wakes up. Boo fucking hoo.)

Her thoughts slow, but they don't stop. The Elena/Louise roulette wheel spins, ticks to a stop, lands, finally, on Elena.

Elena was asleep in Noor's bed. Her eyes were closed, her gaze dancing about under the lids, off roaming other lands, with other people. Elena never had any problems sleeping, not even under a strange roof. She'd slept soundly the very first night she'd stayed. Noor hadn't actually been sure if Elena would *want* to stay – or if Noor wanted her to – but Elena settled the matter by falling suddenly, deeply asleep. That was six months ago, and Elena had stayed more and more often since then. She'd been here now for a couple of weeks. Noor still wasn't sure how she felt about this, either.

She got in carefully next to Elena, who – unusually – woke up, and put her arm over Noor's shoulder. Her skin was warm.

How is it you can remember the helicopter crash? Noor asked, switching off the light.

Oh, right, Elena said.

She sat up and rubbed her eyes. For the first time, she looked evasive.

She said: Look. It wasn't exactly the crash I had deleted. It was the stuff . . . around it. Some *circumstances*. That it was better for me to forget.

Okay, Noor said.

She was trying to work out what she wanted from this conversation. If she really pushed Elena, Elena would more than likely tell her that she had been sleeping with her boss. Because what was a memory of *circumstances*, if not a memory of context? The context being that Elena and her boss must have been having a relationship. His death upset her so much that she was celibate for a long time. She must have wanted to make the memory of him less painful. Maybe she'd erased the day he told her he'd leave his wife. Presented her with an engagement ring. Or maybe it had gone the other way: he'd dumped her, and she couldn't bear to remember it.

Do you want to talk about it? Elena asked – and now she sounded hesitant.

No need, Noor said. I just wanted to check there weren't any procedural issues.

Of course you did, said Elena. She laughed, but her laugh didn't sound very happy. She said, I thought for a moment there you might have some personal reason for asking.

Sorry, said Noor.

So, as we're awake and talking, can I ask about *your* work? For my own personal reasons.'

Okay, Noor said warily.

You got very prickly the other day: when I said about you getting in so late. So I dropped it. But I'm curious. You work crazy long hours. You're always talking about Louise and your work. It all seems very . . . devoted. Did you two used to date or something?

Noor was shocked.

Absolutely not, she said. Christ. I don't see Louise like that at all. She's been a mentor to me. I *admire* her. I don't want to have *sex* with her.

Oh, so the two things can't go together? You don't admire me?

I didn't mean that.

Okay. Don't be offended. You're just obviously committed to your work, that's all.

I am committed about my work, said Noor. And to Louise, too. She's trying to make the world a better place. That's what I want too. What you need to understand about Louise is –

I've met her, remember? Elena said. She didn't seem all that amazing to me. But I'm glad she inspires you.

Noor was annoyed by this.

Don't *you* want to be inspired by a job? Noor said. Are you going to get another one of those, by the way?

I got a lot of compensation from the crash, Elena said. Her arm had retracted; Noor hadn't noticed when that had happened.

Fine. But if you did something you loved, maybe you wouldn't be here all day, focusing on me, noticing what time I get in. I mean, you can do what you want. It's just a suggestion.

There was a long pause. After a moment the sheets moved around Elena's shoulders. Noor, facing the dark ceiling, guessed that Elena was shrugging.

Okay, Elena said. Maybe we should get some sleep. You have work tomorrow.

Okay, Noor said. Night.

Night.

(A growing coldness across Noor's collarbone, where Elena's arm had been.)

When Noor woke up, Elena was gone.

Noor sits at her desk, half her attention on the sliced-up view, wondering at what point the slices of Louise's Tesla are going to slide silently in under the slices of the pines.

I'm not ready, she wants to say. *I need more time.*

Because if Louise arrives now, she's going to look at Noor and know that Noor's worried.

Which puts Noor at something of a disadvantage.

The memory wheel spins.

Louise is up this time.

It's four or so years ago. Louise's hair is longer; it's hot outside; there's a weeping fig in the corner of Noor's office, still alive. Louise was talking to Noor about something, and then she stopped, looked at Noor closely, and said, What's wrong?

Nothing's wrong, Noor said.

Don't lie, Louise said gently. You're a decent liar usually, but being in love makes you obvious. You should know that about yourself.

Love? said Noor.

Louise laughed. She said, It might shock you, but you behaved exactly the same way everyone else does when they fall in love. You gazed through things. You smiled more. You looked softer. You didn't sing, though I honestly thought you were about to at times. Then you took a week off work. Now you look terrible. So what happened?

You and I don't usually talk about personal matters, Noor said.

Louise just looked at her.

I got involved with a client, Noor said.

She hadn't really been planning to say it. But that was what she said.

It was said now.

Noor looked at Louise not in terror, or relief, but an exact midpoint between the two that felt strangely like calm. A stillness descended. She felt limp, placid. Like she'd given up on survival and let herself float out to sea, allowing whatever happened to happen – possibly the first moment in her life that she'd done so. It was just a shame that she was allowing her life to be ruined.

Louise, for the first time, looked surprised.

That was unexpected, she said. So, you fell in love with a client. What, after you did her final interview?

Yes. I met up with her after that. It's over now.

I can see that, Louise said. Her eyebrows were returning from the heights they'd just scaled.

I know that makes no difference, Noor said. I mean, my career's over in any case.

Oh for God's sake, Noor, Louise said. You didn't do anything wrong. I know there are *rules*, but rules have to make way for common sense from time to time. The clients are almost out of the door when they get to you. You assessed this woman objectively, right? Right. You won't see her again in a professional capacity. The way I see it, no harm done. The main concern is if she's likely to make a complaint, or say something publicly.

No, said Noor. She . . . wouldn't do that.

Noor couldn't tell what she was feeling now. Uncomprehending. A second ago she'd been floating out in the sea. Now she was back on land, towed back by Louise; Louise bearing her weight; Louise's arm round her neck.

I can't ask you to keep a secret for me, Noor said. This is serious. You could get sacked just for knowing about it.

So don't tell anyone that I know about it, Louise said. Problem solved.

But – said Noor.

Stop, Louise said. Stop being so noble.

Okay, Noor said. Uh. Thank you?

Louise moved across to Noor, patted her shoulder, and said, These things happen. I mean, *you* probably never thought these things would happen to you personally. But it did. You got involved with someone, and it ended. Welcome to the world of everyone else.

It's shit, Noor said. But anyway, you're in that world and *you're* having a great time.

Louise laughed. Is that what it looks like? she said. I suppose I don't talk to you much about my family. Well, I'm divorcing my husband. My daughter is also experiencing some issues. Unrelated to the divorce.

Oh. God. I'm sorry, Noor said.

She didn't say, I don't know why you married your husband in the first place. She remembered Mei sitting in the darkness on a swing, talking about being an outcast.

I had no idea, Noor said.

You weren't meant to, said Louise.

I met Mei once, said Noor. A while back, at your party. She was only twelve or so.

She's sixteen now. She's not very . . . resilient. I worry about her.

I'm sorry, Noor said again. Your husband . . . uh –

Oh Christ, don't be sorry, Louise said. She looked at Noor. Then she laughed, and said: Oh yes. You met Alistair. You're wondering what I saw in him.

Well, Noor said. Maybe.

He was a lot of fun in our twenties, Louise said. And good-looking. I didn't see it as a problem that I never really took him seriously. Then he ended up not being a serious person. Not that that's *my* responsibility.

Of course not, Noor said. Then she thought – *but.*

Noor'd noticed over the years that the things Louise believed often ended up being true. And it made sense: Louise's perceptive eye naturally covered the future as well as the present. But she was also reminded of the reason experiments are double blind: to prevent researcher expectations influencing the results.

Anyway, Louise said, I've had unrequited university crushes that hurt me worse. Much worse. Maybe that's the key. The newness of being hurt. The first is the worst. After that it's just . . . routine.

Thanks, Noor said. That's depressing but also quite helpful.

Well, good, Louise said.

Uh . . . I'd rather not talk about this again, if that's okay?

Fine with me, Louise said. We'll go back to not talking about personal matters.

And that, as Noor remembers, is what they did.

With everything else that's going on, Noor's plan to ask Louise to help her erase the memory of the very end of her relationship with Elena has been pushed back, almost forgotten. What's stupid is that she'd been dreading asking, but she sees now how simple it would have been.

Do you mind conducting the procedure? As I can't tell anyone else how the relationship started, is all she would have needed to say.

And Louise, as Noor's friend, would have said: *No problem*.

But *is* Louise Noor's friend?

The thing is, Noor thinks she is. She's just not sure why. Maybe Louise is only Noor's friend so she can know where Noor's bodies are buried. Or to have a useful person to blame when the phone calls come to light. Or both.

She was a bad egg from the beginning, Louise would say at the inquiry. *First the affair with a vulnerable client. Then the illegal calls to clients, trying to sabotage the restoration programme. I suppose I do bear some responsibility, for allowing her too much free rein. Oversight procedures will be examined, I can promise you that.*

'What did you do, Louise?' Noor whispers this at her desk, to an imaginary Louise opposite. (The imaginary Louise being a lot easier to question than the real thing.) 'Why did you break the rules?'

Rules have to make way for common sense, says Louise.

'Did you do it for something good, or something bad?'

Stop being so noble, says Louise. *Don't tell anyone. Problem solved.*

She pats Noor on the shoulder.

No harm done.

Noor looks up the clinic schedule again. The first week of November is nearly here. She checks all the four people who are coming in. Nobody has cancelled.

She takes out the notebook. She shouldn't keep it in her bag, really. Though it's not like anyone else would be able to make much sense of it. Noor herself hasn't made any sense of it. It's covered in question marks. Underlined question marks. Three or more question marks in a row.

What is RASA?

Why did Louise prevent only a small number of people from getting their memory back?

Why are the clients lying about speaking to Louise?
Who is Louise looking for now?
Has she already found them?

. . . and then the other questions, written at the back, that have nothing to do with anybody,

Why did Kirk –? How did Orlando –? What did Clementine –?

Questions, questions.

A philosophy lecturer Noor knew told her once that philosophy wasn't about answers. It was about asking questions.

He said this like it was a good thing.

Noor thinks: I need to do something about this notebook.

She burns it that evening in the log-burning stove she never uses – leaving the door open, which makes her cough. She's got all the questions memorised anyway. And when she goes to bed, her hair lying around her face, smelling of smoke, the questions come back. They circle and swoop:

. . . *why is Louise lying?*
. . . *what is Louise going to do next?*

In less than two weeks' time, the people on the schedule will be arriving at the clinic. M. Lewarne, W. Hall, M. O'Connor, O. Levy.

Noor knows Louise is spending the rest of this week in Manchester. After that, Noor expects Louise will be back at Crowshill. She'll be running out of time at that point, but she won't be able to let that haste show on her face. She'll arrive in Noor's doorway, looking carefully cheerful and calm, and then she'll try to intercept a restoration.

Which means that without knowing what she's preventing, or why she's preventing it, or how she's going to prevent it, Noor is going to have to do something to prevent that.

Mei

Mei's sitting on her bed in Kuala Lumpur. It's late afternoon. In Amsterdam, people are cycling, ordering pastries, unrolling blankets in the Vondelpark, rolling joints, feeding the small dogs that live on the houseboats, sitting outside coffee shops.

The thought of all the people of Amsterdam leading their lives makes Mei feel inexplicably sad. Their lives are like little pains in her body. The thought of the man – Armand – makes her sad, too. That's not a little pain. It beats away steadily, like a second heart.

(Is Armand his first or last name? Mei doesn't know.)

In the restaurant, when he'd recognised her, Mei had just stared at him. She couldn't do anything else. She was too shocked to move. The room faded out around her; her pulse jumped violently in her head.

The man started to smile.

It *is* you, he said. What the hell are you doing here?

He put the menu down. He was about to walk over to Mei's table, where she was still sitting, staring – as if she couldn't move, or not unless he looked away.

Mr Armand? the waiter said to him.

Wait one second, said the man, turning to him.

And in the moment that the man turned to the waiter, Mei dropped all her remaining euros on the table, snatched up her bag and, for the second time, fled.

She thinks now about how his voice softened, so that his *What the hell are you doing here?* sounded more like *Welcome, I'm so happy you're here.*

She puts her head in her hands.

There's no apparent reason why Mei should have run from this man. There's no apparent reason why she would delete her memory of him.

Except . . . she did. It wasn't enough for her to leave Amsterdam and go back to London. She'd eradicated the knowledge of even having met him in the first place.

There had to be a reason for a move as bold as that.

Are we based on memory? Mei asked her mum once. She was starting her philosophy A level and had been asked to hand in an essay about the ethics of stem cell research, screening of embryos, or memory removal. She'd chosen memory removal, reasoning that it ought to be a walk in the park.

Based? said Mei's mum.

Our personalities, I mean?

This is for school? Mei's mum asked her. She moved to Mei's shoulder to read the assignment.

You may wish to consider implications for the justice system, individual choice, philosophical standpoints, e.g. the argument that personality is based on memory . . . Christ, said Mei's mum. The persistence of Locke.

Locke? We've only done him for social contract theory, Mei said.

In short, Locke said that the self is based on memory, Mei's mum said, rolling her eyes. Scientifically, nobody knows the extent to which our memory forms our idea of self and how much our idea of self forms our memory. In practice, it doesn't seem to matter. Long before Nepenthe came along lots of people were living happy and productive lives with parts of their memory missing. Even quite large parts. Our sense of self is very resourceful. Some people cope with the loss better than others, obviously.

Right, Mei said. So the self *could* be based on memory but some people just learn to get around without it. Like a three-legged dog.

Three-legged dogs are as happy as any other dog, Mei's mum said.

So what about the people who don't cope? That can't come to terms with their missing leg?

Coping is a choice, said Mei's mum. I personally would encourage those people to ditch Locke altogether – I mean, this whole idea that we're one story, one thing leading to another. Talk about a rod for your own back. The happiest people are the ones who take the Humean view. Have you studied him yet?

No. So his view is . . . ?

The self as a bundle of processes. A collection of associations, learned responses, memories, et cetera. Swirling, contradictory, inchoate. Impermanent perceptions, belonging to nothing.

You tell your clients this?

I don't deal with clients these days, Mei's mum said. And if I did: no, of course I wouldn't.

Okay, Mei said. Thanks.

This was fun, her mum said, putting her hand on Mei's. I'm always delighted to talk about your interests, Plum. Let me know if you get any other essays you want to discuss.

Will do, Mei said.

Alone, she felt suddenly miserable. She thought of her own missing leg; her months in the Chinese orphanage in Guangzhou. A phantom limb, still sending out its odd, hard-to-interpret signals. Shyness, anxiety, shots of pain. Her mum might have claimed that Mei wasn't a dog but a bundle of perceptions, but Mei wasn't sure that her mum really believed that. Mei thought that they'd both have been happier if Mei was a normal four-legged dog, running around outside the remit of philosophy.

Later, Mei phoned her dad.

In your opinion, are our personalities based on memory? she asked.

That's your mother's area, Mei's dad said. Why are you asking me?

It's for an assignment.

Oh, very good, said her dad. A presentation in favour of memory removals. Well, I take back whatever I may have said in the past about you not having a business mind. Very good, darling. I'd say your mother owes you dinner.

That's not – said Mei. She stopped, and sighed.

Never mind, she said.

In the end Mei wrote about stem cell research. She was in favour of. She got a B.

Mei picks up her phone. She searches for the Nepenthe Reddit.

She doesn't really know why she spends so much time on this site (though her mum would probably have a theory about it), reading about people who've had memories stolen or added or jumbled up. Most of the people seem pretty jumbled up themselves. Their most frequent complaint is that nobody is listening to them.

I'm listening, thinks Mei. Not that the people on the Nepenthe Reddit know that.

She scrolls down the most recent posts.

User: Fightilluminanti. Topic: *Memory implant's????*

User: AnonTestSubject. Topic: *Secret Research Programme erased ENTIRE childhoods!*

User: Hotmama. Topic: *What they don't tell you about Antidepressants and Nepenthe!*

Alarmed, Mei clicks on the last one, but it's just another theory about antidepressants being used as population control, and antipsychotics too. And for people who realise what's going on (people like Hotmama) and stop taking their meds, the government have nepenthe, the drug that's used to wipe memories. They put it in the water supply and remove the memories of the population en masse.

Hotmama has sent her own tap water off for testing and – *surprise surprise!* – *the testing agency said they didn't screen for memory-removal chemicals.*

Someone else says that the chairman of the Nepenthe board is a Tory donor. Its CFO used to have a high-level position in the Treasury. *They're not even attempting to hide the connections!!!*

Isn't that just your standard Western government/corporation cosiness though? says someone called Johnboy82. *I mean, why would the government wipe all our memories anyway?*

Johnboy82 is told to wake up.

Mei closes the web page.

She imagines her mum overseeing a convoy of lorries, filled with men in black wetsuits holding cases of memory-loss drugs to tip into the water supply.

Do what has to be done, Mei's mum says, hands on hips.

Mei can actually kind of picture it.

But she also pictures the day she left for Kuala Lumpur, her mum dropping her at the airport, trying not to let Mei see her crying.

. . . Is there anything else?

Yeah.

There's a really obvious thing Mei can do, that she really, really would rather *not* do.

She can call her mum, and ask *her* about the memory wipe.

Is this absolutely, definitely, one hundred per cent the only option?

263

This is what Mei is thinking, sitting on her own bed, the phone slippery in her hands.

Is there maybe, another way?

No. There isn't.

She wipes her hands on the duvet cover. She spins the light on her bedside table, a revolving thing she used to have when she was a kid, with birds that moved over the walls and ceiling when the light was on. It doesn't turn any more, but she still finds something about it comforting.

She doesn't know why she's so daunted by a woman who bought her a light with revolving birds on it to celebrate Mei's achievement of going three weeks without wetting the bed, and read her stories as the birds flew slowly round.

She wipes her hands again, and calls her mum.

'Plum!' says Mei's mum. 'Where are you?'

'I'm at Dad's apartment,' Mei says. 'I just got back from Amsterdam.'

'You just . . . *what*?'

Mei's mum isn't ever lost for words. Under other circumstances, Mei might have enjoyed this moment. But she's sweating, the silence increasingly clammy, physically pressing on Mei to explain herself.

'I lied to you,' Mei said. She takes a breath. 'I know I had a memory of a trip to Amsterdam deleted. I was a night client, obviously: I didn't know about it until recently. But I had some traces, so I asked Katya, and she said we'd gone there on holiday, so I went back to find out what had happened.'

'You . . . *what*? Mei? I . . . I don't even know where to begin,' Mei's mum says. 'Why didn't you tell me about any of this?'

'You'd just have talked me out of it.'

'Did it occur to you that I'd have talked you out of it because it was a *terrible idea*?' her mum says. She sounds angry. 'There's a *system* for people who retain vestiges of the original memory. There's *support*.'

'So traces do exist?'

'Of course they do. Nepenthe just hasn't admitted it yet.'

'So what, you'd wipe the traces?'

'Wipe. I do hate that word,' her mum says. She pauses. She sounds less angry now – not shocked, not any more. (That's a bad thing. Mei's mum angry and shocked might have said something unintentionally revealing. Mei's mum having had a moment to collect her thoughts is going to be impossible.) 'But yes, removing the traces is the best thing to do under the circumstances. What were they? What did you remember?'

Mei winces.

'I don't want to tell you,' she says.

'What? Why not?'

Because they're mine, is what she wants to say.

'I just want you to tell me what happened on that holiday,' she says instead. 'I know you're not allowed to, but I need to know.'

'I understand why you'd feel that way,' says her mum. 'And I know you must be feeling frustrated and confused –'

'Don't therapise me,' Mei says. 'Can we just have an actual conversation like we're both adults? Not like you're my mother slash psychologist and I'm your daughter slash patient.'

'Okay,' her mum says. 'But I'd like to point out that you're appealing to me as a mother. You want me to go against my professional code of conduct and tell you something that you agreed – in a legally binding contract – you did not want to know under any circumstances. It's only as a mother that I'd feel an emotional need to give you what you want. As a doctor I'd tell you: no.'

'Okay then, stop being Dr Louise Nightingale. Be my mother,' Mei says.

'I'm not going to stop being either of them,' her mum says. 'As your mother – I feel that what's best is for you to come back and remove these traces. As a professional I *know* that's what's best.' She pauses, then says, softly, 'But it seems like you don't trust me.'

'I don't know what I think,' Mei says. 'I think, I wish you'd only ever been my mother. Not a doctor mother who prescribes me memory wipes – deletions, whatever – and antidepressants. I don't want –'

But she's started to cry, so she stops talking.

I've lost, she thinks.

'Plum,' her mum says. 'I love you. What I care about is *your* happiness. Don't you know that?'

'I suppose,' says Mei, wiping her nose.

'I can't talk about the procedure you had. But I can say that I could never have *prescribed* it to you. Could never, would never. Maybe I've given you advice – with your happiness in mind. And it's advice I gave a lot of thought to at the time, and stand by now. I did support your having the procedure. I still think it was done for good reason. The decision to have the procedure, though, was yours alone.'

Mei looks out at the skyscrapers of Kuala Lumpur, blurry in the fog.

She came here to make a getaway. A *bold move*. What a joke. She thought she'd leave her mother's house in London and everything would be different. But she's still there. Every morning she wakes up in her bed in London, seven years old, in wet sheets. She could dream about Amsterdam, maybe, but it's just a dream.

She thinks: none of my decisions are mine alone.

Not long after that, the message from Nepenthe arrives.

It's November.

Mei is walking through Crowshill, towards the clinic. It's only about ten minutes from the station. Which is good, because it's *cold*. An edge of frost scrapes her throat as she breathes. The light is brighter than in Kuala Lumpur, less hazy. It's strange and familiar at the same time. She passes a tall clock tower, a Tudor pub with black beams and white plaster, a few old trees with benches around their trunks and autumn-coloured leaves, mobile phone shops genteelly tucked away below the arches of an old-style new building.

Mei's mum used to live here, years ago. She shared a house with some other medical students because it was close to St Helier hospital. Back then, obviously, there was no Nepenthe. Mei googled the town before she came. Its Wikipedia page said that Crowshill used to be a dormitory town – or was, before the clinic arrived and it woke up.

Mei wonders where her mum lived; if Mei's walking, now, past her old house. She hasn't been able to ask her: the two of them haven't spoken since Mei told her mum that she understood her mum didn't want her to do this, but nonetheless (she actually said that, *nonetheless*), she was definitely going to get the memory back.

Mei's mum was shocked, again.

Mei wondered at how she could have gone through the first years of her life without shocking her mother once, but now it seemed like a daily event.

Look, Mei's mum said, eventually (once it had become apparent that she couldn't change Mei's mind). Plum, you came back from Amsterdam in a terrible state. You may not remember what happened on your holiday, but you know what happened after you got home. If you restore the memory, I'm afraid that you'll be back in that state. After you worked so hard to recover. I've seen it happen. A lot of the test subjects who underwent this procedure haven't done well. They fell back into the same kinds of problems you've had. Depression, addiction, serious self-esteem issues. It's why I argued against making these procedures available. I'm still against it. And now to think my own daughter –

She broke off.

Mei was horrified to realise that her mother was crying. Her mum *never* cried.

I'm sorry, Mei said.

I'm sorry, her mum replied. I didn't want to tell you that. Aside from anything else, it's professional misconduct. But there's a greater good here, Mei, and if it helps you decide what the best course is, I don't regret it.

Help, Mei thought.

Decide.

Best course.

There was something wrong with the words.

She thought about Armand in the restaurant, the jolt of the tilt of his head, his smile.

She thought about a motionless rat. Lying on its back, eyes closed, nose and whiskers pointed up to the sky.

She called her mum back.

I might not be like one of those people, she said.

People? What people? said her mother.

The ones who fell back into their old behaviours. The ones who couldn't cope. Maybe I could cope. I'm not a teenager any more.

No, said her mum. Of course not. But you *are* only twenty-one. And it's not about age, either. It's about what you're equipped for.

Equipped for? Mei said. (She was starting to feel angry.) You think I'm weak.

Not weak, said her mum. Sensitive. You have a history of finding it hard to cope.

Now who's constructing a narrative Lockean self for me? said Mei.

Don't be facetious, her mum said. I don't claim to know what the self is, but it's usually very predictable.

So, predictably sensitive, Mei said. In my case. Which really means predictably weak, even if you won't admit it.

Listen, her mum said, and now she sounded frustrated. There's nothing wrong with admitting vulnerability. With allowing yourself to be *helped*.

Help, Mei cried. I'm sick of that word. If I need so much help, why haven't you helped me better? If you can cure my bedwetting and my eye and my addictions, why can't you cure this? Why am I not equipped for this? You're the doctor. You're always telling me that the self isn't a fixed quantity. So why haven't you made me into the kind of self that's equipped to know its own history?

It's not like that, Mei.

Isn't it? Mei said. So is it maybe that I *am* equipped? And that maybe you'd rather I wasn't? I wonder if I'd have been so vulnerable and depressed if you hadn't been reminding me all my life how vulnerable and depressed I am. You know, I thought I was the problem. Maybe *you're* the problem.

That's absolutely – Mei's mum began to say.

Mei hung up on her.

It was the first time in her life that she'd hung up on her mother.

She was trembling. She realised she'd pulled all the sheets on her bed up around herself, plucking at them with her hands, tightening them. She kicked them away.

Her mother called back immediately. Mei put the phone on silent. Her mum called again, a few hours later. She left a voicemail saying that she respected Mei's wishes, and she wouldn't keep calling her, but she hoped Mei would call back, when she was ready to talk.

Yeah, and you'll be ready with some counter-reverse psychology hypnosis voodoo routine, said Mei to the voicemail. I don't think so.

She didn't call back.

Recalling that last conversation with her mum now, as she gets closer to the clinic, probably wasn't the smartest thing to do. The anxiety of that argument collides with the anxiety of the impending procedure. She feels squashed, slightly breathless, between them. The past is painful, the future is frightening. She wishes she could just keep walking up this hill forever, past the nice old houses, like that guy who had to roll the stone up a mountain, except in her case it wouldn't be a punishment but a reprieve.

But nobody answers her wish, and before she knows it she's at the gates, and there's a confusing melee of people with camping chairs and Thermos flasks and banners saying 'NOT IN OUR NAME' and 'LIARS' and 'DON'T FORGET JESUS'. Mei doesn't look at them. She walks straight through, up to the security guards. She shows them her passport; signs the logbook; stands still for a camera to scan her face.

'Don't do it!' someone shouts behind her.

'Shut up,' the security guard says to them. 'Sorry, Miss Lewarne. We get some fruit loops round here, as you can see. Now, if you'll please follow me to reception.'

'It's the internet,' Mei says. She laughs.

'Pardon?' says the guard.

'The internet, but in real life. I didn't really think about the internet people being real people. With Thermoses.'

'Real nuisances,' says the guard.

He takes her through the clinic grounds, which are peaceful, with grass in wide plush-looking stripes, neatly edged gravel and tall dark pine trees. In the distance a magpie is hopping across the bonnets of parked cars.

Inside the clinic, which is white and futuristic – as she must once have noticed before – she's left to wait in reception.

Mei looks around warily. She suspects that her mum is somewhere nearby, waiting to subdue Mei with study results and the power of suggestion, but after a while she realises that this is stupid. It doesn't make sense for Mei's mum to waylay her here. It would be totally unprofessional for a start. She could be sacked.

For some reason, the realisation that nobody is coming to stop her fills Mei with a sudden fright. She looks around again; there's a woman here now, standing near her.

'Hi, Miss Lewarne,' says the woman. She puts out her hand. Mei stands up and takes it. The woman has long greying hair in a plait and a friendly face. An emissary of Mei's mother? She can't be sure.

'I'm Karine,' says the woman. 'Can I call you Mei?'

'Yes,' Mei says.

'Lovely. Let me take you through to the treatment rooms, and we can have a chat about the procedure.'

Mei nods. She feels unexpectedly wobbly. Karine is walking slightly ahead, talking about what a bright day it is, and has Mei seen much of the town, and other things that are probably meant to be soothing and monotonous, and only when she gets Mei into the treatment room, sitting in a comfortable reclining chair, does she look at Mei's face and say, with surprise,

'Mei, what's wrong?'

'I've hurt my mum,' Mei says. (Does Karine know Louise is her mum? Probably not. Mei doesn't really care anyway.) 'But she hurt me first.'

Karine takes a pack of tissues out of her pocket and hands it to Mei.

'Go on,' she says.

'My dad texted me this morning,' Mei says. 'He just sent a smiley emoji. I don't know what that even means.'

'Does he struggle with emotional communication, generally?'

'Yes. But it's not that. He pretends to be really important and successful, he's like, this freelance consultant in something financial, but –'

She stops herself. She can't exactly say to Karine: *My dad lives in an apartment that's paid for by my mum, something he claims is just a tax thing he's helping her with, some way of avoiding tax, but actually it's more like she owns him, and he complains about her but he's also too scared of her to give any kind of opinion on anything to do with memory removal, even when his daughter is about to – possibly ill-advisedly, possibly not – get a memory restored.*

'– he's just a coward,' she says. 'He's still . . . Uh. I was going to say, he's still dependent on my mum even though they divorced years ago. But now I'm thinking, *I'm* exactly the same as him. I resent my mum. But I live off her money. And the last time I spoke to her I blamed her for all my problems – but I'm an adult now. I mean, I literally just said to her I was equipped to handle life without really believing that I was. But maybe I *am*. And I am responsible for my own problems. Though I am still angry with her. Yeah, I definitely am.'

'Okay,' says Karine. 'It sounds, Mei, like you're having some really important realisations right now. Do you want to delay the restoration procedure? Normally we have this kind of talk afterwards, but we can delay the procedure, and talk now. It's fine to do that. You don't have to have the procedure today, either. I know the paperwork you got sounds very strict about cancelling and rescheduling, but I personally don't think that's a very helpful approach. So. You tell me what you need, Mei. Your well-being is the key thing: we're here to support you.'

Mei laughs.

'Sorry,' she says. 'I'm not laughing at *you*. I just hear the words support and well-being so often that they don't sound like themselves to me. I think I need, like, a break from those words.'

'Fair enough,' says Karine. 'Consider them obliterated from the English language for now. I mean, they're sort of therapy *staples*, but, well, it's good to be professionally challenged. So. What would you like to do? You don't have to have the procedure now. Or ever, actually. It's completely up to you.'

She smiles at Mei, and Mei feels suddenly better. She says,

'I want my memory back.'

The actual restoring of the memory is nothing more than a nurse bringing in a tray holding a plastic cup half full of a bitter-tasting clear liquid, which Mei drinks, before Karine asks her some questions.

'We'll start with the coffee shop,' she says. 'Armand's. Have a think about it, see what comes up.'

And Mei thinks.

Mei, Katya and Sophia are sitting at one of the small tables outside Armand's. The late-morning sun reflects off the canal; a small dog goes by, riding on the roof of a boat.

They're all hung-over. Katya is wearing a pair of pink reflective sunglasses and says that if she takes just one bite of the pastry in front of her she's going to freaking vom. Sophia is silently getting through a large pile of frites with mayonnaise.

'Have you seen the barista?' Sophia says, when she's almost finished. 'He's hot. I can tell he has a huge cock.'

'How do you know?' Mei asks. 'He's wearing an apron.'

'Oh no,' Sophia says, waving her fork, 'looking at *out-lines*, that's entry-level shit. *I* can work out how big a guy is just from his behaviour.'

'What, like having to sit differently?' Katya asks.

'No, no, no. Listen. According to my research,' says Sophia, 'men who have big cocks are generally more chill. And those, like, attention-seeking, thirsty men usually have little ones.'

'Really,' says Katya flatly. She tends to be unconvinced by other people's theories.

'I'm telling you,' says Sophia. 'So far I've had a one hundred per cent successful prediction rate. It's a straight-up gift from God. I'm going to get that barista over here and prove – shhh.'

'Prove shhh?' says Katya. She and Mei look at Sophia. Sophia is looking over Katya's shoulder. Katya and Mei turn round to see that the barista has arrived, and has begun clearing the table next to them.

A silence descends as he piles cups and plates onto his tray. He wipes the table, moves the little vase with one tulip in it back into the centre, and goes back inside.

'Do you think he heard us?' hisses Katya.

'Probably not. But he totally saw you two spin round in your chairs and stare at him,' says Sophia. 'Though Mei here has already been staring at him like a two-year-old looking at an ice cream or something. So you've basically ruined *my* chances.'

Mei looks down, feeling self-conscious.

Mei's mum once said that she wasn't sure Sophia and Katya had Mei's best interests at heart. Mei denied that. She felt defensive of her friends. Against what, she doesn't know. Just a vague . . . sense. Mei once stayed out late with Katya and slept through a brunch date with her mum, and ever since then, whenever Katya's name is mentioned Louise's eyes narrow. It's probably not even measurable, this narrowing. But Mei can see it.

Anyway, now Mei's on holiday with her friends, she thinks her mum might – maybe – have had a point about best interests.

'You're a major bitch on a hangover,' Katya says to Sophia now. 'Come on, let's get out of here. I need a Bloody Mary.'

*

It's the next day.

It's nine o'clock, and the other two girls are too hungover to even make it out of the Airbnb. Mei's walking alongside a canal in the already hot sunshine, feeling part of things. She feels an energy rising up from the cobbled streets and the tall houses and the brilliant water, moving through her and out again, out into the world.

When Mei arrives at Armand's, this circling of enjoyment stops for a moment. She stands in the doorway, wondering what the hell she's up to. Then the guy from yesterday comes out of a door at the back of the cafe, carrying a sack of coffee beans.

He puts them down, straightens up and smiles at Mei.

His smile is a thing of beauty.

'You were here yesterday, weren't you?' the guy says. 'With your friends?'

'Yeah. They're still asleep,' she says. 'I thought I'd get breakfast.'

She wants to ask if he overheard their conversation yesterday, but she doesn't have the nerve, not yet.

'No problem. What can I get you?'

'One of those pastries. And a cappuccino. With a little jug of milk on the side, please.'

He laughs. 'Why the extra milk? Would you prefer a latte?'

'Cappuccino isn't milky enough. Latte is *too* milky.'

'Can I make a suggestion?' he asks.

(There's something intimate in his raised eyebrows. Mei leans in. She knows he's only going to make a suggestion regarding the coffee she's ordering. But still.)

'Have you tried a flat white?' he says.

'Never,' says Mei. 'But I'm on holiday. So. Why not?'

'Walking on the wild side,' the man says.

Does he mean to sound so warm, so – well – borderline *flirtatious*? Maybe he just has a warm face. Like a bottlenose dolphin. They could be really pissed off or sad or bored, but their faces are still saying, *I like you!*

'Did you, er, hear what we were talking about yesterday?' she asks the man. He's turned away to make the coffee.

'Penises?' he says, over his shoulder.

'Oh. Right. You did. Uh, sorry –'

'I didn't hear anything. That was just a guess. You're all females. You're in Amsterdam. You're worried I heard your conversation. Therefore I deduced you were talking about penises. There's no need to apologise for that. They're a perfectly normal everyday item.'

He turns round as he says this. He's wearing a neutral expression.

Mei has no idea what her own expression is. Probably not neutral.

She wants to look around to see if anyone else in the cafe has heard this – like the girl who works there and is right now only a few feet away toasting some sandwiches under a grill, but this would mark her out as even more unworldly. She laughs, embarrassed for being silly about penises.

'Maybe to you,' she says.

The man acknowledges this with a genial shrug. 'Here's your flat white,' he says. 'I find it funny that, as what – a Gen Z? A millennial? – you've never had one of these before.'

'Millennial. I'm not a very good one,' Mei says. 'Unless by millennial you mean a thousand years old. Sometimes I feel like that.'

He laughs.

'Only young people say those kinds of things.'

'You're not old either,' she says. 'You're a millennial too, technically.'

'I reject that category,' says the man.

'Well, you know what a flat white is,' says Mei. 'So.'

The man laughs. She feels a rush of success. It urges her on, to say, 'Do you have a break coming up?'

'It's my cafe,' the man says. 'So, yes, a break is a possibility.'

'*You're* Armand?'

'I am. Pleased to meet you.' He holds out his hand for her to shake, over the counter. The way he is looking at Mei makes her nervous and confident, light and steely, like an arrow flying right towards its target.

'I'm Mei,' she says. 'So, when you finish, could I buy you a drink?'

'Was it okay?' Mei asks Armand. 'You taking the afternoon off?'

She doesn't really care if it was okay or not. She just needed to hear her own voice, proving her own existence in this exact moment, walking with Armand along the street, in the dark, purplish-blue night, the tables outside the restaurants and cafes taken away, the pavements almost empty, all the flowers folded up. The last bar they were in closed without them noticing. She was enjoying talking to Armand; conversation that didn't stumble or hiccup or just keel over and *die* the way it tended to with Mei and men her own age.

Now they are walking, apparently aimlessly. Mei's having fun, but she's also worried that at any moment Armand is going to say, *It's time I went to bed*, and not add anything clichéd but also exciting, like: *Want to join me?*

'Margreet understood. Did your friends mind *you* taking the day off?' he asks.

'They're probably stoned by now,' she says. 'And also they're quite self-absorbed. They won't miss me.'

'Then you don't need to go back yet?' he says. 'There's another bar round the corner. It's open until four.'

'Why not?' Mei says.

They go into the bar, which is lit up with hanging strings of lights. Mei, having been prevented from paying all night, insists on buying the drinks. Her card is promptly declined. Then, intensely embarrassed, she has to ask Armand to pay while she texts her mum to ask if she can transfer over an advance on her allowance. She tries not to let him work out what she's doing, but he guesses anyway.

'You haven't mentioned your parents,' he says. 'But I see they're good to you.'

'Hm,' Mei says, at the thought of them. Then she thinks she must sound ungrateful. 'I love my parents,' she adds, 'and they're generous – of course – but they're also kind of . . . I don't know. They're pretty big personalities, in different ways. I sometimes wonder if there's enough personality space left for me. I can't say that though or my mum will probably tell me that there's, like, no such thing as personality or whatever.'

'An interesting theory,' Armand says.

'Oh, if you're pro-Hume and anti-Locke I'm sure you'd find her very interesting,' Mei says. She's drunk. She can feel it. The alcohol wants her to embark on a long monologue about her parents. *Nope*, she tells herself. She will *not* be doing that. Armand already thinks she's much younger than him – even though he's not even thirty yet, and she's almost twenty – and whining about her parents will make her look even more like a sulky kid.

'I don't disagree with her,' Armand says. 'But I think she left out the good bits. Like Sartre. I mean, if there's no such thing as an essential self, then it's all a matter of choice. Nothing and everything. You know?'

He leans back in his chair. Mei can see the shoulder muscles shift and resettle under his T-shirt. She looks at them, then thinks *Two-year-old! Ice cream!* and quickly looks away.

'That's true,' she says. 'I like Sartre. I just wish I could *feel* that way, instead of agreeing with him rationally. My mum – argh. I don't want to talk about parents,' Mei says. She taps the table. 'This is officially parent-free space. A safe space. That's a millennial joke, by the way.'

The joke obviously wasn't very good, because Armand looks serious. Then he says, 'I *am* a parent. I have a two-year-old daughter. Emilie. I'm not living with Emilie's mother – Melanie – at the moment. But we're still married. We're . . . going through some things.'

Mei is too taken aback to think. She says quietly, 'What things?'

'Well, when we had Emilie, it was, uh, not intentional. We were talking about breaking up actually. But Melanie wanted to have the baby, and we loved each other, despite our differences. A lot of differences. But we decided to try to resolve them and become a family. That hasn't worked very well. So we're separated at the moment. We're meant to be thinking about what we want.'

Mei didn't realise exactly how much she liked Armand until he says this, the word *married*, at which point her stomach contracts, like a snail trying to pull itself back into its shell. She wraps her arms around her abdomen.

'We agreed we would still . . . meet other people,' Armand says. 'But I know, also, that other people might not like being *other people*. Which is why I thought – without making any assumptions – I'd mention it now.'

He likes me is one of Mei's thoughts.

He's a married father is the other.

The two thoughts make her feel both euphoric and crushingly disappointed, almost at the same time. Then both feelings merge, and she feels only blankness. She wonders what difference the news really makes. What is this, if not a holiday romance? And what does it matter if the subject of her holiday romance has a wife and child she'll never meet?

Still, the blankness persists.

'It's late,' she says. 'I think I should probably go.'

'Oh – of course,' Armand says. He sounds sad, and polite. 'I completely understand. I'll call you a taxi.'

'Thank you,' she says.

He nods, almost a bow. Mei feels, suddenly like crying.

You will *not* cry in front of him, she tells herself. *You will not.*

And it actually works. It's not until she's alone in the taxi that she does cry, travelling down the tear-smeared street past the people talking and laughing outside night-clubs and sex clubs, enjoying their adult fun – because she's a child, so painfully and obviously so, because only a child would feel so hopeful – over nothing – then cry, when it doesn't get what it wants.

The next day.

The coffee house.

Mei is waiting outside, a little way down the street, leaning against some railings. Margreet is putting out the tables and chairs. The early-morning sunlight slants the shadows of the flowers across the tabletops.

Mei wonders if maybe Armand isn't coming in today. She chips at the railings nervously with her fingernails; realises she's touching someone's old chewing gum; retracts her hand sharply.

Then Armand walks up to the cafe.

'*Margreet! Goedemorgen,*' he says. Then he looks over, and sees Mei.

She takes her sunglasses off and waves at him. He laughs.

'*Een minuut,*' Armand says to Margreet.

The two of them, Mei and Armand, are on the balcony of Armand's apartment. From here they can see rooftops, domes and spires, trees, parks, other people on other balconies. On the opposite side of the river some people on a moored-up canal boat are making breakfast, the smoke from their stove rising up against a row of tall houses, red, brown and orange.

Shoulder to shoulder, thinks Mei.

She herself is standing shoulder to shoulder with Armand, a skin contact that would have seemed like the most sexually exciting thing to have ever happened to Mei so far in her life had she not had sex with Armand just half an hour ago. Even so, the touch energises her. She imagines that she can feel each small hair of his arm scraping lightly against her own skin. She looks at her own arm next to his, as small and pale as a peeled twig. She smiles.

She says, 'I was just thinking about when I was a kid and I used to sit in the garden doing things like peeling all the bark off twigs, or opening up conkers, and separating them into piles. I used to do it for hours. My dad had a joke that it was the Chinese in me, you know, like I was biologically predisposed for factory work. My mum didn't like that joke.'

'I can imagine not.'

'Yeah, well, she just watched me and made notes in case I was autistic or something.'

Armand laughs. His own parents – one French, one Mauritian – live in the suburbs of Paris. They're nice people. They call him every Sunday, and tell him all the news from the neighbourhood. They don't ask how he is: they assume he's doing brilliantly.

'Do you know anything about your birth parents?' he asks.

'No. Mum says they were untraceable. I don't know anything about them.'

'I can't imagine giving a child up,' Armand says. 'Their lives must have been pretty desperate.'

'Or they're both dead,' Mei says. But she realises how unlikely that is, as she says it. That all her family in China are dead. She hasn't ever liked to think much about the existence of her real parents. Thinking about it now isn't a good feeling.

'I actually don't want to talk about my parents,' Mei says. 'Birth or adoptive. I'm in a different country and I'm still talking about them. Though maybe if I could stay here for longer I'd run out of things to say, and that would be it. I'd finally be my own person.'

'I know what you mean,' Armand says. 'That's partly why I came here from France. Though Melanie wants to go back, now.'

Mei hasn't got used to him saying *Melanie* yet. If she had the choice it would be on her list of banned words. Along with *married*. She doesn't know what to say, and there's a short silence. Armand turns to look at her.

'Is it okay, me talking about her?' he says. He rubs his hair, grimacing. 'I'm sorry. I've made you uncomfortable. I shouldn't have mentioned it. I just . . . I don't really know what I'm doing. This is the first time anything like this has happened since, well.'

'What?' Mei says, delighted and relieved. 'I had no idea.'

'God,' he says. He puts his face in his hands 'I must seem so old and complicated. This is probably one of many casual things for you, and I'm overthinking it and ruining it.'

Mei starts to laugh. 'One of many adventures,' she says.

In fact Mei has only slept with one person before Armand, and she's not even sure it counted. It was literally three weeks ago. She went on a date with a guy from her course, they had too much sangria at the tapas restaurant, then they slept together. He came when he was halfway inside her. She meant to google *Am I half a virgin?* and then forgot, and anyway it's a moot point now. It didn't feel like it could even share a category with what she and Armand have just done.

'That came out wrong,' Armand says. 'I didn't mean – I wasn't bringing up *numbers* or anything. I celebrate whatever you choose to do in bed, with whomever you choose to do it, whenever you choose to do it.'

Mei smiles to herself. She can smell his fading aftershave, skin-in-sun scent. She breathes it in, picturing it making its way into her lungs, her blood, the centre of her body, setting off an answering hum, a tiny shout from each cell, then down, where it collects, focuses, *sharpens*.

She likes the way he says *in bed*.

'Well, the first thing is sex,' she says – giving it emphasis: *sex*, loitering exquisitely on her tongue – 'and the second thing is *you*, and the third is *now*, if you're up to it.'

'Up to it?'

'Given your advanced age, I mean. I wouldn't want to kill you.'

They're both laughing now. He catches at her hips, but she dodges, running back inside. He comes after her, then he pauses, goes back, and draws the blinds. She lies on the bed watching the lines of sunlight narrow, burning at the edges of each long slat.

Later, she thinks, they'll get up and go out into that sun for some lunch.

After that, she doesn't know.

*

286

Mei goes back to Armand's apartment the next day.

'What did you tell your friends?' he asks, as they're lying in bed. 'Where do they think you are?'

'Right now they think I'm at Anne Frank's house,' Mei says.

'And yesterday?'

'The Rijksmuseum.' She laughs.

'What if they'd wanted to go with you?' he asks.

'I know them,' she says. 'They told me they'd meet me at a bar when I was done.'

'You seem different from them,' Armand says. 'But you all went on holiday together?'

'I know,' Mei says. 'We don't really have a deep connection. But I never expected connection. I thought I'd never really connect with anybody, because there was something kind of . . . wrong, with me. And so the best thing I could do was try to fit in with the normal people that showed an interest in me. But now, I wonder if I *can* connect with people, and I just chose the wrong friends.'

'That sounds more likely,' Armand says. He kisses her neck. 'There's nothing wrong with you.'

'I don't know about that,' Mei says. She looks out at the houses beyond his window, lit up by the sunshine. 'I feel like my life this far has just been waiting for a big moment, you know? A bold move. Except it's got to the point where anything would feel like too much pressure. My bold move. It's hard to do.'

'Well, bold moves aren't such a big deal. Almost as soon as you've made one, it doesn't feel bold any more.'

'Then what?'

'Then you look around for the next bold move.'

'That sounds depressing,' Mei says.

'Does it?' says Armand. He laughs. 'I think it's rather beautiful. Maybe I didn't explain it very well.'

Mei says, 'You know, I think *this* is what my bold move should be. Living in another country. I could just pack all my things and go somewhere totally new. If only there wasn't such a thing as real life.'

'Fuck real life,' Armand says. 'You're on holiday, remember. Real life is a dirty word.'

Mei smiles – but the words are here now, in her head. *Real life*. A world Mei has to rejoin in one day, seven hours and twenty-six minutes, when her flight leaves.

'It was totally freaking gross,' Katya says to Mei, on the plane. She has to lean across Sophia to continue, in a lower voice: 'I almost got hit by semen. I think the guy did it on purpose. Sophia didn't see any of it because she was covering her eyes.'

'It was too real,' Sophia said.

'And then they said no mobile phones allowed,' Katya says to Mei. 'So we were like, fuck this.'

'So you were probably the smart one getting an early night and going to the art gallery or wherever,' Sophia says to Mei.

'Though you could have let us know,' Katya says. 'You did kind of ditch us, Mei.'

'Sorry,' says Mei.

The other two fall asleep in their headphones, and Mei puts on a film on her iPad, which plays through without her noticing.

She said goodbye to Armand yesterday.

What else was she going to do? They'd talked about it and they couldn't think of anything. Mei is a student, in the UK. Armand is a married father, in Amsterdam. That's it. It's over.

Credits roll on the screen in front of her. The plane is coming in to land. Katya and Sophia are stirring. Mei wipes her eyes, trying not to let them see. Though if they did notice, it wouldn't matter. People cry at the endings of films, all the time. Then the film ends, and they go back to their real lives.

Mei goes back to her real life.

Unfortunately, though, everything in her life is exactly the same as how she left it – the arrangement of philosophy books on her shelf in halls, her favourite carrel in the library with the view of the chestnut tree, happy-hour shots at the student bar, the picture of Mei and her mum and her dad in Paris, the gold bracelet she got for her eighteenth birthday, with a specially made diamond-covered plum hanging from it, the revolving nightlight of cut-out birds – all of that seems different. Like it's only surfaces, with nothing underneath – nothing that could give her any pleasure.

A week or so after she gets home, she skips a visit to her mum, because she can't be bothered to get out of bed. This isn't a good idea. Mei's mum immediately calls her, and asks if Mei's okay.

'I'm fine,' Mei says defensively.

Her mum observes that Mei sounds defensive.

'I'm not defensive,' Mei says. 'In fact there's nothing wrong with me at all.' It doesn't sound convincing.

'What? Well, of course there isn't, Plum,' her mum says. She sounds much more sincere than Mei does.

Tears come to Mei's eyes. *What am I doing?* she thinks. Starting a fight? This is unlike her. But then she wonders what is and isn't like her. Who decided that anyway?

'Why did my parents give me up?' Mei asks. It comes out loud, sudden. 'Do you know?'

There's a pause so long that Mei checks the mobile screen. The call is still connected. She puts the phone back to her ear.

'What?' Mei's mum says. 'Your . . . *parents?*'

She's so startled that she's almost inaudible. Mei feels startled by herself.

'You must know something about them,' she says.

'Plum. *We're* your parents,' Mei's mum says. 'Where is this coming from? Do you really want to know about them? When we've discussed genes –'

Mei feels angry at that.

'You've kept it from me,' she says. 'You do know something. I can tell. You can tell when I'm lying, but I can tell when you're lying too.'

'Why do you want to know about them? What would you do – look for them?'

'Maybe,' Mei says. She has no idea. 'I *could* do that.'

'I don't think that's a good idea.' Her mum speaks very gently, but there's something pushing at her voice from beneath, something less calm.

'That's my decision,' Mei says. 'I decide if it's a good idea!'

'Are we not enough for you?' her mum asks. Now she sounds upset. 'I don't understand, Mei. Are you angry at us – at me – about something?'

'No.'

'But you sound angry. What happened on this holiday? You've been avoiding my calls since you got back. Did something bad happen? You can tell –'

'No,' Mei interrupts. 'Good things happened. I met someone, actually, and he asked me about my birth parents. And he said Sartre says –'

'Sartre?' her mum says. 'Asked you about your . . . Who is this person?'

Mei is about to say, Armand, and he's not *this* person, he's the best person I've ever met, but something in the way her mum's tone slows, becoming more considered, keeps her quiet. She can almost feel her mum's eyes, doing their imperceptible narrowing. She has the sense of threat – to Armand, or maybe just the idea of him, the part of herself that's been changed by that idea.

'Just a holiday romance,' she says.

'Plum,' her mum says gently. No – deliberately gently. Mei can hear the strain. 'I don't understand. Why do you want to look for people you don't know, when you know you won't find anything good?'

'But I *don't* know!' Mei cries. 'Why don't you tell me what I'd find? Why are you treating me like a child? You keep things from me. You watch me all the time. Because you don't trust me to cope with stuff on my own. You've made me feel my whole life that there's something wrong with me, I'm not strong enough or whatever. And now I think that actually I *am* okay. I don't need you to look after me. But *you* don't believe that.'

'That's incredibly unfair,' her mum says. She's not gentle now: she sounds clipped, angry. 'You don't want to be treated like a child? Attacking me like this is childish. You –'

'Stop talking about *me*! You can't take any criticism, so you're analysing me. I should analyse you! Why don't you want me to meet my other mother? Because she's poor? Maybe she's not as clever as you! You sneer at stupid people. Yes, you do! I've always been worried that I'm not clever enough for you. Maybe life would be nicer with my stupid, poor mum. She wouldn't be so judgemental and hard to please and, and *controlling*.'

'Yes,' her mum snaps, 'Drug addicts with mental health issues *do* tend to be less controlling. That's why she left you in a railway station.'

There's a silence.

'What?' says Mei.

Her mum draws her breath in. Mei hears it. Louise is trying to calm herself, and then she's going to calm Mei, tell Mei that she's sorry, she hears her; she'll say things like *communication*, *understanding*, *acceptance*, until everything's back to normal.

'Plum,' her mum says, 'I'm sorry. I shouldn't have –'

'So that's my real mother,' Mei says. 'What about my real dad?'

'I don't know. Your birth mother didn't know,' her mum says. 'Mei, I'm sorry.'

And Mei, for the first time ever, hangs up on her mother.

A month later. Mei's missed most of her lectures. She's fucked up one essay, and not handed in a few others. She was meant to be meeting her personal tutor about that, and she couldn't bring herself to go. She's not talking to her mum. There's an exam next week she hasn't prepared for, and she's supposed to be handing in her dissertation a couple of weeks after that.

She feels numb. The buoyancy she felt with Armand, talking about bold moves and connections and choice, feels like a long time ago. Those conversations feel like a joke – a tired, lame old joke. Every now and again something will penetrate her numbness, like treading on a pin. Revelations, but not the kind she'd hoped for. *I'm pathetic*, she realises. *I'm weak. My mother pities me. I can't help but fail. My friends are repelled by me. I'm genetically doomed.*

She looks in a mirror after a night of bad sleep and despises her own flaccid face, her skin as pale and shiny as raw fish, her uncertain mouth, her unwashed hair.

Is this what *she* looked like? she wonders.

How much of me is her?

Mei's personal tutor warns Mei she's at risk of being thrown off her course. At that point, the numbness goes away, and when the cloud clears every nerve in Mei's body is exposed, alive and singing with simple panic.

She gets some modafinil from Sophia: to catch up, the way everyone does, telling herself that by doing this she will also demonstrate that she's *not* like her real mother, she's not weak, or unstable, or predisposed to addiction, but it turns out she's wrong about all of it, and she can't stop taking the modafinil, the way everyone else stops – or stop taking the Xanax either, and before long she's failed, failed everything.

Just like her, she thinks, *just like her, just like her, just like her*. She sits on the floor of her room, out of pills, her face against the wall. The thoughts circle; draw in; pull tight.

She leaves university and travels back to her mum's house; her mum driving, Mei silent, everything in boxes in the back seat – the books and the bracelet and the nightlight – and when they pull up her mum just looks at her, sadly, and Mei, who didn't want to cry, cries after all.

'My darling Plum,' Mei's mum says, holding her hand tightly.

They don't say anything more that day.

It's the next morning, over fresh pancakes with caramel sauce, made by Mei's mum (which, in retrospect, should have been a warning sign), that Mei tells her mum about Amsterdam. Afterwards, Mei's mum presents her plan. Which is: to wipe the entire memory of the holiday.

Mei's horrified at first. She'd actually considered a wipe herself, crying at night and then punching her soggy pillow, in frustration at her own stupid crying, her inability to cope. But she doesn't think the holiday itself is the problem. It was just the start of it. The first domino in the series, a domino that was always going to fall one day, because Mei is really the daughter of someone profoundly, intrinsically damaged, and she's damaged in the same way.

'Failing was my fault,' she says. 'My birth mother –'

'I hear what you're saying,' says Mei's mum quickly. 'And I understand why you're taking that line of thought. Your behaviour was self-destructive, yes. You spiralled.

But there was a triggering event. Something you shouldn't have been exposed to. You're so young. You're vulnerable. And this older man saw it and exploited that.'

'Armand? But I . . . *wanted* that to happen,' Mei says.

'I know,' her mum says. 'Young people in your position often feel complicit. You feel like you invited this attention. You had a perfectly normal attraction to an older man – and it should have remained just that, but he took advantage of the situation. He destabilised your perception of yourself by questioning your origins. He impressed you with his superior knowledge, Sartre and so on. These are the first things predatory men do. He manipulated you, and you convinced yourself that this was what you wanted.'

'But it *is* what I wanted,' says Mei. 'I was happy.'

'Are you happy now?' says her mum.

Mei pushes her plate away. She stares out of the window at the garden.

'Do you feel good?' her mum asks.

Mei shakes her head.

'That's your own intuition telling you this wasn't right,' says her mum. 'And this is why I think a deletion is a good idea under the circumstances. This isn't just one of those things you go through as a teenager. This isn't acne, or your prom date standing you up. This was an imbalance of power. An abuse.'

The word *abuse* startles Mei.

'You never met Armand,' she says. 'He isn't like that.'

'So you say,' her mum says. 'What is he like? A married man, I know that. Did he tell you he didn't love his wife any more?'

Mei shakes her head. The garden wobbles in her vision.

'Well, I suppose he was honest,' her mum says. 'That's one thing in his favour. So, if you were to go back to Amsterdam, get into university there, and then call him . . .'

(Mei's secret hope. Said out loud. It sounds pathetic.)

'. . . what do you think he would do?' continues her mother. 'Would he leave his wife? Invite you to move in with him. The two of you would raise his child together?'

Mei's rigid gaze buckles, slips off the blurred shapes of the garden, down into her lap. Tears follow behind it, specking her jeans.

'Plum,' her mum says. 'My beautiful Plum.'

She comes to Mei's side of the table and puts her arms around her. Mei smells her mother's perfume, that rich amber smell. Her mum's worn the same perfume for as long as she can remember. Mei could be fifteen, ten – a seven-year-old again, watching her nightlight revolve beside the bed.

Her mum moves away; she gets a tissue out of her bag. Mei sees there are tears in her eyes too.

'I'm sorry,' Mei says. 'I've upset you. The things I said –'

'Don't think of it. Don't apologise,' her mum says. 'It's hard to see you unhappy, that's all.'

Unhappy, Mei thinks. It's not a word she's applied to her situation. She's only used words like *stupid, fucked up, pathetic, useless.*

Unhappy, somehow, opens a door. Mei puts her head in her hands and sobs. She doesn't try to stop herself, or even cry quietly. Her mum moves close to her, and strokes her hair.

Through her crying Mei can hear her mum talking gently, about how Mei can draw a line under this last year of university. Money's not a problem. She can take some time off, reapply to other, better universities. They'd be glad to have her. And that traumatic situation in Amsterdam could be made to go away, completely.

'Think about it,' says her mum.

'Do things connected to the holiday also get deleted?' Mei asks.

Her mum hesitates. She looks slightly wary. 'Yes,' she says.

'So when we, uh, argued, and I talked about Armand . . .'

'That conversation would be erased,' says her mum. 'All the conversations about him would be erased. Which is why it's important to do this soon, so you don't lose any more than necessary.'

Mei thinks about her birth mother. She'll forget who she was. She wonders if her mum is thinking the same thing. *Was* thinking the same thing. Her mum has always known what Mei thinks before Mei thinks it.

'What are you feeling?' her mum asks gently.

Mei – wet and muffled – says something like, shouldn't she be learning from the past? (But her heart's not in it. Which means her mum can tell her heart's not in it.)

Her mum strokes Mei's hair. 'This was exceptional circumstances,' she says. 'You weren't at fault: you were a victim. You've had experiences you weren't ready for. Knowledge that you weren't ready for. I believe in learning lessons, but this is too much, too soon. You don't need traumatic memories pulling you back. They aren't helpful, they aren't instructive. You can let them go. Start again, gradually. We work on the depression, give you a chance to build up your confidence and self-esteem. And *then* you get back out there. A fresh start. How does that sound?'

Oscar

'You just put your hands round my neck,' Jess says.

'What if I get too excited and accidentally squeeze?'

'That's kind of the point. If you squeeze too hard I'll elbow you in the ribs or something, don't worry.'

'Hmm.'

'Oh, come on. It's a real high. I can show you if you want. Then you'll get it. You'd have to take off your necklace . . . what is that anyway? Is it teeth?'

'I'm not sure.'

'It's probably teeth from girls you've murdered,' she says cheerfully.

'Ha,' says Oscar uneasily.

He wonders: does Jess *sense* something in him? She isn't the first to see dark things in Oscar. One girl had a theory that he was a sociopath, because of his inability to form meaningful relationships. And she was proved right, maybe, because he never formed one with her. Not that she actually seemed to mind him being a sociopath. In fact, just after she'd said it they had urgent, rushed sex; not so much sex as a collision, a car accident in which nobody wants to admit responsibility, and afterwards nobody looks anyone else in the eye.

Sometimes Oscar thinks he attracts the wrong kind of girls.

Afterwards, Oscar went online and did a test to find out if he was a sociopath. He failed the test: apparently he had too much empathy. He didn't know how to charm, either – let alone how to turn it on and off. And he didn't *do* anything, so he couldn't answer yes when he was asked 'Do you believe you're the best at what you do?' All in all, the only psychopathic tendency he had was to get in trouble with the law. Another friend had once speculated that Oscar was autistic, but when Oscar did some 'Are you autistic?' quizzes, he wasn't on that spectrum, either.

An Australian girl he dated once probably came closest to a diagnosis. She said Oscar didn't talk about anything real. She said, You ask about *me*, right, and I talk about work and what I did today, and people I know. If I know someone really well, I talk about my family and school and exes and stuff. If I know them even better, I start talking about what kind of future we might want. Like, *together*. But I ask about you and I get nothing. You talk about, I dunno, monkeys in space, and what's your favourite type of river, and Occam's razor and Russell's teapot and what if Chekhov's gun shot Schrödinger's cat, and the world's longest beard. It's just all so fucking *whimsical*.

Oscar was interested.

The world's longest beard? I said that? How long was it?

It's just an example. You're lucky you're so fucking beautiful. Or this wouldn't be cute. It'd get really. Bloody. Irritating.

(The way she said it made it sound like she was a bit irritated already.)

Another time, near the end, she said: Hanging out with you, Oscar, is like being stuck in some abstract painting. All swirls and no actual bloody picture.

(Like a Mandelbrot set? Oscar almost said, then thought better of it.)

But that's it. Nobody has ever been able to put their finger on what's wrong with Oscar, because the wrongness comes not from a nameable thing, but an absence of any nameable things, a swirling of *not a lot*, circling a core of nothing at all.

'Oscar?' says Jess. 'Hello? You vanished.'

'Sorry,' Oscar says.

'You looked really weird, actually. Is everything okay?'

'Totally fine,' he says. 'Sorry.'

'Fair enough,' says Jess, dropping the subject. She drops it so quickly that he wonders if she's really one of them. A double agent. But probably a double agent wouldn't keep encouraging him to strangle her.

Jess, apparently abandoning the idea of having sex with Oscar, lies back on the bed now and sighs. 'Anya's being so ridiculous,' she says.

'In what way?' he asks.

Jess embarks on some complicated backstory about a love triangle between her friends. Names she has mentioned before crop up again, and Oscar can't place who they belong to. He topples gently backwards onto the bed next to her.

'Sorry. This is boring,' Jess says.

'No. I'm listening.'

He *is* listening. He envies Jess just for having a story like this to tell. Envies Atticus, too. You can't have a fall out without having a friend; you can't have family problems

301

without having a family. There's closeness there, even if it's angry and messed up. Real people have arguments, resentments, which may or may not be forgiven. They get so close to other people that they can hate them *and* love them at the same time.

Oscar can't imagine what that feels like. He hates nobody. He loves nobody. There are people he likes, lots of them. People he feels guilty about. More of them. People he's frightened of. The men wearing suits. He doesn't know how many of them there are.

Confidential, was what they said, in that meeting years ago. The terms of the money are confidential.

The man who said he was representing Oscar's interests (Oscar had never seen this man before in his life) told him to accept the money. He said it was the best thing for Oscar.

They talked about Oscar while Oscar was still in the room.

He understands what this means, right?

I understand that I have suffered brain damage as the result of an incident I can't remember and as a result my long-term memory has been affected which is why I am being given money but I have to keep this money secret, Oscar said loudly. Or else.

Well – said someone.

He gets it, said someone else. Let's move on.

Now, Oscar didn't know exactly what was going on, but he wasn't a total moron. He could tell when people were lying, for a start. He could also see that everyone in the room wanted the same thing: for Oscar to take the secret money. Oscar was the only one who was unconvinced. He was also outnumbered.

There seemed like only one sensible course of action.

Oscar agreed with everything they said. Then he left the room, went straight to the station and got on the next train. And since then he'd done nothing to draw attention to himself, kept out of trouble, kept the secret; moving all the time, from country to country – at least until the day he got cocky and stayed in a fancy hotel and they came for him again.

Oscar can only guess they want to haul him off to that room he remembers, to the white light, white coat hanging on the door, the fake leather reclining chair with its creaky plastic cover.

Oscar doesn't think so.
Thanks all the same, but no.
Fuck *that*.

Oscar's been staying at Jess's riad for a few days now. There's been no sign that anyone's tracked him here, no phone calls, no men in suits, no letters, and so he's whistling as he heads out to meet Jess, who's been shopping all day and now wants to get a cocktail; crossing the central court-yard of the riad; nearly tripping over the house tortoises. One of them is butting the other. It takes a step back, tucks its head in, then lunges. There is a dull, emphatic clunk.

'What's going on?' Oscar asks a passing doorman. 'They were friends yesterday. What even makes a tortoise angry?'

'They are not angry. They are about to . . . make love.'

'Wow,' Oscar says.

He thinks he ought to remember this, so he can tell Jess that she has the sexual peccadillos of a female tortoise. He's turning to go when he hears, from the riad manager's office:

'Is there an Oscar Levy staying here?'

He looks through the doorway at the back of a man's head. He doesn't recognise it, though that doesn't mean anything. Beyond that is the manager's head, face on. The manager looks up, over the man's shoulder; catches sight of Oscar.

Oscar turns and runs.

He hurries through the front door of the riad behind another couple, nearly crashing into them, shouting an apology to the startled doorman, running, without looking back, straight into the medina. Once he's far enough away he keeps walking, for hours, never entirely sure whether he's losing his pursuer, or circling closer and closer towards him.

At some point, thinks Oscar, he's going to look back and think it's funny that his life was once saved by two tortoises having sex.

The tortoises remind him of Jess. He was supposed to be meeting her at some bar, however long ago. He doesn't know the time: his phone's out of power, and he has no charger. The sky has turned a dark purple. The minaret is unhelpfully silent. He asks a kid the time and he says he'll tell Oscar for 10 dirhams, 5 dirhams, 2 dirhams, but Oscar doesn't have any change.

He keeps walking.

Night falls.

After a while, exhausted, Oscar sits down on a bench in one of the parks just outside the medina walls, in the dingy not-quite-light before the dawn.

The park is as green as it gets here. Scuffed grass dotted with orange trees. A stray dog trots over and collapses with a sigh by his feet. Like it's Oscar's own dog, come to find him. It's sandy-coloured, with a black muzzle. He wishes he could take it with him, but a stray dog can't adopt another stray dog. A home-owning creature is needed, one that can fill out paperwork.

Time passes. The sun comes up in a splodge of orange and gold. The minaret starts up. The dog gets up and lopes away, to start its working day.

Oscar walks back into the medina, to the main square. It's empty; just a few cars, people unloading crates. He's used to walking through and having fifty people shouting at him. It was reassuring. If Oscar didn't exist, he couldn't be asked to sample some lamb. If he didn't have a body, he wouldn't be offered a seat. If he didn't have a future, nobody would offer to tell it to him. *Oscar!* the people cried. *You're alive! We see you!*

Now, in the middle of the city, Oscar misses the city. He misses himself being in it. He's here, but not as a real person. His presence is basically a haunting. He realises Atticus wasn't a ghost: Oscar was the ghost all along. That'd be a good twist. Though he can't help but feel he's seen it somewhere before.

I hate nobody, he thinks. *I love nobody.*

What kind of human is that?

He walks to the taxi ranks, and asks to go to the airport. The driver, comfortingly, recognises him as a person, and promptly overcharges him. Oscar gets into the car and sits back against the cracked leather interior. He opens both of his windows, so that the gritty air currents can flow over him. He notes that the doors are unlocked. He tries not to feel trapped.

He was trapped before, once, maybe other times. He'd shouted for them to let him out. It didn't work. Nobody came and opened the door. Why would they? He can't think of any real-life story or film situation where someone locked up managed to get out by shouting. But he couldn't stop. He shouted until his voice burned out.

Why am I here?

What are you doing to me?

Let me out!

At length they answered:

We're helping you.

Which is what nobody good ever said in any film, ever.

Oscar has to wait a few hours at Marrakech airport before he can get on a flight. He buys a Fanta and a charger for his phone, finds a small table near a power socket, plugs the phone in, sits down to wait in the undercooked fluorescent lighting that colours everything dirty yellow.

He wants to say goodbye to Jess, and thank her, if thanking her wouldn't seem weird. She never seemed to mind if Oscar didn't say anything substantial, which was nice because she was clever (he'd seen her reading *Infinite Jest*) and she had a lot of political opinions which she threw at him from time to time, as if expecting some sort of quick-fire volleyball debate, but it all landed short: thud, thud, thud. The most interesting thing he's ever had to tell her is that she's like a tortoise in bed, for fuck's sake.

She deserves a decent goodbye.

The phone turns on, at last. Texts from Jess appear:

At the bar. Want me to order you something?

Hey, everything ok?

Where are you?

Ok, I'm getting worried now. Where are you?

I'm back at the riad. Text me and let me know if you're dead or something. If you're not dead, don't bother coming to my room later. I'll be asleep.

He texts her instead, to say sorry and goodbye.

She doesn't reply.

Oscar's only ever told one person about the extent of his memory problem: his old flat-mate Karolina, from Budapest.

What have I got? Oscar said to her, once. Nothing. No memory, so nothing.

Karolina thought about it for a bit. Then she said, I don't think you need memory. You *do* have a past. You have influences. Whatever happened, happened, whether or not you remember it. Just because you can't remember the ingredients, it doesn't mean you're not a cake.

It's kind of weird not knowing what flavour cake I am.

But you *do*. I know, and I've only known you six months. You like being in the sunshine, right? You worry about animals going hungry. You're often late. You're kind. That's more than just momentary stuff. Those are traits. Is that the right word?

Don't ask me, Oscar said. I'm shit with words.

That's just memory again, she said. It's not important.

Yeah, said Oscar. Fuck memory. Who needs it?

And he agrees with her, up to a point. He does feel as if he knows things about himself. But because he's not sure if he was any of these things *before*, these traits don't reassure him. He doesn't know how long he's had them, or where they came from, or if they'll persist. And there are things he does remember, partly, and these things seem to contradict the traits he's got now. Like, for example, he isn't really tempted by drugs. But he knows he had a heroin problem in his late teens, early twenties. Where did that go? How does an opiate addiction . . . disappear?

Like how Karolina thinks he's kind. But he remembers – distinctly, and without being able to call any specific crimes to mind – being in trouble with the police.

He remembers being sixteen and stealing his friend's dad's gun.

And let's not fuck about here, Oscar, he thinks. Let's get to the point. All this wondering about traits and cakes because he can't name what's really on his mind. But how *can* he? He couldn't have said to Karolina:

I'd like to know what stealing a gun and keeping it for years might be indicative of, character-wise.

I'm worried that I can't remember what happened in that closed-down supermarket at night.

308

Where those people went. Those shady characters I was friends with. The way they all seemed to vanish. One night I showed them the gun, the next night . . . I don't know.

Where did they go?

Where did the gun go?

Why can I remember everything about the gun except what happened to the gun?

Karolina, I'm worried that I can't remember anything about the first sixteen years of my life.

Karolina, I'm worried that I have a bank account full of money and I have to keep it a secret.

Karolina, I'm worried that one of my traits might be murdering people.

Karolina, I'm worried that I own a necklace that seems to be made out of teeth.

. . . Karolina?

Where are you going?

(Oscar can't go back, either, and ask Karolina what happens when things that were once constant traits, start to shift; to expand. Like his thing about water.)

*

It's almost time to board. He looks at his phone. Nothing from Jess. What did he want from her, anyway? To say, *Don't feel bad, Oscar, I totally get it. You stood me up then told me you had to leave the country and you can't explain why. No worries. Happens to us all. Have a nice life.*

Oscar drops the phone into the bin beside him.

Does he even *want* Jess to care about him? If she did care, and was hurt at him leaving so quickly, then he'd feel guilty. But if she didn't care at all, and doesn't miss him, that's a different kind of pain. He swings between the two.

If the world was a reasonable place, someone who couldn't decide what sort of pain to feel shouldn't feel any.

Unfortunately, it hasn't worked that way.

He misses Jess. He misses everyone. Even if he can't remember their names, he remembers what it was like to be around them for a little while. He feels like he's opening books at random, reading a few lines, putting them back. Never getting to an ending. What's Lonnie doing now? Will Atticus's brother patch things up with their parents? Will Jess forgive Anya? Did Karolina keep anything of his – just to remember the weird guy with no memory, who stayed with her once?

Is that . . .

Atticus?

Or has Oscar finally gone insane, with despair or sleep deprivation or just standard-issue madness?

No. It's definitely Atticus.

He's at a different gate, standing in a queue, about to go through a doorway. He's spotted Oscar at the same time that Oscar's spotted him. Atticus's parents are just in front of him, handing over their boarding passes, oblivious to Atticus waving.

He mouths something that Oscar guesses has to be: *Goodbye, Oscar.*

Oscar raises his hand back. Mouths back: *Goodbye, Atticus.*

He wants to add, *And thanks for being a friend, because that's really what you were, and I know I might have acted like you were just a nuisance sometimes, but actually I was happy, and I'm grateful*, but he doesn't think Atticus would get all that.

Then the queue moves, and Atticus is gone.

(Oscar doesn't often cry, but sometimes his eyes prickle.)

Maybe he has gone mad.

He doesn't know why, but he feels like this – seeing Atticus – is a good sign.

Of some sort.

Of something.

He rubs his eyes. When he opens them again there's a man sitting opposite to him. It's the same man who was asking for him at Jess's riad. He's not wearing a suit, just a shirt and chinos. He's about forty. He has small black eyes, half blanketed in folded skin.

'Hi, Oscar. Why are you leaving?' the man says.

He has an air of tired, saddened affection that Oscar recognises from his extensive experience of movie villains. The ones who say rueful things like, 'Oscar, Oscar, Oscar. Look what a merry dance you've led us,' before suddenly breaking the protagonist's legs.

Oscar stands up quickly, his metal chair giving an outraged squawk. People look over at him. He can't tell which people might be complicit and which are just nosy.

'Wait a minute,' the man says. 'Just wait. Aren't you tired of this? Running?'

Too close, thinks Oscar. Too much his own thought. He wonders if they have some means of seeing inside his head.

But, he thinks – and maybe this is a voice that they've put in his head, maybe it's his own – he's not *wrong*, is he?

Oscar hesitates.

'Oscar,' says the man. His voice, too, is compelling. 'Don't you want to know, at least, what you're running away *from*?'

William

'I just want to understand,' says Annetta, 'why William is so set on not getting the first memory back, and deleting the new one. Isn't it obvious that deleting things doesn't work?'

(William and Annetta are, once again, sitting opposite Marian Dunlop.)

Marian hears Annetta out. Then, as she is wont to do, she refuses to adjudicate, and instead asks them both how they feel.

Annetta is feeling frightened, sympathetic, angry, loving, frustrated, sad, hopeful and conflicted. She's feeling other things too, she says, but those are the main ones. Then she falls silent, arms drawn in, legs tucked, like there's not enough space for her and all the feelings in Marian's small room.

There's a silence.

'And you, William?' Marian prompts.

William hesitates. He's trying to pick the right words to fit his thoughts into, though they aren't thoughts so much as sensations that slither in and out of reach; scribbles, lightning flashes, walls, long drops.

The long, long shadow, sliding into view.

'. . .' says William.

But what can he say?

I'm worried

about

Dad

Marian is looking at him closely.

Has he spoken? No, he hasn't.

'Okay!' she says brightly. 'I want to come back to this. Perhaps in some one-on-one sessions. What I'd like to do right now is an exercise.'

She asks them to think of a favourite memory – a moment when they each felt particularly positive about the relationship, and deeply connected to the other person.

Annetta looks sceptical, and for a moment William wonders if she might object. But then she tells the story about when they first met. It was through mutual friends. There wasn't really any other way they *could* have met: both of them too shy to pick up strangers over tangled dog leads in the park, dropped papers, held-open lift doors. It was at a birthday party, and the two of them had started talking. Annetta says she can't even remember what they talked about, but she *knew*, just from that talk, that she was going to marry William.

It was the same for William, too. Though he'd spent most of the night across from Annetta without really registering her presence, once he was nearly nose to nose with her in the noisy room he felt . . . smitten. Not just smitten, in fact, but suddenly, potentially embarrassingly, turned on. He thanked God there was a table between them.

It was a surprise to him too, though maybe it shouldn't have been, how much Annetta liked sex. She liked it more than anyone he'd ever met. Her initial shyness vanished after two dates and she'd been startlingly articulate: calling him at 3 a.m. when he finished his shift to talk dirty, telling him – over brunch – how he should go down on her. Her hair – straightened back then, braided now – was the only thing off limits. Don't get semen on it, she said, before she'd even taken her clothes off. William struggled to match her: in libido (he was often exhausted), imagination, confidence, vocabulary. All of it. But he gave it a good go, and had fun trying.

Annetta is smiling at him. As if she knows what he's thinking. He smiles back – the good feeling sliding between them – surreptitious, almost, like a note passed under the desk in class.

Outside, next to their cars, the two of them laugh about the transparency of Marian Dunlop's exercise.

'I mean, it's not as simple as that, obviously,' Annetta says. 'It wouldn't work on everyone. Not permanently.'

'You couldn't rely on stuff like that,' he agrees.

Nevertheless, they stand still; they smile on. She's scrunched her gloves in her hands. He notices she's wearing nail polish. He considers telling her it's a nice colour, then wonders how many times she's worn it before, going unnoticed, and whether his saying it now will sound forced, or – worse – a cynical attempt to build on the goodwill of the session.

Annetta's looking at a small collection of cigarette butts next to the wall.

'How many couples do you think have stood here and cried?' she muses.

'Or had another argument.'

'Or proposed. God, I'd just sit at my window all day if I lived in one of these houses. Watching the people come and go.'

'Yes,' William says.

Silence rises.

'Better go, I suppose,' she says. 'I might see you tomorrow?'

'I'll call,' says William. He's trying to think of something to say to keep the conversation going, but he can't. And maybe it's better to part now, on a high note. Their goodbyes are affectionate but slightly awkward, like they've just started dating. Annetta gets into her car. As she turns the corner she glances back, and waves, and William waves too.

He feels slightly ashamed of himself. He thinks that he probably should have said in the session, or – failing that – just now, that he should make it clear what he wants to do. Vis-à-vis the deletion. Vis-à-vis the restoration. About how he intends to do whatever it takes to go ahead with the former and avoid the latter.

But things were going so well, and he didn't want to ruin it.

William is at the bar of The Fox and Hounds, waiting to buy a pint for Carey and himself, allowing himself to be washed gently backwards as other people flood in, deferring the point of purchase. He looks at the time: eight o'clock. If he can draw out this first drink, delaying Carey's turn at the bar, he might be able to plead a work night and get home after only two pints, sober.

William tries to avoid getting drunk these days. Mainly because alcohol and Valium don't mix – he doesn't want Annetta or the children having the burden of Drugs Death Dad for the rest of their lives. The problem is socialising. He'll drink too much at the start of the night in an attempt to feel more comfortable. Then every time someone says something that makes him uncomfortable, he'll drink again. The last time was at a fortieth birthday party he couldn't get out of.

William! All the lavender I planted is dying. What do you think I should do?

William! You'll know this one. Who is the UK's most prolific serial killer?

William. I have a friend you might like. She's a widow but she's very positive. What? Only separated? But it's been what, a year? Oh, right. It feels like much longer.

'Sir?' the bartender says. 'Sir, it's your turn.'

'Is it?' asks William.

'Yes,' says the bartender. The two people to either side of William both nod encouragingly. Everyone in the world, it seems, wants William to buy his drinks.

'So,' William says to Carey, sitting down and putting the pints down on the unsteady table. 'Got any holidays planned?'

Carey looks at him curiously. It's probably the same expression he had when William called him and said he felt bad about leaving it so long, and would Carey like to go for a pint?

'Mauritius,' Carey says. 'With Deborah and the kids.'

'Great,' says William.

There's a pause.

Starting off with this sort of casual conversation was a mistake. William's not a casual man; it looks off. And in any case, there's probably no way for William to casually bring the conversation round to the subject of his memory wipe, or what he wants Carey to do. He can't think of any way to lead in to it – other than saying, Look, Carey, I need you to pull some illegal strings and see if you can get some information on a memory wipe I had. Just the when, why, who and how of it. Be a pal, won't you?

'You okay, Hall?' Carey asks.

'Why?'

'You seem different. Well. You used to be silent and grumpy. Now you're silent and sad.'

'Not a bad summary,' William says. 'You should tell my therapist.'

'You have a therapist?'

William takes a long, delaying sup of beer. By the time the sup has ended he's still not sure what to say.

'Yes,' he says. 'A relationship one. Annetta wanted us to see her. On, er, account of us being separated.'

'Shit,' Carey says. 'I had no idea. I'm sorry to hear it.'

'Well,' says William. 'These things happen.'

They both drink now, long and contemplative. In the dim, beery interior of the pub, no fresh air circulates. Atmospheres descend, and stay put.

Look, Carey, begins William, in his head.

'Look, William,' Carey says (William's line!), with the air of someone *working up to* something (William's air!), 'are the relationship troubles . . . uh, related to this memory wipe you're getting?'

'Actually,' William says gratefully, 'it's more complicated than that. I found out that I already had a memory wipe. The one where you go in at night. I didn't know anything about it when I applied for the second wipe. And now Annetta wants me to get the first one back, and –'

'You're not going to do that, are you?' says Carey. He looks alarmed.

William is taken aback at first. Then he's relieved. Here it is: confirmation that William is right, Annetta is wrong.

It's not about right and wrong, says Marian Dunlop promptly.

It seems Marian Dunlop is in his head now.

'No intention of it,' he says to Carey.

'Glad to hear it. You know – confidentially – the people who've had their memories restored haven't been having a good time of it. The early test subjects. We've had quite a few people brought in for affray, criminal damage – and worse. I mean, no shit, right? You just got a traumatic memory back! What the hell did you expect?'

319

'Exactly,' William says.

Carey is animated now; his voice rises, then he checks it. 'I don't understand what those fucking judges were thinking. Why they forced Nepenthe to offer the restorations. But then . . . *judges*.' He shakes his head.

'Right,' says William. 'You know, Annetta thought maybe this latest thing, my being – Well. The photo thing. She thought that might be some kind of after-effect from the first wipe. Because the photo itself wasn't anything unusual.'

'In that case, all the more reason to get this second wipe,' Carey says. 'If they did miss a bit, or whatever, you can go back and get them to finish the job.'

'That's what I was thinking,' William says. But he's starting to feel, oddly, less certain than he was before Carey started agreeing with him.

'Yep,' says Carey. 'The less you know about that memory, the better. I think you're a hundred per cent doing the right thing.'

'Right,' says William. Trying to think of a way he could maybe still ask Carey for that favour, and realising, no.

No he can't.

The next day William knows he needs to call Annetta. He has to tell her he's planning to get another deletion, and not a restoration at all.

William *really* doesn't want to tell her that. He's feeling a lot of *resistance* to this idea, as Marian would put it.

So, Marian's still here. William's invited her over the threshold somehow, and now she's making herself at home. Wandering around. Looking at things. Asking questions.

Is that the only thing you're feeling? she asks him.

No, admits William.

What else are you feeling?

Panic. Nausea. Dread. The approach of the shadow.

Let's investigate these feelings, is what Marian would say.

Okay, thinks William.

Except he doesn't know where to start. He summons Marian back. Fair enough: if she's going to keep popping up to offer her twopence worth, he may as well put her to work.

Really, William? says Marian. She sounds different, now. Less kind. Less patient. *Because I think you know exactly what your feelings are. Don't you?*

So stop wasting my fucking time.

William closes his eyes.

And here it is, the fear that dare not speak its name:

Dad

Dad

(getting bigger now)

Dad

(fully present, fully realised)

Dad.

Because William's dad killed himself when William was six.

Not that anybody ever put it quite like that.

The way his mum put it – holding William on her lap, the back of William's hair cold and wet with her tears – was that William's dad had been out walking their cocker spaniel Patch along the cliff path and had *lost his footing*. Patch was found wandering around yapping by a woman who lived nearby. William's dad was found at the bottom of the cliff.

It was judged to be an accident, and William and his mum got life insurance, which allowed her to live comfortably in her retirement, and even when William got older and thought: *Bullshit, Dad never walked along those cliffs, he was scared of heights*, he never said that to anyone, not even to his mum – and she never said to William:

He didn't leave a note because he wanted to protect us.

*

Because: William overheard his dad one night, saying to his mum:

You have to listen, they're spying on me, Maura, they've been recording everything I say. Listen! They want me to know they're doing it. Isn't that sick? I turn on the television and they're reading a transcript of this terrorist, this recorded phone call made by a criminal, but it's all me, all my words, Maura, and they want me to know that if I step out of line they're going to use my words, my own words, to put me in prison forever. Do you understand what I'm telling you? You'll never hear about me again. They'll say I'm dead. Maura! You have to listen!

Because: it makes no sense that William contracted PTSD from the sight of a dead girl in a photograph. A deeply sad death, yes, but a small death. A not unusual death.

Because: William added other elements to this memory. The sweets. The tarmac underneath her – he *remembers* that.

But she wasn't lying on tarmac, was she?

Because: maybe William has inherited this psychosis or schizophrenia or whatever it is from his dad.

In which case.

Maybe whatever he wiped the first time round wasn't *actually* the problem.

*

Past William obviously *thought* it was the problem, and why wouldn't he? He was mad. Mad people don't admit they're mad. They find something to blame for their problems, like a memory, and then wipe it. Past William must have slipped through the various Nepenthe assessment stages because (a) he wasn't completely mad yet and (b) because the symptoms of his madness could be mistaken for trauma.

And – obviously – the memory wipe couldn't cure his madness. Which is back, hooting and hollering in his dreams, or passing darkly overhead, or sometimes just lying quietly, one arm outstretched, with a handful of sweets thrown across a road.

And if William wipes this latest memory, then what?

After a short amount of time, maybe something else becomes a problem. He starts imagining things that aren't there, having panic attacks, nightmares, zoning out. Restorations are ruled out by this point – not that he even wants a restoration. He wants another wipe. Maybe he gets a wipe secretly, the way Past William did – because that's the kind of thing mad people do. He goes to the clinic again and again, but the wipes just aren't trimming enough off his madness to keep it back, and it grows strong and brambly and wraps him up. (His breath is speeding up.) He loses more and more of his life. He loses Annetta. Maybe he loses the kids. (The breath is going out but not coming back properly; he can't pull enough of it in.) Maybe he doesn't lose the kids figuratively but literally: zoning out at the wheel, having an accidental nap and sleep-murdering them. After that, he kills himself. Annetta never recovers –

Enough.

He sits still, waits for air to fill him again.

You get the point, he says.

(To who?

To Marian?

But she's long gone.)

There's only one way, William realises now, to find out if he is in fact going mad. And that is to go back to Nepenthe, let them bring his monstrous memory back to life with a bolt of lightning. To let it loose in his brain again, half spoiled, misshapen and scarred, groaning with pain and fright. To go back to Marian Dunlop or another professional and try to deal with it the hard way. Endless talking. Or not, because talking is expensive. Endless medication.

He doesn't fancy it.

But maybe, he thinks, *maybe* it wouldn't be like that. If William's dad hasn't in fact passed any madness down, only a love of Sinatra. If it was the memory wipe itself that's responsible for his problems, as Annetta believes. Then getting the memory restored could make the problems . . . *vanish*.

Stranger things have happened. And seeing as Nepenthe have already pretty much admitted they've got no bloody idea what they're doing at the clinic, William considers that his guess is as good as theirs.

It's been so long since William felt hopeful that it takes him a while to identify the feeling now it's here. He's suspicious of it at first. A brightening inside his ribcage. A lifting of the top of his head. A need to hum. *Fly me to the moon.* And, yes, it *is* exactly what it seems to be.

Hope.

It brings with it William's best dream, his fondest thought. The lights go on; all the horror seeps away; he's sitting up in bed, wide awake, with the birds rioting outside the window and Annetta snoring gently next to him and the kids tapping on the door.

Wake up, Daddy!

Funny that his own life could seem so unreal. The idea of going back to how it used to be, only a couple of years ago.

But why not?

Fiona perched on the end of the bed with her bowl of cereal; Milo sprawled less carefully across their legs, *Watch the cornflakes, Milo!* Is that sun coming through the window? Giving everyone a fizzling gold edge. Reminding William he ought to book a holiday. Spain, South of France, Florida. *Now, don't look so worried, Annetta, we've got the money for it, since I sued the shi— since I sued the shenanigans out of Nepenthe. What do you say, kids? Three cheers for Disney World?*

And in this frame of mind, he calls Annetta and tells her that he wants to go back to the clinic and get his memory restored – and he even smiles as he's saying it, feels it, for a moment, like the sunlight of his vision really is shining on them all.

'Oh, William,' she says. 'I'm so, so relieved. I really think this is right.'

And it could be, he thinks.

No more PTSD checklist.

No more living in a corner of the bathroom cabinet.

No more Marian Dunlop – though he doesn't mind her, really.

No more shadow.

And when this is over, maybe he'll be able to wave Fiona off to meet her friends in the knowledge that there's only a zero point zero zero zero something chance of her being abducted and killed.

Maybe he'll be able to go back to work.

Maybe he'll be able to watch a fucking Scandi drama.

Yes.

That would be nice.

Finn

Finn thinks about the story he tells, of the night he and Mirande first danced, at a wedding in Cornwall.

What does he leave out of the story?

The fact that everyone had argued with their partners.

(Not that anyone knew it at the time. They all thought they were the only ones secretly arguing. David's girlfriend what's-her-name wasn't speaking to David. Mirande and her boyfriend Max were avoiding each other. Finn's girlfriend Diana had thrown a shoe at him the morning of the service, and sat in a different pew.)

What else?

He saw Mirande and David on the beach.

Finn can't remember if this was the night of the wedding or the night before. He can't remember if it was before or after Mirande danced with Finn. He knows he was drunk. It was late, and Finn was walking (staggering) along the beach. He couldn't see the edge of the water for a long time: his eyes refused to adjust. It was just a black, hissing space in front of him. After a while he made it out; darkness rolling in, darkness rolling out. A glass in his hand, a glass on the sand. Whoops. He sat down next to it. Two figures were walking along the beach towards him. He could just about make out the pale peach of Mirande's dress.

Were they holding hands? He saw it; he was sure, for a moment. Then they saw him, and moved apart.

'Remember the wedding in Cornwall,' Finn says to Mirande. 'I was thinking about it the other day. That all the couples had fallen out.'

'Oh God. Max *proposed*,' Mirande said. 'And I said no, and then he told me he hated me.'

'I'd forgotten that. What a mess. And I was almost passed out on the beach, then you and David found me.'

'David?' Mirande looks surprised. 'No, that was Max. That was after he proposed. He'd stormed off up the beach, like he was going to walk to Truro, and I went after him and calmed him down. He said he was sorry and I said it was okay. But I knew I was going to leave him, as soon as the wedding was over. Then we came back, and found you sitting in the sand on your own.'

'Really?' Finn says.

'Yes? Why?'

'How can you remember so much detail? I don't even know why Diana threw her shoe at my head.'

'I always thought it was because you'd kissed Carrie,' Mirande says. 'But I think that was unrelated. She had no idea.'

'What? Carrie? Who the –'

As he says it, Finn remembers Carrie. David's girlfriend. He can't remember what she looked like though. She reminded him of some actress, and now her face is gone,

replaced by the face of the actress she reminded him of –
whose name escapes him.

'I *kissed* her?' he asks.

But that's coming back to him now too. Some of it,
anyway.

'Shit,' he says. 'I'd forgotten. That was later. On the
night of the wedding. But how did *you* know I kissed her?'

'You told me about it a while after we got together.'

'Does David know?'

'No,' Mirande says. 'Of course not.'

'Right,' says Finn. 'Good, I guess. That's good.'

'Are you okay?' Mirande asks. 'You look . . . I don't
know.'

Frustrated, supplies Finn. *Baffled. Fearful. Despairing
at not knowing if this frustration and bafflement and fear
is ever going to end.*

'I'm fine,' he says.

Why did Finn kiss Carrie?

It was in the hotel kitchen. He remembers that now.
They'd gone out to find the wedding cake to eat. The
lights were off and there was a buzzing noise from a big
industrial fridge. They were drunk: that goes without
saying. But there must have been some kind of build-up.
Probably a mixture of things. Maybe it was because he'd
danced with Mirande and felt like he was a hundred times
the amount of *present*, a hundred times the amount of
alive, than he'd ever felt in the past – and then Mirande
went up to bed with Max. Maybe he thought he deserved
it, for being noble and forbearing and waiting to dump

Diana until they got back home. Maybe it was simple envy of David. Maybe longing for Mirande. Or the way someone else's wedding can stick in the craw, the love and loyalty and love and loyalty everywhere you go, remorseless. No wonder he made a grab for David's girlfriend in the dark.

He kissed Carrie.

How could he have forgotten that?

But then, those two faces floating along the shoreline; in that dim silver light off the sea. One was Mirande. One was David. Finn *saw* him. Now he sees Max.

It's around this time that Finn understands what he's up against.

While Mirande might have had part of her memory excised, the rest is so infallible that she *still* has the advantage over Finn. She's probably already worked out the content of the missing memory just from the shape of it, the exact place where the other memories end.

Whereas Finn, at the age of fifty, has an old man's memory. The past eludes him, changes shape, combines, divides, moves from one place to another. It's Mirande, it's Carrie, it's Max, it's David – no, it's only Finn, sitting in the sand on his own.

It's a door, a window, a wall.

Look behind you – no, not there.

Now it's behind you.

Look!

Finn and Mirande have a party.

David is invited, of course.

It gets to 2 a.m. The Good Whisky is out. Someone has just told a story about embarrassing themselves at work. Someone said, shame you can't get a memory wipe right now. Then someone else said, surely that's over for good. The amount of bad publicity they've had is insane.

'It's a good product though,' Finn says. 'It's like Viagra. It offers something unique that people can't refuse.'

In his peripheral vision Mirande is looking at him. Finn can feel the question coming from her direction. When Mirande is hurt, or stressed, her neck flushes. He doesn't look at her, or her neck. He lets his gaze swing out wide, moving over the group.

'I just don't think it's right,' someone says. 'Brains are very delicate mechanisms. You start tinkering with them, you break things.'

Mirande says, 'Did anybody see that they shut down the Vine and Escargot in town? I went past it yesterday and saw the sign in the window.'

'Really?' says someone.

Finn talks over them.

'*I* read this article,' he says, 'that said the brain is capable of much more repair than we give it credit for. So something like Nepenthe isn't necessarily dangerous.'

Agreement, disagreement. People start talking loudly about memory traces. Finn doesn't really care. He doesn't know if he's right or wrong. He's just waiting for the moment at which someone will inevitably ask one of the doctors present for their opinion. One of the doctors, Mirande, has left the room. But David is still here, and soon enough someone says, 'Come on, David, what's your professional opinion?'

Finn looks at David, who to his disappointment is leaning back in his chair, smiling.

'Nepenthe was never a totally perfect solution,' David says. 'I heard it wasn't actually that marine snails study that prompted all this restoration furore. They'd already realised that some patients were starting to remember things again after a couple of years or so. It would usually be in dreams, or unexplained flashbacks. Memory traces. It became apparent that any "deletion" they did – short of burning out the neurons, and maybe not even then – might only ever be temporary. As Finn says, the brain can find surprising ways to repair itself.'

'That's so sinister though, the company hiding that,' someone says.

'Like a *film*.'

'How do you know all this?' someone asks David. 'Do you know someone who works there?'

'Actually, I do,' David says. 'I live in Crowshill, where the biggest clinic is. My neighbour works there. And when I was doing my surgical training at St Helier I lived with a psych graduate – Louise – who's pretty high up at the company these days. But I didn't hear about it from either of them. My boss knows one of the company heads. They play golf and they gossip.' He shrugs.

. . . *Louise*, thinks Finn.

Finn knows Louise.

How does he know Louise?

'. . . Oh, no, I haven't seen her in years,' David is saying. 'Back when I knew her, she was working with the team that would go on to invent Nepenthe. I didn't know that then.'

'I want to hear about what it's like living next to the Nepenthe clinic,' Finn says. 'It must be like having Huntingdon Life Sciences in your town. Or the Scientology headquarters.'

'It was strange when I went back,' David says. 'It must have been, what, fifteen, twenty years since I left. Nothing physical about the town had changed. There had been an old glass factory, that was demolished, and the clinic was built – but that all happened behind a big wall. I've only ever seen pictures of the clinic. But the town felt different.'

Interesting, thinks Finn.

'You're not missing much,' he says. 'That building is quite a well-known fuck-up, architecturally speaking. Curved glass burning cars, wind noise, that kind of thing.'

At this point, the conversation of the group divides. Someone starts talking about frying eggs under the Walkie Talkie in London. Other people are making jokes about how Nepenthe doesn't actually zap memories with a laser, it just makes them stand in front of the building on a sunny day.

Finn wants to ask David more about Louise. He turns to him. But something about the way David is looking at him makes Finn change his mind.

He stands up instead, smiling.

'I'll get more drinks,' he says.

It turns out that Finn didn't need to ask David after all, because when he's lying in bed later that night, the name arrives, sudden, fully formed, as if dispensed by a machine:

334

Louise Nightingale.

Saying: *You're very tolerant.*

Finn looks up Dr Louise Nightingale. It's not hard. She's the only search result for her own name. There are pages and pages of her, in fact.

Louise looks much the same as he remembers. No: she looks *better*. Her silvery blonde hair is fuller, her teeth whiter. Her eyes are a gentle blue, her mouth has a *don't fuck with me* shape.

Finn only met Louise once, at that university reunion of Mirande's. An unofficial thing in a cocktail bar in Soho. He and Mirande had just moved in together, so it must have been in the late nineties. Nobody knew anything about Nepenthe yet. Louise must have known all about it, this thing that was about to happen to the world, but she said nothing. At that time Finn knew only that Louise was a psychologist; he'd heard Mirande's reaction when another woman pointed her out.

Great, Mirande said. Now she's weaponised.

Finn had been introduced to Louise early on, then didn't see her again all evening – not until she slipped into the empty chair next to him and said:

I must say, you're very tolerant.

I'm sorry, what? said Finn.

He didn't get it at first. He was drunk, as usual. But Louise was looking pointedly in one direction and he eventually came to understand that he ought to look in that direction too. When he did, he saw David and

Mirande. They were at the bar, near a speaker; talking closely. David had stooped down so his mouth was at the level of Mirande's ear. Mirande had tilted the ear up towards him, her head on one side.

How so? Finn asked Louise.

Louise opened her mouth. Then she closed it again.

Never mind, she said. I'm sorry. I spoke out of turn.

I don't understand, Finn said. What did you mean?

But Louise wouldn't say anything else. She apologised again – though she didn't *look* particularly sorry – then made her excuses and joined another group of people he didn't know, and even if Finn had known them he couldn't exactly follow her. And now it's twenty years later (how? How?) and Finn lives in Arizona and Louise lives in London, and is a well-known psychologist with whom Finn could have no way of getting in contact, even if he could think of a subtle way of asking her about that night.

So he'll never know any more than this.

Another get-together, organised by Finn, a small one this time, in the garden. Smoke from the barbecue rushing up to meet a sunset that's as violently beautiful as always: pink, purple, gold. The red rock behind is lit up like it's on fire. People are laughing. Finn doesn't know why; he'd stopped listening. He laughs along, slightly too late.

We've done a lot of hosting lately, Mirande said to him last night. We've barely had an evening together. Don't you want a break from it?

A break? Finn said incredulously. From our friends? From *fun*?

(He might have overdone the incredulousness.)

Never mind, she said.

David is talking to Mbali, making her laugh about something. She's laughing more than she does with Finn.

The other day David had managed, during a ten-minute stroll in the garden, to impress their gardener by knowing the Latin name of some plant. Apparently it used to be an old remedy for something.

Finn knows he shouldn't think: *my*.

But still.

Finn's wife, *Finn's* friend, *Finn's* gardener. If Finn owned a dog, David would have bought it biscuits.

Stop, Finn thinks.

He's feeling annoyed about a dog he doesn't even own. That's not reasonable. He notices Mirande, across the garden, looking at him. She looks worried, and wary. Why? He sees himself: standing with people he's not listening to, glaring at nothing. It jolts him. A moment of clarity. Well, he's had a lot of them. After a while they're easy to ignore.

He excuses himself and goes inside to haul another crate of wine out of the larder. They've been getting through more wine these days. Finn himself has accounted for a lot of it. He picks up a couple of bottles, and carries them back outside.

Unusually, Mirande is up before Finn the next day. She's toasting some bread and has made fresh orange juice. Eggs are cooking in a pan. When Finn comes in she turns quickly, wearing a nearly convincing smile, and slides a glass of juice across the counter towards him.

'Thank you,' he says. It comes out very formally. 'Need any help?'

'All good here,' she says. 'Almost ready.'

'Delicious.'

An awkward silence arrives. Finn strains orange pulp through his teeth, chews it. Mirande stirs the scrambled eggs. Then she turns off the gas.

'Finn,' she says. 'I've been thinking. Why don't we go home?'

'Home?'

'Back to England. Or Ireland. Ri keeps saying she wants to go to sixth form in Ireland. And we did always plan to move back. Remember?'

'I dimly recall.'

'It would be nice to be close to her.'

'Ha,' says Finn. 'Nice for her, or for us?'

Mirande acknowledges this with a lift of her spatula. That the two of them are, as always, chasing their daughter. As their daughter moves away from them in her usual way, without a glance back.

It's not that Ri isn't loving. It's just that her love has a more than usually independent quality to it. She'll sit curled up with Mirande – sometimes – she'll fall asleep with her head on Finn's shoulder – sometimes. She kisses them goodnight every night, and occasionally at random: kisses bestowed with the element of surprise, a glancing blow on the side of the face. But if she needs something, she sorts it out herself. If she hurts herself she doesn't come to them. The only time they can remember it happening was when she fractured her wrist jumping off a swing.

You know, she's going to break someone's heart, Mirande said once.

Yes, said Finn. Ours.

Mirande has a fear that Finn's never been able to talk her out of: that the bout of postnatal depression she suffered – her distance at this critical time – was what made Ri so preternaturally self-sufficient. The depression wasn't helped by her anxious online searches. Looking up what would happen if Mirande didn't get her shit together, couldn't feel love. (*Look, Finn! Look at this study. This is what happens to babies that don't get touched enough.* Or: *She won't latch because she can tell that there's something wrong with me.*)

And so it was Finn, the not-so-convinced parent, who spent the most time with Ri after she was born, while Mirande saw a therapist who promised to get her back to her usual self – and did, as far as Finn can tell. As far as there *is* a usual self.

And that time!

Finn was worried about Mirande, yes, and about Ri, but still, left alone with his daughter – what a mysterious time of wonder that was. Not something that can even be described. Blathering on about tiny fingers clenching one's own or little feet or translucent skin, translucent hair, lit up that first summer, falls short of expressing even a fraction of it.

Finn can't remember, now, what he and Mirande were talking about. He smiles at Mirande. If she hadn't been on the other side of the counter dishing up eggs he'd have reached for her, without even thinking about it. She looks surprised, and then she smiles back.

Then Finn remembers everything else. The rest of it. Like waking up in another bed and taking a moment to realise where you are.

He's not in his own bed any more.

He must have stopped smiling, because Mirande's own smile vanishes, as quickly as if she's a mime, copying his responses. About as funny as that, too. These days she often looks at Finn uncertainly, cautiously, like she's trying to guess what he's thinking. And she guesses his thoughts now, maybe, and looks pained.

She talks on, blinking. 'Anyway, it doesn't have to be Ireland. I think it could be good for her to have a more international education. Your project's almost finished; there's no need to stay in America. And I'm at a point where I can leave things here. I've been training my own replacement for the last year.'

'I don't know,' Finn says. He feels suspicious. He's wanted to move back to Ireland for years, but Mirande found the prospect of continual rain unappealing. He has the sense that he's being distracted.

'I thought maybe it would be good to have a change?' she continues. 'Change always revitalises us.'

'On a superficial level,' Finn says.

Mirande looks stricken. 'Okay,' she says softly. She comes round to his side of the counter, and takes his hand. 'Finn, I don't know what to do. You've seemed . . . unhappy lately. I'm worried about you. Please, talk to me?'

He wonders what he might suggest they talk about.

What David meant when he wrote, *The way we were.*

What Louise meant when she said, *You're very tolerant.*

Whether Mirande left Max because she was in love with David, but David was with Carrie, and then by the time David was free, Mirande was with Finn. Until Singapore, when she wasn't – not all the time.

'You're worried about me?' Finn asks. 'I'm worried about *you*. Bringing up this idea of moving now. Do you think perhaps you're just doing it because you're worried about Nepenthe? Are you trying to distract yourself from it?'

Unfair, yes. Pompous, undoubtedly. And the tone was all wrong. It was supposed to sound concerned, but instead it sounded angry. No wonder, really, that Mirande dropped his hand, and went over to the sink. She turned on the tap. Then she turned it off, and leaned on the countertop, not looking at him.

'I don't . . . I honestly . . . Look. What is happening? Something's wrong, I know it. You aren't telling me everything.'

He doesn't mean to say it, but he does:

'I could say the same about you.'

'What *is it*, Finn?' she says. She doesn't sound tired any more. She sounds desperate. 'What do you mean? I'd tell you anything. What do you think I haven't told you? Whatever it is. Ask me. I'll tell you. Please.'

But he can't answer.

'*Please*,' she says again.

But he can't ask.

Later, after a while of not talking, Mirande went to town. She had her bag in her hand when she told him, pausing

341

briefly in the doorway. She didn't say what she'd be doing in town, or when she'd be back.

Finn remembers standing outside Winchester Palace, looking up at the sky through the empty rose window, Mirande looking at him, with that closeness, that interest. He felt the look running all through him like lightning.

What happened next?

David arrived.

Finn wants to go back to that exact moment, the two of them standing alone, the others disappeared around one corner, David not yet visible beyond the other. It's Finn's story, it's fake, maybe, but at least partly true, and Finn was happy there. For over twenty years Finn's been standing in that moment, he and Mirande outside Winchester Palace, with nobody else in sight.

But now David has come around the corner to join them.

It's MY story, Finn wants to say to David. *I tell it. Not you.*

Give it back.

That night Finn goes into the bathroom. He thought Mirande was in bed, but he finds her sitting on the edge of the bath, crying. She jumps when she comes in.

'Mirande? What's wrong?'

'Oh, just . . .' she says.

Don't say *nothing*, Finn thinks, at the same time as he thinks: please, please say *nothing*.

She says nothing. She takes some tissues and wipes her eyes. Finn stands in the doorway, not knowing what to do. Eventually Mirande blows her nose, looks up and says:

'I called the clinic. I'm going to get the memory back. I've got an appointment in early November. I booked a flight.'

'Really?' Finn's taken aback. 'But I thought you didn't want to? What made you decide to do it?'

'It's like you said,' she says. 'It's been on my mind. I'm not happy, either. Life won't go back to normal until I do it.'

Finn stares at her, dismayed.

He understands, suddenly, that this isn't going to be how he finds out the truth. Of course it isn't. Not if she doesn't want him to. It's why he hasn't asked her if anything happened with David: she wouldn't tell him. And now Mirande could fly to England, spend a day sightseeing, come back, tell him she got the memory back – some patient dying in horrific circumstances, or whatever – and that will be that. Even if Finn went to Crowshill with her and sat in the Nepenthe waiting room, she could still come out and tell a lie.

Really, Finn? go his thoughts. *Has it come to this?*

And he is ashamed.

Ashamed – and . . . still suspicious.

The two things coexisting: self-hatred, fear. Thinking at the same time, *I love my daughter*, but with something else running underneath that, a stream of thought that goes, *My? Or His? Mirande called her Rionach, she looked it up in a book, I said I'd never heard of it, it was totally archaic, but pretty, absolutely, and Mirande was determined to give her an Irish name – why? Calling the cuckoo in the nest, O'Cuckoo?*

343

I love my daughter.

Or: I love his daughter.

Which is it?

Does it matter if she isn't my daughter? Does it matter if Mirande was his lover before she was mine? His after she was mine?

Mine.

His.

And it doesn't stop.

When did Finn become so obsessed with what's *his*? It's primitive, it's everything he hates, but knowing something is stupid and deplorable doesn't make it go away. He hears it at night, the thought, starting back up again. *His. Mine. His or Mine.*

Finn wonders if he's always been this person, somewhere – a paranoid, tense, manipulative person – or if he's just responding to circumstance.

He remembers the conversation in which Mirande rejected the concept of self. That party was three weeks ago. It feels like a lot longer than that. He can't even remember what she said. It might even have been helpful, but he can't exactly ask her about it now.

When Finn's company won the contract for the neighbourhood project, Finn gave a talk to the staff about what he wanted to do. As Finn had said to David, he tended to resort to bullshit when he talked about architecture. Telling people that design and history were *in conversation*; that his own role was merely, humbly, to *facilitate* this conversation.

But the thing was, this spiel wasn't complete bullshit. Though he may not be able to translate the conversation, Finn can still sense it taking place. It's an interplay, an energy flow. When there's a true sympathy between the old and new, Finn can *feel* it.

He tried to explain this to his team, some of whom lived in the neighbourhood they'd be redeveloping. He said that the new draws its strength from the old without crushing it, or ignoring it. The old – anything lost or unwanted or fragmentary – is to be protected, restored, gathered up into the arms of the present to live again.

Continuity of story, he said. Whatever was there before can't be ignored. We can't just tell a new story. We have to find a way to include the old story too.

When he thinks of that speech now, it makes him angry.

Maybe the best thing to do would be for Finn himself to get a memory wipe. Forget the day he saw the email from Nepenthe, the last few weeks. What was it Othello said, when he found Desdemona's handkerchief in Cassio's possession?

By heaven, I would most gladly have forgot it.
Thou saidst – Oh, it comes o'er my memory,
As doth the raven o'er the infectious house,
Boding to all – he had my handkerchief.

But Finn has to know, that's the problem. Is he right or wrong?

He doesn't know what happens if he's right.

He can't be right.

A week passes and they hear nothing from David. *Where are you?* wonders Finn. It's only another few days, now, until David flies home. A great stone is rolling into place, and if Finn doesn't run towards it, throw himself through the closing gap, he'll be trapped underground forever.

Finn starts an email to David.

Hi David

Hello David

Dear David

He abandons it. He can't get the tone right. Affable Finn, the old charmer, is too far out of reach.

So he waits.

It's Mirande who brings him the news that David had to leave early. Some patient of his back in London suffered complications of some sort, and David decided to fly back immediately to check on her, missing his last weekend in Phoenix, his own goodbye drinks. He's already gone. So that's it. The end came and went without Finn even knowing.

'He said he had a great time and was very grateful for our hospitality. He's sorry not to say goodbye in person, but wishes you all the best,' Mirande says, reading out David's text.

All the best? Finn wants to demand. That's *it*?

All the best?

346

He wants to sit down heavily, like someone who's had a shock. He *has* had a shock, but not one that can be shown, or soothed. He can only shake his head and murmur something about it being a shame, and he'll drop David a line to say he was very welcome.

All the rest of the day Finn feels . . .

. . . not much.

He doesn't feel relieved. He doesn't feel disappointed or angry. He feels only absence: a perfect, empty flatness. All his energy up until today has been directed at David, or what David represents, and now he can't remember what his life was before David arrived.

This is what purgatory must be like, he thinks. Heaven is knowledge of goodness, hell is knowledge of evil. Purgatory is not knowing which is which.

In one possible story, David is a decent man who probably fancied Mirande once – maybe even kissed her, or slept with her – then, when Finn came along, decently stepped aside. Went to Canada. Got married. Kept a safe distance.

It's just Finn isn't sure if this is the story he's living in.

When he thinks of Mirande these days he sees different women, from different possible stories, inhabiting the same space. The starry, crucial Mirande of the wedding in Cornwall. A smiling Mirande among the sweet peas outside their first house in London. A hopeful Mirande on the step in Singapore in the rain. Mirande looking at him outside Winchester Palace. Mirande saying something in David's ear in a bar. *The way we were*. Mirande arriving home, resting her head on Finn's shoulder. Mirande sitting on the edge of the bath, crying.

When he thinks of Ri he thinks –

No.

He can't think about Ri.

Mirande is working at the table, facing away from Finn. She's pulled her ponytail over one shoulder and is twisting it with one hand, concentrating. A familiar gesture. The pale back of her neck is visible. The fabric of her shirt pulled across her shoulder blades. Is she thinner? Her shoulders are tight. Tenderness and sorrow come over him, pass away.

It's a strange feeling not knowing who you live with. In what story. It puts him on the outside of things. He's watching a film. He can feel the ending on the horizon.

Fin.

The problem is, he suspects it's going to be one of those arty, ambiguous endings he pretends to appreciate, while secretly preferring endings with answers. Rosebud, Keyser Soze, Norman Bates's mother.

But then, he's chased an answer without really considering what it would be like to get one, without really believing in any of the things it might be.

It's all so extreme, that's the problem. Betrayal or safety. Despair or happiness. War or peace. But if he gives up the chase, what happens then? The in-between, the nothing, the numbness.

This?

Forever?

*

Finn and Mirande have been avoiding each other. Neither of them says this is what they're doing. They just do it.

On Sunday morning Mirande gets up and goes to the grocery store before Finn wakes up. Then she says she's got a headache and is going to have a nap in the garden. She opens up a sunlounger and lies on it, fully clothed. She's wearing sunglasses, so he can't tell if she's asleep or not.

Finn works in his study for a while, then, stifled by his own company, makes up an excuse to go out. He writes Mirande a note (*I didn't want to disturb your sleep* . . .) and puts it on the worktop. He drives to Tucson, where fewer people know him, and sits in a bar with a beer.

His sense of being behind a glass wall has not faded. He isn't enjoying the beer. But he knows if he says to the barman, *This beer has no taste*, the barman will say something along the lines of, *No, sir, I'm afraid it's you that's the problem. What did you expect? You're not in the story. You're looking at the world through glass. On your side of the glass you're in darkness. But if you like, I can get you another beer.*

Finn doesn't want to have that conversation, even by implication. So he pays and drives back to the house, where he finds Ri.

. . . *Ri?*

Ri.

Finn is so stunned that he comes to a halt in the doorway. If he had been carrying anything he'd have dropped it. Rubbed his eyes, mouth agape. But here she is, standing in the kitchen, an inch taller or just his imagination, facing away from him and fiddling with the coffee machine. Then she turns round, and laughs.

'Hi, Dad!' she says. 'Surprise!'

Ri.

She has a few more freckles, her fringe has overleaped her eyebrows to brush her lashes, she really does seem (she can't be) taller. There's a light coming out of her, not soft or luminous but active and rippling, like the light that comes off the North Atlantic, off Dunquin. It moves when she moves, turns when she turns. She raises one eyebrow.

'Look,' she says. 'I drink coffee now. And I can raise one eyebrow.'

Then she bounds over and wraps her arms around him; in her enthusiasm, bellowing, 'I missed you' accidentally straight into his ear.

Finn welcomes the volume. He wants the sound to hit him, knock him over, roar through him. He wants obliteration.

He's trying not to cry into her hair.

'So what did you do without me?' she asks. Over his shoulder he hears a giggle, a sniff, a wipe of her nose, possibly on his pullover. 'Was it awful?'

He finds his voice:

'It was worse than you can even imagine.'

She giggles again and disengages, rubbing her face. Slightly embarrassed, as she always is by emotion. 'Oh, *good.*'

'But I thought you were back on . . .'

'Tuesday. Yeah. But our teacher Miss Hobart got caught buying cocaine in Berlin and got the sack on the spot, and then we didn't have the legal number of teachers to keep an eye on us, which is funny really because, you know, turned out it was more like they needed *us* to keep an eye on *them*, and anyway there'll probably be a massive fuss about it, you and Mum will laugh your heads off.'

Tuesday.

He'd even forgotten she was coming back this Tuesday. 'I'm sorry,' he mumbles.

'Why do you look so horrified? I don't care, I hated Miss Hobart. And now you can be like *I told you so* to Mum, cos it proves your point about modern schooling or whatever. Anyway, I did call to tell you but your mobile was off and Mum's rang out. Then I thought it would be funny to surprise you. I got a lift back with Nandi and her dad. Anyway, then I got home and you were out and Mum's fast asleep so it's not actually as dramatic as I was hoping. But' – she laughs – 'you still looked pretty surprised, Dad.'

Finn looks out of the window. Mirande is still on the lounger, one arm thrown over her face, like she's warding off some nightmare – dreaming of Finn, maybe.

Forgive me, he thinks.

'Well, we'll have to get your welcome party started,' he says. 'I'll cook something nice.'

'Oh yeah. I'm a vegetarian now. Is that a problem?'

'That's fine. Is there anything else I should know, besides the vegetarianism and the eyebrow and the coffee?'

'Nope. That's it. Obviously I'm more cultured and cosmopolitan from all the travelling. But you probably noticed that already.'

'It was the first thing I noticed. Shall we make some coffee then? We'll take an espresso to your mother.'

'Cappuccino for me.'

'Oh?'

'With lots of milk. Lots of foam. Lots of chocolate dust.'

'Percentage of actual coffee?'

'About thirty.'

'Darling girl,' says Finn.

She cringes, physically, away from the sentiment. Roots in a cupboard for the cocoa. Says, over her shoulder, 'You know the tour missed off Dublin? We didn't visit Ireland at all. Can we go there? It's actually stupid that I haven't been, what with being named after an ancient queen and everything.'

'Sure,' he says. 'We can go to Ireland.'

(Mirande sleeping outside in the sun.)

(Ri here in the kitchen.)

It doesn't matter, Finn thinks, what story he's in.

Ri is looking at him in horror.

'Dad, you're *crying*.'

'My apologies,' says Finn. 'If I'd known you were coming home I'd have done it beforehand like a respectable father. I'm just . . . well. I'm sorry.'

But the tears won't stop. He reminds himself, finally, not of Othello but of King Lear.

I am a very foolish, fond old man.

And Ri – tutting, still looking faintly scandalised – doesn't sidle away. She leans against him, and strokes his arm.

She smells different: some intense vanilla and Parma violet combination, a pop-star perfume bought at the airport, no doubt, lovely only to young girls.

For no reason this makes him cry more.

'Oh dear, *Dad*,' she says. 'You've got to get it together.'

I know, Finn answers, in his head, where his voice can't give way. *I will.*

PART FOUR

Noor

Tell me a story.

I've told you all the stories I know.

I mean our story.

I've told that.

You missed the ending.

Noor doesn't want to tell the end of it, her and Elena's story. It's not a happy ending. And no questions are answered. She'd rather just leave it out.

But Elena just waits, she's not going anywhere, and so Noor has to do what Elena wants, which is to go back to the last time she saw her, and go over it all again.

It wasn't long after the morning that Elena left Noor's apartment, collecting all her things and disappearing before

Noor woke up. Only a couple of weeks had passed. In that time Noor didn't hear from Elena, and she didn't call her. She supposed that by leaving, Elena had made herself clear. She didn't want to see Noor, or speak to her. This outcome wasn't surprising to Noor. She'd been ready for something like it from the beginning.

Noor was adjusting to having her apartment back, taking a bleak pleasure in its cleanness, its quietness. She was getting on with work, which had slipped slightly over the last few months. Noor had been distracted. She'd made some minor errors, and now she was going back over everything, a kind of self-audit, to make sure she'd caught them all. This work took her all evening, and exhausted her so much that she'd tip herself into bed at eleven and pass out, without having had time to think about anything to do with Elena.

And then Elena arrived at the door, slightly tipsy, holding a pair of Noor's reading glasses and one of Noor's bras as justification for her presence, both thrust awkwardly out in front of her, before she started to cry.

Look, she said. I needed to give you these back. And also I don't like how we left things. I didn't *want* to leave things. I just realised, that night, how things . . . were.

Things? said Noor.

I'd been trying so hard to get you to open up to me, Elena said. To have a proper relationship. But it's impossible. I saw it when you were talking about Louise.

Louise, Noor said. She felt defensive.

I know you aren't in love with her or anything, Elena said. You admire her.

I also trust her, Noor said. And I understand her. I understand her goals. They're the same as mine. To do our jobs well. To make people better.

Exactly, Elena said. She wiped her face. And I realised, those are the things that are missing with us. You don't admire me. You don't trust me: you keep me at arm's length. You don't understand me, or what I want. You don't even want the same things. I want intimacy, communication. Actually I think you're ashamed of the part of you that loves me.

Her voice went up at the end, as if she was asking a question. She looked at Noor, eyes wet. Noor felt obscurely *under threat*. She stepped back.

Well. Thanks for explaining, she said.

Elena's eyes widened. She blinked. Then she did something Noor didn't realise people actually did: she threw up her hands. She cried out, I don't know why I came! You're such a, a *robot*. I don't think you're even capable of being a proper person!

Noor felt the force of Elena's anger as if she'd been physically hit by it. Then she felt angry, too. She said, I may not be as emotionally *demonstrative* as you, but I happen to think that's a good thing. I'd rather be emotionally stable.

Oh, right, Elena said. I'm the damaged one, am I? Come on, Noor. You're as fucked up as I am. That's why you won't talk about anything in your past.

Maybe because you talk too much about the past, Noor said. I didn't need to hear it all. Did you consider that? I saw your history on your medical notes. Childhood trauma, suicide attempts, criminal damage, rehab, unhealthy sexual attachments, depression. But you insist on telling me it all again, in the name of openness and

359

honesty. Why do you need everyone to be fucked up? Why can't we just get on with it?

Wow, Elena said. You're sounding really emotionally stable right now, by the way.

Fuck you, is what Noor nearly said then. She *should* have said it. It would have been infinitely better than what she did say, which was:

I don't know how you even passed the screening.

Elena looked shocked. Then she laughed. There was a bitterness in the laugh that Noor hadn't heard before.

Oh and Nepenthe's screening processes are of course totally irreproachable, Elena said. Developed and monitored by your hero, Louise.

At least I admire someone who's worth it, Noor said. Unlike you, having an affair with a man who abused his power and cheated on his wife.

What did Elena say then?

No, Noor remembers. Elena didn't say anything. She just looked at Noor. Then she visibly drew herself together, turned, and walked away.

And Noor closed the door, and said,

Fuck you.

(And of course it's probably too late, now, to ask Louise to help her delete this memory forever.)

The first week of the restoration programme is loud, and fraught. Noor's car has to nudge its way through crowds each morning, a jumble of noise. Journalists have joined the protesters outside, extending their microphones towards her car window. Security guards shout at them. Cameramen filming the scene get in the way, get tripped over. Then the security guards shout at them too.

Noor barely registers the convulsions outside the clinic. She's more occupied with her own anxiety. The second week of the programme begins: the week that Louise went to such lengths to look up. Noor is waiting for Louise – back now from Manchester – to come in and ask Noor if she wouldn't mind just quickly authorising access on another client file.

At which point Noor will – well, Noor still doesn't know exactly what she'll do then.

And then Tuesday comes, and she goes in to work, and sees Louise's daughter sitting on one of the long white sofas in reception.

'*Mei?*' she says.

Mei looks up from her phone. For a moment Noor thinks she's made a mistake, but no, it's Mei, minus her swing and white pyjamas, and a few years older, but still with the same small, teardrop-shaped face, the sharp little chin.

'You?' Mei says. (Noor realises Mei probably has no idea what her name is.) Mei looks panicked. 'Is my *mum* here?' she says. 'Is this some kind of set-up?'

'You're M. Lewarne?' Noor says, at almost the same time. 'That's your name? Not Nightingale? You're here for an appointment?'

'Answer my question first,' says Mei. She stands up and looks around. She looks ready to run out of the door.

'Everything okay?' asks the receptionist.

'It's fine,' Noor snaps. She says, more quietly, to Mei, 'Your mum isn't here. I don't know if she plans to come in. I could find out for you?'

'No,' Mei says. 'It's okay. I don't think that's her style.'

'Can we talk outside?' Noor asks.

Mei looks at her for a moment. She frowns. 'Okay,' she says. 'But you'd better not be planning to get me to talk to her. I can tell you now you'd be wasting your time.'

(*This?* is what Noor thinks then. *This* is the too-sensitive girl?)

It's cold outside, and Mei draws her large woolly coat around herself. She looks back at the clinic. The curved frontage reflects the sky, clouds passing quickly, the sun appearing and vanishing again in the glass.

'I'd never been to one of these until last week,' she says. 'I guess you guys don't do *bring your daughter to work* days.'

'It's discouraged.'

The wind picks up and flings strands of Noor's hair across her face. It gets in her mouth. The shutters emit a low, querulous cry.

'Was that the . . . building?' Mei asks.

'The wind gets behind the shutters,' explains Noor. 'I'm Noor Ali, by the way.'

'I know,' Mei says. 'And Lewarne is my dad's surname. In answer to, you know, your question earlier.'

'Are you okay, Mei?' Noor asks. 'You obviously don't have to tell me any details.'

'It's okay,' Mei says. 'I'm okay. I was a night client, I got my memory back, and I'm glad I did. This is my follow-up appointment.'

'And Louise didn't want you to?' Noor says.

'No,' Mei says. 'It was her that talked me into the deletion in the first place. Not even to protect *me*: it was to protect herself. She said something she regretted and she didn't want me to be sad, or angry, and make her feel guilty and not perfect. That's probably why she talked me into taking antidepressants. She tried to talk me out of getting the restoration, but I was, like, done with being talked into and out of stuff. And now I'm done with *her*.'

Noor's too shocked to know what to say.

'I know you're her friend or whatever,' Mei says. She looks defensive. 'You probably don't believe me. Everyone usually believes her. It's her superpower. Talking everyone into things. Even my dad always does what she says, but he has to because she has all the money. And I guess you're on the payroll too. Ha. Literally. So yeah, I don't expect you to believe me.'

'I'm sorry,' Noor says. She experiences her own horror like a block of ice. She's standing inside it, unmoving. She wants to ask more, but she can't: it wouldn't be ethical.

'Uh, my appointment's starting like, *now*,' Mei says. They look inside. Karine is standing in reception, squinting out at them. 'I should probably go.'

'I'll walk you in,' Noor says.

Outwalk, she thinks.

'Remember when I met you?' she says to Mei. 'You were weighing up whether to become an outcast. I always wondered what you'd decided.'

'Really?' Mei says. 'I don't remember that. I mean, that sounds kind of like me at the time, and I remember meeting you, but I don't remember what we talked about.'

Noor persists. 'We said how if you choose to be an outcast, it's more like, an outwalk. It was a joke.'

The two of them stand just outside the door of the clinic. Karine is waiting inside. She's already got her warm smile on. Noor isn't sure why she feels disappointed; why she needs Mei to remember their conversation.

Mei turns her hands palm up, lifts them to her shoulders. She looks pitying.

'Uh, no,' she says. 'Sorry.'

Noor sits at her desk, hands locked around a cold mug, listening to the whistling of the building.

She focuses on putting things together.

The person Louise must have been looking up was Mei. M. Lewarne. Maybe it was Mei she'd attempted to call from the clinic because Mei was – understandably, after Louise put her on pills and persuaded her to get a memory deletion – ignoring her calls.

But this still leaves other things Noor can't put together. Like RASA. Or the Access Denied clients. Or why Louise interfered with several other clients' procedures.

Noor feels a crunching inside her body. Like a large hand has just closed around her internal organs. Her breath squeezes through the gaps.

What have you done, Louise? she thinks, with a plaintiveness that makes her wince.

Is this the end of it?

Louise?

*

After Elena left, Noor thought she didn't mind.

She thought she was fine.

In retrospect she did some strange things for a person who was fine. For example, a few months after Elena left, Noor went to London. She wore a hijab and sunglasses. She had a new car, and she parked it opposite The Cat and Pigeon and sat in it for two hours, watching the door to Elena's flat. Then she drove back to Crowshill.

She went back to London, several times. She hesitated, once, at the door of The Cat and Pigeon, but didn't go in. She saw Elena coming out of the flat, but she never approached her.

Elena didn't see Noor.

Elena seemed happy enough. She showed no signs of the deep and irreversible damage she'd joked about in her interview. Not that Noor even knew how deep and irreversible damage might look.

Like Noor's own face, maybe: still and flat, looking almost two-dimensional. Like a picture of a face.

Then, after a year of this, Elena moved, and Noor couldn't find out where she'd gone. Her landlord didn't have a forwarding address, and she didn't appear on the electoral roll when Noor looked online. The only thing Noor was left with was Elena's number, which may or may not have been changed. Noor never called it. She kept it in her phone contacts, in the event that, maybe one day, she'd think of something to say.

. . . So, yeah.

Maybe Noor wasn't fine.

Because of the increased traffic in town these days, Noor arrives at work at the same time as everyone else. She's annoyed when she gets into the kitchen to find several other people there. She doesn't bother to hide her annoyance; the stress that's been snapping at her through the night, over her uneaten breakfast, through the car-clotted streets. There isn't an *exodus* exactly, more of a slipping away, in ones and twos, very quietly. But within five minutes Noor has the kitchen to herself. A clean teaspoon, too.

She almost smiles.

She's making herself a tea when Jim Stokes passes by. He looks as tense as Noor feels.

'Hi, Jim,' Noor says. He so clearly doesn't want to stop and talk that Noor becomes perversely determined to force him to. 'How's everything going?' she asks.

'Fine, fine,' he says. He hovers in the doorway. He frowns, blinks a couple of times, and twiddles with his tie. He's doing everything but wring his hands.

'Well, that's good to hear,' Noor says. 'I'm certainly convinced. How are the restorations going?'

Jim sighs. He comes into the room and sits down heavily. 'I have no idea,' he says. 'I sometimes think I know ten per cent of what goes on in this place. I'm supposed to be the clinic director. That's what it says on my door.'

He looks at Noor. The look is questioning.

'It definitely does,' she says.

'But if you're asking about this thing today, I'm sorry, Noor, but I simply have no idea. I can't fill you in because nobody has filled *me* in.'

'Hang on,' Noor says. 'What's "this thing today"?'

'Oh,' Jim says. 'It's one of the restorations. The senior management are going to be handling it, apparently. Clifford Byrne's here, and someone from legal, and one of the chief psychologists, and a couple of other people I've never heard of. All from London.'

'Louise?' asks Noor.

So this is it, she thinks, with a feeling of dread and relief. *Whatever it is.*

At least she'll finally know.

'I don't know,' says Jim. 'I haven't seen her.'

Noor can hear Clifford Byrne's voice outside. It starts as a small low rumble, like far-off thunder, then gets louder, then louder still, until it's filling the corridor.

'I'd better . . .' says Jim. He nods towards the sound.

Noor – nervous as she is, shaky as she is – finds she can't *not* follow him out. They find Clifford Byrne and a small group of men standing outside, a little way down the corridor. They are all wearing identical suits in dark blue or dark grey. It's impossible to work out which is a lawyer or a doctor or a board member.

'Ah,' says Clifford Byrne, seeing them. 'Jimmy! I was just saying, we'll be taking treatment room four and therapy room two for the duration of the morning. We need the rooms around it cleared. Corridors clear. Absolute confidentiality for this client. I don't want anyone unauthorised – i.e. anyone who didn't arrive with me – wandering in and out of reception, either.'

'You want me to move the neighbouring staff members to other offices?'

'You got it.'

'And tell everyone not to move around the building for . . . how long?'

'Rest of the morning.'

'Right.'

Clifford slaps him on the back. 'Good work, Jimmy.'

'Excuse me,' Noor says. All the men turn to look at her. 'Hi. Is Dr Nightingale with you?'

Clifford Byrne is looking at her with a confused expression. She realises he's trying to remember her name.

'This is Dr Ali,' Jim says quickly. Clifford Byrne looks blank. 'She's our head of aftercare.'

'Oh, right,' Clifford Byrne says. 'Well, your aftercare team won't be required today.'

'I worked that out,' Noor says. 'Absolute confidentiality. Shall I lock them all in their rooms?'

Clifford Byrne looks at her, properly this time. His eyebrows go up. They stay up for a moment, and she's reminded of a Roman emperor's thumb, hovering in mid-air, about to turn up or down. Then Clifford Byrne laughs. The noise of it, both unexpected and loud, makes the two men closest to him blink.

'Very good,' he says to Noor. 'Very good. What were you saying about Dr Nightingale?'

'Is she with you today?'

'Dr Nightingale isn't part of this particular team,' one of the other men says. 'We're dealing with a few, very . . . specialised cases. The first of which is today.'

'Right,' Noor says. She nods as if she understands. In reality, she has no fucking idea what's going on.

'Get the case notes to Dr de Oliveira, okay?' Clifford says to another man, who nods and heads away.

Karine, thinks Noor. Interesting.

'Excuse me,' Marie the receptionist says, appearing round the corner, nearly colliding with the departing man.

'Yes, Maria?' Clifford Byrne says. 'Didn't I tell you to stay at your desk? We can't have a client arriving and no receptionist. You stay at your desk until the client arrives. Then you call therapy room two. It's a simple set of instructions, Maria.'

'I *did* stay at my desk,' Marie says. 'And I called the room several times but there was nobody there. And Jim wasn't in his office. I didn't know what to do. But the client's *here*. He's been here for nearly half an hour.'

'Shit,' says Clifford Byrne.

All the men start walking quickly, towards reception. Marie hurries after them. When they turn the corner, Noor and Jim are left alone.

It seems suddenly very quiet. Jim's sigh echoes in the empty space.

'Cup of tea?' Noor asks, feeling sorry for him.

'Yeah,' says Jim. 'Why not.'

When Noor gets back to her office she goes to the window first. She can see several expensive cars in the car park, presumably the ones that Clifford Byrne and his team arrived in. Louise's car isn't there.

Noor looks again at the clinic schedule. O. Levy. A specialised case, one of a few. Access Denied.

Today confirms at least that Louise isn't looking for O. Levy. She didn't bother showing up ahead of the appointment, and she's not going to show up now that the restoration has begun. Her interest in this particular week must have begun and ended with Mei.

Is this *it*? Noor wonders.

She's forced to confront the possibility that she'll *never* know what was going on. She'll never know why Louise called those other clients to stop them getting restorations. She'll never be able to ask her about it. She'll spend the rest of her working life wondering: not only about the wrongdoing she failed to prevent – or worse, helped to happen – but about the likelihood that one day someone will come into her office and fire her and it won't even be because of Elena.

And while possibilities are being *confronted* . . .

Noor's forced to confront the possibility that she's been hoping someone *will* come in and fire her over Elena.

That – once that happens – at some point in all the tribunals and interviews, Noor'll find herself in a solicitor's office (she's imagined it already: wood panelling, handshakes, neat files arranged at right angles on a shiny wooden table) and there, opposite her, will be Elena herself.

And afterwards, what: the solicitors will somehow magically fade away, leaving Elena and Noor on the pavement outside, alone?

Jesus.

What trash.

*

She's left – again – with her questions.

Louise, what have you done?
  Why did you do it?
  What's next?

Oscar

Oscar's in England.

Surrey, to be precise. On his way to the town of Crowsbeak, or Crowshat, or whatever it's called.

After Morocco the English landscape still seems absurdly green. The car made him feel uneasy at first but he rolled down his window and watched the hills outside rising and falling and it made him feel better. The green looks delicious. He wants to smell the colour of it; stick his head out, open his mouth and taste it: the just-gone frost, the tender blades of grass.

Look, Oscar, the guy at the airport had said. His name was Frobisher. The problem is that we need to speak to you. But you don't have an email, you won't take calls, and you don't answer letters. So we end up having to track you down.

He sounded baffled, as if he expected Oscar to explain himself. But Oscar had decided early on that he was going to maintain an unyielding silence. So he did. He folded his arms and tried to look impassive, even though it was probably obvious to both of them that Frobisher had a full house and Oscar had dropped all his cards on the floor.

We don't want to harass you, Frobisher continued, I mean, I personally have got better things to do than follow you around Marrakech.

He gave a friendly laugh, but Oscar's arms stayed folded.

Do you even *know* what we're trying to talk to you about? said Frobisher, and now he sounded almost exasperated.

Oscar wasn't falling for that one. He gave Frobisher a long stare.

I don't know if this is a trust issue, Frobisher said, or you're just angry, or what. That's understandable. What happened should never have happened. Now it can be put right, if you want. You don't want to talk to me, that's fine. All you have to do is listen. My job is to explain the situation – I can do that right now – and give you your options. That's it. You can do what you want after that. Is that okay?

Okay, Oscar said. Fire away.

(He regretted the choice of words immediately.)

And ultimately it comes down to this:

Nothing.

It's not like Oscar believes Frobisher. Frobisher said he came to give Oscar information, but Oscar has no way of knowing if any of it is true. Frobisher said 'options', but that's essentially bullshit. There's one option, one story, one source of information: Frobisher himself. He laid it all out over the wonky-legged airport table and Oscar went along with it, because it's Frobisher or nothing, and Oscar has had enough of nothing. It's like that riddle: *What's greater than God, more evil than the Devil? The poor have it, the rich want it, and if you eat it you'll die.*

Well, Oscar had been living on nothing for a long time, and he knows that if he has to do it any longer he'll die.

Frobisher seemed to understand this. His experienced eye saw that Oscar was a thin fox, ready to drop. He said: You can change your mind at any time. Just go to the clinic. Talk to them.

And Oscar said:

Okay.

When they landed at Heathrow – a flight organised and paid for by Frobisher – Frobisher said a driver would be waiting for Oscar in arrivals.

You're not coming with me? asked Oscar.

No. I'm catching a train and going home. You're going to a . . . place. It's nice. Like a hotel, but with doctors. You'll stay with them for a couple of weeks and get evaluated and interviewed and so on. Everyone's expecting you. You only have to give your name. Have you got everything you need?

He was looking at Oscar's mostly empty backpack. (Contents: Passport. Squashed Moroccan pastry from the airport. Credit card. A few dirhams.)

I have no idea what I need, Oscar said.

Maybe some warmer clothes, Frobisher suggested. I know you haven't been back to the UK in a while, but flip-flops in November are a no-no.

Is that what month it is? Oscar said. It's hard to keep track.

Frobisher seemed now to want to get away. He was looking at Oscar like Oscar was on his doorstep trying to sell him cavity wall insulation. Oscar reassured Frobisher that he did have a credit card, and he would clothe himself appropriately.

Good, said Frobisher. Then I'll leave you to it. He shook Oscar's hand and wished him all the best.

And that was that.

Oscar wandered the shops; bought himself some jeans, a coat and some brown leather shoes. Then he went to arrivals, and there was his driver, holding a card that said *Oscar Levy*, which sent the usual electric shock through Oscar, before he remembered that he was *meant* to be known.

That his name, maybe for the first time, was a good thing.

It only takes half an hour to get to the clinic. A bit too fast for comfort. Oscar isn't quite ready for it. Not the gates, the tallness of them, or the protesters, the number of them, or the clinic itself: the fact of it, its existence in real life. The car comes to a stop.

'Is this it?' he asks stupidly. Of course this is it. His hands are trembling.

'This is it,' says the driver.

'Oh. Are you sure? Okay. So, I just get out here then, and go inside. I suppose I do. Yep. That's what I do now.'

Oscar pinches off the shakiness by making fists. Unfortunately this just has the effect of moving the shakes up his arms, and into his chest. Now his heart's going.

375

He gets out reluctantly, and walks towards reception. He looks back. The driver is still sitting in the car, watching him. And so Oscar has to pass through the large glass doors, into . . . white.

Everything is white. In the corner is a receptionist, sitting behind a curved white desk. He walks over to her across the shiny white floor. He notices that when the receptionist greets him there is something careful about her politeness, as if she's as tense as Oscar.

The receptionist asks for his name, nothing more. She asks him to take a seat and wait. Oscar goes over to the other corner of the room, and sits down on a white sofa.

Nothing here jogs his memory. Maybe that's intentional, that's why the design brief was 'blank and white' – though in its absolute blankness and whiteness the place *is* kind of memorable. It doesn't remind him of the place he remembers, with the chair and the white coat. That was white, too, but there was something different about that place. The vibrations of the noises, the density of the atmosphere. He can't explain it. It's just not the same.

After about twenty minutes, the receptionist leaves. She says she'll be back in a moment. She definitely looks edgy. He hasn't seen anyone else in all the time he's been here. As if everyone here is so frightened of Oscar that they're hiding in their offices until he's gone.

He looks out at the grounds, filled with a sportive light, bouncing about on the grass. Beyond the wall of pines is the road out of here.

He wonders if anyone's ever escaped over the wall.

Maybe he'll be the first.

The thought's a half-hearted one. Oscar already knows he's not going anywhere. They all know it; that's how they can leave him here alone. He's not going to run away now, just because he's got no idea what this procedure will do to him – if it will flip him neatly inside out like a surgical glove, left to right, all his ins now outs.

Just because he's fucking terrified.

The receptionist comes back as Oscar's leg is starting to jitter.

'Mr Levy? Would you come this way?'

He follows her ushering arm through a door.

It leads to a white corridor.

Oscar knows, now. At the end of it there's going to be a room, with a reclining chair upholstered in pale grey vinyl. A coat hanging on the door. A lifeless kind of light.

So this is it.

Well, fuck it. He walks towards the final door with a weird feeling of acceptance. The sweating in his hands has stopped; his fingers hang at his sides. This is how everyone says death is, this volition-less floating towards the end, only minus the sense of euphoria, the singing in the ears, the blinding beauty.

'Oh, sorry, Mr Levy, it's this way.'

'What?'

'It's this room. Er, this one here.'

The woman is holding open a door behind him, the first door they'd come to, off to the right.

'Oh,' says Oscar. Walks back to it. 'Sorry.'

Inside this room there's no reclining chair. Just a desk, some large plants in pots, four men in suits, and a framed black-and-white picture of a beach.

All the men get to their feet. They smile, with varying degrees of sincerity. They take it in turns to shake Oscar's hand and tell him who they are.

Man number one says he is Clifford Byrne, director of something and something here at Nepenthe.

Man number two says he is Francis Hathaway, a Nepenthe solicitor, though Oscar is not to worry about this as Francis Hathaway's presence is really only a formality.

Man number three says he is Alex Medvedev, a Nepenthe psychologist.

Man number four says he is Michael Goldman. He is the youngest of the four and is apparently Oscar's solicitor.

'I'm here to represent your interests,' he says.

'Because I don't know what they are,' says Oscar.

'Er,' says Michael. 'Basically, yes.'

'Okay,' Oscar says. 'Have we met before?'

'Actually the solicitor who originally represented you retired. The case was passed to me. We haven't met but I know your family. Your uncle Simon . . . ? Your aunt Rebecca . . . ?'

'I don't know those people,' Oscar says.

'Hopefully they'll come back to you,' says Michael Goldman.

The talking after that takes a while. The men say mostly the same things that Frobisher said, which means either Frobisher was telling the truth or they're all in on the same lie. They tell Oscar about the restorations. Everyone wanting memory refunds. A giant rewind button pressed. People walking, backwards, to the clinic; coming out as younger versions of themselves. Money flowing out of the clinic's bank accounts, confidentiality agreements unwriting themselves.

'I don't get it,' says Oscar. 'If someone spent a load of money to get rid of a memory, why would they want it back?'

'Most people don't,' says Clifford Byrne.

'But you're telling me that *I* do,' Oscar says. 'That this is what's best for me.'

'We're not making any claims as to your future condition,' says Francis Hathaway.

'That's reassuring,' Oscar says.

'It's true that we can't guarantee what the results of this procedure will be,' Dr Medvedev says. 'Your case is very different to that of the average client. It's not a matter of one unwanted memory. It's more complicated than that.'

'Because you scrambled my brains,' says Oscar.

Then everyone starts talking at once, at Oscar. They use a lot of words – *clinical trials, government approval, rigorous methodology, full and informed consent, settled in court, generous compensation* – stacking the words up in front of them, one on top of another, like a wall. Oscar almost feels sorry for them, rushing to protect themselves. From Oscar! It's actually funny.

'It's okay,' he says to them. 'You can stop explaining it.'

At this the wall is dismantled. The men come out, cautiously, from behind it. They're still talking, but this time they're using lots of words that aren't exactly *sorry* but are clearly meant to stand in for it.

Regrettable. Unfortunate. Hindsight. Best intentions.

'Okay,' Oscar interrupts. '*If* you're telling me the truth, the gist of all this is: you only wipe the short memories, but not the long ones. Or the old ones.'

'Wipe isn't exactly the word –'

'And you don't wipe those, because it doesn't work.'

'Well, the procedures in themselves were successful, but there were some adverse consequences –'

'And you know about the adverse consequences because you guys were doing dodgy secret research –'

'– I have to point out here that there was no illegality about the RASA clinical trial, and confidentiality was necessary to protect –'

'And these RASA experiments ended up messing everyone's brains up.'

'That's not the terminology we would use.'

'No. I guess not. I have problems remembering the right terminology though, which I guess is technically your fault, so maybe you'll let me off?'

Silence.

'Oscar –' Michael Goldman murmurs.

'And I apparently volunteered for this, when I was twenty-one, though obviously I can't remember it.'

Michael again: 'You did volunteer, yes. We have all the documentation you signed. Which is available to you –'

'Sure, sure,' Oscar says. 'Look: let's just do this. Hook me up. Un-wipe me. Un-zap me. Whatever you do. Then we'll see afterwards what happened to me. Or what I did. *Then* I'll read the paperwork.' (Side-eye to Michael Goldman.) 'That's okay, right?'

'It's your choice,' says Michael.

'My choice,' repeats Oscar. He looks at the men, sitting there so gravely. They could be anyone. This place could be anything. He's getting twitchy. His palms have started sweating again.

Maybe he is dreaming. He could be in the riad beside a snoring Jess. He could be a child the age of Atticus, having dreamt his whole life. If it turns out that he's in a coma, like the guy in that film, what's this procedure going to do? Is this his way out? His way of . . . waking up?

'Let's do it,' he says.

They go into another room. Just Oscar and Dr Medvedev this time.

In this new room the light is white, but it's still not the same as the light he remembers. There's a smiling nurse in here. A window onto a room of computers and people who ignore Oscar's arrival. A white-sheeted bed in the corner.

'Where's the chair?' Oscar asks. 'The reclining chair?'

'I'm sorry: the what?' asks Dr Medvedev.

'Never mind.'

'If you lie down here . . .' the nurse says. She's holding a small plastic cup.

'Where's the laser?' asks Oscar, looking around.

'No lasers. It's a chemical compound. Once it takes effect, we pass electrical waves gently through –'

'*Gently*? How do you electrocute me gently?'

'It's a very mild current. It just works to activate areas of the brain.'

'You're waking up my memories?'

'That's a good way of putting it.'

'Well, what do you know. That's the first time someone around here has liked my way of putting things.'

They are looking at the cup.

Oscar raises it to the nurse, Dr Medvedev and the people beyond the window.

'Bottoms up,' he says.

And drinks.

They've turned the lights up to full beam. Faces dissolve in the intensity of it. He wants to tell them, but his throat is too dry.

'Bright,' he whispers.

A hand is in front of him, holding a plastic cup.

'What is it?'

'Just water. Drink it slowly. And when you're ready, sit up slowly. It's going to take you a while to feel steady, so don't rush.'

'So how does this work?' Oscar asks.

'Just try to think of something you know. Something you can remember. You should find it connects to another memory now.'

Oscar thinks of the white corridor. And he's *there*: as soon as he thinks it, he's walking along it, in a smaller body than the one he has now, his feet tiny, in their new fluorescent trainers. The feet hesitate. The flat, artificial light spreads beneath the closed door.

He stops, looks at his dad.

'It's fine,' his dad says. 'Appointments are over. Go on.'

His mum looks up when Oscar runs in. She's taking off her white coat, hanging it on a peg behind her. Beside the empty chair are the traces of pink swill in the sink, cold spit and tooth-polish grit. (Spit and grit, a good rhyme.)

His mum removes her gloves; holds out her hands.

'Ozzie-man! Where's my hug?'

He goes and wraps his arms around her. She smells minty.

'Home?' says his dad.

'Absolutely. You too, Tara.'

Tara the dental nurse is switching off the light above the reclining chair. She turns on the tap and the pink of the last patient disappears. 'What's up, Oscar?' she says. Tara once gave him a sheet of stickers, each one with a smiling canine on it.

I'm a happy tooth! I get brushed every day!

Oscar has wondered before if there are stickers with crying teeth on them.

I'm a neglected tooth! I'm a rotten tooth that never got brushed. I'm a sad tooth.

'Night, guys,' Tara says, leaving. 'See you tomorrow, Rachel.'

His mother puts on her coat, a grey moleskin velvet; a nap that would raise up if you rubbed it the wrong way, making a dark streak on the fabric. He brushes it now, the cuff, as he takes her hand.

The exact feel of it, under his fingers.

*

383

The necklace, Oscar thinks.

And then he's in his garden. The sun coming down in bits and pieces, scissored up by the trees. He's eating strawberries from the large terracotta planter beside him, three so far. He'll stop at five, which he's calculated is the number he can eat without it being noticed.

His mum comes out just as his hand's reaching for number seven. He drops it; acts nonchalant.

'Ozzie, we need to get some suncream on you. It's getting hot out here. Hotter in the kitchen, though. Dad's making a cake. Don't ask me why.'

'Chocolate cake?'

'Carob and apple. But just as delicious.'

The problem with both parents being dentists is that nobody sneaks him anything when the other one's back is turned. They're both on the same side: the side of good dental health. Oscar has tried to argue that his baby teeth are all going to fall out anyway and so it only makes sense for him to start eating healthily when the new ones arrive. They ignored that.

His mother strokes his hair. As if she hears what he's thinking, she says, 'When your milk teeth are all out, I'm going to get them cast in gold and made into a necklace.'

'Really?' his dad says, from the kitchen doorway.

'What?' says his mum.

'It'll be hideous. And macabre. Didn't some serial killer do that?'

'What's a serial killer?' Oscar asks.

'Nothing. Your dad is being silly,' his mum says. 'Listen Ozzie-man, my necklace will be beautiful, because *I* think it's beautiful.'

Oscar's father laughs. Surrenders. 'Fine. Lovely. What-ever you say.'

Something else is worrying Oscar.

'Aren't you going to give the teeth to the tooth fairy?' he asks.

'Ha!' says his father. 'Answer that one, Rachel.'

'Of course I am,' his mother says. 'But we dentists have a special arrangement with tooth fairies. It was a pact made thousands of years ago. By the very first dentist and the very first fairy. They met on the moon, on a mountain in the shape of a tooth and they carved the words of their pact into the side of it. That the tooth fairies still take the teeth, and the children still get their money, but later on, if they have some special plan in mind, like my plan, the dentist can send a message to the fairies and ask for the teeth to be returned.'

'How do you send the message?'

His mother doesn't even blink. 'Under my pillow, of course. But only on a full moon.'

'Of course,' says his father. 'The first thing we learned at dentist school. I don't know how I forgot.'

'Silly Daddy,' says his mother, and they laugh, and Oscar joins in, wondering why it's funny, with half his mind on the security of his tooth fairy money, now assured, the other half on the forgotten carob cake still baking – maybe burning! Like the last time his dad got distracted when he was making avocado muffins, and they went and got ice creams instead.

Oscar's eyes swim and well.

He needs water, but his throat is too tight to get the request out. He signals instead. Gets water, in a plastic cup. Tears spurt from his eyes as he drinks, as if the water is cycling up and straight back out.

He hands the empty cup back.

Lies back.

Closes his eyes.

Water, Oscar thinks.

Oscar and his parents are on holiday.

They'd loaded up the Volvo and off they went, first visiting Uncle Simon and Aunt Rebecca near Le Touquet, then heading on to a villa near Deauville owned by his father's friend, which they'd got the use of for a couple of weeks in exchange for some free dentistry.

Oscar, squinting in the back-seat sun, is relieved that his cousins, Leah and Nat, are getting further and further away every minute. Both of them black-eyed and black-haired, like two apprentice witches. They were bloody annoying. He told them that, then got ticked off for saying bloody, though in the corner of his eye he could see his mother trying not to smile (maybe because she was the one who'd said it in the first place), and was made to apologise. Then the cousins knew they'd won that one and Nat said that if Oscar didn't help them with the castle they were making in the rockery (stupid bloody castle), they'd tell their parents he said *bloody* again, and it'd be two against one. So he helped move stones and re-pile them, and got bitten by some weird French ants. Then on the last day of their stay, when the castle was discovered and Uncle Simon blew his top, the bloody twins claimed it was all Oscar's idea.

On the plus side, Uncle Simon and Aunt Rebecca had let him have ice cream at the beach, and biscuits out of a green glass jar, and his mum had unexpectedly allowed it, shrugging and saying, 'Well, we are on holiday.'

He wonders how long this permissiveness is going to last. The wondering is slow and enjoyable; a drowsy reel of Soleros, Ferreros, Polos, Rolos. A long, unwinding strawberry string of rhymes. The sun wraps him like a blanket, heavy and familiar. It seems easier to close his eyes than to squint against it.

'Look at Ozzie,' his mum says now. 'He's half asleep. Those girls tired him out.'

'No, they didn't,' Oscar says immediately. Eyelids snapping up. He clarifies: 'But I do hate them.'

Her eyes float in the rear-view mirror. One of them closes, reopens. She's the only one in the family who can wink. But Oscar and his dad can roll their tongues.

'Why, Ozzie. What a thing to say. Two young girls.'

But she's laughing, and his father says, 'Young in years but old in wickedness.'

'Well. It'll just be us at the villa.'

'The four of us,' his dad says. Side-eye to Oscar's mum's football-sized, apparently soon to be beachball-sized stomach.

Oscar asks, 'Can we call the baby something that rhymes with Oscar?'

'What rhymes with Oscar?'

'Nothing rhymes with Oscar,' his dad says. 'That's partly why we called you Oscar. I was Adi at school. Adi the baddie. Addo the saddo. Et cetera. Whereas your mother never got bullied because she was called Rachel.'

'Hang on. I never got bullied because (a) I didn't wear glasses and (b) I never told anyone I wanted to be a dentist.'

Oscar presses on. 'It could rhyme with Oz. Like Loz.'

'Or Roz. Actually, Roz is cute. Rosalind. Rosamund.'

'Look, Oscar! Look at the water.'

His mother points. Below the bridge the wide river is shivering silver. It's like a giant sparkling piece of silk, pegged to the ground, trying to shake itself free.

'Or Fozzie,' says his dad. 'Like Fozzie Bear . . . *Shit!*'

Oscar looks up. He can't understand what he is seeing. Then he can. It's a truck. All the windscreen is truck. And it's moving too fast to see, and the noise is louder than all of them.

He's trying to get to his feet and they're trying to stop him.

'Try to stay calm, Mr Levy.'

'Just breathe.'

'Please, sit down.'

A new cup of water is offered. He reaches for it, misses, knocks it out of the nurse's hand. It hangs for a moment in the air, trembling.

Then – as it was always going to – it hits the ground.

*

Later, they say his dad died immediately.

Oscar doesn't say anything to that. He could have told them that actually there was a moment after his dad's head was obscured, in a red crackle of surprise, that Oscar heard him speak, but he didn't know what his dad said, the noise was so squashed by whatever had happened to his face, and so there didn't seem any point in explaining it.

His mother had spoken. She screamed at first, as the car hit the water, but then she stopped abruptly, and turned to Oscar in the back.

Her eyes were wide and clear and rational. She got this look when she was making a plan. She'd be silent for a moment, the look would appear, and then she'd say something like, 'Right, Oscar, we need to get you to the shoe shop before term starts,' or 'I'd better let Tara know about the 9 a.m. cancellation.'

She looked at him then and said, 'Oscar, can you undo your seat belt?'

Oscar was crying and didn't listen. There was too much. The strange side of his dad's head, what he could see of it. The water flooding through the smashed windows. It was foaming pink. It was so loud. The car rocked like he was shaking it, like it was his own voice doing it, drowning them.

His mum twisted and pulled her body, as much as she could, back past the front seats. She couldn't get all of herself through, and Oscar thought it was because of the football-sized stomach – but they explained later that it wasn't that, it was because her legs had been trapped when the lorry crushed the front of the car. She got hold of Oscar's seat belt and undid it; pulled him between the seats, past his father, out through the empty jagged hole of the windscreen.

Her hair was pressed wet against her face.

There was no blood on her at all.

Eyes wide.

Calm.

The water came in over them.

Then the car was travelling downwards and Oscar was going up, holding his breath, beating his arms and moving up to the surface where the grey light jittered, because he knew she was coming too; she was right behind him.

Oscar felt for a long time after that as if he'd been tricked, by someone he couldn't be angry with.

They said he couldn't have helped her. Her legs were trapped, they kept telling him. Nothing could have been any different. It wasn't a sacrifice, it wasn't a matter of her or him that had to die.

He doesn't say, *But why couldn't it have been both?*

If she hadn't looked so calm, maybe he'd have understood what was going on; stayed with her, so she wasn't all alone at the bottom of the lake when she died.

Instead he got to the surface and bobbed about screaming for help, like a bloody idiot. He got pulled out by people he never thanked, because at some point he twigged and started to fight them instead, trying to get back into the water. Someone held him and he kicked them, to stop them carrying him away, back past the jackknifed lorry with its wheels steaming, the gathered, staring crowds. A woman had her hands pressed against her mouth. Away from the hanging metal of the bridge barrier, the water below.

It was calm.

The car was gone and the surface had mended itself quietly back together, rippling gently in the afternoon light, like nothing had happened.

They give him her necklace.

There's the house in Chippenham, too, but Oscar is too small to live in it by himself, burrowed into his parents' bed; an eternal Sunday morning, waiting for them to wake up. Instead he and the necklace go to Uncle Saul and Aunt Bee's creaky, high-ceilinged old house in Bristol.

After a year or so Uncle Saul (who is old, and ill) and Aunt Bee can't cope with Oscar any more, so he goes to Uncle Matthew and Aunt Nicky's house in Poole. When – a few years after that – it turns out Uncle Matthew and Aunt Nicky can't cope either, Oscar is sent to live in France for the summer, with Uncle Simon and Aunt Rebecca. (Everyone agrees – all the executors and guardians and legal representatives – that it'd be better, more stabilising, for Oscar to stay in England. But he's run out of uncles and aunts in England, and family abroad is considered better than strangers at home.)

He doesn't want to go back to Le Touquet. It wasn't Aunt Rebecca and Uncle Simon's fault, obviously, but the last holiday he'd spent with them didn't turn out all that well. But Uncle Matthew and Aunt Nicky are divorcing and (according to Nicky, whispering, at night) this is in large part Oscar's fault.

He'll send you to an early grave.
    How can you say that?
    It's just an expression. But anyway, it's true. And anyway, I can't deal with him. I just can't.

Everyone thinks Oscar has turned a corner after he gets to Le Touquet. *Healing,* they say. What they mean is: *easier to cope with.* Really it's that the proximity to the crash has knocked the fight out of him.

What was he fighting?

Everyone. Everything. Not in the obvious kind of way. He never raised his voice, or hit anyone. He just ignored people until it drove them mad. He wore them out with nots. Not eating. Not talking. Not listening.

In Le Touquet he sits by the old rockery and digs the weeds out, waiting for the weird French ants to come out and bite him, but they don't.

Nat and Leah have actually turned out okay. Still blackhaired but not witch-like, not really. Not that it matters. They want to help him and be his family, but Oscar isn't up for more family. Been there, done that. Thank you very much but no.

He isn't able to explain this, so he just avoids them and in the end they give him a respectful berth; watching him across the space he's created, with their sad dark eyes.

After the summer he says he wants to go back to England, to boarding school, and nobody argues with him. They probably all hope it will help. He's twelve by now;

old enough. And it's not like money is an issue: there's the life insurance, and a payout from the haulier company, none of which Oscar gives a shit about.

As soon as he's escaped Le Touquet, Oscar goes back to *not*.

Not listening in class. Later, not going to school. Not seeing his relatives in the holidays, not answering their calls. Stealing a gun; not giving it back. Not coming back to his dorm, for entire nights, then entire weeks. Not contesting his expulsion. Not stopping drinking, then, when he got taken to hospital, not telling the nurses his identity. A protracted turning of his back: a long, messy *not*.

'This isn't the first time you've got into trouble,' says Oscar's solicitor.

He stares at her, and says nothing.

'Oscar, we want to help you.'

Oscar can't see how that's possible. He's finally got beyond help. That was the entire point. He's eighteen, no longer a minor, he's dropped out of school, and he's into heroin by now, which seemed like the biggest *not* anyone had or could ever come up with, and so he took it, gratefully.

. . . But heroin wasn't the biggest *not*, was it? There was one more.

The ultimate and final *not*.

This *not* was contained in a chamber of the cylinder of a gun once found in the possession of a famous musician, then in the house of Lonnie's dad, then under Oscar's bed, now in Oscar's hand, in an empty supermarket, being discussed by a group of junkies and ne'er-do-wells.

Things to do with a gun

(Because something must be done.)

Suggestion 1) Stage a heist.
  Too risky. And also, hassle.

Suggestion 2) Find a quiet place and shoot some inanimate objects.
  Too boring.

Suggestion 3) Mug someone.
  Bad karma. And also, hassle.

At this point it was starting to look like the gun wasn't going to fulfil its destiny after all. Not unless Oscar stepped in, with

Suggestion 4) Russian roulette.

  . . . Russian roulette?
  Hahaha – wait.
  Man, you're fucking crazy. Are you serious?
  He's serious.

Oscar, don't do it.
Oscar!
Is it loaded?
Three bullets.
Aren't you meant to do it with one?
He's going to fucking kill himself.
Oscar, stop it!
Oscar, this isn't funny.

He sees his parents. Water separates them. He'd like to say it was the ripples that obscure his vision, but the truth is he can hardly remember their faces.

One *not* to part the water.

Oscar!

Oscar, don't!

Bang.

. . . Nothing.

Oscar sits on a wall, alone. The sky is black and the Thames looks like a dirty piece of glass, small lights reflecting off its broken edges.

They took the gun away from him, wrestling it off him, as he shouted at them. One of the girls said she'd hand it in to the police.

Fuck you, Oscar said to her. Then he said, Sorry.

Then he left.

They all stood there behind him, not saying anything. He walked down the empty aisle with its signs hanging overhead. CEREAL said one. If he'd actually shot himself they could have called him the cereal killer. It would have been his first successful joke.

He'd walked the rest of the night and morning, finally ending up here, in the heart of the City. The skyscrapers stare impassively at the sky, like they're averting their gaze from Oscar below.

He stares at the water and feels a corresponding shifting, oily misery flowing through him. The river comes up through him. It reaches his eyes, leaking polluted water; if he opens his mouth it will pour out and out and never stop.

At dawn he buys a newspaper and sits in a coffee shop without reading it. He has no plan. The day overtakes him. The sun comes up, then the rain comes, people with suits and umbrellas come in, order coffee to go, then go.

At the time it feels like a sign.

'Latte please. Grande. I hear they're paying a lot for the trials at Nepenthe.'

So says a woman in a skirt suit.

'It's pronounced Nepenth*ee*,' says her colleague. She has a small, sarky smile. 'And they'd *need* to pay. I mean, who *are* these people . . . ? *Hey, let's find out if wiping my memory has catastrophic long-term effects.* Jesus. Espresso, please. Double. Thank you.'

They both laugh, passing to the end of the counter, beyond Oscar's hearing.

And Oscar thinks: what was that, if not a sign? A word from a higher power, or the universe, or his parents, even, saying:

This is better than killing yourself.

Oscar gets up and leaves the coffee shop; moves with new purpose across the lightening streets, heading for the station.

'I'll do anything,' he says to Nepenthe.

They say this isn't considered informed consent. First he has to hear all about the procedure they're testing (wiping the memory of early childhood trauma), how secret the nature of the RASA trial is (top secret), and what could go wrong (a lot), and then he has to sign a large number of forms.

'Whatever,' he says. 'Just make it go away.'

He isn't at the actual clinic yet. It's some other office in London. A woman named Dr Nightingale is there.

'Like Florence,' he says to her.

'Florence Nightingale was a nurse,' she says. 'I'm a doctor.'

'What does Nepenthe mean?' Oscar asks her.

'It's an old word. Quite obscure, really. It was a forgetfulness potion.'

'Was that on purpose?' Oscar says. 'Naming a procedure to make people forget after a word that everyone's forgotten?'

'Perhaps,' Dr Nightingale says. She doesn't smile. 'Listen, Mr Levy, I need to make sure you are fully aware of the risks of this kind of experimental procedure. Because the risks are numerous. And significant. They could be life-changing. Do you understand this?'

'I don't like my life,' Oscar says. 'I don't care how it changes. I don't honestly care if it ends. Anything is better than this.'

Dr Nightingale looks at him. She sighs.

'Okay. I'm satisfied with the results of your evaluation. However, please bear in mind this is only the first stage of assessment. I'm going to hand you over now to Dr Russell, who's running the RASA trial, and his team.'

'You aren't running it?'

'No. Absolutely not. I'm just conducting the assessments. You won't see me again.'

'That's a shame. On the bright side, maybe Dr Russell will find my jokes funny,' Oscar says.

'Probably not,' Dr Nightingale says. 'But on the bright side: you won't remember if he doesn't.'

Which *is* funny, and Oscar laughs.

'Bring on the next stage of the trial,' he says.

They warn him the necklace will confuse him, afterwards, but he says he wants to keep it. They seem confused (and why wouldn't they be?) that he can get rid of everything – his parents' house, their things, every memory of them – but not that.

'Your choice,' they say.

They say that a lot.

'We really do think,' says Dr Russell – leaning forward, earnest – 'that this can give you and other survivors of trauma the best chance of a happy life.'

The weird thing was, Oscar felt like he meant it.

Oscar's sitting up.

They've cleared up the water he knocked out of the nurse's hand, and he apologised, and everyone raced to be the first to say that it wasn't a problem, that this was a stressful time, and so on.

He's taken back to the first room, to rest and await his chat with Dr Medvedev. He notices a box of tissues within arm's reach on a small table next to the sofa. They're expecting him to do some more crying, then.

His solicitor Michael Goldman must still be around somewhere. He remembers Goldman & Bude now, the firm chosen by his uncles and aunts. Michael Goldman wasn't lying: he is here on Oscar's side. Or, as much as any solicitor is ever really on anybody's side. The only time Oscar ever heard his dad swear was when they were buying a new house and he found out about the solicitor's fees.

Shifty fuckers. I could do it myself, he said.

Not this again, said Oscar's mum. No, you couldn't.

Well, no, and that's because they've made it impossible for people like me. We can't even access our own records. It's a conspiracy! It should have been simple but instead it's a fu— a *flipping* Masonic illuminati ritual.

He turned to Oscar. Listen, Ozzie, if you're paying someone to do something that you don't understand, they're probably screwing you over.

Adi. Let's not embitter him too early.

I'm preparing him for the world. Right, Ozzie? Don't forget your father's wisdom.

Oscar covers his eyes.

He forgot.

He pulls tissues out of the box, too quickly, tearing them. He's never cried much, before. Not even after his parents died. Maybe because it's been so long coming, all the things he could have cried over appear again – in no particular order or weight, like someone's picked up a box and turned it upside down.

His dad asleep on the sofa as a film played, because he could never make it through a film without nodding off. Atticus on the flight home, worrying about his brother. His mum singing Madonna, better than Madonna, but being too shy to ever do it in front of people; just a voice slipping out under the bathroom door. Not saying goodbye to Karolina, to Jess, to anyone.

He's out of tissues, but the tears are easing off. The images have slowed to a trickle. Just one last kick, from a hurt-looking teacher whose class Oscar disrupted, and that's it. When Dr Medvedev comes in, Oscar feels like telling him it's too late.

'How are you, Oscar?' asks Dr Medvedev. 'Obviously there's a lot to take in –'

'A lot is right,' says Oscar. 'You guys took a lot away. You really fucked it up, right?'

Dr Medvedev hesitates.

'One moment,' he says, leaving the room.

When he comes back he's accompanied by the solicitors.

'Do you mind if they sit in?' he asks Oscar.

'Be my guests,' Oscar says.

'So. The results of the first phase of the RASA trial weren't promising, sadly,' says Dr Medvedev. He speaks carefully. 'We decided to end the programme. What this meant for you and the other subjects is that the memory of the early childhood trauma *was* successfully removed, but it turned out that too many secondary memories were connected to that primary memory. We're still not sure exactly how it works at a neurological level, but the theory is that you'd probably spent a lot of time thinking about your parents, and this content was entangled somehow with other moments in your life. As a result, a lot of your other memories would have seemed dissociated, patchy or disrupted.'

'Dissociated, patchy and disrupted,' Oscar says. 'Yeah, that's basically it. So, then what? I sued you?'

'Well. You weren't considered – legally – to be in possession of sound mind at that time. You couldn't remember visiting Nepenthe, so bringing a suit was difficult. It was your former legal guardians – your aunt and uncle – along with other people acting on behalf of the other subjects who brought a suit against Nepenthe, and Nepenthe settled.'

'I was living with my relatives, then?'

'No. You spent some time in a private hospital. You were . . . disoriented.'

'No shit,' Oscar says. 'Wasn't it in the newspapers? The case?'

'No. It was confidential.'

'But why was it confidential to *me*? Why didn't anyone explain what happened to me?'

Dr Medvedev says that before the study began, Oscar signed something to say that no matter what happened to him, he didn't want the memory back. Later on, when it became obvious that Oscar's brain was fucked, teams of people argued about this in court. The decision was made to honour the original agreement, because they thought that it might do even more damage to tell Oscar about a past he couldn't remember.

So it was agreed that they'd tell him that he'd suffered brain damage affecting his long-term memory. And maybe if so many people in suits hadn't been involved in this telling process, or so many legal documents, or – later – so much money, they might have been more plausible. Or maybe Oscar remembered his dad's warning after all, because he didn't trust any of them.

'I ran,' he says.

'Yes.'

'But then Nepenthe was looking for me. The man in Brighton. The guy in Budapest. The calls to the hotel. How did you know I was there – was it the card? I didn't use the card at the riad.'

'I'll answer this, if I may,' says the Nepenthe solicitor. (Oscar's already forgotten his name. Probably a normal person would have forgotten it too, under the circumstances.) 'Your family hired someone to look for you after you absconded. They were worried. But you disappeared, and after a few months they couldn't afford to pursue you. Then this year, we engaged a firm –'

'Wait,' Oscar says. 'This year? So I've been on the run for *years*, and nobody was even looking for me?'

The Nepenthe solicitor nods.

There's a long silence.

'Do you need a minute?' says the Nepenthe solicitor eventually.

'Use your eyes,' Michael Goldman says. 'He needs a minute.'

Some minutes pass.

The Nepenthe solicitor resumes. 'In spring this year, we engaged a firm to track down the former RASA patients and make them aware of their right to a restoration procedure. Your bank account is administered by family trustees, and they gave Nepenthe permission to use the account information to trace you. As for the riad, it says here . . . yes, a social media user named JesstoImpress posted a picture of you on the Instagram app, a public forum, which was picked up by our facial recognition software. She also included the name of the riad as a "hashtag".'

'Right,' Oscar said. At least now he could contact Jess and send her a proper apology. 'But then they found me at the airport. Frobisher did.'

'Uh. That was actually a coincidence. The investigator had submitted that you could be considered to have refused contact, and he was moving on to the next assignment.'

'*Synchronology*,' says Oscar, momentarily delighted. 'Typical. So, hang on: you were just *giving up*? You were going to leave me alone?'

'So to speak, yes.'

'Then why chase me so hard in the first place?'

'After the news came out that memories could be reclaimed, Nepenthe committed to make every reasonable

403

effort to notify the RASA test subjects, and offer them the memory back.'

'That's a lot of effort,' Oscar said. 'Tracking down a load of nutters like me, I mean. You'd think that was above and beyond.'

'Actually,' Michael Goldman says, 'the representatives of some of the other RASA patients sued Nepenthe, and won. They argued that as Nepenthe were going to offer their self-confidential patients the chance to have the memory restored, the same went for the RASA patients. More so, given that the impact on their mental health and quality of life was so much greater. It was another sealed case: you wouldn't have heard about it in the media. Anyway, the ruling was that Nepenthe had a duty of care to track down the former patients and offer them restoration.'

'Which we committed to do,' says the Nepenthe solicitor. 'And this is important, Oscar: the details of the case are still confidential. You'd be in breach of the terms of the settlement if you discuss it with anyone now.'

'Yes. Nepenthe fought for that one, and they won,' Michael Goldman says, without looking at the Nepenthe solicitor.

'We maintain that anonymity continues to be in the best interests of the patients,' says the Nepenthe solicitor, without looking at Michael Goldman.

'How kind of you,' Oscar says.

He's not really listening. He's running the knobbles of the gold necklace between his thumb and finger.

Michael Goldman looks worried. 'You understand, right, Oscar? You can't tell anyone about this. You could challenge the decision legally, of course, but I have to warn you that this –'

'I don't care,' Oscar says. 'It doesn't matter.'

After all this time, it was his own teeth.

Jess was right.

The teeth of someone he'd killed.

Noor

The good thing about having all her meetings cancelled and everyone being confined to their offices, Noor reflects, is that it leaves her at leisure to sit by the window of her own office with a cup of tea, waiting for O. Levy to come out.

A few hours go by. Nobody passes the window. The light moves slowly across the lawn. Noor falls into an awake-asleep state. Her tea sends up distress signals into the air next to her as it cools. When something finally happens, Noor jumps. O. Levy has come out of reception, flanked by Clifford Byrne's squad of specialised whatevers, and is walking towards one of the black cars that's waiting there for him.

He looks *young*, from what Noor can see of him. First Mei, then this boy. Another kid?

Noor gets up and puts her face close to the glass. The thin view between two shutters expands. She watches the man stop, facing away from her, and look at the trees circling the grounds. He turns towards the gates and looks at them, then the car park. Then he completes a full revolution and faces the clinic. He looks like he's never seen a building before and now, having seen one, it's more beautiful than he could possibly have imagined.

His eyes travel over the place where Noor stands, without penetrating beyond the glass. An odd feeling: seen yet not seen. With his face upturned Noor can see him now, clearly. He is really quite extraordinarily good-looking. Older than she first thought, too. More like late twenties. It's only his manner that made him seem younger. Where Mei was closed and wary, this man looks as if he's been opened out. In anyone else that look of wonder could have seemed fey, but this is . . . *convincing*.

Then the men escorting O. Levy gather around him, subtly pressing him in the direction of the open car door, blocking Noor's view, and when they move out and away, the car door is closed and the man is gone.

And Noor has to wonder:

What the fuck?

But that's that. Noor's going to have to go home that night without knowing what the fuck. Chances of ever finding out what the fuck are decreasing by the minute, she realises. She might live out the rest of her life, years and years of it, and die, without ever knowing what the actual fuck.

Of course, she does have another option. She could tell senior management or even the media or police what Louise has been doing – which might, in the resulting catastrophic mess, throw up a few insights. But Noor, for various reasons, not least of which is the fact that she herself has personally signed off on every single one of Louise's illegal activities, would rather *not*.

RASA, Noor thinks.

Then it comes to her. Not RASA, but rasa. As in *tabula rasa*.

A blank.

A complete erasure.

Noor remembers what Louise said, when she was here with Clifford. Something about large amounts of memory being lost. Louise said later that she was talking about people with head injuries, but Noor wonders now if this was another lie. Because what did TotalWipeOut73 experience? Well. A total wipeout. Maybe Martin Noye was another person who'd developed memory loss as a result of a botched procedure.

What if RASA is a code word for procedures that went wrong, somehow, and had to be covered up?

Noor gets up and goes out into the hall crowded with newly released Nepenthe staff – noisily excited to be out of their offices – steering a path through them, shutting down attempts at small talk, until she arrives at Dr Karine de Oliveira's door.

'Hi, Karine,' Noor says. 'How's it going?'

Karine looks up. She seems surprised to see Noor, but not unwelcoming. Karine's office is very different to Noor's. It has about thirty more plants in it, for a start.

It also smells faintly of something that Noor suspects –
with a shudder – to be burnt sage.

'I'm not interrupting anything, am I?' Noor says.

'Oh, no,' Karine says. 'I like to have a brief meditation
session after I see each client, but that's over. What can I
help you with?'

'As normal operations have been suspended, I'm running
errands,' Noor says. 'Clifford, you know.'

(She hasn't actually said Clifford is the one who tasked
her with this. Noor is the one who set the errand. Then,
in an unconnected sentence, she said Clifford's name. So:
not a lie.)

'Right. Clifford,' says Karine. For a moment she looks
somewhat less spiritual. Noor even thinks she sees a tiny
eye roll. But maybe she's imagining it.

'Have you received the notes yet for the RASA client?'
Noor says. 'Mr Levy? He just left.'

'Yes,' Karine says. 'Thanks. I didn't realise you were on
the RASA programme.'

'Communication round here, right?' Noor says.

(Not a lie.)

Karine laughs.

'Well, that's all. Thanks,' Noor says. 'I'll speak to Louise
and Clifford.'

(Not a lie.)

'Dr Nightingale? Is she on RASA? I thought she was
very anti the, well, the whole thing. Which is understandable.'

'Oh, totally,' Noor says. 'She should just know that the
clinic is open again. I don't think anyone's been keeping
her in the loop, either.'

(Not a lie.)

'Sounds like you have a fun day ahead of you,' Karine says.

'Right,' says Noor. 'If they work out how to use their mobile phones I'll be obsolete. See you later, Karine.'

So there's an answer.

RASA is definitely something shady. The Access Denied clients are RASA clients. But this has nothing, apparently, to do with Louise.

So: not a very satisfying answer.

That night Noor doesn't take her sleeping pills. She doesn't sleep. She thinks about Louise. She thinks about Elena. She thinks about Captain Kirk and Clementine; Orlando Paladino, dipped in the silent water.

Tell me a story, she thinks.

No: not good enough.

Tell me an ending.

She knows what a happy ending is now. A happy ending is an answer. It doesn't even have to be a happy answer.

Just something that allows the book to be closed, so that everyone can move on with their lives.

At about midnight Noor's startled by a loud noise from outside. A sharp bang; two hard surfaces suddenly brought together. She goes to the window and looks out. The girl from the next-door garden flat is walking unsteadily up her drive. Behind her, a wheelie bin lies on its side.

Noor hasn't seen the girl or her boyfriend since last week. After a weekend with no music or voices or smoke or laughing or breaking of glasses, she'd assumed they were away, bothering someone else's neighbours.

She looks at the girl curiously. Noor's always thought of her as a happy, noisy drunk, but that's not in evidence tonight. The girl is wrapped in a large hooded jumper, pulled up over her nose. Above it her eyes are negatively haloed in a glistening black, smudged down onto her cheeks. There's something about her expression that Noor recognises: the same thing she noticed before, when she was reminded of Elena. Like the girl knew all along that the secret of life is that it's shit, and unfair, but she laughed and talked and smiled anyway – and now she's decided that there's no point fighting it any more.

Noor remembers the way Elena looked at her, before she turned and left Noor's flat, and Noor shut the door firmly behind her.

Of course, her look had said. *What else was it ever going to be?*

The girl outside stumbles, and falls onto her knees. Noor winces reflexively. The girl doesn't get up immediately, despite Noor willing her to. She just sits there, on what must be the freezing paving of the drive, her arms wrapped round her knees.

'Okay,' Noor says, to the girl. 'I'm coming.'

She puts on a coat and boots over her pyjamas and goes outside. The girl doesn't look up as Noor approaches, insulated as she must be by alcohol, by misery. She only looks up once Noor is basically standing over her. Her expression is like a closed door. (The inside of Noor's newly closed door, vibrating minutely on its hinges.)

What's her name? Nina?

'Hey, Nina,' Noor says. She isn't sure what to say. 'You can't sit out here.'

She means it to sound gentle, but it doesn't come out that way. She tries to think of something softer, but it doesn't matter, the girl seems to be far beyond tone. She turns her face up, not trying to wipe her eyes or her running nose, and Noor's not even sure the girl really sees her. A gust of alcohol comes off her, hot in the icy air.

'Where's your boyfriend?' Noor asks. 'Shall I get him?'

'Gone,' the girl says.

'Gone? When is he coming back?' Please, she thinks, let him arrive and deal with this. 'Shall I call him for you?'

The girl doesn't just look drunk: she looks ill. Possibly she's about to throw up. Noor can't help herself; she moves away from the girl, eyeing the wavering, unpredictable edges of her mouth.

'Coming back?' repeats the girl, wonderingly. 'Back? No. Not coming back.'

'What? Why not?' Noor asks.

'We met. We *slept* together. Then we found out. Then we deleted it. Then we met again. We've been living together. *Living* together! Then we got the memory back.'

The girl suddenly focuses on her. As if the sight of Noor has roused her, she gets, surprisingly quickly, to her feet.

'You,' she says. 'You work at the clinic.'

'Yes,' Noor says.

'You shouldn't have let us in in the first place,' the girl says. She sounds almost *angry* now; an anger fighting its way up through the wet weight of booze and tears. 'Shouldn't have let us delete it.'

'Delete what?' Noor asks. The girl seems very close again. Noor steps back, into the flower bed. But the anger, if that's what it was, never breaks the surface. The girl is crying. She sways towards Noor.

'How can . . .' she says. Then something incomprehensible.

She sways again, her eyes fixed on Noor, as if her question is skewing her own gravity. Noor puts out an arm to steady her, and to hold her away.

'What?' Noor says. Something of the girl's fright has got into her. She doesn't want to hear the answer, but she asks again anyway: 'What did you delete?'

'He's my *brother*,' the girl says. 'My brother.'

Then she shakes off Noor's arm – Noor incapable of letting go, or holding tighter, or moving at all – and walks unsteadily into her own flat.

Noor goes to bed in a daze. She gets up the next day in the same daze, unreset by sleep. She doesn't see her neighbour as she goes outside to her car.

She stands the bin back up, and drives to work.

The fog doesn't break until Noor gets into the empty kitchen at Nepenthe. She stands in the familiar space and feels, at last, like she's woken up.

413

Not into anything good.

She feels suddenly dizzy. She leans on the worktop and puts her head in her hands. Her fingers are so cold against the skin of her forehead that she flinches.

She thinks of the girl, saying, *You shouldn't have let us*.

But that was just wrong. The girl was upset. Nepenthe couldn't be responsible for –

The girl was right.

It's all out of control. What is Noor a part of? Something doing damage, harm spreading out across the world, each harm dividing and multiplying. People are booking restorations every day. People still want deletions. The clinic doesn't care, she thinks. The clinic rolls on, gathering money. Someone in pain extends a hand, and Nepenthe plucks the cash out of it. Sometimes their interventions make people better, sometimes they make them worse. Sometimes they destroy them. Her fingers press into the skin of her forehead. There's no order, there's no system. It's chaos. And . . . Louise. Noor thought Louise at least was administering her philosophy of least harm, protecting the ideals of health, of *sanity*, guarding the sanctuary doors against the painful confusion of the world. But there is no sanctuary, and Louise is playing both sides anyway, order and confusion.

That's when it comes back to Noor what Mei said the other day. About her dad being on the payroll.

Not a joke then, from Alistair. Louise really was the one who made the money. For as long as Noor has known her, in fact, Louise has been making a lot of money. Enough to pay for the Japanese-inspired house, the perfume, the Tesla, the art, the overseas property.

So where does money like that come from? Not from mentally ill Access Denied patients, obviously. Money like that comes from important executives in the arms and energy industries, rich housewives, solicitors, fraudsters. Maybe it doesn't come from the people themselves but from people around them.

'Oh God,' she says.

She googles Guy Cazalet, Elena's old boss. Her mind is ahead of the search results: when they come back with his history – missing links, dodgy connections, accounting discrepancies and fraud allegations at his chain of casinos and bars – she isn't even surprised. He'd been stabbed on the street in Rome a year before the helicopter crash. A mugging gone wrong, apparently. He was in intensive care for weeks.

What did Elena say?

... *Oh and Nepenthe's screening processes are of course totally irreproachable.*

... *She didn't seem all that amazing to me.*

Noor puts her phone away.

She thinks of her dreams when she arrived. A straightening, a streamlining, a brightening of people's minds. A doing of good, a making of sense. She thought she and Louise were going to do it together.

She thinks of Mei, saying, *I'm done with her.*

She closes her eyes. Tiredness and sickness, anger and panic, make her head swim.

When she opens her eyes again, Louise is standing in front of her.

'Morning, Noor,' says Louise.

Louise looks almost beatifically calm. Her hair is in perfect order. She looks like she's had plenty of sleep.

Noor stands up straight. She tries to look equally calm and at ease. Then she thinks, bugger that. There's not even the slightest chance Louise is going to be fooled. Louise can probably tell right now that even Noor's attempt to stand up straight is shaky. Noor's legs don't feel like her usual legs, that's the problem. Like some trick has been played, her good solid legs swapped for a pair made of rubber.

'Hi,' Noor says, doing her best Noor impression. 'You're a day late. Everything important and secret happened yesterday.'

Why are you here? Noor is thinking. *Why? Why?*

But she knows. Today's appointment is M. O'Connor. This must be the person Louise is after.

'I heard,' Louise said. 'Are you okay? You look, uh, well –'

'Bloody awful?'

'Yeah.'

'I tried to get a natural night's sleep. Terrible decision.'

'Agreed,' Louise says. 'Drugs are the answer. Nature had her chance and she fucked it up, right?'

(Noor thinks about Louise writing Mei a prescription for antidepressants.)

'So,' she says, 'what was all that confidential stuff yesterday? Can *you* tell me?'

'I would,' Louise says. 'You know I would. But I can't.'

'Guess we'll have to wait for the impending court case,' Noor says.

'Given how poor Nepenthe is at burying bad news, I'm sure you won't be waiting long.' Louise smiles at her. 'You know, Cliff was asking me about you. He remembered your name, which is unusual. Seems you impressed him yesterday.'

It occurs to Noor that Louise is pretending to be Louise as much as Noor is pretending to be Noor.

'I was rude to him,' Noor says. 'He chose to take it as a joke.'

'He'll probably want to promote you now. And not that I like agreeing with Cliff, but that *is* something we should discuss again. It's long overdue. Anyway, were you on the way to your office? Do you mind helping me with something?'

'Sure,' Noor says. 'But – is it urgent?'

Louise hesitates. Then she waves her hand, and smiles. The smile is bright, wide – and brief, as if Louise knows it wouldn't stand much scrutiny. 'No, no,' she says. 'Not at all.'

'Oh, great,' Noor says. 'I'm meant to stop in and speak to Jim Stokes. Probably about yesterday. It won't take long, and then I'll be back down with you.'

'Perfect. I'll be here most of the day: we can have lunch.'

'Great,' Noor says.

*

Noor leaves the kitchen and takes the stairs that lead to Jim's office. On the first storey there's a recessed window-sill. She puts her tea on the floor, already knowing that this is goodbye, and sits on the sill, her back against the wall. The rubbery feeling has expanded, crept from her legs up through the rest of her body.

Noor holds her phone in her rubbery hand. She calls Clifford Byrne.

She's put through quickly. Not because he recognises her name (he doesn't, despite Louise's claims, and Noor has to explain twice who she is) but probably because she says the words *urgent, misconduct* and *security breach* to his secretary. And even once Noor has filled Clifford Byrne in on what Louise has been doing – looking up clients and calling them, presumably to convince them not to have restorations – he seems, if anything, somewhat baffled.

'Whew,' he says. 'Well. And you say that you will be implicated? You co-authorised this malpractice? Whatever it was. And you're doing this . . . because . . . it's the right thing to do? Okay. No, that's a good enough reason. All right then.'

'Okay,' says Noor.

'Is there anything else?'

'Yes, actually.'

'Okay,' says Clifford Byrne. He sighs. 'What else?'

'I heard about something called RASA –'

Clifford Byrne interrupts her. 'Where did you hear about that?'

'A former client said it,' Noor says. 'A protester. I don't even know what RASA is.'

'Okay,' Clifford Byrne says. 'Well, Nora, forget what was said. It's all above board. Obviously. But it *is* confidential.'

'Yeah,' Noor says. 'I'd got that impression.'

'Right,' Clifford Byrne says. 'So. That's everything?'

'You tell me,' Noor says. 'What do I do now?'

'Oh, nothing,' says Clifford. He sounds almost . . . cheerful. It makes Noor feel uneasy. 'There's due process now. Thank you for telling me, Nora. We'll take it from here.'

'Oh,' Noor says. 'Okay.'

And that's it. The conversation seems to end very quickly. Noor finds herself faced with the prospect of going back downstairs. She stays wedged into the window for a little longer, her adrenaline sputtering, dying. Eventually she hears a door open further along the corridor. Footsteps approach. She has to get up, and walk down the stairs.

It's fine, she thinks. She'll just go down to her office and explain to Louise that the meeting with Jim took longer than she thought and she doesn't have time to sign off on anything for her right now. Louise will be pissed off, but there won't be much she can say. Obviously further down the line she'll work out that Noor has betrayed her, and be *really* pissed off, but she'll be back in London by then.

Noor can hear voices as she approaches her office. Jim is one. Louise is another. As she rounds the corner she sees the two of them standing outside her own office door, with two security guards.

'I'm your boss,' Louise is saying to Jim. 'You don't have the authority –'

'Uh,' Jim says. 'This hasn't come from me. Clifford Byrne called. You've been denied security clearance.'

'What? What the hell is going on?'

'That's all I know. You need to go back to London and speak to him.'

'Noor!' Louise says, as Noor approaches. She looks relieved to see her. Clearly nobody has told her that Noor is responsible for the denial of her security clearance.

Noor goes over to them, feeling something rotten turn and flop inside her. Perhaps it's her stomach. Or it could be the heart. Something rotten, anyway, in the state of Noor.

'I need to speak to Noor,' Louise says to Jim. 'Give me a few minutes.'

'Er . . .' Jim says.

'I'm not going to take her hostage, for fuck's sake,' Louise says. 'You and these two gentlemen can stay right here, in the corridor. You won't get in any trouble.'

Say no, thinks Noor.

'Okay,' says Jim. 'But just a couple of minutes.'

He and the security guards retreat a few feet away, where they stand, in silence, looking rather foolish.

Louise takes Noor's arm. She leans in. Her perfume surrounds Noor. It feels as if it's in Noor's mouth.

'Listen,' Louise says. 'This is important. I have to speak to a client. I can't explain why, but it's urgent. I need you to get me some information, privately. I'll explain later.'

'You want me to illegally access a client file, so that you can illegally contact them?' Noor says.

'Yes. I know you can do it. You're good with computers. You can cover your tracks, can't you? I need to stop something. I need to protect someone, a client. It's going to be disastrous. Trust me, Noor.'

Up close Noor can see that Louise's forehead is shining with sweat. She removes her arm from Louise's grip.

'But I don't trust you,' she says. 'I think the only thing you care about protecting is your cash flow.'

There's a silence. It feels long, and painful. It's like all the air is being pressed out of Noor. If the silence goes on too long, she'll have no breath left. Her anger has gone too; it can't hold her up. She'll fall on the floor and Louise will stop looking stunned and become furious and will step on her head, or kick her in the ribs – and Noor will accept it.

'I see,' Louise says. '*You* told them.'

And Noor says: 'Yes.'

Louise takes a breath in. Now – finally – she looks angry.

Noor has no idea why this comes as a relief.

That's a lie.

Noor *does* know why. She needs Louise to behave like a villain so that Noor knows she definitely is one. Villains, when they get caught, shout and rage and vow revenge and say they'd have got away with it if it hadn't been for those pesky kids.

They don't stand quietly and look shocked, and – worse – betrayed.

Say something villainous, she begs Louise.

'You absolute. Fucking. Idiot,' Louise says.

Thank you, thinks Noor.

'But why did you do that? Why couldn't you have come to me first?' Louise says.

Slightly off-script, but Noor decides to ignore that. She's full of her own righteous outrage now. She says, 'Because you involved me in gross misconduct and fraud. You lied to me. Your own daughter warned me about you. *She* didn't trust you either.'

Louise opens her mouth. Then she closes it again.

There are tears in her eyes.

Noor's hands are trembling.

'You fucking idiot,' Louise says again. But it lacks conviction.

'You fraud,' says Noor. Also lacking in conviction.

At this Louise shrugs. The tears, if they were ever imminent, are gone.

Behind them, Jim Stokes coughs.

'Oh for God's sake,' Louise says to him. She turns round. 'Lurking in the corner coughing. You're not standing in a line behind a queue jumper. You're the clinic director. Grow up and throw me out properly.'

'Throw you out?' asks Jim.

'Yes. This conversation is over. I'm ready to go.'

'Wait. What were you even doing?' Noor asks her.

Louise looks genuinely startled.

'You don't *know*?' she says.

She looks at Noor as if she's so bowled over by Noor's stupidity that she can only marvel at it, in silence. Then she gives one of her angry laughs. 'You'll find out,' she says. She beckons the security guards. 'Come on. Aren't you going to handcuff me or something?'

'No,' says one. 'Er. We're just meant to see you off the premises.'

'Fine,' Louise says.

She doesn't look at Noor. She turns round and walks away, and Jim Stokes and the security guards have no choice but to hurry after her. After a moment they all disappear, around the curve of the corridor.

Silence descends.

Noor feels . . . right. Yes. What she did was right. She thinks of Louise calling her a fucking idiot. It makes her feel better.

She also feels terrible.

But she assumes that will pass.

Noor waits a few minutes, then goes into reception. Marie is at her desk and Jim at the window. Neither of them are looking at each other or speaking. The white space is full of held-in shock. Noor goes to the window to stand beside Jim, and the three of them watch as Louise's car pulls out of the gates, and disappears.

'What the hell was *that*?' Jim asks her.

'What?'

'I get a call from Clifford Byrne saying I have to get Louise out of the clinic and send her to see him. Do whatever is necessary.' He looks upset. 'What would I have done if she'd resisted?'

'I don't know,' Noor says. 'Got her in a headlock? Fended her off with a chair?'

'This is funny to you?' Jim says.

'Not especially,' Noor says. She sighs.

She's about to explain to Jim that – But what can she explain? Nothing.

She's going to have to stay silent, because whatever she does and says now is going to be thought about later, as *that stuff Noor said when she was trying to get herself off the hook.*

Let it go on the record that Noor said nothing, she thinks.

'I'm going out,' she says to Jim. 'For a walk.'

Jim looks surprised. Before he can think of what to say in response, she's through the door.

And then, she thinks, *Dr Ali just walked out. Which was an admission of complicity if I ever saw one.*

Never mind.

She can hear the protesters now, just about. They're quiet; caught between protests. She can hear the pigeons cooing, more loudly. The hoarse hum of the passing cars. A security guard with a pot belly, talking on his phone as if it's a special forces walkie-talkie.

'All clear,' he's saying. 'All clear.'

Noor walks round the clinic to the back of the building. Here there is an unlovely secret corridor of air-conditioning vents and a concrete path tufted with untrimmed grass, leading to the gravelled area where laundry vans and bin collectors pull in. She used to smoke there, once upon a time, before Louise saw her one afternoon and said, You ought to stop doing that, you know.

Noor wishes she had a cigarette now.

Elena wasn't in love with her boss, Noor thought. Those weren't the circumstances. Elena was a witness. A victim.

The only one who had an unhealthy relationship with her boss was Noor.

*

424

Noor's first day at Nepenthe.

Here she is, new suit, with two stubborn pieces of hair getting out of their ponytail and curling above each ear, like two apostrophes. Here is Louise, her own hair in a perfect bob.

What is Noor saying?

I want to change lives.

Change lives? asked Louise. She looked amused.

Or, restore meaning to people's lives. Improve quality of life.

Well, those are three different things.

I'm sorry?

You talk about them as if they're synonymous. But they're not. Take meaning. If you ask somebody what gives their life meaning, they'll probably say it's family, or work, maybe some kind of religious or ethical crusade. They *choose* a narrative thread. And after a while they convince themselves that they didn't choose it at all. And that's how people make life make sense.

Oh, said Noor.

She thought: *I've blown it.*

But then Louise smiled at her. She said: And it's our job, we psychologists, to play along.

Our, thought Noor.

We.

Noor doesn't take her sleeping pill again that night. She allows herself to lie in bed and think about Elena; about Louise saying, *You fucking idiot*; about Elena; about her neighbour crying on the step. About Elena.

She turns over in bed.

Ask one question, and the rest come in behind it.

What did Louise actually do?

Does wiping a note change the rest of the symphony?

Who is O. Levy?

Did Captain Kirk ever dream of Rayna?

Was Louise ever Noor's friend, really?

Can love change you, as a person? Can that change be undone, if the memory of love is undone?

If Noor erased that last argument with Elena, would it give her peace? If she thought their relationship had ended with Elena leaving without warning, and never coming back. At that point Noor had just assumed Elena hadn't loved her. And Noor could get over it, because what was there to get over?

The problem was that she'd *seen* it in Elena's eyes when she came back to Noor's door – love – before it got chased off by hurt, and anger and finally that weary, fatalistic look, that *of course*.

If Noor forgot that day, she'd forget that Elena had loved her.

Meaning: nothing to hold on to.

Meaning: letting the idea of Elena go. Noor going back to how she was before. If not *contented*, exactly, at least *calm*. Stable. Functioning.

A factory reset.

Would that work?

Is there such a thing as Nepenthe, as Homer and Poe and Spock meant it?

The theory, the dream?

Noor knows all the questions, now.

William

William is sitting in the back seat of a black car, on the way to the Nepenthe clinic. The car they've sent is electric; he's still adjusting to the strange lack of sound. The driver, too, is silent. William supposes that in this line of work it's difficult to make conversation. You can't ask people about their holidays, for example, in case they're off to wipe the memory of a holiday disaster. Nor can you turn on the radio, in case it plays 'Don't you forget about me' or 'A night to remember' or something.

He tries not to yawn, not to have that be the only sound in the car. He's hardly slept for the past seventy-two hours, benzos being one of the prohibitions on the long 'Not To Do' list that Nepenthe gave him, along with alcohol, prescription drugs, illegal drugs, herbal remedies, caffeine and any activity that might result in something colliding with his head.

William's head has never been so well looked after. Still, it feels awful; both wired and fuzzy, alert and slow.

It's turning into a sunny day. It was drizzling in Hassocks when William left; he wonders if it's drizzly there still. Thinks of Annetta in the wet grey morning, waking the kids up. A kiss for each of their foreheads. Schoolbags waiting downstairs by the door.

William tries not to think about them. It's that superstitious fear: that if he thinks about them too much he'll lose them.

Don't look back, that's how the wisdom goes. Even if you can't hear their footsteps behind you, don't turn round. Not until you're safe, on the other side.

A couple of days ago Annetta came over, without the kids. To talk, she said. The sun was going down behind her; a tangerine glow over the chimneys. William very much did not want to talk, but he wanted to be near her just as powerfully. He welcomed her in and she went around the house curiously, touching things, as if being there was as strange for her as it was for him. She didn't say anything. Her fingertips ran over photograph frames and sofa arms, and he couldn't read her expression.

I want to go with you, she said.

No, he said, before he could think of a 'because'.

Because, he began.

Look, William, she said. You don't want support, I get it. But what if you come out of there and it turns out you *do* need it?

Mmm, said William.

He personally wasn't sure what Past William, once he was back, might want.

Annetta had seated herself on the chair opposite him, in a way that looked temporary. Thighs half on, half off the seat. Now she came and sat beside him on the sofa. He caught her perfume. She smelled like the Annetta of nights out and babysitters waiting at home; of getting drunk too quickly, because they were out of practice; of sex in hotels, one ear out for a tapping at the door between the rooms.

Anyway, she said, suddenly brisk, so that all William's inappropriate thoughts went scurrying out of sight. Are you on meds or anything yet?

William explained the list of seventy-two-hour prohibitions.

In the same awkwardly matronly tone, Annetta calculated the hours they had before William had to start protecting his brain.

Then she said they had about three left for a glass of wine.

When the bottle of wine was gone Annetta's briskness and awkwardness fell away. William saw it happen. She put down her glass, inhaled, then there was a moment like a little shrug, and they were gone. In the window the sun was gone too.

Annetta smiled, and leaned forward.

She said: Please tell me sex wasn't on that list.

At the clinic William speaks to various people, one after another. He's being very careful. He knows that if he tests positive for madness, they won't restore his memory. He's avoiding mentioning his dad, his suspicions about his own mental stability. He can't avoid the subject of his recent application for a memory wipe, though. When he's asked about it he admits to a few PTSD symptoms. To throw them off the scent, he wonders aloud if perhaps his previous wipe went *wrong* somehow. At which point everyone gets very defensive.

'That is highly unlikely,' says the psychologist. 'These other symptoms you have sound like a completely separate issue.'

And with that, the handing over of William from person to person comes to a conclusion. The psychologist leaves and William sits with his secrets intact, in another white room, on a reclining white couch thing, next to a computer.

'Won't be a moment,' says the nurse. 'Everything okay?'

'Yes,' says William.

Because what else is he supposed to say?

In the end William told Annetta that he didn't want her to come with him. He told her several times, in fact, as she argued with him rationally and calmly for about half an hour – then stopped abruptly, gave up, and cried.

I'm sorry, he said, wondering if she even actually heard him saying *I'm sorry* any more, or if with overuse he's wrung all the meaning out of it. Pared it down to a string of phonemes. *Ai-m s-or-ee*.

Annetta left at midnight, so she wouldn't have to explain to Milo and Fiona and her mother why she'd slept in her own house that night. Her leaving was a desolate thing. Then the next morning William found the fractal T-shirt had got into the wash accidentally – he hadn't

430

meant it to, and now there was nothing of her inside it any more.

He didn't know why this bothered him so much. It wasn't like she'd died and that T-shirt was all he had. She was half an hour away, for God's sake. He could call her and she'd answer. But he picked it out of the washing machine drum and the sadness came on slowly, in low pulses.

'William?'

Someone's standing in front of him. The nurse.

'How are you doing, William?' she says, smiling at him. 'Are you ready?'

'I'm ready,' he says.

What else can he say?

She hands him a cup.

He drinks.

The way the memory hits, it's like it happened just a moment ago.

In a way, he supposes, that's true.

William is walking down a street.

And not just that. It's . . . *everything*. It's remarkable, how much detail there is. The waft of bonfires in the air, the slippy layers of chestnut leaves under his shoes – his smart leather shoes, with no traction whatsoever. The sky a ludicrous sherbet pink, deepening to red nearer the roofline.

It's half past eleven and William's slightly drunk. His feet fumble along the uneven paving stones, almost but never quite tripping. He's humming Sinatra songs. He's just had dinner – sushi – with Annetta, and he loves her, not that he's told her that yet.

He loves her.

He's mouthing the words. Maybe he's more drunk than he thought. He mainly wants to hear how they feel. A drop of the jaw, tongue to the roof of the mouth, top teeth resting on bottom lip, a final push of air.

I. Love. You.

He meant to say it to Annetta tonight, but was hesitant, and hadn't found a good moment. Really he'd prefer to text it to her – LV U. Or maybe shout it at her window, then run away. That way if she doesn't feel the same it's easier on both of them.

Still, Annetta introduced him to her mum a couple of weeks ago. That must mean something. It certainly did to Judy, who asked him about his job and prospects as if he were a 1950s teenager. Then she'd made him take some food home. It was clear from the way she offered it that she thought William had no food in his house. He tried to tell her he did, but she cut him off. Supermarket ready meals, she said, in a tone of deep reproach. You bachelors and your ready meals. But now you have food.

Thanks for putting up with her, Annetta said afterwards, apologising. You were great. You have more patience with her than I do.

I can't actually eat ready meals, William said. Which is inconvenient. I'm mildly allergic to them. There's something in one of the preservatives they use that makes my lips swell up.

Don't tell her that, Annetta said. You'll break her heart.

William would like to bring out some parents of his own for Annetta to meet. But it's a bit early to take her to the nursing home to meet his mum. Maybe he could show her his dad's record collection, which has been sitting in storage since he died. A lot of them are rare: Billie Holliday, Sinatra, Johnny Cash's first LP. Annetta seems to like old music. But that's not the same as liking old records: maybe she'd be unimpressed.

Maybe he could take her away for a weekend instead. Yes. That's actually a great idea. Rome, maybe. Venice. His perennial failure to fit words to feelings wouldn't be so noticeable in a gondola. He could let the city do the romancing for him.

William turns towards his own road. He hears two teenage boys, talking and laughing up ahead. They're messing around, jumping up onto the bollards along the road, slipping and half jumping, half falling back down. One balances for a triumphant second, before having to bail.

The smell of weed drifts over to William. It reminds him of university. He finds himself gazing at the two boys with nostalgia. They're calling an end to their own night, now. One boy answers a phone call, waves to the other, slouches off. His laughter fades out as he rounds the corner. The other boy leans on the bollard for a moment, looking at his own phone. He gets something out of his pocket, a bag, possibly tobacco. William hopes the kid isn't going to skin up, right there, right in front of him. He doesn't want to be a police officer today. He wants to think about summers at university and gondolas with Annetta.

But the kid doesn't roll anything up. Just as William's about to pass him, he pushes himself gently off the bollard and saunters into the road, without looking, straight in front of a taxi.

What William does then isn't in any way a conscious decision.

His brain isn't involved. There's nothing but a klaxon in his ears. It sounds like a car horn. The sound is pure urgency. It's saying: *must*.

You must.

Must *do*.

And so his body does.

William's lying on the ground, his brain coming back to awareness. It fires up sludgily, like the klaxon wiped it somehow, and it needs time to reboot.

Why is he on the ground?

His body hurts. His hands are stinging where they scraped along the tarmac. The noise of a car horn is dying in his ears.

Then it comes back to him that there was a boy.

The boy walked out in front of a car, and William threw himself after the boy, to push him out of the way. Which he did: his hands punching into the boy's slender back, knocking him forward, forward, safe.

He raises himself up slowly, to see where the boy is. It turns out he can get onto his hands, and then his knees, and then his feet, without his body giving way. He's not in too much pain. Standing, he looks around. The taxi is a few feet away. It stopped before it reached William. The boy himself is almost on the other side of the road, lying down. He isn't moving. William hobbles over to him.

'Are you okay?' he calls.

The taxi driver is by his side; they reach the boy together.

The kid is not okay. It's obvious. His head rests on the kerb. Blood moves from this resting place outwards, across the tarmac.

His right hand is extended, almost as if he's reaching out for help, or offering something to William – and William sees now that he does have something to offer, a bag of sweets, except most of them are scattered across the road.

His face is turned away.

There's an absence all around him, like a black hole, drawing in light.

Not the girl, then, that girl who had never meant William any harm, except to fall in the same way as the boy fell then.

He can picture her now, like the ghostly reflection of the boy. Two of them lying, two arms outstretched, two hands reaching out.

Afterwards, William is cleared of any wrongdoing. The coroner's report ruled: death by misadventure. The fact that William was drunk, and the taxi driver was able to stop with feet to spare is hardly mentioned.

The taxi driver says the boy – Michael Graham – walked out in front of him. Michael was stoned, and drunk. A woman who lived in one of the houses says that the teens had been mucking about in the street all night, causing a disturbance. She'd phoned the police before about them. It was only a matter of time, in her opinion, before there was an accident.

The incident doesn't even get into the press. Michael was from a family of small-scale gang members, so William's name isn't released, for fear of reprisals. His boss calls him in to reassure him of that.

'So, that's good news,' he says to William. 'I knew you'd be relieved.'

He's looking at William like he's expecting William to shake his hand.

Congratulations, thinks William. *You got away with it.*

'It's not your fault,' Carey says to William. 'Are you listening to me? It's not your fault.'

'You did the right thing,' the person from the police welfare department says. 'How can you be blamed for that?'

*

'Look, son,' says William's boss. 'Take some time off. Welfare's obviously not cutting it. Have therapy. Come back to duty once this is . . . under control. Okay?'

But therapy, which is meant to shrink William's guilt to a practical, controllable level, doesn't work.

He doesn't see why he, William, is alive and well and walking around unpunished while the kid he recklessly hurled into a kerbstone is dead.

The therapist says that what William is experiencing is survivor's guilt.

William asks how you could be said to be a survivor of yourself.

The therapist says that's just semantics. The emotional effect is the same.

What the fuck do you know? William says.

No, he doesn't.

He says thank you. He says he feels better.

He goes back to work.

'Are you okay, William?' some of his friends ask. He hadn't told any of them about what happened. He hadn't told Annetta, either. He can't bear to. He doesn't *have* to. There's no overlap between William's friends in the police (Carey) and his friends outside work, so he's able to keep it to himself. But something seems to be leaking out, and worrying people.

'Are you really okay, William?' says Annetta. There are tears in her eyes. 'You don't *seem* okay.'

'I know you're not better,' Carey says to William. 'You're just pretending.'

When Carey says this, William sees the boy, Michael Graham, lying in the road. The generosity of that open hand. Open eyes.

What happened? his eyes were asking.

No, they weren't. They didn't look confused or horrified or sad or serene. They weren't asking or telling. They looked like all dead people's eyes look. Dead.

At night the sky is a pool of blood and all the stars glitter in it like sour sugar crystals. William's dreams tell him to fly up into the sky and choke in it.

'Don't be ridiculous,' William says to Carey. 'I'm fine.'

'Yeah, right,' Carey says. 'I've seen people like you, right before they kill themselves. Is that what you're thinking about?'

'What? You're out of your mind,' says William.

'Weren't you going to take Annetta away this spring?' Carey asks. 'Well? Have you booked the flights? What are you doing for Easter? Name one thing that's in your diary.'

'I don't own a diary.'

Carey shakes his head. 'You can't fool me, William. That boy is on your conscience. Listen. Have you thought about a memory wipe?'

'What?' William says. 'I was involved. I was the subject of an investigation. Even though I've been cleared, I can never wipe it. You know that.'

Carey lowers his voice. He says: 'There are other ways to get a wipe.'

'Any wipe under the circumstances would be illegal,' William says.

'Yeah, I *know*,' Carey says. 'Why do you think I lowered my voice?'

'Oh sure,' William says. 'I could be one of those poor bastards who try to lie to the machine. The ones that don't go mad get twenty years. Hard to choose which option I'd prefer.'

'That's not what I mean,' says Carey.

'Then . . . *what*?' says William.

'Look,' Carey says, 'Chief Superintendent Rathbone told me about it. There's a woman I can put you in touch with. At Nepenthe. She can get you that wipe. It's not legal, obviously. But it happens. You could –'

'No.'

William turns and walks away. Carey follows him. He takes William's arm.

'Listen,' he says. 'Annetta called me.'

'She called *you*?'

'Yeah. Funny way to meet the love of your partner's life. She wanted to know if I knew what was wrong with you. She didn't have anyone else to ask. I could hear she was at her wits' end. She wouldn't have called *me* otherwise. She's frightened for you. She loves you. Which means, if you fuck things up for yourself, they're fucked for her too. Do you want *her* to feel the way you're feeling now?'

William stares at him.

'No,' says Carey. 'The answer is no. So, stop being so fucking selfish.'

William is sitting opposite Dr Louise Nightingale. She's a composed blonde, hair up, suit uncreased. He's noticed that she speaks better than other people. Not a posh accent – though she's got one of those. It's more that she doesn't hesitate, or repeat herself, or say *um* or *er*. Which is rare.

They are in Louise's office in the Nepenthe building near Baker Street. The building is undoubtedly swanky, but in an ordinary way – which struck William as deeply strange. It's Monday afternoon and people go in and out holding Pret A Manger bags, or talking on their phones, just like ordinary working people everywhere. He supposes that to *them* they are ordinary. Everything they do here is strange, so strangeness is ordinary. No wonder Louise Nightingale is so calm, sitting here explaining to William how they break the law.

'So I don't have to lie, when I describe the memory to you?' he says.

'No,' she says. 'Forget all that Carol Kurtz stuff. You tell the truth. Remember, nobody will hear the content of the memory except me. The technicians and nurses aren't in the room when you tell me the memory. It won't go on your police record because it'll be filed as a personal memory. The deletion itself will be on your medical record, but not the content. Meaning, I'm the only person who would be able to report that you're trying to delete something you're not supposed to.'

'Okay,' William says. 'Thank you.'

'No need to thank me,' Louise says. 'You're *paying* me not to report it. This isn't a favour.'

'Right.'

'So. The money. The cost of the basic procedure is £4,000. Which leaves the issue of accounting for the payment. For the self-informed clients, this isn't a problem.

440

You'll just need a cover story for what you chose to forget –'

'I don't think I can do that,' William says. 'I've got a girlfriend. She seems to be able to tell when I'm keeping something from her. Or lying.'

'Then lie better,' Louise says.

'I . . . don't think I can,' he says. 'I'm sorry. I think I've wasted your time.'

There's a silence. Louise looks at him for a long time. Then she sighs.

'Okay,' she says. 'I really prefer not to do this. Self-confidential is a lot more difficult. Almost everyone I do this for is self-informed.'

'How many people *do* you do this for?' William asks.

'Here's some advice for when you're doing something illegal,' Louise says. 'Ask fewer questions. Otherwise people might start wondering if it's a sting.'

'Oh, right,' William says. 'Sorry. It's not. Please don't shut this down.'

'It's okay,' Louise says. 'I trust Rathbone, and he trusts whoever it is that vouched for you. And I think you're asking me about numbers because you're worried that this is some shoddy under-the-counter operation that might accidentally destroy your brain. Is that right? Well, it's not. It's a very professional under-the-counter operation, and you're one of many. Well. Many self-informed procedures. I've only done a few self-confidentials. About ten people, maybe. Mainly because, like you, they're just in too sad a state for me to refuse. The main concern for me is that if I ever needed to, I can't keep track of you. Self-confidential clients tend to move to different jobs or houses or countries, and they obviously don't let me know.'

'You could ask Rathbone,' says William. 'He's not going anywhere.'

Louise acknowledges this with a nod.

'Fine,' she says.

'Thank you,' says William.

'Don't thank me yet,' says Louise. 'There's the issue of money. What *usually* happens with the private self-confidential clients is that Nepenthe has agreements with most of the major banks. You pay the fee out of your savings. We erase your memory of those savings as part of the procedure. Then, for a small admin fee, the bank will backdate your statements so that the money effectively vanishes. You'll also destroy any hard copies of statements, obviously. Any relevant lawyers and accountants will be notified, and will sign confidentiality agreements. The information will be visible to the tax office, but nobody is allowed to tell you about that.'

'That makes sense,' William says.

'Now. I charge £10,000, on top of the Nepenthe fee. It's usually more, but I don't think you could afford it on a police officer's wage. I'm sure you'll agree it's reasonable given the risk I'm taking. The difficulty here is that you, as a self-confidential, would need to find the cash for this in a way you won't miss later on. Obviously I can wipe your memory of however you get the money.'

'What kind of people are able to get £10,000 in cash and not notice?'

Louise gives him another long stare. This one harder than the first.

'Never mind,' says William.

He wonders how many people Louise has helped in this way. If *helped* is the word. Much as he'd like to convince himself that she's some saviour figure defying an unfair system, he doubts she's doing this out of altruism. Her hair and clothes are too sophisticated, for a saviour. The fact that she charges £10,000 is also not very saviouresque.

'If you want to wait and get the money together . . .' Louise says.

'It's okay,' he said. 'My dad died and left me a record collection. It's been in storage because I didn't know what to do with it. Nobody knows I have it. I could sell it for cash. My mother died recently, so it's not like she'd know. And I haven't told Annetta about it yet. I thought I'd wait, and –'

He stops. Louise Nightingale watches him politely.

'You don't care, do you?' he says.

'Not really,' she says. 'But it's good that you have a solution. I can delete your memory of what happened to the collection, of course.'

'You can wipe more than one memory at the same time?'

'In the same session, yes, it's standard. We delete the memory itself, plus your memories of requesting the removal, the interviews et cetera.'

'Right,' William says. 'So that takes care of that. My dad's record collection.'

There's a short pause.

'Is that a problem?' Louise asks. 'You see, you just presented it as a solution. But now your face says that it's a problem.'

'No,' William says. 'It's not a problem.'

*

It's almost midnight when William arrives at the clinic for the removal. He can hardly make out the town of Crowshill. It appears in spotlit fragments. A clock face that seems to be hanging in the clouds. Beech hedges glowing under lamp posts. Dark shopfronts reflecting the car headlights.

The clinic itself is a big, white building, phosphorescent-looking, like a research base on another planet. It's lit so brightly that it's hard to see anything else. The trees are a black rustling wall against the slightly less black sky; the ground is black, the gravel just a crunching noise under his feet. Then he gets inside, and everything black is abruptly white.

He rubs his eyes. When his vision adjusts he sees Dr Nightingale (not *Louise*, he must remember) in front of him. She asks William a few questions – how was the journey? How are you feeling? – with a look that warns him not to answer honestly.

'Come this way, Mr Hall,' Dr Nightingale says.

She leads William down a curving corridor, into a white room containing a normal-looking, fake-wood desk and office chair, and a plastic-covered bed, next to a white, plastic-covered piece of machinery. Wires come out of the machine, attached at the other end to what looks like a transparent swimming cap, hanging up above the head of the bed.

Along one wall there's a long window, behind which a couple of technicians are seated at some monitors. They aren't as crisp-looking as Dr Nightingale. One has a striped jumper visible under his lab coat. The other has a pen behind his ear.

There's a hum in the air, hardly audible.

'Sit here, please,' Dr Nightingale says to William. He climbs onto the plastic chair, which hisses gently under his weight.

'I –' he says.

'Wait,' she says.

A nurse comes in, holding a cup of water and a small dish containing some pills. She hands them to William with a smile. He swallows the pills, hands the cup and dish back to the nurse, who thanks him, smiles again, and leaves.

'Right,' Louise says, turning to him. 'What do you want to know?'

William's worried that he'll finish talking about the memory and then his first thought will be, *I hope I don't forget Annetta.* And then whatever it is they're doing will wipe her too.

'What happens if I think of other things by accident?' he asks. 'Would they get erased too?'

'Oh yes, that's a common question,' Louise says. 'The drug we give you is only activated when we pass an electrical current through the relevant areas of the brain. We know which areas hold the parts of the memory because they're the brightest spots. If you think about something else, it'll come up as an anomaly on the scan. As soon as that happens the current switches off, until you're back on track.'

'Okay,' he says.

'Now, I'm going to fill in some of this paperwork while you sit and wait for those pills to take effect. It'll be about half an hour, okay? Do you want a magazine or something?'

'I'm fine,' William says. He's feeling tired suddenly. He leans his head back. When he opens his eyes Dr Nightingale is very close.

'You fell asleep,' she says.

'Sorry.'

'Not a problem. Lots of people do. Anyway. It's time.'

'Okay,' he says.

Dr Nightingale presses a button, and the chair starts to recline.

William tries to detect the presence of drugs in his body, but he doesn't feel any different. Tired, maybe. He doesn't feel stressed, or frightened. He realises that's probably an effect of the drugs. They don't add things, they take them away. They have also taken away his headache, the slippery, seaweedy tangle in his stomach. He floats in a temperate bath, the chair flexing and creaking gently underneath him as it lowers his upper body to near horizontal.

A nurse he hadn't noticed before attaches the cap to William's head.

One of the technicians looks up at Dr Nightingale. He raises a thumb.

'Okay then, William,' she says. 'We're going to activate the drug now. I want you to keep your mind on what happened.'

Her voice comes from far away. It sounds gentler, sweeter – probably softened, like everything else, by the drugs.

It says,

'Tell me about your walk home.'

*

William opens his eyes.

He's almost surprised to see that Dr Nightingale is gone. Years have passed. The technician in the striped jumper and the one with a pen behind his ear have been replaced by other people. There's daylight coming in, a nurse standing beside him.

'Don't try to sit up too soon,' says the nurse, beside him. 'How are you doing? Okay?'

He can't answer. Without sitting up he moves his eyes around the room, looking for someone from before. He doesn't recognise anyone.

None of this lessens his alarm.

'Did you . . . *see* my memory?' he asks the nurse. 'Did anyone . . . ?'

It's not how he meant to say it, but she seems to understand.

'No. You're the only one who knows what it is,' she says. She must be used to explaining this. 'Would you like some water?'

William thinks for a moment. Where is Dr Nightingale? Does she know he's come here for a restoration? She can't. She'd be here too, surely, if she knew.

But *why* doesn't she know?

He's trying not to give his thoughts away. He puts on what he hopes is the expression of a typical Nepenthe patient. Then he realises that most restoration patients probably look as panicked as William, as stunned, as desperately calculating.

He says: 'I need to use the loo. Is that okay?'

'Of course. You should get up carefully, though. Take your time, and if you feel dizzy, call us. There's a button in the lavatory.'

447

'Okay. Thank you.'

He wants to run. He gets up slowly; forces himself to walk slowly towards the door.

Not the girl in the picture, William thinks, not that poor girl.

Michael Graham.

William can see him now. A figure of a person, so recently vacated. How could he have left so quickly? There was a second in which William and Michael were in close contact, a fraction of a moment of the very nearest intimacy. Then what? Then nothing. By the time William picked himself up and walked over to Michael, Michael was gone.

I'm afraid Michael just left, said the sweets in the road.

You just missed him, said the blood.

Sorry! said the outstretched hand.

As William opens the door (slowly! Slowly!), the nurse says, 'When you get back we'll give you a brief medical check, then Dr de Oliveira will be here to chat to you.'

'Not Dr Nightingale?' he asks.

The technician at the computer looks up now. He looks at the nurse. Then he says, 'Dr Nightingale doesn't work on individual cases any longer,' at the same time as the nurse says, 'Dr Nightingale is on leave' – and William knows that Dr Nightingale has been sacked.

William walks down the corridor, thinking about the crimes he has committed.

Crime one.

Killing somebody.

Which was technically not a crime, in the eyes of the law, not officially judged to be so. William got away with it. Which is insane, because how can killing somebody ever not be a crime? William didn't mean to kill a boy. But he *did* kill him. He was drunk, and stupid, and it turned out that a man's life was safer in the path of a moving vehicle than it was in the hands of William.

He sees it clearly, the killing. Detailed, defined. Like how frozen food companies claim that food is actually fresher for having been frozen, this memory is pristine from lack of handling.

(The girl in the picture, the boy on the road, the girl's hair, the boy's hand, holding the sweets he was about to eat, then not.)

This is what the word *unsparing* means, he thinks.

Crime two.

Erasing the memory of killing somebody.

Technically very much a crime in the eyes of the law. Aside from the gross misconduct, and tampering with neural evidence, illegally obtained memory deletions can get you twenty years.

William could go to prison not for killing someone, but for forgetting that he killed someone.

Not quite a life sentence, though he deserves it, doesn't he, because a life is what he let escape, when he cracked Michael Graham on the kerb like an egg, and that's what everyone says, the victims – *a life sentence is what my daughter got, my dad got, my wife got, what I get, so that's what the killer should get* – so many different victims yet they all believe the same thing, the same truth: life for life.

William walks past the lavatories, checks behind him, sees nobody around, and continues on towards reception. The receptionist is at the desk, facing away from him, her head bent over something. Trying to look neither panicky nor casual, he walks quickly towards the door.

The sudden movement makes the receptionist jump. She does a muffled 'Oh!' when she sees him. She's halfway through a sandwich, which she knocks out of sight behind her computer.

'I'm just going out to make a phone call,' he explains.

She looks at him warily. Then she says, 'We have a room you can use.'

'I also need a cigarette,' he says. 'I'm staying in the grounds. Back in twenty. They said it was okay.'

'Uh,' she says. 'Okay. Sorry. It's just we've had people leaving and not coming back. We have a duty of care . . .'

As she says this, William realises that there's nothing the clinic can do right now to actually *stop* him leaving.

He almost smiles at her, with the relief of it.

'Thanks,' he says. He heads towards the door.

'I'll be right here, Mr Hall,' she calls after him. 'Just press the button to come back in.'

He raises his hand in a small wave. The glass doors slide open as he approaches. The security guard standing there seems absorbed in his own thoughts, head tilted up at the sky, the icy burn of the blue. As William approaches, the guard nods at him, allowing William to walk past, on through the main gate, and out into the street.

William starts a text message to Annetta. He tells her he loves her. He says it turned out the wipe was to do with his dad's death, he'll explain the details later. He doesn't mention Louise Nightingale. He wouldn't want her to get into trouble. He's strangely grateful to Louise for making at least a few years possible. A decent amount of happiness, for a good number of years.

A bargain at the price.

He doesn't say sorry to Annetta. He wishes he could. He wishes he could say all kinds of things. But he's got to think about how this message will be read, later.

I'll be home soon, he types. *Tell the kids I love them.*

After he sends the message, pain comes over him.

It's a different sort of pain from the kind he felt under the shadow, which was final and flat and pressed the sense out of everything, like a truck tyre rolling over a mouse. This misery is rich and nuanced. Complex notes, different layers. A symphony. It encompasses Annetta's T-shirt, Fiona's boyfriend's dog, Milo's ice-cream sundae. It's the past: Fiona as a toddler, low-browed and ferocious. Milo as a baby with the hiccups he got so often that they took him to the doctor, who said she'd have expected this sort of overreaction from new parents, but not from them.

It's also the future: the bed in the sunlight, with his family on it. Lifting up, now, rising into the sky like the bed in that old Disney film, and William running to get on it, even though it's too high already – but he runs and runs anyway, and finally gives up, out of breath, bent, squinting after it, smaller and smaller, until it vanishes into the light he'd liked so much.

William walks until he comes to the fastest flowing part of the road. Nobody stops him. He can walk or stop. Absolute freedom of choice.

He has a strange sense that he is being given a choice so that he can make the right choice.

He's never really believed in redemption before. He's not sure if this is it. But that's probably the thing about redemption. You have to do it without knowing that it will work.

Otherwise it doesn't count.

It was as if William hit Michael so hard he divided in two, in mid-air. His body fell to earth, his soul flew up, knocked out of the park.

At the time William was horrified at how easy it was. How effortlessly something like that could be done. It disturbed him. Now he finds it almost consoling.

Here, gone, blink of an eye, simple as that.

A woman is walking on the other side of the road, holding the hand of a child. William waits. He watches them walk round the corner, until they're almost out of sight.

His phone starts ringing.

A lorry comes round the corner. It moves neatly, almost deliberately, in front of the receding woman and child.

The lorry seems larger because of it; like it's filling the whole street, blotting out the light. There's that kind of inevitability about it.

The way the sun reflects off the window of it, a flat glare, like the gaze of God, looking at William, saying: *You understand.*

And William says:

Yes.

Noor

What with all the unanswerable questions, and the travelling between uncomfortable past and uncertain future, back and forth, Noor gets about two hours of sleep. She moves through the morning in a fog, looking at herself in the mirror closely as she brushes her teeth, trying to work out if she's still dreaming.

She's not sure. The familiarity of the toothbrush with its splayed bristles and the one defunct spotlight around the bathroom mirror, the apple on the car seat at the traffic lights, the gates of the clinic – all these say: not a dream.

But then, arriving at work to be met by Jim Stokes and a security guard, with Marie in the background trying not to stare, and being told that she's been temporarily suspended from her post while investigations are carried out into whether or not serious misconduct took place on her part – all that feels distinctly *dreamlike*. When Noor looks at Jim she half expects him to turn into her father, or for all her teeth to drop out.

Noor stands for a second, waiting. Nobody changes into anybody. Her teeth are still in her jaw, trying not to chatter.

'Okay then,' she says. 'What happens now?'

'You can take what you need from your office,' Jim says. 'Personal effects, obviously. No company property. Mark here will go with you, er, while . . .'

. . . *while you scuttle back to your office*, Noor mentally fills in.

But that's not fair. Noor's quite fond of scuttling into an office herself. She and Jim are both this way: industrious, tunnelling creatures.

As opposed to Louise, who is . . . not.

But then Noor's still not quite sure what sort of creature Louise is.

She goes to her office with Mark. They don't make conversation, though she considers asking him where he's going on his holidays.

I hear the Maldives are lovely this time of year, Mark.

She opens her desk drawer and takes out her tea and sugar. She puts them into her bag, takes the drawer key and her office key off the fob, and puts them down on the desk.

'There you go,' she says.

'That's it?' says Mark. He looks surprised.

Noor considers the room, in case there's something she missed.

It looks like *her* room.

It also looks a lot like nobody was ever there.

What now?

But she doesn't really have much say in that, does she? Go home. That's all she can do now. Go home, live her life. Hope that whatever happens next is for the best.

*

What happened to Orlando Paladino?

Love made him insane, so they took it out of his brain. History does not record what happened after that.

Noor's sitting in a coffee shop near the river. The window has a partial view of the water. A swan crosses it, slowly.

Who else?

Clementine and Joel.

Whether or not their second attempt at love was doomed to fail, their efforts to forget each other were misguided. When Joel is first seen, waiting at the train station, his head emerging from the shuffling rows of commuters, both questing and hopeless, it's obvious that he's miserable. When he lies upturned in his bed he looks like a dead man floating in the sea. The facts of the love are gone – the biographical notes redacted – but the love is still there. There is no eternal sunshine; there is no spotless mind.

There are three types of memory. Noor learned that when she did her second degree, in psychology. (At the time she considered it just a different type of software programming. Thinking herself superior software, of course.)

The first type of memory is episodic. A memory of something *happening*. For example, a memory of playing the piano at a concert.

The second type is conceptual: the knowledge that you can play the piano. Amnesiacs actually retain their conceptual knowledge. They might know they are a pianist even if they can't remember a single performance.

The final type is procedural memory: remembering *how* to play the piano. Like conceptual knowledge, it can survive the destruction of other memories, which is how amnesiacs can sit down at the piano and actually play.

The problem with *Star Trek* is that it didn't show that Captain Kirk was different after the death of Rayna, Noor thinks. He would have known that he was a man who had been in love, even if he'd never learned how to do it properly, or couldn't remember one single person he'd loved.

He would have lain upturned in his bed, and thought: *Something is missing.*

Two women come into the coffee shop. The barista says hello to them as if she recognises them. They order their drinks and sit down, talking about a new documentary series one has seen and says the other one has to see.

Back at the clinic, W. Hall will be in the middle of his or her restoration. Staff from various departments will be talking in the kitchen, probably about Louise's departure, or Noor's disgrace, or maybe just about TV shows.

At Noor's house, empty spaces. Clean floors. A neatly made bed. A TV planner full of unwatched shows, none of which Noor has been told to see, or told anyone else to see.

On the other side of the river there's a small park. A few people sitting on the benches, in the cold, waiting patiently for the sun to come out from behind the clouds. A woman pushing a pram, accompanied by a Dalmatian. The woman sees an older man, waves, stops, and the two of them talk as the Dalmatian circles the man's legs and tries to push its nose into his palm.

457

Noor feels very far from the town, the people, the dogs. Even when she goes out into the town she doesn't walk with people. She walks *amongst* them.

What else walks amongst? Death. God. Murderers. Monsters.

Nothing good.

Outwalk, she thinks.

She wonders, for a moment, what an inwalk would feel like.

Out of the coffee shop's other window Noor can see a man standing, facing the road, waiting to cross. He's holding his hand up to shield his eyes from the sun, which is pointing right at him. He waits for a long time. She thinks the sun must be strong, because the man obviously can't see that the road is completely empty. It's a main road, and cars do travel down it quite quickly, but there hasn't been a car in a while and here he still stands, squinting up and down. And when something does come down the road, a lorry, he lowers his hand and lifts his foot and looks almost as if he's decided that *now* is the time to cross.

And then the man steps out.

*

Everything is so nonsensical, then, that Noor registers it as elements only, floating pieces.

A howling mechanical noise.

Sun.

Her tea, overturned, spreading across the table.

A man in the road.

A human noise: a crying out.

Noor runs out of the cafe, past the lorry, which has swerved
a little further down the road, mounted the kerb and come
to a stop. She reaches the man, who is kneeling strangely,
next to the pavement. As she crouches down beside him he
topples sideways and she catches his weight, which sends her
half sprawling on the ground, holding his body. An abrupt,
wet warmth spreads across her own stomach and legs.

She's saying something, but she has no idea what it is.

One side of the man's head is dark and tangled with
blood. His face is turned up to her own. His eyes are still
open. They're green. She's never seen green eyes before,
or not up close. They don't have much consciousness in
them. They waver over the rooflines, the sky; the lids drop
and open like mouths trying for words.

For one second they catch on Noor's, and there it is:
his self.

'Annetta,' he says. Then the self passes out of his eyes.
The lids come down.

Noor holds her fingers against the warm skin of his
neck. She doesn't even know what she's doing. She's never
checked a pulse before. There must be a pulse there: she's
just too ignorant to find it.

Other people are gathering, now, around the two of
them. The lorry driver is here; an unsteady man who moves
towards them, then away, and throws up over a wall.

He thinks it's worse than it is, Noor thinks. It's fine. It's just a lot of blood, making everything look dramatic. Look: his face is so calm. There's not much blood on his head, not really. He's just passed out.

She wants to tell the lorry driver not to worry, but he won't hear her over the noise of people shouting and talking around her. Passers-by, a security guard and a sales assistant from a nearby shop, both uniformed, the waitress from the coffee shop. No police or paramedics – but they're on the way, that's what the people around her keep saying. And then sirens can be heard, and everyone says, see, that's them, they're coming.

'He's dead,' someone says. They're crying. 'It's too late.'

Noor ignores that.

It's the blood, she thinks. And the strange way the man's body looks, maybe. People have glanced at him and made the casual assumption that he is dead. They aren't looking at his face. It's a pleasant, uneventful face. He looks like he's dozed off, in fact. Like it's that lull-time of a Sunday and he's been on the sofa, watching TV and the afternoon sun slipped in and drowsed him into a peaceful nap. His hair is grey-brown, with a slight bald patch on the top of his head. Lying next to him is a plain brown shoe with a scuff on one toe. On his wrist is an inexpensive digital watch, its broken face reflecting the sunlight. She notices one of his eyebrows is disturbed, but she can't smooth it back, not with blood on her fingers.

How could someone so normal be dead? How can someone die in a small town, on a sunny afternoon? It's too dramatic, it's not plausible.

A police car and an ambulance appear, and pull over. People run towards Noor and the man she holds. A paramedic crouches down and takes hold of the man's wrist. He listens to his heart. He opens one of the man's green eyes and shines a torch into it. He looks up at another paramedic, and he shakes his head.

'Do you know him?' a female police officer is saying to Noor, crouching down beside her. She has one of those warm, gentle voices that usually annoy Noor, but doesn't just now.

Noor nods. Feeling like it's true. She knows this man better than they do, anyway.

She notices that the crowd has grown. People are standing all around her. People with shopping bags, some of the protesters from the clinic, the security guard, the waitress, texting now, tearfully. There's a Nepenthe technician here too, a woman she knows is called Kath, holding a half-eaten baguette, talking to another police officer.

'He just left the clinic,' Kath says. 'He said he was going to call his wife. I saw him in the grounds when I was leaving. I was on my lunch break. You need to call the clinic. Get someone down here. No, I don't know his name.'

W. Hall, thinks Noor.

'But . . . that's Dr Ali,' she can hear Kath saying. 'Noor Ali. I don't know . . . no, she's a doctor at the clinic.'

'Dr Ali?' the police officer with Noor asks.

Noor nods.

'The paramedics are going to take over now,' says the officer. 'We need you to come and sit down.'

Paramedics surround Noor and gently lift W. Hall up, off her. The police officer holds out her hand.

Noor takes it.

She gets up. She allows someone to put a blanket on her, noticing as they do that her blanket is different to the one they are putting on W. Hall, after they lift him onto the stretcher. One blanket for the living, one for the dead.

'William Hall,' a paramedic says, holding a wallet open.

Before the ambulance leaves, she asks if she can sit inside it for a moment. The police officers and paramedics look at each other, as if they're hoping one of them, someone else, will say no, but nobody says it, and so they agree: Noor can get in. So she climbs inside, and stands next to William Hall's covered body.

'Me again,' she says.

She'd take his hand, but it's been wrapped up with the rest of him. She touches the corner of his dead-people blanket instead. The blood has dried on her own hands, cracked, splintered into dark flakes.

'Goodbye, William,' she says.

Seeing as nobody else has said it.

Finn and Mirande

Mirande and Finn are in the garden. It's autumn, but it's still warm. The desert is changing over for the season; the colours of their view go blue, purple, red, beyond the long-shadowed green of the lawn. A small coolness in the air says time has passed, time will pass.

Mirande sighs, like she can feel it. Then she sips her gin and tonic, and smiles at Finn.

From the house behind them there's a shriek of laughter. Through the glass Finn can see the grey-blue shapes of Ri and a friend of hers on the sofa, watching TV with their hands sticking out in front of them. Drying nail varnish, probably. The friend is wearing a panda onesie, Ri a tiger onesie. (Cute, said Finn, though we all know the real endangered species in this house is me.)

Finn's scrolling through his phone, looking at houses in Ireland. Not houses, really. More like ruins, of castles and towers and manors. Falling-down castles at knock-down prices. There's a medieval keep in Waterford that'll be a nightmare, undoubtedly. But. It's on a hill, there's no landslip – he says to Mirande – and from its battlements you can see the Celtic Sea.

'I like it,' says Mirande. 'Are we still aiming for spring?'

'Yes. No point doing it now, right before Christmas. What's the date . . . huh –' Finn's checking his phone. 'Did you know it was Guy Fawkes Night a couple of days ago? I forget it, over here.'

'What night was it?' Mirande asks.

'Monday, I think.'

'Really?' She starts to laugh.

'My forgetfulness amuses you? Or is it the festival itself? It *is* possibly the weirdest of the English rituals. Not to mention the most macabre. Though I have to say . . . Jesus emerging from his grave: that's also weird. Halloween's got nothing on that.'

'No,' Mirande says. 'Maybe I never told you. This is the date Nepenthe gave me to have my memory back. It's today. I'd forgotten it.'

'Today,' Finn says.

There's a moment of silence as both of them contemplate it.

'Did you manage to get the airfare refunded?' asks Finn.

'Sort of. They'd only give it to me as a voucher. And I've got to use it before the end of the year.'

'So we could go to Ireland for Christmas,' says Finn.

'Yes. Look at cheap castles.'

'Hey, what about Rome? You know, it's been fifteen years since we last saw it. There are things we haven't seen. Ri was telling me about this museum designed by Richard Meier.'

'She remembered the architect's name?'

'No. I filled that part in. The building is designed around this altar, the Ara Pacis. No idea how you pronounce it. The Ara – the altar was built for Augustus, who'd been away for three years in Gaul and Hispania. Like a welcome home gift.'

'City ruins,' Mirande says.

'*The* city of ruins. Remember the Forum? The Aurelian Walls? That kid who stole your watch?'

Her gaze defocuses; off to Rome. 'I remember,' she says. Finn takes her hand.

He doesn't *know*. That's his choice. But Mirande had her choice too – whenever it was made, in the nineties or years later or a few weeks ago – and he knows the outcome of that.

Mirande smiles again. Looks away, looks back; a look Finn can't quite get the gist of, maybe because there is no one gist. An excess of gists. If there's reassurance, it's perhaps only part reassurance. But if there's trouble there, it's only part trouble. Parts and possibilities, and haven't they always lived like that, even when they didn't know it?

'What was that other wall called?' she asks. 'The oldest one. Older than the Aurelian Walls. We saw a section of it on the Aventine. Remember? That Japanese tourist asked for a photo, and you were going to take one of him, but it turned out he wanted one of *us*.'

'And quite rightly so,' Finn says. 'We're a beautiful pair.'

'We should go back and revisit that wall; I just can't remember its name.'

'Don't worry,' says Finn. 'I'll look it up.'

PART FIVE

Mei

'. . . Just three houses,' Mei says. 'And a conversation about a bold move.'

'It's like a film,' says Margreet. She's supposed to be working, but the cafe is quiet, so she's pulled up a chair next to Mei's, so Mei can tell her the whole story. Margreet smiles now as if she's finished a good meal. She takes a sip of Mei's flat white. 'I like romantic stories,' she says.

'Well,' says Mei. 'I've only been here a month. We don't know if it's a romance yet.'

'This *is* it,' says Margreet. 'This is when it's romantic. Nothing is romantic after a few months.' She sits back contemplatively, taking another sip of Mei's coffee. 'Yes,' she says. 'A good story. The part in which you became a drug addict. And then the uplifting ending, with you about to attend university here in the Netherlands.'

'I'm not there yet. I've only just applied.'

'Oh, yes. Where to?'

'Maastricht, Erasmus, Leiden, Amsterdam. Doing philosophy. It's actually cheaper to study here than in the UK, did you know that? It could work out really well. That's if they accept me, I mean.'

A customer comes in and stands at the counter. Margreet looks up at the woman, then rolls her eyes at Mei. The customer looks embarrassed.

'I'd better go,' Margreet says.

'Thanks for the chat,' Mei says. 'I'm going to meet Armand at the Van Gogh Museum.'

'I doubt you will enjoy it,' Margreet says, getting up and going back to the counter. 'Van Gogh is not a very good painter. But it's not so crowded, at this time of year. You probably won't have to spend long there.'

Mei drains her cup of coffee, and checks her phone.

She has a message from Armand (*Hey Mei-lennial, see you at 3, ok? Under the sunflowers. X*) and her dad, who wants to visit. (*About time I gave this Frenchman of yours the once-over. I jest, of course. The words cheese, garlic and surrender will not pass my lips*).

Mei won't reply to her dad for now. He only wants to visit because Keiko has dumped him.

She wanted me to move out of my flat – he said, outraged – because it gives her some imaginary condition, and buy somewhere else with her. On the ground floor! I told her hell would freeze over before Alistair Lewarne descended to ground level. Ground zero, as I called it.

No, Dad, said Mei. You can't call it that.

She'll be back, said Mei's dad.

Will she? Isn't she dating someone else?

It won't last, Mei's dad said. She's stayed with me all these years – drinking and, er, socialising with other women and whatnot – *because* of those things. She likes the unpredictability. The excitement. This new Jeremy is a nice guy by all accounts. Ha! That'll get boring.

470

What if she doesn't come back? Mei said. Would you move out of the flat for her?

At this Mei's dad talked loudly and quickly about Mei's mother's name being on the lease, and tax loopholes, and property markets and other complicated reasons he couldn't actually move out. Then he sighed, and said, with what sounded almost like a tearful note in his voice, that Mei should come back to Kuala Lumpur.

We had a bloody great time, didn't we? he said. Father and daughter. That's how it should be.

Are you drunk? Mei asked.

I've been drinking, her dad said haughtily. I am not drunk.

Dad, said Mei. This is ridiculous. You miss Keiko. Go and talk to her. I know you can't afford an apartment as fancy as the one Mum's paying for. So move somewhere less fancy. Keiko would appreciate it.

You don't know women, Mei, her dad said.

I am a woman, Mei said.

You know what I mean, her dad said.

Not really. But never mind. Keiko's not with you for money! You're the one who's obsessed with money. You're the one who couldn't decide between an actual human female who *likes* you and a stupid apartment.

Fortieth floor, said her dad. With a pool.

Mei sighed.

I'll give it some thought, her dad said. Also. Have you called your mother? She's phoned me. Very upset about you doing a runner to the lands of Neth. Seems like there's some trouble at her work, too. Her buddy Dr Ali stitched her up, apparently. Some whistleblowing antics. You really ought to speak to her.

I will, Mei said. Just . . . not yet.

471

She felt guilty, then, about what she'd said to Dr Ali.

When Dr Ali had appeared at the clinic, just before Mei's follow-up appointment, Mei thought she'd been sent by Louise. Then she realised she hadn't. She wanted to say to Dr Ali: Why *didn't* she send you? She wanted Dr Ali to say, *You should call your mum.*

But Dr Ali didn't do that. She seemed to have her own problems. She half dragged Mei back outside, and asked Mei a lot of questions. Then she seemed shocked at most of Mei's answers. Mei wondered if she was officially shocking now: if this was the start of her new life, shocking people.

Mei had remembered more about Dr Ali as she talked. It came back to Mei that they'd met at one of her mum's parties, when she was a kid, and Dr Ali had come out to the garden. Mei couldn't remember what she and Dr Ali talked about that night, but she remembered Dr Ali looking back towards the house, at the party happening behind the glass doors. Dr Ali was looking at Mei's mum. She'd had this wondering look, as if she was looking at the Northern Lights. *Starstruck*, Mei thought. She'd heard her mum mention Dr Ali since then as her best employee. Capable. Bullshit-free. Loyal. Perceptive.

Not *that* perceptive, thought Mei.

Remembering it, she felt obscurely angry. She wanted to strike out at this unperceptive doctor's picture of her mother. Scribble the eyes out, draw an evil moustache on it, devil horns. Wave it in Dr Ali's face.

So she told Dr Ali what her mum was actually like, and Dr Ali looked shocked again.

The stupid thing was, almost as soon as Mei had spoken – and she could tell that Dr Ali *listened* to her, with this horrified, but also strangely *comprehending* expression – she regretted it.

It's all true, she reminded herself – reminds herself. But still, she wished she hadn't said it. She wanted to get away then, from Dr Ali. As if leaving the scene would undo the crime.

What happened after that? Dr Ali started reminiscing about some embarrassing kid-thing Mei said. Mei almost wanted to ask her if she was okay, but it was obvious she wasn't. When Dr Ali left she walked away slowly, as if fatally stricken.

Mei felt stricken herself.

Loyal, Mei thinks.

The word makes her feel unhappy.

You really ought to speak to her.

Mei's conversation with her dad was a couple of weeks ago. Mei still feels the same way now:

I will.

Not yet.

Mei hasn't answered her mum's calls, or read the emails from her.

She loves her mother. She's angry with her mother. She loves her mother. She can't trust her mother. Her thoughts go round like that a lot.

Sometimes she thinks that her mum couldn't bear to see Mei – via her first romance – becoming more independent. When Mei thinks this, she pictures the woman whose photograph she sees in the papers sometimes, Dr Louise Nightingale, walking out of the Nepenthe headquarters in London in a steel-grey suit, expressionless. The doctor with her hands on her hips, supervising the tipping of chemicals into the water supply.

She's pretty sure, though, that the main reason her mum wanted Mei to wipe her memory was so that what Louise said about Mei's birth mother would be swept away too. More than that, she thinks her mum would do it again. If she had the opportunity to put a headset on Mei while Mei was sleeping and wipe the memory all over again, Mei thinks her mum would probably find a way to justify that.

But did her mum want the deletion to spare herself, or Mei? And where was the line between the two of them, anyway? Mei's mum was pained by Mei's pain. To comfort herself she had to comfort Mei.

And sometimes Mei thinks that maybe her mum didn't *know* why she did what she did. That for a moment she wasn't Dr Louise Nightingale but a normal person: doing something without understanding why she was doing it. And if she'd acted according to her own unconscious fears – her fear of losing her daughter's love, of Mei moving out of reach – could that be . . . forgivable?

And then she pictures her mum reading to her in the light of the revolving birds, or crying at the airport. Saying, *My beautiful Plum.*

Maybe all of this can be true.

Except the contamination of the water supply.

Probably.

Mei thinks about her birth mother sometimes.

She feels sorry for the woman whose circumstances were so desperate she had to give her baby up. Or maybe, had to give birth to a baby she never wanted. Before, Mei'd been so horrified at being like her birth mother – weak, addicted, unstable – that she didn't even consider that maybe her birth mother didn't start like that either, that she'd just taken that shape to fit into the space that was available.

Mei – and at times she feels guilty about this, and about not wanting to track her mother down – has more space.

Mei's not so worried, either, that she's going to repeat the same story. She doesn't believe in *story*, for a start. She doesn't really believe in strong or weak any more – not when it comes to people. Maybe she's turning into a true Sartrean after all. With Humean overtones.

Not that she'll ever tell her mum that.

It's not like Mei plans on ignoring her mum forever or anything. She even knows what she'll say to her, when they finally do talk. Something about having spent her life being scared of bold moves, longing to make one, but feeling that she didn't have what it took. And she didn't get it right at first. She thought that her bold move was geographic. London to Kuala Lumpur to Crowshill to Amsterdam. But that wasn't it. Then she thought it was romantic: her turning up here, finding Armand standing on a ladder, hanging up Christmas lights.

Want a hand? she said, like she was in a film and it was ending happily.

But that wasn't it either. She's enjoying the Mei and Armand film, but it's not the end. She doesn't know how it's going to end. Right now she wants to be with him, have a lot of sex, get married, have children, die in the same bed in their old people's home. But if they don't, Mei will get over it.

It turned out, Mei will say to her mum, that my boldest move was just doing something you didn't want me to do.

And then she did it anyway and – just like Armand said – there was this sense of things being . . . *calm*. Unknown, but okay. Like going over a waterfall and landing in a deep pool. Maybe she'll swim to shore, maybe she'll flail around and sink to the bottom and have to struggle back up.

But she's not going to float.

Something like that, that's what she'll say.

For now she's just enjoying having a bit of time to herself.

She puts on her coat and scarf, picks up her bag, opens her umbrella, and goes out, into the sudden rain and cold, feeling the ceiling lift off her, flying out and away in cloud swirls, like the Van Gogh paintings she may or may not enjoy, thinking:

This.

Oscar

Oscar's kept for a long time at the Nepenthe clinic after his appointment, talking to various people. He isn't sure that the talking is very helpful for anyone involved. He, for one, feels like a watermelon that has been dropped from a great height. Then various Nepenthe people stand over him and ask him how he feels about being a smashed watermelon.

'I don't know yet,' Oscar says.

After that he's sent back to the private hospital, the implication being that he's going to stay at this hospital until he bloody well does know what he feels about it.

Not that anyone put it like that.

Oscar doesn't mind the hospital, though. He cries in his room, then he chats at the salad bar to rich people with drug problems and eating disorders, then he cries in his room again. Sometimes he cries at the salad bar. Nobody minds.

After a couple of days he's meant to go back to Nepenthe for more appointments. They send a black car for him after breakfast, and he gets in – but as soon as he's out of the gates of the hospital Oscar decides he's had enough of being *in* things. The dim, broken lighting of Marrakech airport, the processed air of the plane, the hooting brightness of Gatwick, the clinic, the hospital, the cars.

Enough.

'I need fresh air,' he says to the driver.

The driver isn't sure about this. He says something about Oscar needing to be under observation.

'Yeah, I know,' Oscar says. 'You lot want me *in*. But I need to be *out*.'

The driver says the concern is that Oscar isn't ready to be out. That at this stage Oscar might not be exactly stable enough for a stroll around the town.

'But,' says Oscar, 'you can't actually *stop* me, can you?'

'Well, no,' said the driver.

Which is how Oscar – unready, unstable – ends up having a little stroll around Crowshill.

The town is very pretty. Well-behaved children sitting in the coffee shops with their parents, watching cartoons on tablets; well-behaved dogs slyly cocking their legs against the Tudor buildings. Interesting-looking clock tower, trees, a post office, a school playground with an empty set of swings –

Oscar stops.

The feeling of *not* has just come back to him.

No to everything.

Oscar was going to kill himself before he heard about the trial, he remembers. He could definitely have killed himself since. The world was his oyster when it came to ways to die. He'd stood on high buildings and bridges and cliff edges. He'd had unsupervised access to heroin, Valium, sleeping pills. Rows of razors in the pharmacies, rows of knives in department stores. Stolen cars, brick walls.

But he didn't do it. In that sense, Nepenthe had worked.

Oscar wonders if that longing, for *not*, would come back. He searches for it, gingerly. He remembers how it felt, like he can remember how being high felt without actually *being* high, or wanting to be high. But the feeling itself isn't here. Or, to be precise, it isn't here at this moment. There's no way to tell how long that will last. Or what will happen the next time he's unhappy.

Well.

He'll get to that.

And on the plus side: he's found out that he isn't such a bad guy. His biggest fear was that he'd done terrible things – and it turns out he'd never intentionally hurt anybody at all.

This is a good thought. He tucks it into his body, like a penguin with an egg. He could sing it. Head back, beak up, penguin style.

People of Crowshill! I, Oscar Levy, have no idea what's going on or who I am but I have NEVER TRIED TO HURT ANYBODY.

That'd go down well.

When Oscar gets to the main square of the town he sees two parents, swinging a four-year-old boy in school uniform between them. This makes him cry. He tries to keep his face the same, so that people passing hopefully won't notice the tears streaming down his face and dripping into his collar. He can't do much about the tears, though. They won't stop. In the end he buys a newspaper, sits down on a bench, and pretends to be immersed in the news as he cries.

After a while, he realises that between the bouts of crying he's feeling something else. Feeling – what?

But come on: Oscar knows exactly what this feeling is. He just isn't sure he should be feeling it right now. This wonder, this *happiness*, taking its turn with the memory of his mother sinking through the water – or the memory of what he imagined, because he never saw her, did he? She didn't get smaller and smaller. She didn't wave. She didn't mouth anything.

Goodbye, Oscar. I love you. Go.

He bends his head over the newspaper again. But then he looks up, and the day comes over him and says, *Look at me. I'm so beautiful, Oscar. Look.*

His father's face, taken violently away from him.

The wonky cut-out of the windscreen, like a cartoon *Pow.*

Bang.

His dad's speech bubbles

(. . .)

The beautiful day.

The calmness of his mother's face, knowing she was heading downwards to die.

The day.

He wishes that beauty and horror would get themselves straight, or at least take longer turns in his brain.

While all this is going on people are walking past Oscar without paying him much attention. They've got their own thoughts to wrestle with, he supposes. He wonders if any of them are in the same position as Oscar himself – but then, even if they were Nepenthe clients, they wouldn't be quite the same sort of client as Oscar. For most of them it was just fucking and fuck-ups. When they visited for their refund they'd get back a manageable, bite-size chunk of time. But Oscar has been given a whole childhood. A heap of childhood; an avalanche of childhood.

He can't work out what to do with it yet.

After a while of crying, he thinks that maybe the driver was right and Oscar isn't quite stable enough to be out yet. That maybe he ought to head back to the clinic.

That's when it happens.

Bang.

For a second, Oscar is back in the water. Then he's in the street, wondering if that noise just happened in that moment or if he's starting to fall apart – if the fresh air he'd been inhaling has *undone* something and now his brain is dissolving into soup. But the sound of it is fading in the air, still, and the people around him are looking around too, alarmed.

Oscar walks to the end of the road, where people seem to be gathering. It's hard to see in the sun. He sees a lorry, stopped at a strange angle in the road; a woman, running past, towards a figure that appears to be kneeling down, right in the middle of the road. A few other figures in the distance are moving towards them. Running.

Oscar stands a little distance away from the man who had been hit by the lorry, the woman holding him. He watches the people trying, hopelessly, to save the man's life. There's a puddle of blood around the man, on the tarmac, sending out long, questing rivulets. There are cracks spreading across the windscreen of the lorry.

Oscar wonders if this is really happening, or if he's gone mad. He's able to move backwards, a few steps, and sit down on a wall. That's all he can do.

He knows, somewhere, that he ought to find his driver again, hand himself back in to Nepenthe. He just doesn't feel able to move. The heat and electricity have seeped out of his body, leaving an inert mass, that sits, and watches.

Time passes without him. An ambulance arrives, police arrive. The dead man is taken away. The lorry is driven away, by someone who isn't its original driver. The driver is taken away, a tiny person emerging from that large, brutal block-shape, tiny and crying. The police talk to the woman wrapped in the blanket. The crowd gradually breaks up, draws away.

The woman moves away from the police officers. She's holding up her hand, palm out, fingers up: the signal for *enough*. No. She sits down on a wall of her own. The police are still around her, taping off the area, but she's alone among them.

Then she looks up, and looks at Oscar. They're not that far apart. She can see him clearly, but she squints at him, then her eyes widen. Like she *knows* him.

Oscar is startled. With it, he finds he can move again; like this contact is a line thrown out in the water. He takes hold of it. He doesn't think; he's not there yet. He walks over.

'O. Levy?' she says. 'Really?' She sounds disbelieving.

She's small, with long dark hair coming out of what once must have been a neat knot. She looks at him calmly, but there's a refusal in her calmness, as if he's part of a bad dream, and she's not going to panic, but she's not going to accept this dream figment, either.

'Oscar,' he says. 'But . . . I don't know you?'

'No you don't,' she says. She looks down. The refusal drops away, and she just looks blank. Oscar realises she's shaking.

His head is back now; it comes to life like a screwed-in bulb. He finds he's able to think.

This woman, he thinks, needs my help.

The idea of *help* feels audacious. The idea of Oscar being substantial enough for someone else to be supported by him. But he gives her his hand. She holds on to it, tightly. Her own hand is covered in blood, but she doesn't seem to notice.

A police officer has come over. She looks at Oscar warily.

'We're going to take you home, Noor,' she says to the woman. 'Do you have someone there, or someone that can be with you?'

'No,' Noor says. She's still gripping Oscar's hand.

'Do you want me to come?' Oscar asks her.

483

Noor is silent for a moment.

'Do you . . . know this man?' the police officer asks her.

'She knows me,' Oscar says. 'I don't know her. I don't know why that is.'

The police officer looks confused.

'He's coming,' Noor says.

Oscar makes a cup of tea in Noor's empty kitchen. Her whole house looks empty. It would resemble a corporate let, except corporate lets have pictures on the walls. Noor's walls are as white as those of the clinic, the floor is polished wood. In the large sitting room there's a sofa, a table and chairs, and a television, and nothing else. Noor sits on the middle of the big sofa wearing the bathrobe he found upstairs, in silence.

Oscar brings the tea in and hands it to her.

'Thank you,' Noor says. He's relieved to hear her speak. She takes a sip.

'Hot tea,' she says. Then she starts to cry.

Oscar watches her crying with approval. He'd been worried by her calm blankness. Grief, from what he's seen, is seasonal. First everything is frozen solid. Then it thaws, and the ice rains down, water crashing everywhere. Then, later, the leaf buds start to appear. (Or so Oscar hopes.) He'd wondered, from her rigidity and her obvious force of will, if Noor might be the kind of person who just wouldn't ever defrost.

He shivers. It's not just his own analogy: it's cold in here. There's a log-burning stove with a heap of dusty wood in a basket next to it. He looks around for some matches.

'You don't need to stay,' Noor says. 'I just had to get rid of the police. I'm actually fine.'

'But you're crying,' Oscar says.

She makes a dismissive gesture.

'But your friend . . .' Oscar says.

'I don't actually know him,' Noor says. 'He was a patient at the clinic. Not my patient.'

'And that's how you know me?'

'Yes. Well, not officially. You're Access Denied. RASA. I don't know what that is and I'm definitely not meant to talk to you about it.'

'Oh really?' Oscar says. 'So it's a secret inside your company too? They really like keeping secrets, don't they? Well, I don't care if you want to talk about it. I mean, we'd both get in trouble, probably. I think they'd make me give the money back. Though personally I'd rather *talk* than have a lot of money. But I wouldn't want you to get in trouble.'

'Trouble,' Noor says slowly.

Her tears, which have been dropping steadily, seem to gather up and overwhelm her. She puts her head in her hands.

Oscar makes the fire. When he opens the door of the stove a few small pieces of paper drift out. He picks up the largest one. It's black at the edges. It says, *All there are, are endless questions.*

He fishes it out and puts it to one side. When the fire is burning and Noor has wiped her face and stopped crying, he says,

'This is beautiful. Why did you burn it? Was it an accident?'

He holds it out and she reads it. She frowns.

'How on earth is that beautiful?' she says.

'Isn't it saying: you have to keep asking questions? That sometimes you get an answer, sometimes you don't, and you'll never really know anything beyond all doubt, but you never stop asking questions. The questions are the point. Isn't that it?'

'Uh,' says Noor. 'If you like.'

'If you don't want it, could I . . . keep it?'

Noor rubs her face. She looks baffled. 'Sure,' she says. Then she puts down her empty mug, and falls asleep.

Oscar puts the piece of paper in his pocket. He waits around for ten minutes, in the bare room filled by the sound of Noor's low, regular breathing.

Oscar's got himself a phone now, one attached to his own name, so he writes down his number on a notepad and puts it on the table. He writes: *It's okay that you know me* – then, in case that's too ambiguous or maybe even creepy-sounding, adds: *i.e. we can be friends*. Then he lets himself out of the house and walks back down towards the town centre to find his driver, who is probably asking a lot of questions of his own right now, uppermost of which is where the fuck is Oscar.

Oscar's out of the private hospital now, living in a flat with his cousin Nat in Islington. He was worried that she'd only offered him the room because she felt obliged to – and was probably dreading his arrival, a blast from the bleak past of *not, not, not* – but when he arrived his uncle and aunt were there too and they'd hung up a sign that said 'Welcome Back Oscar' in coloured letters and there was a cake. They all cried.

Leaf buds, he thinks.

Oscar's enjoying living with Nat. She remembers his parents and often references them in a way that makes it feel like they're still alive – just not right here, at this moment. He and Nat both like Monty Python and the hundred-year-old walrus at the Horniman Museum. They have parties and make paellas for people. Oscar's accumulating new traits every day.

He still goes back to Nepenthe, to talk to Karine de Oliveira. Oscar likes talking to Karine. She's not very professional, despite being a high-up doctor at Nepenthe. Their meetings happen at the London offices now because the Nepenthe clinic in Crowshill just got shut down for mysterious and apparently shady reasons that nobody at Nepenthe will talk about. Even Karine, who normally swears and laughs and makes jokes, speaks as carefully as the others when Oscar asks her about it. She uses the same words as the others, too. Alleged misconduct. Fraud inquiry. Under investigation. More information in due course.

'Is it to do with RASA?' Oscar asks her.

'No,' Karine says. 'Something else.'

'So, RASA: that's all still a secret?'

'Yes,' Karine says. She rolls her eyes. 'Though, who knows for how long. There are a lot of people who can't really be said to have given informed consent to their confidentiality agreements.'

'Because they're mad, like me?' Oscar says.

'Mentally ill,' Karine says. 'And you're not mentally ill. Which means you also have to keep it to yourself when I accidentally say too much, like I did just now.'

Oscar taps his nose. 'No problem,' he says. 'Doctor–patient confidentiality, right?'

Karine laughs.

'So were they mentally ill before they signed up to RASA? Or afterwards?'

'Not before,' Karine said. 'But that doesn't mean they were *okay*. People who sign up to a trial to remove childhood memories don't tend to be. Bereaved people like yourself, abuse survivors . . . A lot of emotional damage. Then, after the trial, there was a high rate of mental illness. As you would guess. As, some might argue, Nepenthe *should* have guessed.'

'How many of us were there?' Oscar says. 'Us RASA patients?'

Karine looks at him for a while.

'Oscar . . . I'm not going to regret telling you this, am I?' she says.

'I won't tell anyone,' Oscar says. 'I just want to know what happened to them. Do you know?'

'Listen, Oscar, the RASA trial *did* have good intentions. It was hideously wrong-headed, and the doctor behind it was sacked – but it was originally supposed to help people.'

'So did it? Did it help anyone?'

'Not really. There were about sixty participants, aged between eighteen and forty. The older people were, the worse they were affected by the procedure. Of the total, I think maybe around ten are missing; unaccounted for. Twenty more live in institutions. Roughly twenty are

488

working or leading relatively independent lives. They have
varying degrees of mental health issues. Some of those
people will be offered the restoration –'

'What about the other ten?' Oscar asks.

Karine hesitates. She has an expressive face, but Oscar
realises he's never actually seen Karine look *angry*. So he
can't say for sure if the look that appears, momentarily,
on her face is anger. It's just a guess.

'They're dead, aren't they?' Oscar says.

She nods. 'I'm sorry, Oscar.'

'It's okay,' he says. 'Well, not really.'

'How are you feeling?'

He thinks about it.

'I feel . . . it's like I was on the edge of a cliff – and I
nearly fell off. But I didn't. But thinking about it now . . .
it takes a while to stop feeling shaky. It's frightening.
Thinking how close it was.'

'Yes,' Karine says.

'And then I think about *them*.'

'Who?'

'The others. The people who fell.'

Later.

'Are you glad you got your memories back?' Karine
asks him. 'Or is it too soon to know?'

Is Oscar glad?

Is it better?

*

489

The windscreen gaping onto the receding sky like a shocked mouth.

Bang.

His dad toppled forward on the sticky dashboard.
  His mum, falling away behind him.
  Down, down; darkness.
  Calm.

'Yes,' he says.

(*Yes?*)

But yes – yes – it's true.
  'All I wanted was to be *with* people,' Oscar says to Karine. 'Have friends, girlfriends. But I was scared to, because I didn't know what I was. I mean, I didn't know if I'd done something bad, or if I might do something bad in the future. I couldn't explain anything. I couldn't promise anything. You know, a girl once told me I was like an abstract painting: just swirls, no real picture. Anyway. Now I might be able to see what the picture is.'
  Karine frowns. 'Not very fair to abstract art, or to you,' she says.
  'I can see how I was quite annoying,' Oscar says. 'She probably didn't mean it about the art.'
  'I don't see that there's anything wrong with swirls,' Karine says. 'And I'm not sure about the quest to find out what you *are*. A lot of people don't think that's even possible.'

'I actually remembered the other day that I took LSD once,' Oscar says. 'Sorry –'

'Don't apologise to me,' Karine says. 'I've done it myself. It was great. I don't recommend it for you, though. Not at this time. Anyway, please go on.'

'I was fourteen and I thought it would make my maths class more interesting. Also, I was hoping it might kill me. Anyway, in the middle of maths, I vanished. My body didn't vanish. My friends had to hide it in the cupboard because I was unresponsive. But *I* vanished. I remember panicking at first, and then there was no *me* to feel panicked, if you see what I mean. I can't really describe how that felt. It was beautiful. When I remember that, I think I probably *am* a load of swirls. But so's everyone else. We're all just swirls, pretending to be real pictures.'

'That sounds very Buddhist, actually,' Karine says.

'Maybe I could go on a Buddhist retreat,' Oscar says. 'Go to Nepal or Tibet, even. Live in a monastery. Do they let troubled Westerners stay in monasteries to learn about Buddhism?'

'Uh, yes,' says Karine. 'To the point that it's now something of a cliché.'

'Excellent,' Oscar says. 'Maybe I can ask them about my acid trip.'

Asking questions, he thinks. His hand nearly moves towards the pocket with his wallet in and the folded-up, sooty bit of paper. He stops it. He hasn't told Karine about Noor. He knows he's not meant to know her. She has something to do with the Nepenthe clinic being shut down. Not that Oscar gives a shit about that. He likes Noor. If she ever calls him, he'll go and see her.

'Let's finish our sessions first, though,' Karine says.

'Oh sure,' Oscar says. 'There's no rush. I want to stay in London for a while. I actually want . . . is there any way I could meet any of the other RASA people? I was thinking, maybe it would be helpful for them. In some way.'

She thinks about this. 'I don't know, Oscar. Nepenthe probably won't like it. But I'll look into it. I can't promise you anything. I'll do my best, though.'

'Thanks. Don't worry – it's not just them I want to meet. I'd like to make some *friends*. The lifelong type. See my aunts and uncles and cousins. Maybe get a girlfriend.'

'That all sounds good to me,' Karine says.

He sits back in his chair and smiles.

His hand has crept up to his neck, his mother's necklace. It's always warm, this necklace. He never thought of that before. It's warm because of Oscar's own blood, twitching and roaring and singing so close to the surface of the skin.

There's blood in him. Of course there is. The same thing that's in everyone else.

He smiles.

He thinks:

Just like everyone else.

Noor

The problem is that to go almost anywhere, Noor has to pass the clinic.

This used to be a good thing. It was why she bought her house. She'd get up at nine, wash, dress, put on a coat, pick up an apple, get into the car. Eat the apple at the traffic lights at the foot of her road, six, maybe seven bites; throw the core into the garden of the man who once called her a terrorist. By half past nine she'd be at her desk.

In the days after everything happened, Noor sometimes found herself halfway to the door with an apple in her hand – before remembering that there was no journey to make. Because there was no desk to sit at. Because she no longer had a job. That's happening less frequently now, though. Only once in the last fortnight. She's getting used to the new routine, of no routine.

Admittedly, Noor could be making more of this time. These could be her last days as a free woman, for God's sake. She probably ought to be skydiving or swimming with dolphins or having orgies.

Though to do any of these, she'd still have to drive past the clinic.

*

She's in the car now; stuck in the traffic climbing the road that leads past Nepenthe and out of town.

It's quieter now, in Crowshill. The police were the first to go. The yellow tape and traffic cones were carried off to another, fresher incident. Then the reporters left – reluctantly, not wanting to leave without answers, called away only by other stories, with higher chances of answers. Then the clinic closed and the protesters left too.

Without the usual crowds the street seems wider, unnaturally bare. Leaves blow across the pavements and pile up along the high walls of the clinic grounds – in sight now – the tall trees behind them, the sky grey behind the trees.

The traffic jolts forward, then compresses to a standstill. Noor drums her fingers arrhythmically on the wheel. This is like a punishment from Greek mythology. She can't just drive by – no, Noor's going to have to *crawl* past the clinic at two miles per goddamn hour. Unable to look away, even though there's nothing to see except a wall and some trees and a pair of shut gates.

But that's just it, isn't it?

It's the shutness of the gates that's the point.

After William died, there were bouquets left outside the clinic, leaning up against the nobbled flint of the wall. Carnations in pink cellophane, lilies in green cellophane, sunflowers in purple cellophane.

Noor thought it was strange at first. It wasn't like anything had happened right outside the clinic gates. It was further down the road, in the town. Now she

494

wonders if the people who brought those flowers weren't confused; had known what they were doing. Going not to the site of the death but the origin point, where the death began.

She wonders where they would have laid the flowers had they been allowed inside the gates.

Reception? The treatment rooms?

Or further in?

Down the hall, up the stairs, into Noor's office, on the desk.

Noor called Louise, not long after the two of them were suspended.

She hadn't planned to speak to Louise, and in fact the board had warned her *not* to speak to Louise, in one of the many interviews she was attending around that time, to establish how involved Noor was in whatever it was Louise was doing.

But one morning Noor turned on the television, and saw a picture of the clinic.

The text scrolling along the bottom of the screen said . . . *Fraud Probe * Nepenthe Clinic Closed, Employees Under Investigation * Fraud Probe* . . .

Noor watched several revolutions of the same words before she understood them.

Then she called Louise. When Louise answered, it was as if the smiling Louise who had just appeared on the screen was speaking directly into Noor's brain.

Her voice didn't sound as if she was smiling, though.

Noor? she said. What do you want?

Noor switched off the television.

It's public, she said. It's on TV.

You called to tell me that?

The clinic's closed, Noor said. I didn't expect that.

They had to suspend restorations until they could establish how many procedures have been compromised, Louise said. What did you *think* would happen?

Right, said Noor. So now I'm naive for thinking the clinic would hush something up?

They would have hushed it up if it suited them, Louise said. But having this taking centre stage in the press may suit the board better. They can fire or prosecute a couple of rogue employees, say that lessons have been learned and safeguards have been put in place, and the whole thing draws attention away from anything else they've been up to. So: get ready for your fifteen minutes of fame.

What else have they been up to? Noor said. RASA? Right? What is RASA? I know that you know.

I do, Louise said, but *you* know I'm not allowed to talk about it. Is that why you're calling me?

I want to know other things, too, Noor said. Why did William Hall die? What did you have to do with that?

Noor had seen William's death reported in the news as a tragic accident. There was speculation that it was a suicide. Either way, he clearly shouldn't have been allowed out to wander around the town right after getting a traumatic memory back, and a negligence claim had been brought against Nepenthe by his widow, Annetta. Noor hadn't had much opportunity to follow how that'd been going, having been kept busy with her *own* investigation.

She did know that, so far, the two things – William Hall's death and Louise's malpractice – were being treated as separate cases. Nepenthe was undoubtedly aware that William was a former client of Louise's, but it didn't seem to know any more than that.

There was a silence on the line.

Noor carried on, talking into it,

And what about Oscar Levy? What did Nepenthe do to *him*?

More silence. Then Louise said,

Listen, Noor. I know you want answers. You think having them will help you sleep at night. And, even if that were true – which it isn't, by the way – why would *I* give you what you want?

So you won't tell me why you talked those people out of getting restorations? Or what Elena had to do with it?

Louise laughed.

That still gets me, she said. You didn't know anything. You get me sacked, and *then* you try to find out if you did the right thing.

There were things in her tone that couldn't coexist. Spite and pity, anger and resignation, affection and dislike. Noor wondered which of them were real, and which she was imagining.

What I want to know, said Louise (and her voice changed again, becoming neutral), is: what exactly did I do to you?

To me? said Noor.

Because all I know is that Nepenthe wasn't going to hire you – you had no experience – but I argued for you. I nurtured you. I didn't air my suspicions about your unethical relationships with female patients, or your inappropriate interest in me. I hoped you'd take personal rejection professionally. Even when it became apparent you had a grudge against me, I still helped you access client files. Because I trusted you. But you wanted to frame me. Do I have that right?

Partway through this, Noor realised Louise was recording their conversation. That this statement was a warning. She didn't know if it was a warning of what Louise might do, or what she'd already done.

I'd better go, Noor said.

Just a moment, Louise said. I've decided I will give you an answer to your questions. The ones you really want to know. The first answer is yes. You fucked things up with Elena, because you were terrified of intimacy. And the second answer is also yes. This *is* your fault. I spent my career helping people. Saving people. I know that everything I did was for the good. William Hall is dead because of *you*. Other people's lives will be ruined, because of you.

Noor flinched. She took the handset away from her ear, quickly. But it was too late, the words had already got inside.

She could hear Louise still, more distantly now.

There are your answers, said Louise. And fuck you.

After this phone call Noor didn't sit down heavily, or throw her phone across the room. She didn't stare out of any windows. She went upstairs and pushed herself, flat on the floor, underneath the bed in her spare bedroom slash study (used as neither), sweeping with her arms until she hit a laptop bag. She backed out with it, snakelike, and set the laptop up on the empty desk.

She'd borrowed the laptop several months ago to get some reports filed over a weekend. She hadn't bothered to tell anyone she'd taken it; nobody would have cared. Nobody knew it was here. Noor herself had forgotten it was here.

The lighting up of the screen, the Nepenthe logo, its bland lower-case optimism – gave her pause. A memory of when the logo felt different. When *Noor* felt different. If she did this now, she couldn't ever go back to that logo's former, comforting constellation of associations; to her tidy office with its single plant, the tea and sugar in the drawer, light striping the pale walls.

She glanced out of the window, at the silent garden of the house next door. *Least harm*, she thought.

She broke into the Nepenthe legal department's database of contact details. It didn't take long to find what she was looking for. Only a few minutes, to carry out an act that would get spotted as a breach immediately, traced back to this laptop – and from there, eventually, traced to Noor.

When she shut the laptop, she realised she'd been holding her breath. Her head was ringing with the pressure.

But what will they do? she asked herself, taking large, tattered breaths. Sack her? She's as good as sacked anyway. Add a few more years onto the prison sentence?

The logo is just a logo. Her office is a distant dream. It's all over anyway. The rest doesn't matter.

Noor is at the gates of Nepenthe now.

The gates are tall and made of dark, solid wood. They fit so tightly against the stone gateposts that it's impossible to see the building behind them. The curved white front, the glass doors; closed.

Eerie, she thinks – but is it really? It wouldn't look eerie to anybody else. It's a normal gate on a quiet road in a small town. Which is eerie to Noor. All the things that made it normal to *her* are gone. No guards. No protesters. And inside, no technicians, no clients, no Karine or Jim, or Marie on reception, nobody sitting at the screens in the treatment rooms, nobody in the kitchen wasting time talking about their holidays. The lights off, the white dimmed. The shutters all drawn, like somewhere closed for the night – except it never closed at night, did it?

Noor left in early November. A month later, in December, the clinic closed. Now it's nearly March. The daffodils on the grass banks of her road have come out en masse. Noor saw a butterfly yesterday, a small white one. The people that Noor overhears in the park and the shops hardly talk about Nepenthe any more. They used to say things like, *All the children in school have colds right now – probably something to do with that clinic.* But the passers-by these days are talking about how much better the traffic is on Belsey Road, by the old Nepenthe clinic (already the old Nepenthe clinic!), or what the theme for the school fete will be, or where does good gluten-free cheesecake, and has anyone seen that the old Odeon cinema on Watlington Street has reopened as a Picturehouse, which means you can have a glass of wine while you watch a film. Maybe soon they'll be talking about how the old Nepenthe clinic has reopened as a community theatre or a rehab facility or a hotel.

And there are daffodils everywhere, and a white butterfly.

*

The pace of the traffic picks up, carrying Noor away up the road. Nepenthe's gates shrink in her rear-view mirror.

Stop, she wants to say. *I'm not done.*

But done with what?

What she means is:

I still don't know.

Doesn't know what Louise did, doesn't know if the clinic should have closed, doesn't know why William died, doesn't know if she was wrong or right, doesn't know if Elena still loves her, if she ever did, ever would again, or if Noor should have deleted that last memory when she had the chance, and tried to move on.

Endless questions, says Oscar.

Still looking for answers, says Louise mockingly.

Noor finishes the line for her.

Fuck you.

Noor reaches the bottom of the hill. She takes the turning out of town, towards the coast.

David had advised against this.

He'd told her not to involve herself any further. That was a couple of weeks ago. Noor had run into him throwing some bottles into the recycling bin on Saturday morning, and he'd said he was going to walk along the river. Did Noor want to come?

She surprised him by saying yes.

The two of them sat on a bench overlooking the water. The sun was out, bouncing off the ducks' backs, just like water was supposed to. Maybe everything bounced off a duck's back. The morning green of the grass was freshly rinsed and sparkling; undented, crossed only by spiders and snails. The tree above them was covered in tiny hairy buds.

So what's going on with Nepenthe? David asked.

Noor sighed.

They've been tracking down the clients that Louise got in contact with, she said. None of them are saying anything. Several of them are so scared we might make them say something that they've got themselves legal representation.

David started to speak, then waited, as a jogger went past. Her breath sandpapered the air in short, hard strokes. They watched her shiny back disappear round the next corner.

David said, So, you're not off the hook yet?

They know I didn't carry out some of the checks I should have, Noor said. When I was authenticating Louise's access, I mean. I told them that. I just don't know if there's a way to prove that Louise made the calls and not me. I don't know if she's even blaming me or not. I guess if some of these people do talk, or decide to get their memories back, that will be evidence. But they're not doing any new restorations, as far as I know.

I can't believe Louise did all that, David said.

You used to know her, Noor said. What did you make of her then?

David lifted his hands. I lived with her for a couple of years, a long time ago, he said. I barely remember it. Maybe because I had . . . other things on my mind at the time. I wasn't paying attention.

Another pause, another passer-by. This time a middle-aged woman with a French bulldog that leaned, yearningly, towards their feet, before the woman noticed, and pulled it onwards.

You probably knew her better than I ever did, David said. I mean, I don't even know how her life turned out – before this, I mean. Was she with someone? Did she have children?

She's divorced, Noor said. She has a daughter, about twenty. Mei.

Really? David said. Jesus. In my mind *Louise* is twenty. He looked sad.

Are you okay? Noor asked.

Yes, David said. It's strange how things turn out. I was just thinking about Louise. We slept together once. In a field. It was beautiful, actually – not just the, uh, sex – the field and sunset. She'd brought a joint. Now I think about it, she could have set the field on fire. And I had hay fever. It's probably more beautiful in my memory. She'd been celebrating some milestone with her research team, I met her for a drink. I had no idea at the time that it was probably the day they worked out how to delete memories.

Noor tried and failed to imagine Louise, twenty-something years old, lying in a cornfield with David, smoking weed.

Why didn't you get together? she asked. Because you liked someone else?

Yes. I assumed it was a one-off. For both of us. But then she basically ended our friendship, ignored me when we crossed paths, so now I don't think that was true, maybe? Anyway. We were talking about *your* life. Not my youth, a thousand years ago. I'm sure you'll be exonerated, Noor. Eventually.

It's not just that that bothers me, Noor said. It's the clients. Not just the people who were Louise's clients, who have to deal with whatever it is she's done. But all the people who think that the restoration ruined their life. All the people who think having a memory deleted ruined their life.

She thought about her former neighbours. She hadn't seen them again, after that day. There was a To Let sign outside their flat. She looked at it every time she came home, but the driveway was always empty and the blinds in their flat – some up, some down – never moved.

We're ruining a lot of lives, she said.

Not you personally, said David.

Noor looked at the ducks. She said nothing.

I actually know someone who decided against getting a restoration, David said suddenly.

Oh? Noor said. Really? Has their life been ruined?

They seem okay, David said. But you never really know, do you? If it's really okay, and if so, how long for. But they seem happy to me.

I take it you never had a deletion? Noor asked.

No, David said. I thought about it once. Years ago. In the end I felt like even though it was a painful memory, I wanted to hold on to it anyway.

Because you never know when it might come in useful? said Noor.

Because then you might just be able to let it go, naturally, said David. And then . . . it's really gone.

The traffic vanishes once Noor gets out of town. She drives southwards for an hour, before arriving at Annetta's door.

She stands on the doorstep and rings the bell. Then, as she always does, she starts to feel that she's standing slightly too close to the door, and moves back off the step, so as not to end up nose to nose with the door opener.

The first time she came here she stood way back. Almost at the bottom of the path. That was because she wasn't sure if she should have come at all. She hadn't planned to, but then she saw a picture of Annetta in a newspaper; her hair blowing across her face in the wind, struggling with the bags she was carrying.

She looked desperate.

No, she was quoted as saying. *They haven't told me anything.*

I just want answers.

And so Noor decided that she would go to Annetta's house, whether or not it constituted professional misconduct (in for a penny, in for a pound) and speak to her.

She had to examine her own motives for this first. She didn't want to bother a grieving woman in pursuit of her own agenda; trying to find out exactly what Louise had to do with his death.

. . . And if it might, in some way, get Noor off the hook.

But no: she didn't believe it was that. Maybe it was, but only a little bit. More than that, it was the desperate look of William's wife.

Mostly, it's because Noor knew it was what William would want.

William, a total stranger – and yet.

Noor felt – feels – a connection to him. An intimacy. She doesn't know why. Maybe because she saw him die.

She didn't tell David she was going to Annetta's house, that first time. She didn't tell anyone. When a shape appeared in the rippled glass of the front door it occurred to Noor that she could pretend to be someone else, a Jehovah's Witness or a charity collector, and nobody would ever know that she'd been there.

(*Hi, could you spare a minute for Save the Children?*)

The door was answered by a short woman in her sixties. She was already frowning. Noor wondered if this was Annetta's mother.

I'm Noor Ali, she said, before she could change her mind.

The woman scowled at her. She said: No journalists.

She started to close the door.

Wait! Noor said. I'm a doctor at Nepenthe.

Bullshit, said the woman.

The door slammed.

Then it opened again. Like a magic trick, the older woman was gone and a younger, exhausted-looking woman whom Noor recognised as Annetta Hall was standing in her place.

Is that a lie? Annetta said. Are you really a doctor at the clinic?

I am, Noor said. And I'm sorry to turn up like this. But I thought you might want to know more about William. I read that you hadn't been given any information. And I don't know how much more I can offer you, but I came anyway.

Are you allowed to speak to me? Annetta asked.

No, Noor said. Not really.

How did you know where I lived?

I broke into the legal department's files.

Okay.

Uh, Noor said. I also need to tell you that you might have cause to . . . I mean, I have a role . . .

Annetta stepped back.

Come in, she said.

'Come in,' says Annetta.

Noor follows her into the house. She takes off her shoes and puts them next to the various small- and adult-sized pairs of shoes scattered around the porch. She hangs her coat up between a red jacket with ladybirds on it and a large navy windbreaker. William's things haven't been put away yet. His electric razor and aftershave are on the bathroom shelf, next to the cartoon character bubble bath and the headlice lotion. His wellingtons are in the utility room; his credit cards are in a kitchen drawer with the spare keys and batteries and rubber bands.

'I really appreciate this,' Annetta says.

'Please don't thank me,' Noor says.

'Milo!' Annetta shouts, leaning into the kitchen. 'Fiona! Noor's here.' She turns back. 'They're outside. They're making a coffin for a dead bird they found. Marian – our counsellor – said stuff like that was normal, given the situation. If they ask again to cremate it though, that's still a no.'

'Fair enough,' says Noor. 'No cremations. How are they?'

'Fiona's still angry. Milo . . . I don't know.'

'And how are you?'

Annetta sighs. 'I don't know.'

When Noor first came here, she told Annetta that Louise had been trying to get in touch with William to stop him getting his restoration. That Louise had already done the same thing successfully with several other people, before Noor reported her. Nepenthe was in the process of tracking down and interviewing the clients in question, but whatever Louise had said to them had obviously left an impression, because they'd all refused to cooperate. They didn't want their memories back, and they didn't want to talk. And because they didn't want to sue, either, Nepenthe might well leave it at that. Which meant that the only person who knew what William's deleted memory actually *was*, was Louise.

Right, said Annetta. She frowned. Then she cried.

Noor had to acknowledge then that she'd had – in a very small and secret way – an idea that she might say to Annetta, *This was all my fault.* And Annetta would say, *No. It was not your fault. It was going to happen anyway.* Or, *I forgive you.* But at that moment Noor saw how stupid and wrong that idea was.

Instead she said:

Tell me how I can help.

'How's your mother?' Noor asks Annetta.

'I think she's okay. Just a slippery step. It's her hip, apparently. She's also got herself into a state because she thinks she ought to be with me night and day. She's driving the hospital staff mad. I don't suppose they'll be persuaded to keep her for longer. After I see her I'll go to the solicitors' office. I hope it's not too long? The kids will be pleased to have you here, I know that.'

'Take all the time you need,' Noor says. 'Any news on the . . . ongoing . . .'

'The lawsuit? Well, the solicitors are really good. I suppose everything's going smoothly, there could be a lot of compensation for the children – though they'll already have the life insurance . . .'

Her eyes fill with tears.

Noor puts a hand on her shoulder. 'I'm sorry,' she says.

'No. It's okay,' Annetta says. She looks at her watch, then wipes her face. 'Shit. I really don't have time to cry. I have to go.'

Milo and Fiona come in. Their hands are muddy.

'Are you here for the order of service?' Milo asks Noor.

'Why not?' she says. They stand either side of her. Each of them puts a muddy, possibly bird-bloody hand into her own, and they lead her out into the garden.

By the time Annetta gets back it's five o'clock. The sun has gone down and Noor turns on the lights in the house. Under one lamp is a picture of William, Annetta, Milo and Fiona in a place that looks like Spain. There's a sea behind them, dramatically blue. William's wearing a straw hat. His face is in shadow, his nose lit up. His green eyes are hidden in the deepest darkness, under the hat.

*

Later that night, with Milo and Fiona asleep in bed and Annetta asleep on the sofa under a blanket, Noor gets up and puts on her coat and shoes, quietly. She writes a note and puts it on the hall table. Then she leaves the house, gets in her car, and drives towards London.

It's past midnight when Noor arrives at Louise's house. The house itself is set back from the road behind a plain wall, with a door and intercom in the wall. She can just see the edges of the illuminated glass cube behind some trees. Louise is awake, as Noor knew she would be.

She presses the intercom and Louise answers.

'It's me,' Noor says. 'Please let me in.'

Noor hasn't been in this house for years. It's not that different to what she remembers. The Japanese art, which she had ample time to commit to memory, still hangs on the walls, lit simply and elegantly. There are a few lamps on, but the rest of the house is in darkness. Acres of dark floor, acres of dark glass. No lights on in the garden, and no champagne tonight.

'What the fuck are you doing here?' Louise asks.

She says it without force. In fact she seems more curious than anything. She's wearing a pair of jeans and a cable-knit jumper. Neither of them have holes or stains, though why Noor was expecting Louise to look anything other than immaculate she couldn't say. It's not likely that

Louise would have stopped washing. Or sacked her house-keeper, come to that.

'Well,' Noor says.

'Hold on,' Louise says. 'If you actually want to *talk*, you can't record me.'

'I didn't plan to,' Noor says. She puts her phone on the table and takes her jacket off. 'Do you need me to take anything else off? I'm not wearing a wire.'

'The fact you think people still wear *wires* shows that you have definitely not been sent by any official law enforcement body,' Louise says. 'Want a whisky?'

'Why not,' Noor says.

They sit on Louise's long sofa, in a lone circle of light. Noor sips the whisky. She doesn't know why she accepted it. It tastes disgusting. There isn't a coffee table anywhere in sight – perhaps the Japanese frown on coffee tables – so she puts it on the floor beside her.

Louise observes her dispassionately.

'I didn't expect you to come here,' she says. She tips her head. 'You've surprised me.'

Noor feels a familiar thrill go through her – approval, from Louise! – but she slaps it down.

'I'm not here for myself,' she says. 'I'm here because I've met William Hall's wife. Annetta.'

'I know who William's wife is,' Louise says.

'Well, she doesn't know what happened to him. She's trying to move on, but she's devastated. She needs to know what his reasons were. For –'

There's a short silence. It fills up with tarmac, blood, low sun, the weight on her wet legs. Noor picks up the whisky and drinks it, too fast. She coughs. She puts the glass down again.

'So, you came to ask me?' says Louise.

'Yes. I don't know how much of what you've said to me over the years is true. If you really did see me as a friend. But I think we *were* friends. And I don't think you're a cruel person. I'm sure you hate me now, but this isn't about me. Annetta hasn't done anything to you.'

Louise looks at her for a few moments. It's impossible to tell whether she agrees or disagrees with any of this.

'I think this is *a* reason why you're here,' Louise says eventually. 'But it's not the only reason why you're here. Is it? Listen, Noor. If you tell me the truth, maybe I'll be honest too.'

'Okay,' Noor says. 'I still want to know what the fuck happened. I want to know what RASA was, and what you were doing, calling those people, taking money. I want to know if someone paid you to wipe Elena's memory. Forced her to do it. I want to know if William's death was my fault. I want to know if I did the right thing, calling Clifford to report you. I want to know if you're secretly a good person that seems bad now or a bad person that seemed good then. I want to know if Nepenthe is a good thing or a bad thing. If there is such a thing as Nepenthe, if it's even possible. I want to know if I'm a good person or a bad one. I want to know what the point of it is. What the point of *me* is.'

'Not *quick* questions, then,' Louise says.

Noor wipes her eyes, which have inconveniently started to leak.

'You know I can't help you with all of that,' Louise says. 'I can tell you the doings. The goings-on. I can't tell you the abstract stuff. Come on. How many times have I said this to you? It's not linear. There are no *stories*. There are no rules. There are no answers.'

Noor realises she's begun to lean forward. She's reminded of the conversations she and Louise used to have in the early days, Louise sitting opposite her, usually across a desk. Her expensive perfume crossing the space between them to reach Noor every now and again, like a touch, a brush on the nose. There's none of that perfume tonight, no detectable scent of any kind. Noor wonders what she herself smells of. Whisky, probably. Fright.

'Just tell me the goings-on, then,' she says coolly, shifting back.

'Fine. I help people who can't get deletions, get deletions,' Louise says. 'There've been a lot of them, mostly self-known. A few self-confidentials. The ones you looked up yourself. The problem with the self-confidentials is that when they got the letter offering them their memory back, they didn't know that I'd helped them. They thought everything was above board.'

'Criminals?' Noor asks.

'People on both sides of the law, actually. I decide the merits of each case individually. I've never lied to you about my beliefs, Noor. I told you, the best anyone can do is reduce harm. That's what I do.'

'By breaking the law?'

'Okay.' Louise looks impatient. 'Let's pretend for a minute that civil law is analogous to moral law. If we lived in a simple world, morality might have relevance. But it's *not* simple. And yet people persist in acting like it *is* simple, and one rule can be applied to every situation. Nepenthe has a set of rules, the law has a set of rules, but those rules can't cover everyone. There are people like William, who have a PTSD memory that they aren't allowed to delete. Then there are people who might be at risk from others. From criminals.'

'Like Elena?'

'People who needed to be kept quiet used to be kept quiet in pretty heavy-handed ways, Noor. I offer a more humane solution. I can't stop crime – obviously – but I can reduce the body count.'

'So she knew something about her boss being murdered, and they forced her to forget it?'

'Yes. And if they hadn't, she wouldn't have been around for you to fall in love with. Against the rules, I might remind you.'

Brief pause: for Noor to writhe, for a second, in the full knowledge of what a fucking idiot she's been. The things she said to Elena. Her stupid, cruel theory about Elena and her boss. She's lit up with hatred for herself. But Louise is here, hating her too, and Noor needs *someone* on her own team. She refocuses.

'So all these different people get in touch with you?' she asks. 'How? How do you find out that a police officer needs a deletion? How do the criminals find you? Is there a directory for this sort of thing? How do you even *know* all these people?'

'Influential people and corrupt people?' Louise asks. 'I was at Oxford, Noor. Alistair went to Eton.'

Noor is irritated to see that Louise looks amused. 'It's not funny,' she says.

Louise lifts her hands. 'You did set me up for that one.'

'Right. I'd ask how you justify what you do, but I expect I'd just get some shades of grey bullshit.'

'Don't get sulky, Noor,' Louise says sharply. 'You came to *my* house. It's only polite to listen to some of my bullshit. And of course it's shades of grey. Like I said, the world isn't simple. Only *ideas* are simple – and pure, and good: until it comes to the execution. Take Nepenthe. It's a beautiful idea. It's why I signed up, believe it or not. Like you I thought that we were improving the lot of humanity by removing some of its pain. But then when we actually *set up* Nepenthe, in the real world, and put real people in charge of it, it wasn't so pure and good any more. I'm not saying that it was a bad thing, necessarily. It just went very . . . *grey*.

'I mean: at the top you've got a board that has known about resurgent memories – traces – for years, and sat on it, until that marine snails research came out and forced them to admit memories could be restored. A little lower down you've got ridiculous, reckless research programmes like RASA. Off to one side you get private doctors paid off to say their clients' drugs tests came back negative or that they aren't mentally unstable. Actually: here's a story for you, Noor. I had a client who did that: paid a doctor to say she was clean so she could get a memory deleted. After she removed the memory, her coke problem went away. What's the moral there? And finally, right at the bottom you get clients trying to cheat the system, like that Kurtz woman. Or psychologists sleeping with clients.'

'Okay. I get it.'

'And fuck knows what *sales* are doing,' Louise says.

'I wish you'd stop making jokes,' Noor says. 'So what made *you* stop bothering with pure and good?' She picks her whisky up again. It goes down a bit better, third time round.

'It was RASA, actually,' Louise says. 'I fought it. Nobody listened. I nearly quit. Then I wondered what else I'd do. Find another job but in a pure, good medical tech firm, run by pure, good people? So yes, I changed my expectations. I did still believe in Nepenthe: I still thought that it would reduce harm. I just decided that I'd stop following rules, because they were being decided by arrogant pricks who didn't give a shit about human lives, and that I'd administer Nepenthe my way.'

'Reducing harm,' Noor says.

'Actually, yes. Giving people in desperate situations another option.'

'And making a huge profit.'

'Don't forget I was taking a huge personal risk. Plus, I have a daughter. I want her to have money. The way the world is going she'll need a state-of-the-art bunker.'

'Art,' Noor says. She looks around the room. 'Where does *that* fit with least harm? If you were in it for the greater good, you would have donated the money to Amnesty instead of buying Japanese paintings.'

'Woodblock prints,' Louise says. 'And I'm not going to justify my decisions to you. I don't expect you to believe that it's possible to do a good thing *and* make money.'

'I expect you think I'm childish and reductive,' says Noor, bitterly.

'I think you don't know the world yet,' Louise says, 'because you're not part of it. Live in it for a little while, then come back to me.'

This lands, as Louise knew it would.

'Thanks for the advice,' Noor says. She hears herself, again, sounding more riled than she'd hoped to let on. But why even bother pretending? Louise has always been able to read her. And Louise, though she's refrained from doing so up until now, knows how to injure her too.

'What's RASA?' she asks.

'Sorry, Noor,' Louise says. 'I'm going to need RASA. That's *my* leverage. I have copies of all the files. It's the main reason Nepenthe haven't publicly executed me. You should find some leverage of your own, you know. They're looking for a scapegoat.'

Noor finishes the whisky. Louise doesn't offer her another. She just looks at her. Her eyes are a light grey-blue. They can look stony in some lights, hard and unreflective.

'I'll tell you about William,' Louise says. 'He needed a deletion, but he was a police officer at that time, and he wasn't allowed to have the procedure.'

'How much did that cost him?'

'A fraction of the amount I charge other people, actually.'

'So you means-tested criminals,' Noor says.

Louise shrugs.

'And why couldn't you find him, later?'

'He needed to be self-confidential. Then he moved house, and left the police. The contact who put me in touch with him unfortunately died. I had no way of getting hold of him. That's why I came in: to ask you. I thought maybe you could hack into something, I don't know. It was a last resort.'

'You thought I'd *help* you?' Noor asks.

Louise shrugs again. It's an eloquent shrug. And Noor feels the approach of – no.

No.

But here it is:

Shame.

Get down, Noor snaps at it, like it's a dog. *Lie down. Stay.* She's not going to let Louise make her feel ashamed for following the rules. For obeying the law! It's Louise that has abused their friendship, not Noor.

'So William was corrupt?' she says.

'Not to my mind. He accidentally killed a boy, years ago, trying to save him from an oncoming car. But he developed PTSD, and he was clearly suicidal when he came to see me. So I deleted the memory. And that's why I was trying to stop his restoration. But yes, what he did was illegal, so I suppose you'd see him as corrupt.'

Noor puts her head in her hands.

The shame is here, now.

'No,' she says. 'No. You weren't doing a selfless thing. You were protecting yourself. Because William could have exposed you, and everything you were up to would come out, and . . .'

She realises as she's saying it that she's way off.

Louise doesn't speak unkindly, or triumphantly. She just sighs, and says, 'William wouldn't have done that. He'd have ruined his own life if he said anything. That's the only reason I'm telling you this. Annetta won't go public either. She'll be given a lot of money not to, which she can pass on to her children. The other option is that her kids grow up with no money, and a criminal for a dad.'

So he did die because of me, Noor thinks.

Is this true?

Yes, it is. She doesn't know if Louise – a presence Noor is dimly aware of, sitting in silence, watching her – told Noor this as an act of kindness or cruelty. It hardly matters.

Noor is the reason that William died.

She stands up.

'I'm going to go,' she says.

'Okay,' Louise says.

She follows Noor to the door. In the low light Noor's feet catch on rugs, door thresholds. Louise moves silently, unerringly. Something about this makes Noor angry. By the time they get to the front door she's full of rage at both of them.

Louise opens the front door without saying anything. The cold air fills the hall almost immediately, lifting their hair.

'I'm going to have to live with what you just told me,' Noor says to Louise. 'You know how difficult that's going to be. But at least I didn't *mean* any harm. Your "do least harm" is shitty. It means: do *some* harm. You *mean* to do it. You think you're the one in charge of judging how much harm, and for whom. But your judgement is off. That's how you turned into a mother who puts her perfectly normal kid on antidepressants and pushes her into getting a deletion. Where's Mei now? How does she feel about "do least harm"?'

Louise's face tightens; her mouth changes, twitches. Other than this she stands still, holding the door.

Noor realises she's seeing something she hasn't ever seen before, never in her life: Louise, devastated.

She almost says, *I'm sorry.*

She doesn't say it.

She says, 'I *am* going to live in the world. And I'm not going to end up like you.'

Noor doesn't sleep that night. She falls asleep by accident the next morning, holding her phone. She wakes up when her phone falls onto the floor with a bang, opening her eyes to the cold spring day, the sky blindingly bright.

It's evening before she feels able to go to Annetta's. She texts and asks if she can come over once the children are in bed.

I've got to talk to you about Louise, she adds – because she suspects that by the time the hour of the visit approaches, she might have lost courage, and try to get out of it.

She's right about that. As she stands on the doorstep, waiting for Annetta to answer, she realises she's shaking. The sun is just going down behind her. Birds are still singing in the darkening periwinkle sky.

Annetta appears, a pixelated shape flickering and expanding in the textured glass panes, and Noor inhales – deeply, like it's the last chance she'll get.

Tell me a story.

This is what Noor thinks, as she sits opposite Annetta, having refused tea because she's not sure if and when she's going to be asked to leave. A story without a good, solid villain, and no heroes at all. No answer, no justice, no happy ending.

But when the story ends, Annetta tells Noor it's not her fault. She waves away, too, the idea of blaming Louise. She says she doesn't care about Louise. (It's almost comically shocking to Noor, actually, the realisation that there are people who have lived their entire lives without admiring Louise, being advised by Louise, wondering what Louise would think about this or that, hoping Louise would approve of them.)

It's William Annetta is furious with.

'He should have got therapy, Noor,' she says. Tears haven't made her less articulate: she talks faster, even, with a lucid fluidity. 'That's what people did before Nepenthe was invented. It wasn't binary. It wasn't death or deletion. I can *see* him now, making his decision between honour and disgrace. Like some medieval *idiot*. Even after he got that wipe – so *what*? – even if he'd gone to prison, and I'd have had to support myself and the kids, we could have got through it. He'd never have allowed that, obviously. But he was *wrong*. And I can't even argue with him! Not that he'd have listened to me anyway. I could have helped him, but he'd never have talked to me. I know he loved me, Noor, but he never really opened up. I'm being honest. I miss him; I loved him more than anything, but it was hard to love him.'

Noor shakes her head. Tears have shut her up. Faintly, she's aware of the sting of *hard to love*. A nerve somewhere, probably in the heart, being hit.

'And I know why he did it the way he did it,' Annetta says. 'If it's an accident, we get life insurance. If it's a suicide, we get nothing.'

(– the memory of William's blood, so much of it by the end that afterwards Noor's clothes were heavy and hard, it was hard to move her legs.)

Noor stops the memory. A technique from the days of blotting out Elena. She simply visualises herself pressing a button on an old video recorder. The screen goes black.

'It still might not have been suicide,' Noor says. 'I wasn't close enough to see it properly.'

'Nobody was,' Annetta says. 'I'm sure he was very thorough, in that respect. Checking out the CCTV on the street. The angle of the sun. They said the sun must have been in his eyes . . . Oh, I know exactly what he did. So conscientious. Is it bad, Noor? That I want William back just so I can shout at him? Slap him, even, tell him what a bloody fool he's been?'

Then she cries, so much that she can't talk through it any more.

Noor watches her cry. She thinks she should put a hand on Annetta's shoulder, so she does. The gesture feels strange to her – an imposition – but Annetta puts her own hand over Noor's, and clenches it there, so that Noor is effectively kept with her, taking part in this grief that travels through Annetta's hand and into Noor's own body, until it's over and Annetta says,

'I was always trying to get something from him that he wouldn't ever give to me. It was exhausting. I'd do anything to have him back. But part of me would dread it, too. I'm sorry. I don't mean that. Or maybe I do. I don't know.'

'I understand,' says Noor.

Noor wonders if things like that can change a person.

Holding on to someone as they experience such extremes. Grief, death, love. If Noor hadn't held William, she wouldn't have gone to Annetta's house. If Noor hadn't held Annetta's hand, she wouldn't be here the next morning, watching Milo and Fiona eat the porridge that she made them for breakfast. Admittedly they've taken so long to pick out all the pieces of raisin (Fiona) and banana (Milo) that the porridge is basically cold, but still.

Noor Ali, sitting at a kitchen table with a family, eating breakfast.

Who'd have thought it?

Hard to love, Noor thinks.

She has been hard to love. She has been hardened against love. She has found love hard.

Oscar Levy held her hand, when she was incapable of anything.

The questions are the point, he said.

Noor thinks of what Louise said.

There are no stories. There are no rules. There are no answers.

Funny, that this is what comforts her: things said by a possibly brain-damaged former patient and a woman who probably hates her.

Something she isn't even sure Louise really believed, or if she just said it because it suited her purposes at that time.

But it comforts Noor, regardless.

*

She thinks about Oscar Levy a lot. She wonders whether to call him.

Clifford and the Nepenthe management *deserve* to have their activities made public, without question. But that's as far as the absolutes go. Noor thinks about the damaged people crying out about RASA, online and among the protesters. That damage has been done, it can't be un-done – but could it be made worse? And in which case, maybe there's an argument for not bringing RASA to light, but using the knowledge to save herself. Is saving herself so bad? She's not a bad person. Maybe she deserves to be saved.

But what about Oscar? Whether for justice or self-interest, if Noor finds out more about RASA, she'd be using him. Maybe putting him at risk of getting sued. Or just hurting him. He said he wanted to be her friend: she can't let him be hurt. But then, she wonders, is there a way to find out what happened to him without doing him any harm?

Harm, she thinks.

Every day she thinks: should I call him?

Every day she thinks: no.

But the next day she thinks again: *could I?*

Noor leaves Annetta's house in the late morning. It's a slightly milder day, today, a clear bluish sky. The sounds of her feet on the stone path, her scrapings through her bag, her little cough, rise up through the air, past the closed windows of the houses, the branches of the ash tree in Annetta's front garden.

She gets into her car to make her call. She sits there with the fasten seat belt warning binging, listening to the phone ring.

It goes to voicemail.

'Hi, Elena,' Noor says. 'It's me, Noor. I know I behaved horribly to you. I was stupid, and wrong. And now I've lost my job and I might be going to prison. *But*. Is there any chance that when I get out, I could take you for a drink?'

... Of course, she doesn't know if it's even Elena's number any more. And even if it is, she doesn't know if Elena remembers her. And even if Elena does remember her, Noor doesn't know if Elena has got over her a long time ago, or if she's with someone else now, and happy.

But maybe none of that matters, she thinks.

Asking the question.

That's what matters.

ACKNOWLEDGEMENTS

With grateful thanks to . . .

Felicity Blunt, Rosie Pierce, Luke Speed, Sarah Harvey and the team at Curtis Brown, and Hillary Jacobson at ICM. Charlotte Cray, Ailah Ahmed, Rose Waddilove and the team at Hutchinson Heinemann. Valerie Steiker, Kara Watson, Nan Graham and the team at Scribner. Jo Unwin and the team at JULA. My early readers, Mimi, Nicole, Michael, Diane, Bib and Shelley. Amy Pendergast, Emma Stonex and Lucy Clarke, for their help and support.

And thank you to Cian – for everything.

NOTE

To give Nepenthe a place in the novel's part-fact, part-fiction history I have done more than a few real-life scientists a disservice. I left out several important studies, and I haven't given Nader, Schafe and Ledoux the proper credit for their groundbreaking work demonstrating the existence of memory reconsolidation. This novel comes with full apologies to them.